The Rabbi's Gift

Retelling an Ancient Tale

Chuck Gould

Published 2017 by Neoteric Publishing, LLC.

Copyright © 2017 by Charles Gould.

All rights reserved. This book or any portion thereof may not be reproduced or used in any manner whatsoever without the express written permission of the publisher except for the use of brief quotations in a book review.

Printed in the United States of America
First Printing, 2017
ISBN 978-1-64056-006-2

Neoteric Publishing, LLC.
180 N. University Ave.
Provo, UT 84601
www.neotericpublishing.com

TABLE OF CONTENTS

PART I 1
I,I   Racing the Sun 3
I,II   The Tektons 8
I,III   Babaziah, Masmasiah, Kaskasiah, and Sharlai 15
I,IV   The Promised 20
I,V   Tekome Bakah 26
I,VI   Four Figures at a Fire 31
I,VII Yericho Ford 35
I,VIII Setting Fire to a Dragon 40
I,IX   The Water Level 45
I,X   Separate Shadows 51
I,XI   Seedlings 57
I,XII Mazzeroth 61
I,XIII Butter and Smoke 67
I,XIV Graining the Dove 73
I,XV Passage Through Samaria 76
I,XVI Seen and Unseen 79
I,XVII Goats and Lions 85
I,XVIII The Heresies of Lesser Nature 96

PART 2 100

- II,I   Uranus and Neptunus *103*
- II,II   Liquid mouse *107*
- II,III   Headlong into Darkness *109*
- II,IV   Between Death and Dishonor *113*
- II,V   Opus Caementicium *119*
- II,VI   The Scent of Sacrifice *122*
- II,VII   An Aureus for Mithras *125*
- II,VIII   More for the Wine than the Candle *131*
- II,IX   "The Stone Rejected by the Master Builder" *136*
- II,X   Challah, and a Good Red Wine *141*
- II,XI   Planets and Prophecies *144*
- II,XII   Complicated Equations *147*
- II,XIII   Price and Privilege *150*
- II,XIV   Master of a Dark House *152*
- II,XV   Yetzirah *158*
- II,XVI   Grief and Abundance *174*
- II,XVII   Plain of Gan Sarim, The Garden of the Prince *176*
- II,XVIII   In the Image of the One God *178*
- II,XIX   Owl *181*
- II,XX   Short Tether *183*
- II,XXI   The Coin is Spent *185*

PART 3 189

- III,I   Prophecy and Sons of Light *191*
- III,II   Blood Sacrifice and the Seal of Solomon *196*
- III,III   Laughter of a Sparrow *201*
- III,IV   Protocol and Horse *203*
- III,V   The Tree of Life *206*
- III,VI   Reunion *212*
- III,VII   A Wink and a Blessing *215*
- III,VIII   Folds in the Curtain of Time *220*
- III,IX   Forgiven *224*

PART 4 231
- IV, I   One Plus One Equal One Anew 233
- IV, II   A House of Shame 238
- IV, III   Disaster in the Upper Room 243
- IV, IV   Straw Heart in a Stone House 248
- IV, V   A Future Unforeseen 250
- IV, VI   The Forge and Mustard Seed 254
- IV, VII   Rubies on the Road to Yafo 259
- IV, VIII   Yellow Silk and the Family Name 264

PART 5 271
- V, I   Ambush of the King 273
- V, II   Enriched by What is Given Away 277
- V, III   Into and Out of Egypt 282
- V, IV   Unwelcome Guests 288
- V, V   Hawk at the Fountain 290
- V, VI   Healing the Flesh and Blessing with Water ...293

PART 6 299
- VI, I   Consigned to Augustus 301
- VI, II   The Handmaiden's Ruse 306
- VI, III   Thirsty for The Rabbi's Gift 307
- VI, IV   Aching Heart, and Feet of Clay 311
- VI, V   Greater and Lesser Rewards 312
- VI, VI   Fear of Flogging 315
- VI, VII   All Options Considered 316

Epilogue 321

Dedications

To my wife, Jan.
To my son, Zeke
To my daughter, Jessica

Acknowledgements

Friends and associates helped make this book possible. Beta readers, proof readers, and fellow authors who critiqued the nascent rough draft include

Catherine Dook
Mary Pat DiLeva
Heather Strong
Dawn Fitzgibbons
Hafidha Acuay
Margaret McNulty
Elizabeth Mitchell
Rita Hart
Teri McGrew
Tom Thorogood
Stephen Crippen
Joshua Perme

PART I

I,I
Racing the Sun

Fickle, the wind lost its western breath. Among the chartered Phoenician convoy, the trailing galleys were first affected. Sails slacked, then flapped and snapped, hanging limp on the bleached and pitch smeared masts. Odors and sounds intensified as the clock of the great sea appeared to stop. Chains rattled as robust but exhausted slaves dug deeper with their three-man sweeps. The effect was disappointing. Ships laden with ore from the isle of the Britons and trade goods from Tarshish slowed to a strained and reluctant pace.

On the aft deck of the vessel leading the trade convoy, two Roman guards flanked a pavilion topped with a silk canopy. The pair stood proud and erect, round bronze shields strapped to their left forearms. Each gripped a seven-foot spear, the butt of the shaft resting next to laced leather boots. The door to the pavilion opened. Eli bar Joachim, sensing a decrease in the sailing velocity, stepped out to investigate. The Roman guards slapped the spears against their chests. The late afternoon sun struck the copper fire buried in the points of the weapons. The guards extended their arms in smart salute.

Eli, a skeletal figure with a wild shock of white hair and meticulously trimmed beard emerged on deck. He glanced over the stern to forecast sunset. A four-finger width of pale pink sky separated the blazing star from the unrippled mirror of the Mare Nostrum. Two hours, no more, with Caesarea just barely visible beyond the bow. Eli frowned.

This year's expedition had succeeded beyond all expectation. Celtic miners in the southwest regions of Britannia sold larger quantities and at lower prices than any time in memory. The layover at Tarshish, situated centrally between Rome, Espangna, and Gaul, resulted in extravagant profits. Monarchs and metal smiths paid generously for the tin required to convert copper to bronze. Eli was sailing home to

Yudea, ships filled with his remaining metal, Sardinian bronze, and Roman luxuries.

Eli was a Decurion of Rome, personal friend of Augustus, Chief among the Sanhedrin magistrates representing the House of Yudah, and by some accounts the richest man in the Roman Empire. Without a doubt, the richest man in Yudea. Also without a doubt, unlikely to make Caesarea before sundown and the beginning of Shabbat. Arrival after sundown would require Eli and his son, Aban, to spend another night in the pavilion, rather than the family's opulent compound in the hills beyond the port. They had already been too long at sea. Eli sought out the tall Phoenician with the shaved head, bushy beard, and heavily tattooed arms.

"So, Nasir," said Eli. "How many more hours to Caesarea?"

"At this pace? No less than four. Could be slightly longer. Maybe you could ask that God of yours to blow a little wind our way? It helps a lot when we're this heavy."

"Shabbat's going to begin. The journey ashore is longer than permitted. We won't make it without an early start. I don't want to wait another entire day."

"All the more reason to ask your God for wind, Eminence."

Eli smiled. "Perhaps The One God will send a wind. Perhaps not. Perhaps God expects us to use what is already at hand."

Nasir arched his eyebrows. "And that would be?"

"Send the word to the rowers. If we make landfall early enough to travel home, we'll have them draw lots. I will buy the freedom of whomever wins the lottery."

Nasir grinned. "Really? For some of these men, the youngest and the strongest, I would need quite a bit."

"I'm not fool enough to make such a promise and not follow through. You, of all people, know we've had a successful year. You can name any reasonable price. Let's race the sun. And, let's win."

Nasir descended to the lower deck. His remarks to the overseer were repeated in Aramaic. The oarsmen responded enthusiastically, shouting encouragement among their company and establishing a brisk, rhythmic chant. The leading galley almost doubled its speed, leaving behind the rest of the convoy in a freshly energized dash for shore.

Eli noted the increased cadence, and the mounting wake. He nodded his approval to Nasir, while pointing at the sun approaching the western horizon. Shadows grew longer on the deck. The Roman bodyguards saluted stoically as Eli returned to the pavilion.

Aban slumbered on a pallet, but awoke to the noise of chanting and the sound of his father's return. "Are there pirates or something? The timing of the oars is much faster."

"No, son. Just a pirate sun trying to rob us of our first night back in Caesarea. I promised to buy one of the slaves if they get us ashore before Shabbat."

"Do we need another slave, Father? They're not cheap to keep."

Eli laughed. "We're not going to keep the slave; we're going to set him free. Call it a celebration of profitable trade and safe arrival."

Aban remained skeptical. "Is that a good use of the money?"

"For now, the money is mine to use however I choose. I can buy and free a slave if it pleases me to do so. I am anxious be home, and see your sister."

"I wonder what mischief Miriam has been up to."

Eli sighed. "I hate to imagine. She's been more difficult for her chaperones, lately."

Aban's twin sister was a challenge. She was born several minutes earlier than Aban and was technically the elder. Custom decreed that her marriage should be the first arranged. Finding another father willing to pair a suitable son with the daughter of the richest man in Yudea should be easy. Her dowry would be more than many entire families would earn in two generations. She was clever, physically attractive, and well spoken. She was also notorious for refusing to accept her ordained role in society. Some dared murmur that perhaps she dabbled in dark magic.

The trouble with Miriam began at an early age. It was normal for girls as well as boys to learn reading and writing, permitting everyone access to the Laws and Prophecies. Miriam excelled in her studies. She presumed to speak in class, and asked complex questions. Astonished rabbis often mistook her precocious capabilities for impertinence. Many suggested that Eli should "do something" to rein in his daughter. To Eli's profound distress, he had no real idea what he could do.

Miriam often eluded her chaperones. Even assigning two at a time proved insufficient. At least she was easily found, especially during the intervals when the family resided in Yerushalayim's upper city. Communities of Therapeuts and Zealots clustered just beyond the city walls. The Essenes remained isolated, a walk of only several minutes beyond. When Miriam escaped supervision she was invariably mingling with these groups of mystic healers, fanatic militants, and ascetic scholars. The outliers could not be bribed or intimidated into turning her away. She could not be persuaded that her behavior was unsuitable for a young, unmarried woman of her status.

Miriam's visits to the Therapeuts were most troublesome. Gossip was that she showed too much interest and no small ability in the healing arts. Eli's money and status couldn't protect his daughter from rumors of active witchcraft, even if those same assets prevented her official denunciation and persecution.

Miriam's rebellious behavior and unseemly associates ensured that the only fathers approaching Eli to discuss prospects of marriage had mercenary motives. Marrying her away would make Miriam the problem of her husband and his family. However, the same man who was willing to free a slave to reward heroic effort resisted any temptation to market his daughter as if she herself were property.

It was time to resolve Miriam's situation. She was of age a full year ago. Surely this winter, at one of the festivals the father of a suitable candidate would come forward. Miriam deserved special care and handling. She deserved a husband prepared to love her, not merely possess her. A capable, honest, man from a good family with notable social status. A man both patient and sincere. Surely Eli's stewardship would be rewarded. Surely God would provide.

Nasir called from outside the pavilion. "Eminence?"

Eli appeared at the door. "Yes, Nasir?"

"The wind. It's picking up in the west. The sails are filling on the ships behind us. Soon we will ride her breath as well."

"That's good news," agreed Eli.

Nasir savored the moment with a smile. "Good news indeed, Eminence. If the rowers keep up the pace, the wind will drive us ashore before your Shabbat. Remember, sir, the stronger and younger the slave- the higher will be the price."

I, II
The Tektons

Since earliest childhood, Yusuf bar Yakob was fascinated by the stones. Via Maris, the major Roman road, traced the eastern shore of Mare Nostrum from Egypt to Constantinople. Eight feet wide, the highway tickled the hems of low, forested hills, through Syria and Lebanon and the lush aromatic woodlands of northern Galilee. It twisted around, rather than over Mount Carmel, where the Legions established their northern outpost on slopes overlooking the sea.

The abstract symmetry of the paving cobbles reminded Yusuf bar Yakob of scales on snakeskin. Yusuf's place was behind the heavily laden two wheeled timber cart. He typically trudged along head down, pushing to assist his father's donkey on the steepest uphill stretches. Yusuf looked for patterns in the stones. He developed a sense for line, arrangement, and dimension. He began to believe that the only shapes he could not see would be those he lacked the courage to imagine.

Clusters of salted mist fled into evergreen shadow as the bronze star climbed over the Levantine rim. The death cries of a wild goat, not far ahead and barely within the tree line confirmed a kill by the lions. The cats would be distracted by the fresh carcass, and unlikely to harass two craftsmen and a donkey. Even so, it was wise to be wary on the Via Maris.

Yakob placed his hand on the hilt of his sword. A gift from his father, Matthan, who received it from his own father Eleazar. Nearly everyone believed the weapon had passed through ten generations, down to Yakob from a young, depraved and self-indulgent King of Yudah, Yeconiah. During the monarch's disastrous, ninety-day reign, the prophet Jeremiah condemned Yeconiah with a curse, "It shall be as if you were childless. None of your offspring will ever sit upon the throne of Israel. Our God discards you, as if removing a signet ring from his hand."

Like the sword, the curse passed down through the generations as well. The curse of Yeconiah was officially revoked after the Babylonian exile, but the blotch on the family name proved as durable as the crusty rust along the spine of the ancestral weapon. Yusuf was almost seventeen and still unmarried. Only fathers of the lowest possible estate ever contemplated wedding their daughters into a family legacy stained with a curse. Yusuf's age as well as his ancestry was now working to his disadvantage. Yakob wondered if he would die without grandchildren; "it shall be as if you were childless". Nevertheless, the old sword and the family curse would in time be passed to Yusuf. Yusuf deserved better, but would only receive what tainted little his father possessed.

The cart was almost overloaded with cedar planks, easily worth a hundred times more than Yakob would earn by shaping and fitting it for door jambs in Herod's new palace at Sephora. Bandits were plentiful in the forest. Keeping constant watch was essential.

Yet another small incline. The donkey strained in harness. Yusuf, powerfully built and blessed with youthful exuberance, leaned into the back of the cart. Yakob tugged insistently on the rigging, urging his animal along. Progress nearly stopped when one wheel dropped into an unnoticed depression in the cobbles. Yusuf lifted and pushed until the wheel cleared the depression. They advanced again.

Yakob was the first to hear the thumping cadence as they crested the rise. He stopped the donkey cart. "Listen! Sounds like a centuria behind us on the road. Could mean trouble."

Yusuf heard the drum, and nodded in agreement. "How far do you think we are from Nazareth?" The tiny village of Nazareth, a short walk from the building site for Herod's northern palace at Sephora, was populated by Tektons; craftsmen skilled in a variety of disciplines; dressing stone, joining timbers, or finishing with plaster and mosaic tiles. Nazareth represented safety in numbers and the family home, as well as the initial destination of their load.

Yakob was already assessing the variables. He had a carpenter's instinct for mathematics. "There are four steps to a drum beat. At that tempo, it's a fast march, maybe 4 miles in an hour. With this load, we're lucky to make 2 miles. If they are less than six miles behind us, we won't make Nazareth."

Yakob and Yusuf had little reason to fear for their personal safety. The cart, however, was another matter. A centuria consisted of about 80 troops, led by a Centurion, and approximately 20 camp followers and scavengers. The legionnaires would not bother the Tektons, but the provisioning corps routinely used Empirical authority to appropriate donkeys, carts, and even human labor to help advance the supply line.

"We still have time to hide," suggested Yusuf.

"We do, but I didn't like the sound of that kill just up ahead. If we have to choose between the supply train and the cats, we're better off taking our chances with the Romans."

Yusuf was doubtful. "The master builder will be furious if anything happens to this cedar. We could wind up losing our cart, our tools, and everything else we own. We have to get this load back home to Nazareth."

Yakob recognized the wisdom of his son's counsel. He remembered a thicket of brambles, about two miles ahead and close to the Via Maris. Last week, on the journey north, they passed almost fifty Roman slaves cutting firewood near that location. Faced with such human activity, the cats would choose to prowl elsewhere. The thicket would be an excellent hiding place.

"There's a good hiding spot in an hour. We'll get off the road and rest the donkey until they pass."

Shadows retracted their long fingers stretched across the road. The sun ascended in the east. Father and son pushed the cart, pulled the donkey, and avoided the largest holes in the highway. The drums increased in volume. The Roman force was still unseen on the road behind them, but the Tektons realized their margin of safety was shrinking by the minute. As Yakob predicted, they reached the brambles in a little over an hour. No sooner than they off the road and concealed in the brush did the Romans crest a rise and march into view.

An officer on a white horse led the procession. A banner man, bearing a gilded Imperial Eagle of Rome, paraded immediately behind. Forty rows of soldiers, two abreast, stepped with disciplined gait. A kettle shaped drum set the tempo. Behind the soldiers, a rag tag band of sheep herders, wine merchants, food vendors, and prostitutes generated a perpetual windblown cloud of dirty yellow dust.

Yakob reexamined their hiding place. The brambles were seven feet high, and the small gap through which they drove the cart was invisible from the road. All that remained now was to wait; perhaps half an hour until the centuria reached their location and another half hour to allow them to get out of sight. "We'll be safe here, as long as we're quiet."

Air in the thicket smelled of hot donkey, fresh dung, new leaves, and the oil of cedar. Yusuf sat on a rock, closed his eyes, and dreamed of stones. He visualized the great plaza at Sephora, one of the largest mosaic works in all of Palestine. A detailed profile of Herod Antipas dominated the middle area, surrounded by images of quail, concubines, and constellations. The border, laid in concentric rings of red, blue, and yellow created a mysterious halo around the rest of the tile figures. The work was only half complete when the master builder ordered Yakob and Yusuf to haul planks from Lebanon, but Yusuf was confident he could predict any progress made during their absence.

Although an older and higher ranking artisan officially claimed the credit, every Tekton in Nazareth knew that the visionary genius responsible for the design was Yusuf bar Yakob. The lead mosaic artisan frequently demanded that Yusuf report to the plaza for "advanced instruction" in the stone layer's art, but nobody was fooled. During those supposed lessons, it was Yusuf who resolved the more complex arrangements of pieces, and Yusuf who clarified the intricate details contained within the enormous work.

The drum grew louder. Each beat followed by the precise military tramping of 160 feet. The soldiers did not speak, but Yakob and Yusuf heard conversations in the supply train and the bleating of herd animals. The centuria was directly abreast of the thicket. The vibration of the earth disturbed a snake. The serpent slithered out from under a rock, frightening the donkey. The donkey brayed and reared up. The snake wiggled out of sight, but concealment was lost.

The Centurion, fearful of an ambush, barked orders to his troop. Eighty shields raised to form a phalanx. Eighty spears protruded toward the thicket. The Centurion wheeled his horse to the rear of the protective wall. The supply train jerked to a noisy and uncoordinated halt.

"Come out of there!" yelled the Centurion. "Come out now. Come out slowly. How dare you lay in wait for Imperial troops?"

Yakob pushed the brush aside, and jerked the frightened donkey into plain sight. Yusuf followed the cart. There was apparently no threat of ambush, so the Centurion ordered the phalanx dissolved.

"Are there any more of you?" demanded the Centurion.

"No, your excellency," responded Yakob. "Just us. We're bound for Nazareth, and stopped along the road to rest. Sorry we interrupted your column. Truly, we are."

The quartermaster supervising the supply train ran forward. "We'll take that cart and donkey. Some of our people are carrying more than they should be."

Yakob was angry. He reached for his sword. Before he could draw the weapon Yusuf restrained his arm. The Centurion rode up to the confrontation. "Smart move, there. Had the old man pulled that sword, he'd already have a spear in chest. Whatever you have on that thing, get it off. You can pick up your animal and cart this afternoon at Mt. Carmel. Assuming the bandits don't beat you to it, you can come back and get your cargo."

Yakob mumbled and spat on the ground. Defeated, he turned to unload the cedar planks. Yusuf took a bolder approach. As the Centurion turned his horse back toward the column, Yusuf grabbed the bridle. Everyone in the column and supply trained gasped in shock. The Centurion kicked Yusuf to the ground, and leaped from his saddle with sword in hand. "You can't touch an officer, or his horse!" The Centurion raised his sword to strike, but was startled by Yusuf's calm and fearless response.

"Herod will be very unhappy with you."

The Centurion was astonished. "Herod? Herod you say? Are you a madman as well as a fool? First you touch my horse. Now you use the name of the King in your defense! Amuse me! Before I cut you up for the buzzards, why would Herod care at all?"

"Those planks, Excellency, are a special order for Sephora. If we cannot continue with our cart and even a day is lost, the master builder will have to explain the delay to the King. If the planks are stolen before we can return for them, a huge sum of money, as well as many a day's time will be lost. Herod would be very unhappy."

The Centurion shook his head and let his sword slide back into the scabbard. "You're either the boldest liar in Galilee or your story is improbable enough to be true. You have a fool's courage; I'll grant you that. Nazareth, you say? I'll send a runner tomorrow. Be there. And be involved with turning these boards into doorways for Sephora, or I'll confiscate your cart and anything else you own. And then I promise it will be the two of you, not your donkey, pulling a cart in the supply train."

Yakob beamed with admiration for his son. He bowed to the Centurion. "Thank you, Excellency".

The quartermaster was displeased. "Can't we take their cart? I think he's lying sir. That's quite a lot of wood for building a doorway."

Yusuf extended his arms, palms upturned, and shrugged. "The king's house will have many rooms, and almost as many doorways."

The Centurion almost succeeded in suppressing a smile. He motioned to the quartermaster, who returned fuming and empty handed to the supply column. The Centurion regained the road. The column dressed sharply. At a command, the drum sounded and the legionnaires resumed their march.

When the centuria was a few hundred yards away, Yakob and Yusuf pushed the cart and pulled the donkey, rattling onto the pavement of the Via Maris. Yakob watched carefully while the faster military column grew ever smaller in the distance. Yusuf walked behind the load, once again studying the stones.

I, III
Babaziah, Masmasiah, Kaskasiah, and Sharlai

Miriam, wrapped in a grey gown and black cloak, crept warily from her bedchamber. She stepped lightly to avoid waking anyone else in the family quarters. She glanced in all directions from the servant's door, then raced across the courtyard to the protective shadows of the outer wall. She listened for the watchmen, but heard none. Miriam edged along the wall to peer around the edge of the arched gateway.

Moonlight. Enough to illuminate Eli's daughter's path to the midnight shore, but also enough to expose her escape. Early in her surreptitious studies of the healing arts Miriam developed an appreciation for natural and cosmic balance. The same aspects that foster greatest advantage can be the essence of greatest vulnerability. So it was with the moonlit night, but so was it also with her father's cadre of Roman guards. The richest man in Yudea employed pensioned soldiers to guard his several estates. Their military discipline made them formidable as well as fearless. Soon after she began her nocturnal ramblings, Miriam learned how to exploit that discipline to her advantage. Tonight would be no exception.

The guard rotated every two hours, always following a routine that left this minor approach to the compound unwatched for at least 30 seconds. The guard stood where Miriam expected, about 20 feet distant and facing away from the gate. The guard always stood there, but it would be time to change stations very shortly. The guard turned, unexpectedly. Miriam pulled her head from the arch and flattened herself against the wall. Why was the guard breaking routine? Had she been discovered? Her father would be so displeased if she were caught sneaking off again.

Miriam pressed hard against the wall, as if hoping it might embrace and conceal her in return. She held her breath as she heard the guard approach, scabbard slapping lightly on his leather tunic. The footfalls ceased, just beyond the gate. She smelled urine, and heard a stream of running water. The guard was relieving his bladder on the other side of the wall.

Someone called from a short distance away. "Cassius! Shake that thing more than three times and we'll know you're playing with yourself!"

"No need, Cletus. Not with your mother coming around every night." Both men laughed softly.

"Quiet, isn't it?" asked Cassius.

"As ever. Let's go make our reports and trade places. But Mithras curse me if I'll stand too close to your puddle of piss. You ought to use the bushes."

"There's more satisfaction with the wall. Eli may be richer than Herod, but all that money still can't stop an old soldier from pissing on his front gate, can it?"

Miriam listened until the guards and their conversation turned a corner at the end of the wall. This would be her chance. Her only chance tonight. She must go, now. She gathered her gown and cloak up around her knees, and sprinted toward the hedge on the perimeter of the clearing. Once concealed again, she stopped to catch her breath and double check for tracks. There had been a night, with the foreyard freshly raked, when sandal tracks led to her almost immediate discovery. There was no risk of that this evening. Miriam was thankful the servants had been inattentive.

From Eli's palace in Caesarea, it was less than a 30-minute walk to the shore of Mare Nostrum. Most people would avoid walking alone after dark. There could be bandits or lunatics on the road, or wild beasts lurking in the shadows. Miriam considered balance. Being somewhere that nobody expected her to be was more a shield than susceptibility. Besides, she wouldn't be alone for long. Nora and Yetro would be waiting on the beach, just beyond the docks and warehouses. Miriam smiled as she imagined them entwined in unsanctioned embrace, pending her arrival.

Miriam reached the shoreline. Several ships were in port, with lumbering night watchmen casting and absorbing ponderous shadows. The wind was down, so the full moon cast a frayed silver ribbon on the obsidian colored sea. The air was a warm kettle of soft, airborne salt. Miriam turned to her left, taking a familiar path to the low flat rock to meet her friends. On such a night, they would tell stories, gather remedial seaweed, and discuss both Torah and Kabbalah. Yetro was an elder scholar, at risk of prosecution or even stoning for sharing secret knowledge with women. His affection for young Nora made him careless. Miriam took intellectual advantage of his infatuation with her friend, and realized that her presence at these gatherings afforded Nora an easy excuse to restrict Yetro's carnal advances.

Nora and Yetro should have been sitting on the rock. Miriam approached to find them kneeling at the water's edge and very animated. As she drew nearer, she saw a body- with the torso dragged up above the rippling surf. Miriam ran to join her friends.

"What's this?"

"We saw him bobbing, face down, out about waist deep. Probably fell off one of the galleys" answered Nora. "Yetro waded out and pulled him in. We're pretty sure he's dead. He's not breathing. There's no heartbeat."

Yetro added, "There still might be some hope, depending on how long he's been dead. Quickly, Miriam. Nora and I will work his arms back and forth. Try blowing the spirit of your life into him."

Miriam knelt in the dark and placed her mouth across the stranger's cool, bluing lips. She breathed, there was no response.

"It's not working."

"Do it again."

Nora complained, "Looks like it's too late. He's gone."

Yetro remained persistent. "No. It's not too late. Miriam, you remember the four primary angels of healing?"

Miriam stopped blowing down the victim's throat to answer, "Of course."

"Quickly, speak their names, then close your eyes."

"Babaziah, Masmasiah, Kaskasiah, Sharlai." Behind her closed eyelids, Miriam observed a glowing white spot radiate from the bridge of her nose. It rapidly expanded, forming a circular pool of light that enveloped the region where she visualized her head must be. Shapes coalesced in the light. Vegetation, metallic utensils, a fountain, humble buildings, a pen of sheep at market, a village square. A figure emerged from the fountain. Miriam recognized the face, it was the same visage she and her friends were trying to revive.

The vision took both of Miriam's hands and placed a kiss on her forehead. "Thank you and your friends for calling me back. But this is my appointed hour. I'm beyond your efforts. Beyond any efforts. My place is elsewhere now. I have more desire to go there than to remain here. Shalom."

Miriam collapsed onto her back. Yetro and Nora stopped manipulating the corpse to be certain she was unharmed.

"We can stop now," reported Miriam. "He told me it's his time, and he wants to go to some other place."

Yetro nodded. "If we heal with light, we can't manifest any cure that violates the will of the patient. We cannot raise anyone who chooses death over life."

Nora glanced sideways at Yetro. "What do you mean, if we heal with light? Are there options?"

Yetro became somber and answered slowly. "Yes. You can heal against will with darkness. Summon a demon, assign the disorder to the demon, and then banish the demon again."

Miriam frowned.

Nora smiled. She was obviously intrigued, "Really, can you show us how that works? Maybe start with this body here?"

"I'll have no part of that!" insisted Miriam.

Yetro stared at Nora in alarm. "It's ridiculously dangerous. No matter how often you ask, you'll never learn that from me."

A small wave washed over the corpse. Miriam sat on the low rock, and wept.

I, IV
The Promised

Colors flowed slowly back to place as a cool half-light massaged and dispersed the darkness. Two grooms waited at Eli's stable gate, with horses saddled and provisioned for a long day's ride. The white mare was Eli's favorite. She was of premium Arabian lineage, a personal gift from Augustus. The dark horse, preferred by Eli's son, was a muscular steed with chiseled contours, a gleaming coat, and eyes that seemed to penetrate all bystanders. The Roman escort, already mounted, waited 20 yards beyond the outer wall. Aban bar Eli and his father planned to avoid the heat with an early start, a late return, and a luxurious repast at one of the finished portions of Sephora. Eli and Herod shared a strained history. Herod's invitation was informally phrased, yet not to be disregarded.

Father and son approached, speaking in low voices in deference to family members and servants still sleeping at this early hour. The white mare stomped a forefoot, whinnied, and shook. The dark stallion arched its neck, tugging impatiently at the bridle. The jerking arm of the dark horse groom flailed like a cloth puppet. Eli smiled. There was reason to expect a spirited ride.

The grooms bowed as Eli and Aban prepared to mount. With no ceremony and utmost discretion, a small stepstool appeared at the flank of the mare. Eli launched his aging frame from the stool, mounting as proudly as if he required no help at all. Aban eschewed any assistance, merely leaping astride the stallion and striking a proud figure once balanced in his seat. Eli nodded to the grooms, the bridles were released, and the riders cantered through the outer gate. One of the Roman guards proceeded a discrete distance ahead, and the other followed closely behind.

"Looks like a fine day for a ride, Father. No sign of rain."

"A fine day indeed. Let's let Moravius get a bit farther ahead and we will eat less dust." The four horsemen clopped along the road. The trailing guard must have been concerned that Eli and Aban were lagging far behind the leader. He closed to an inappropriate proximity before a stare and a raised brow from Eli inspired him to back off a regulation distance.

Eli sensed that his distrust of Herod was mutual. Each secretly feared what the other might be communicating to Augustus. Herod represented Imperial control of civil authority in Palestine. Eli was part of a small network asserting Roman dominance of economic affairs and protecting Roman interest in the administration of Temple justice.

Herod had a long history of turning his back on friends and switching alliances for personal profit. As a young man, Herod supported Mark Antony's conquest of Yerushalayim. Herod petitioned Antony for a high role in Yehudi government. Antony allowed Herod to name his seventeen-year old brother-in-law high priest. A year later, the high priest was killed on Herod's orders.

Eli was at the right hand of Octavian, eventually known as Augustus, during the defeat of Antony's forces in Palestine. Herod should have been executed for his role in Antony's administration. Incredulously, Herod, the Edomite convert to Yehudism, convinced the victorious Emperor not only to spare his life but to name him "King of the Yehudim." Eli accepted exclusive license to trade with the tin mines in Brittania, eschewing political power for almost unlimited financial opportunity.

Over the years, Herod had nine wives. Many died suspiciously, others were executed for treason. To his credit, he financed the Olympic Games in Athens, expanded the Temple in Yerushalayim, enforced civil order in Syria, and built the port facilities at Caesarea. All accomplishments hailed in Rome, but bewailed in Palestine by ghostly hordes of aggrieved and dispossessed victims.

Aban cleared his throat, preparing to broach what might be a delicate subject. "There was a courier yesterday, in the mid-afternoon.

Any news from Yerushalayim?"

Eli suspected his son wasn't especially interested in political or financial news. Even the servants were gossiping about an interminable chain of rumors. It was time for the twins to marry, for Eli to arrange a good match for each.

"The courier wasn't from Yerushalayim. He was from Ha-Ramathiam, sent by Tadeo. You know Tadeo."

Aban knew Tadeo. "Yes, of course. The Greek. He always impressed me, considering he's a gentile. His family often stays at our house in Yerushalayim during Passover. Was he making arrangements for this year?"

Eli chuckled. Aban thought he detected an ominous tone. "You could say he's making arrangements. And not just for this year. What do you think of his eldest daughter, Lydia?"

Aban reacted with an involuntary jerk. He spoke slowly and deliberately. "Think of Lydia? Think of her how, exactly?"

"I think she would be a good match for you. But you must agree. We won't go forward without your approval."

"Her father's a Greek!"

"True, but her mother's Yehudim, so she is too. Tadeo has been respectful and supportive of our traditions. I think he's at least monotheistic. He would have been a splendid Yehudi." Eli laughed. "We should consider him among the almost-chosen."

Aban grimaced. Tadeo ranked among the most successful merchants in Yudea. Tadeo and Eli partnered in various trading schemes. It wasn't difficult for Aban to appreciate his father considered financial variables before he suggested marriage to Lydia- but why not? Marriage was a young adult's responsibility to the community. In some marriages, an affection might develop between husband and wife.

Lydia? Aban realized he could do far worse. As the families

socialized over the years, he watched her sprout from an awkward little girl into a desirable woman. She was smart. While likely to assume her traditional submissive role she would perhaps like his stallion prove enough of a challenge to be interesting. Olive skin, raven hair, ivory teeth, and nut brown eyes. A healthy and definitely female form. Small hands, dainty feet, and a voice that sparkled like water as it gurgles past stones in a stream.

"Do you think she'd have me?"

Eli nodded. "Of course. In fact, Tadeo already asked if she would be willing. She is. So now it's up to you. She'll have a dowry of course, Tadeo's estate at Ha-Ramathiam."

Aban scowled. "What would I do with an estate? If I marry Lydia, I would want to build a new wing onto your house. That's the custom. I have no desire to live on the shore of Lake Tiberius."

"You don't have to live there. But there are good vineyards, and fields of wheat. You can live in Caesarea, or Yerushalayim, or anywhere else. And of course you can build onto any of my houses; it's expected. It would be a fine marriage, but only if you're willing."

"I don't have to decide now, do I?"

"Not this very instant, but…"

Moravius, on the lead horse, pulled up short at the brow of a hill. He turned, and raised his palm to bring the other riders to a halt. He put two fingers to his lips, calling for silence. A cluster of figures stood at the tree line, about a half mile ahead. It would not be wise to proceed without determining their identity and intentions.

The sound of a bronze axe, thumping into a smoke barked pine, raped the morning silence. Within seconds, additional woodcutters joined the abstract rhythm making war upon the landscape. Moravius relaxed his shoulders, and signaled it would be safe to advance. Yusuf and Eli crested the slope.

"More woodcutters," grumbled Eli. "Sometimes I worry that their wasteful practices will destroy every forest in Yudea."

"Every forest? How could that be, Father? The trees are as thick as the hairs of a dog."

"As many trees as there are? There are even more Romans. It takes a lot longer to grow a tree than to breed a Roman."

Aban considered his options for response, then changed the subject.

"So, if I decide to marry Lydia I'll need a new name. What would I be called?"

"Take the name of your new estate. You can be Aban of Ha-Ramathiam. I'll give you more responsibility in the tin trade. Eventually you will travel to Brittania without me. When I die, you will inherit my seat on the Council of the Sanhedrin. But for now, don't marry Lydia. Not if you think it will make you unhappy."

The air smelled of pitch and wet chips as the riders pasted the foresters. All stopped work to face the guards, Eli and Aban when they passed. The raggedly dressed slaves bowed, slightly.

"But what about Miriam? Have you found a match for Miriam?"

Eli shook his head. "No. Your sister? She is a blessing, and a curse. There's no shortage of young men hungry for the dowry they imagine she would bring. I want you to be happy, Miriam deserves happiness too. The right match, the right situation, hasn't presented itself. At least not with anybody I would dare ask her to accept. One of you at a time. You're the easier of the pair."

"How productive are the vineyards?"

"Which?"

"Those at Ha-Ramathiam."

"The fruit is rich, the vines abundant. Some of the best wines in Galilee are harvested there."

"In that case, I will trust that The One God is working through you and Tadeo. I will be Aban of Ha-Ramathiam, and Lydia will be my wife."

"May God be praised, Son. I'll send a message to Tadeo from Sephora. Let's take a careful look at what Herod is building. Perhaps he will lend us some master Tektons, the better to build you a more impressive house."

I, V
Tekome Bakah

Legends. There was no shortage of legends in Galilee. Some Yehudim claimed that an ancient prophet fractured the incongruous boulder with a single, omnipotent, whack of his walking staff. The Greeks imagined that Zeus accomplished the task by projecting electrical energy across the universe, while the Romans ascribed the lightning to Jupiter. Whatever the actual cause; mortal, divine, or natural, a transparent stream of cool water burbled from the top of a rocky outcrop.

Sheets of foam and aquatic polish slid down the face of the midnight colored stone, fracturing the reflection of the sun into gleaming rainbows, brilliant sparks, and fertility prayers. Once, the emerald grasses flourished along the stream banks. Once, herd animals and predators engaged in endless survival ballets near a series of waterholes. Once, the energy of the great spring, Tekome Bakah, inseminated a luxuriant valley leaping deeply into the Plain of Megiddo.

Now the valley below turned yellow every summer, and the ground was barren in the winter. Just below the great black monolith, Herod's waterworks intercepted the flow. A mammoth bronze cauldron funneled the creek into an aqueduct, carrying the precious water high above the parching valley to the palace at Sephora, many miles away. Isolated patches of green growth indicated the occasional leak in the royal design, but the theft of water was otherwise absolute.

The final reservoir rested an arrow's flight from the outer walls, situated just above the rooftops of Herod's palace. Water flowed to Sephora through four-sided, underground, stone causeways, erupting in the dramatic pillars of central fountains in reflective pools. The palace water marshal introduced it, as needed, into heated baths.

Yusuf, son of Yakob, dipped his calloused hands into one of the palace pools. The cool water soothed two bleeding knuckles. The mosaic courtyard was finally complete. Yusuf splashed the dust from his forearms. While it was still early in the afternoon, this was a logical stopping place for his day's labor. There were voices, behind him across the plaza and under the perimeter arches topping the access stairs. Yusuf turned to see who approached. He recognized King Herod, and the master builder, accompanied by two richly dressed strangers. One of the unknown men was probably his father's age, the other somewhat younger than Yusuf. Washing in a royal pool was a minor, but punishable transgression. Yusuf crossed his hands in front of his waist and bowed deeply, remaining stooped for an extra moment as a silent apology for his offense.

The master builder called, "Yusuf! Come over here. Beg the King's mercy. You violated the pool."

Yusuf crossed the courtyard, and stopped at the base of the steps. He bowed again, careful to avoid eye contact with Herod.

Herod stared at the master builder. "Who is this man?"

"He is Yusuf, son of Yakob. He's one of our hired workmen."

"What does he do, exactly?"

"Yusuf is skilled in mosaic tile. He had much to do with the design and construction of this courtyard, under the supervision of your own tile master, of course."

Herod turned his attention to Yusuf. "Stand up, man! How do you explain defiling the pool? Why shouldn't I have you whipped and discharged?"

Yusuf stood erect as commanded. Every pore of his body was sweating. His tongue felt swollen in his mouth. Trouble with the king was trouble unneeded. The sun was behind the figures at the top of the stairs. Yusuf resisted the urge to shade his eyes, and kept both hands at his side.

"Eminence, I apologize for my behavior. I had only, moments before, finished the final adjustments to the courtyard. I only thought to soothe my bleeding knuckles."

The master builder was aghast. "What? You dared bleed into the pool? Everything will have to be drained!"

"I am very sorry. It won't happen again. Is there something I can do to make up for my mistake?"

Herod addressed the older of the two men unrecognized by Yusuf, son of Yakob. "It's unfortunate that you, my guest, have to tolerate this incident. What do you think I should do with this character? Flog him, or forgive him?"

Eli stroked his beard as he examined the mosaic worker at the base of the steps. He did not speak until his gaze had encompassed the tiled courtyard, appreciating the profile of Herod, and the detailed portrayal of concubines and quail.

Eli addressed Yusuf, son of Yakob. "How much of this mosaic is your work?"

The master builder rushed to answer, "Sir, the mosaic is the work of King Herod's tile master. Yusuf is merely a skilled apprentice."

Eli was not convinced. "Really? And where is the tile master, at this important moment when the apprentice believes the work is finished?"

Eli repeated the question, "Yusuf, son of Yakob, how much of this mosaic is your work? Who did the design, chose the stone, created these images? Speak, and do not lie."

Yusuf felt vulnerable. In truth, he was primarily responsible for the mosaic work. He had been more often the teacher than the student as he and the tile master solved the riddle of a hundred thousand shapes and colors. The stranger was obviously on good terms with Herod, making him a powerful man. There might be some risk in lying about his role, but at the same time there was more risk in embarrassing the king or the master builder.

"Sir, I did much of the work and most of the design. But all of it was under the supervision of the royal tile master. I am a humble laborer, working only to glorify His Excellency, King Herod." Yusuf bowed again, when mentioning Herod's name.

Eli turned slightly to face Herod, and nodded his head, before addressing the king's question about a suitable fate for Yusuf, son of Yakob. "It might be wasteful to flog such a man. If he's poured his heart into your plaza, a bit of knuckle blood in the reflecting pool may be of less consequence. I suspect he is at least as shrewd as he is humble. If you have him beaten, that might damage his eyesight, or his hands- and it would appear both have served you well."

"So," responded Herod, "shall I just let him go, and forget about the incident?"

Eli attempted to suppress a mischievous smile, but Herod was amused rather than fooled.

"No, Eminence. I suggest you banish him from the project. At least for a while. Perhaps three months will give him time to consider the error of his ways."

Yusuf dared speak. "Mercy, Your Excellency. I beg mercy. Flog me if you will, but please do not send me away. My father labors here as well, and as he grows old he more often needs my help."

Eli questioned the master builder. "What does his father do?"

"He's a joiner of wood. Doors, furnishings, cabinets, and so forth. A skilled man, with excellent tools. He also owns his own cart and donkey."

Eli turned again to Herod. "In that case, Eminence, I suggest you banish the father as well. My son will be building an addition to my house in Caesarea, we could use some skilled labor. If it pleases you, we will take this trouble maker, and his father, off your hands for three months."

Herod laughed deeply, aware that he had been manipulated. He could save some face by participating in the charade. "I trust you will work them very long and very hard. Teach this fellow the error of his ways. We need to be sure he will not defile our pools when he returns."

"Sir, before you employ these people, you need to know about the curse," asserted the master builder.

"What curse would that be?" asked the younger stranger.

"They are descended from Yeconiah."

Eli paused a moment. "That curse was officially lifted after the Babylonian exile. Still, blood is blood. The stain remains, if not the shame." Eli closed his eyes, and put his right hand over his ear. "But, nevertheless, I'll put them to work for ninety days in Caesarea." He nodded to Herod as he concluded, "And I hope to send them back to you with improved attitudes and more respect for authority."

I, VI
Four Figures at a Fire

Lydia. Miriam knew Lydia well enough. Tadeo and his family visited once or twice a year. The eldest daughter was adequately clever – perhaps surprisingly so. Lydia masked her more adventurous side with a layer of orthodox conformity, but she often confided her secret thoughts to Miriam. Lydia would prove a surprising challenge for Miriam's self-absorbed and mercenary brother. Like most people, Miriam's brother was easily distracted by Lydia's physical beauty. Lydia's Greek father and Yehudi mother made beautiful babies together. The roots of the family tree tapped pure water from disparate wells, permitting Lydia to spend her life hiding in plain sight.

Childhood was finished. Yusuf elected to live in Caesarea. He would build an extension onto the family home. The marriage feast would begin when the dwelling was finished. Eli always hired the finest craftsmen available. Miriam was not surprised when her father and brother returned from a visit to Sephora, trailed by a pair of the king's own workmen.

"Father and son," Eli explained. "Wood and stone. Your brother's house will have a mosaic courtyard, much like a synagogue. It will rival Herod's new addition, but we'll want to be sure ours doesn't surpass his."

Her brother's future was determined, but Miriam's remained uncertain. With Aban matched to Lydia, Eli was free to concentrate on finding a husband for her as well. Miriam recoiled at the concept. She was the intellectual equal of any man she ever met, and despite common stereotypes was more emotionally secure than most men as well. How could The One God have ordained a system under which she remained her father's property, until bartered, like brood stock, to another man and his son?

There wasn't a problem with men. Miriam liked men. She was even jealous of Nora's clandestine relationship with Yetro. Miriam was once enraptured with a young Roman official, but her father was concerned about the intense friendship. Eli used his influence to have the official recalled to Rome. There had been one letter, intercepted by Eli.

The problem was with expectations. Much, but in some ways very little was expected of Eli's daughter. Miriam bristled that her life would be more restricted than most due to her father's financial achievement and political connections. Miriam dared to dream of owning her life. She treasured this interlude of freedom. Nothing was more valuable than self-determination. There could be no greater sacrifice than entirely surrendering her independence to a man. Any man.

Salt wind from Mare Nostrum wafted through the window like the voice of a lover. Miriam rose from her low couch and stood in a splash of sunlight to draw the linens across the opening. She paused to contemplate the gardens below. With the salt, there was the fecund scent of masquerade; ordinary green stalks audacious in conceit, erupting with vibrant and eccentric blossoms. While Miriam stood in the window, a tiny fledgling sparrow landed on the sill. "You must be fresh from the nest," thought Miriam. "You'll learn to fear soon enough, or you won't survive. Covet your first flights, little bird, before you choose fright over freedom. Don't we always?"

Miriam returned to the couch, lying on her back. She took a deep breath, held it a moment, and exhaled as slowly as possible. She took another, held it longer, and did not deliberately exhale at all. She closed her eyes, finding the tiny pearlescent presence behind the bridge of her nose. The circle expanded, encompassing first her eyes and mouth, then her chin and forehead, and ultimately surrounding the space where she perceived her head must be. As always, the imagery began.

Stars. There were more stars than Miriam remembered. The sky was blacker, but the celestial sparks were as radiant as sun kissed diamonds. The earth was flat, stony, and totally barren of vegetation. Shards of broken pottery, fired with intense and unfamiliar colors, littered the ground and reflected the starlight.

Four figures, wrapped in white robes, were gathered around a fire. Miriam wondered where, in such an arid environment, they found the wood. The fuel snapped and cracked. A swirling tower of sparks, but no smoke, hovered above the flames. A voice, vaguely familiar, called "Miriam. Shalom. We saved a space for you, come join us."

Miriam knelt and took her place in the circle.

"Why do I recognize your voice," she asked.

"We've met before. You and your friends tried to save me, the last time I drowned in Mare Nostrum."

"The last time?"

"That's a long story, and not important."

"Who are you? Who are the others?"

"Me? I am often called Elishua. Sometimes I am called Ben-gabar, or Gabriel, or Almodad, or Israel. Only The One God knows my true name, it's even secret from myself."

"So, your friends are?"

"You have always known them, but have yet to meet them. In due time, Miriam. In due time. Every step in sequence. Patience, daughter."

Miriam noted the companions remained motionless. The only face she was able to see was that of the drowning victim addressing her now. Miriam was amazed- she felt secure and beloved in an alien environment with four total strangers.

"Am I here for some purpose, then?"

"Yes. You need to carry a message."

"To whom?"

"Your second cousin, Elisheba."

"Yes, I know her. She's married to that old priest, Zachariah. What's the message?"

"Tell her she's with child."

Miriam was startled. She leaned back and stared in astonishment.

"What? She has to be many years beyond any function of her womb. And Zachariah? At his age? Physically unlikely."

"Nevertheless, you will carry the message. The child will be a boy. He shall be named Yohan."

A warm and reassuring sensation of love and security rushed through Miriam's body as perfectly as blood in an artery. She surrendered easily, and without alarm. "Yes, I'll carry the message."

Miriam sensed her purpose at the fire was accomplished, at least for the moment. She stood up to leave, but was called back.

"And, oh, Miriam. When you visit Elisheba, she will have a gift for you as well."

Miriam inhaled slowly until her lungs were completely filled. She opened her eyes. As she sat up on the couch, she noticed the sun cast the shadow of a small sparrow- taking flight from her sill- against the linen window sheers.

I, VII
Yericho Ford

Regimental discipline empowered the Roman Legions. Duriel of Archeleus chose to bet his life, and the lives of seventy Zealots, that regimental discipline could render his Roman enemies vulnerable as well as invincible.

Yarden, the "River of Descent" began in the north. It shed all suspended solids in Lake Tiberius before the pristine flow twisted lazily through a flourishing valley skirting Agrippina, Alexandrium, Archeleus and Yericho. The Yarden progressively silted along the way, interminably scrubbing off layers of old soil to reveal new earth below. There were those who believed the Yarden could carry away human iniquities with equal effectiveness. The river ultimately dumped into Lake Asphaltitus, so saturated with sins, sands, and salts the undrinkable waters were commonly considered dead.

The best ford was at Yericho. It was here the Roman patrol crossed. Always on the third day each week, and always within an hour of cock's crow. Duriel imagined that the Romans knew nothing of Gideon's slaughter of the Midianites or Jephtha's victory over the Ephriamites at Yericho ford, but Duriel was well versed in the Torah. There were symbolic as well as strategic reasons to stage his ambush here.

The Romans would send thirty-eight men. They always sent thirty-eight. Two scouts, an officer, and thirty-five men afoot. Duriel's volunteers wielded less elaborate weaponry, but they enjoyed numerical advantage. If surprise were properly maintained, and if The One God heard their prayers, the battle would be short and decisive.

For many weeks, Duriel of Archeleus watched the patrols cross the ford. He learned they arrived in a tight formation, broke up when wading the stream, and formed up again on the far shore. This morning, Duriel's archers and war slingers lay just downstream in the reeds. All were motionless- belly down in cold mud, with a thin layer of muck smeared across their backs. Other patriots, similarly concealed on the upstream side of the ford, were armed with swords and spears. Many of the better weapons were stolen from barracks, or looted from Roman corpses. When the patrol was disorganized, the Romans would be exposed to a volley of arrows and kill stones. Close combat with shaft and blade should make swift work of any survivors.

Duriel and four archers lay in wait, behind a minor hillock only short distance beyond the ford. The unfamiliar Roman armor fit poorly, chafing his shoulders. There was an objectionable smell. Repeated washings did little to remove the former owner's blood from the crimson tunic. However, the armor was a critical portion of his plan. "Roman to defeat Roman," thought Duriel.

As always, not long beyond first crow, the patrol quick marched into sight on the Yericho bank of the Yarden. As always, the formation paused at the brow of the river's edge. As always, two mounted scouts descended into the broad shallows and splashed slowly through the current. As always, on the far shore, the scouts pressed ahead to ensure there were no bandits lurking beyond the riverbank. Unlike a hundred previous patrols, the scouts were felled by arrows the moment they were out of their commander's sight.

The horses reared and whinnied. Duriel and an archer snagged their bridles. Duriel knew the officer must have heard the horses' panic. There was no time to waste if there were any hope to avoid arousing suspicion. Duriel leaped into an empty saddle, rode calmly around the knoll, and waved an "all clear" signal to the patrol. The officer would assume that, as always, the second scout had continued on ahead.

Lucius Petronius, commanding the patrol, felt apprehensive. Something might be different; different beyond a pair of unusually noisy horses. Two scouts crossed the river, one of large frame on a roan mount and one of smaller build on a bay. The figure signaling safe passage was a person of smaller build, astride the roan. They would not have switched horses. Following a short period of indecision, Lucius ultimately concluded his memory might be faulty. Perhaps the larger man actually rode the bay. "I must learn to be more attentive to details, if ever I hope to advance in rank," thought Lucius. Lucius could not know that overconfidence, rather than inattention to detail, was about to prevent future advancement.

Lucius turned in the saddle to face the footmen. "Cross and reform."

Duriel watched until the commander's horse was in midstream. The scout always remained on station until the patrol was partway across, then moving on ahead to join his companion. Lucius was reassured by the routine. "There's nothing to fear at Yericho," thought Lucius. "Farmers, herdsmen, and shopkeepers here. Nothing else. If there's any danger at all, there could be brigands beyond- skulking about in the Golan hills. There have been reports of unrest in Betharampta, and Mecaerus, but even there we seldom en…"

Four arrows sped from the brush atop the low hill. One crippled Lucius' horse, two bounced off his breastplate, and the fourth penetrated his neck below the helm to open an artery. He was unconscious before he hit the ground, and dead when his heart pulsed the last geyser of blood into the Yarden.

Downstream, the Zealots arose. Legion soldiers carried their shields on their left arm, so the downstream volley from archers and slingers landed on the more vulnerable right hand side. Fourteen soldiers fell in the first flight, and nine more in the second as the disoriented patrol struggled to reform in the Yarden.

Duriel drew his sword and charged on horseback into the river. There was no initial resistance from the surviving patrolmen, all assuming he was a fellow Roman riding to battle on their behalf. The Romans advanced, raggedly, toward the archers. Duriel took two lives with as many sword thrusts, distracting the confused soldiers with the treachery. Swords and spears emerged from upstream cover, and a desperate melee began. Men grunted, cursed, and shouted. Steel clanged on steel, or opened flesh and bone with the sound of a liquefied crunch. The ten remaining Romans were no match for seventy Yehudi patriots, sixty-eight of whom were still standing when the ambush rapidly resolved.

Some of the Zealots began to cheer. Duriel, still mounted on his horse, called for silence. Only the pleas and wails of wounded Romans endured beyond the order. "I saw Amos of Zia fall," said Duriel. "Did we lose anyone else?"

"Some wounded, but none too seriously. Silas from Adasa was speared through. A long way to come to die. He leaves a wife, and several children."

"What about Amos?" asked Duriel. "Any dependents?"

"No. He's a widower with nobody left at home. You are bleeding on you right leg."

Duriel extended his leg from the saddle. There was a shallow gash. Dark red traces of tacks flowed toward his ankle, already congealing like cooling candle wax. "So I am. Nothing serious. I scraped my leg on a thorn while mounting the saddle."

Duriel dismounted to join his men in the river. "We can thank God for our victory today. But the cost was high. Silas and Amos were worth more than all of these gentile invaders combined." A wounded Roman soldier struggled to rise in the current, lifting a hand in supplication. Duriel severed the appendage with a vicious swing of his sword.

"Kill all of their wounded. Strip the bodies. Stash the weapons and armor in the cave. Any coins or jewelry, we'll send to Adasa to support the family of Silas."

Duriel's Zealots went grimly about their butchery, until the pleas of the wounded became the silence of the dead. The Yarden whooshed and gurgled in its course, unaffected by the morbid drama unfolding in its bosom. The River of Descent scraped off old soil, to reveal new earth below. All was carried away to Lake Asphaltitus; the sand, the soil, the sin, and the blood- to disappear where even the water was considered dead.

I, VIII
Setting Fire to a Dragon

The massacre at Yericho Ford inspired the Roman Commandant to apportion a centuria of additional guards for Sephora. He also assigned forty to the family compound of the Emperor's close friend at Caesarea. Treasonous Zealots ordinarily targeted Roman soldiers. Yehudim with close ties to Rome, like Eli in Caesarea and non-Yehudi political appointees like Herod were not exempt from occasional, sometimes deadly attacks.

"We're now more of a target, not less!" protested Eli. "I appreciate the concern, but tripling the number of soldiers around my home? It's more likely to anger the Zealots than frighten them off. Call them back. Or send them up to Sephora with the rest. I don't need them."

"Do you have some doubt we can protect you?"

"That's not the point, Commander. Your reinforcements increase my exposure. But go ahead and send five men to bolster my personal guard. I'll note your dedication to duty when I thank The Emperor for his concern."

***

Miriam tiptoed from the compound, eyes scanning the moonlit shadows for any evidence of the additional guards. Tonight's escape might prove more challenging. Men could be stationed in unexpected places. The pattern of patrol might be altered. She pressed into some fragrant vines growing against the outer wall, watching for an opportunity to sprint across the clearing.

Someone gripped her firmly on the shoulder. Miriam gasped and turned. There stood her brother, Aban. "You think you have been getting away with this, don't you?"

"What do you mean? I couldn't sleep. I'm just taking a short walk."

"Sure you are. A short walk down to the beach. You'll be meeting those friends of yours, again."

"What?!"

"I followed you. A couple of times. You're not as quiet as you think when you get up to leave."

"You had no right!" blustered Miriam. She rethought her demeanor and softened her tone. "Please, you can't tell father. He'll lock me in my room."

"Perhaps he should. There's been too much trouble this week. I can't let you go. Not alone, anyway."

Miriam considered her options. Within a day or two, the massacre at Yericho Ford would be less prominent on her father's mind. There was the unfinished business of message delivery. She would be asking Eli's permission to travel to the home of Elisheba and Zachariah. A request that might require Aban's support, a journey perhaps conditioned by his accompaniment. Aban wouldn't be welcomed by Nora and Yetro, but she couldn't afford to alienate him now.

"So, you think it will be alright if we both go? And what about once we're there."

"I don't want to intrude. I'll wait in the shadows under the piers, like I've done before. With the Zealots and all, I think it makes sense for us to walk down together."

Miriam squeezed her brother's hand. "Thanks. Do you think you can make it across the clearing?"

Aban looked around the corner of the wall. "This actually looks like a good time to go. And remember, every time you made it across here, so did I."

The twins ducked low and sprinted for the brush at the edge of the clearing. Once concealed on the far side, Miriam took a breath and grinned. "By the way, not every time. Far from it."

Brother and sister trailed the dark roadway to the waterfront. Each aware that with the impending marriage of Aban and with Eli's efforts to find a match for Miriam, the number of sibling moments would be severely reduced in the future. The twins cared for one another, even as Aban was confused and concerned by his sister's unorthodox activities and Miriam considered her brother too concerned with money and politics. They made idle small talk, deliberately avoiding any speculation about an immediate future that would be profoundly and inexorably changed.

At the base of the trail, the stone quay stretched into Mare Nostrum. There were more galleys than usual. A row of torches outlined the crease where rusted iron rings penetrated the angular sides of the pier. Additional guards strolled slowly along the length of the pier, capes gathered at the breast and belt to ward off a saline chill. The twins sensed it would be wise to exercise more than typical caution.

Aban crouched down in a shadow. "Be careful. Don't get caught. If your friends aren't there, don't wait around. Come back, and we'll go home. And don't be all night if they are there."

Miriam hugged her brother farewell, then hurried along the shoreline, careful to remain above the torchlight. Yetro and Nora were leaning against the flat rock, on the far side where they would be unnoticed by the guards on the pier.

"Shalom, Miriam."

"Shalom."

Nora was more engaged than usual. There was an excited tone to her whisper. "We've been talking about the uprising. Nobody knows who is leading the Zealots. I think it could be the Messiah foretold by Isaiah. Such a complete victory at Yericho. Surely that has to be a sign."

Yetro used a short stick to draw random lines in the sand. "I'm not so sure. There's a new rumor about a Messiah just about every year. Nobody can agree exactly how the Messiah will throw off the yoke of our oppressors, bring us to account for our sins, and restore the kingdom of Israel."

"True," agreed Nora. "But killing off all the Romans would make a good start." She pulled a wineskin from beneath her robe, and handed it to Miriam. Miriam took a short sip, noting the wine was warm and smooth. Miriam extended the wine toward Yetro.

Yetro stabbed his stick into the sand, reached for the wineskin, and then reconsidered. "Thanks, but not tonight. I'm trying to keep a clear head. Trying to listen to my heart. Miriam, what do you think?"

"About the uprising at Yericho? I wouldn't be too quick to say it has anything to do with a Messiah. Father often remarks how these heroes rise and fall. Most of them have a short lifespan, once they come to the attention of Rome. It's been hundreds of years since Isaiah. Obviously God's not in any hurry. Everything in sequence."

Nora tucked the wine back under her robe. "Well, maybe I hope, more than think, it might be the Messiah. How long do we have to wait?"

Yetro twisted around and rose up sufficiently to get a view of the Roman docks. Nothing seemed out of place, their gathering at the rock must be undetected.

Yetro sat back down. "I guess my question wasn't about the situation at Yericho, exactly. More about whether the Messiah, when he comes, will be able to slay so many Roman soldiers."

Miriam pressed her thumb against her lower lip, considered the question for a moment, and replied. "Samson killed a thousand Philistines with the jawbone of an ass. If the Messiah had ten Samsons, or a hundred Samsons- maybe he could kill enough soldiers. But maybe, killing the Romans isn't the answer to the riddle."

Yetro stroked his beard, nodded, and then gestured toward the heavens. "That constellation coiled around the north star,"

Nora interrupted quickly, as if eager to please her instructor and advisor. "The dragon!"

"Yes, the dragon. Tonight, I think that might be our sign."

"How so?" asked Miriam.

"Only a fool sets fire to a dragon. Fire is the dragon's element. The more fire you bring to the fight, the stronger the dragon becomes. That's going to be true with the Romans. If we want a victory over the dragon, we can't fight the beast with its own element."

Nora was disappointed. "So how will the Messiah defeat the Romans and set us free?"

Yetro put his palms over his eyes, spanning his forehead with his fingers. He bowed his head and did not speak. Miriam and Nora sensed that he should not be interrupted. Yetro trembled a moment, then relaxed. He placed his hands in his lap, smiled, and opened his eyes.

"Maybe, when the Messiah finally comes, he will use the Romans to set us free. Maybe, when the Messiah finally comes, we will ultimately be liberated by the occupation- not from the occupation."

None among the three spoke for several minutes. All considered Yetro's revelation. Miriam felt suddenly compelled to leave.

"I've got to go. If I'm not here next week, it's because I'll be visiting my cousin Elisheba."

"Oh yes," said Yetro. "The wife of Zachariah. I'd have you give my regards to my old master, but of course he can never learn that you know me- or especially how."

Miriam retraced steps along the margin of the beach to meet her brother in his concealment at the quay. Miriam was unusually quiet as the twins trekked back to Eli's palatial estate. They slipped unnoticed back into the family quarters. Miriam was pleased that Aban revealed himself earlier in the evening. It was far better to have him as an accomplice than an accuser.

I, IX
The Water Level

Shoshanna, eldest female servant in Eli's household, didn't need to genuflect. Her bent back ensured she stooped even when attempting to stand erect. Shoshanna smiled softly as she entered Eli's library. She carried an ebony tray rimmed with sapphire chips and fitted with elaborately carved silver handles. On the tray were five figs, dipped in honey and rolled in crushed almonds.

Shoshanna knew she must not listen. She could not overhear, remember, or especially repeat any conversations between the master and anyone else. Still, she realized that if she were to listen she would overhear Miriam asking her father's leave to travel to a small town southwest of Yerushalayim. The figs were Eli's favorite treat, delivered at Miriam's instruction "either when it sounds like Father is about to give in, or if he starts to get angry." The old servant willingly conspired with Eli's daughter, admiring the young woman's instinctive ability to manipulate a situation.

Eli raised his eyebrows and chuckled at the timely appearance of the figs. He knew he was being maneuvered, but what else could he expect from strong-willed Miriam? He acquiesced with a theatrical reluctance. "Three days. If after three days there is no more news of Zealots or bandits, you can go visit Elisheba in Ain Karem."

Miriam beamed. "Thank you, father."

Eli wagged his index finger toward his daughter. "It's better to give you permission than to have you sneaking off. You have to promise not to elude your chaperones."

"Agreed."

"You'll travel with three guards, the six of you dressed as poor villagers on a pilgrimage to Yerushalayim. The weapons will be concealed in the cart. I'll have Moravius take you through Samaria rather than east of the Yarden. That's one less day on the road, and there will be fewer Zealots among the Samaritans."

"Remain with Elisheba and Zachariah for a week, assuming you are welcome. Then move into our apartments in Yerushalayim. I'll be in Yerushalayim within a fortnight to attend to affairs of the Sanhedrin. We'll all travel back together, after the Feast of Tabernacles."

Miriam rose from her seat and kissed Eli on the forehead. "You're the best father anyone ever had."

"We'll see if you feel that way when I finally find you a match. This little indulgence should be the end of your childhood. If The One God is willing, the next time you want to travel you will be asking permission of your husband- not your father."

Miriam answered with obviously feigned fervor. "Yes, Father. God willing." She smiled as she left Eli alone with four of the five almond figs.

Miriam skipped joyfully into the garden, selecting a path that terminated where her brother's addition to Eli's mansion was under noisy construction. Cartloads of materials arrived from every quadrant of the compass. Squads of laborers ferried stone, wood, copper, and bronze to Tektons working under supervision of the master builder. The lack of activity in a central area, marked off with a cord stretched between pegs driven into the ground, piqued Miriam's curiosity. She resolved to investigate, and approached the roped off area.

"Hold up there!" hailed a voice from a patch of shade. "Please don't step over the boundary. You might wreck my work!"

Miriam turned to learn who was addressing her. A muscular man, perhaps only a few years older than herself, was seated next to a stack of green reeds. There was something about his voice. Miriam couldn't identify exactly what she found so fascinating- was it the confidence with which he spoke? The solid sound of every syllable, seeming to resonate from a deep and expansive chest?

Miriam approached the man with the reeds. "Shalom, stranger." As she entered the shade she could discern additional details. First, she noticed the eyes. Almost impossibly white around the brown pupils. Like the voice, there was something about those eyes. Something perhaps she now remembered, from a previously forgotten dream. The man chopped reeds into segments as short as a knuckle joint. The sinews of his brawny forearms flexed as he gripped handfuls of vegetation to efficiently cut several at a time. He stood as Miriam approached, revealing a pleasingly slender but sturdy frame. His face seemed to catch fire as he smiled, and Miriam's entire body basked in the heat.

"Shalom," he answered. "Maybe I should say, 'Shalom, mistress'- aren't you Lord Eli's daughter?"

Miriam glanced quickly in all directions. For some reason, it seemed as if she should not be seen talking to this fellow- even though conversation with bondsmen and hired workers was allowed.

She returned his smile. "That I am. But, you can call me Miriam- as long as nobody else is listening. And you are?"

"Yusuf, son of Yakob. At your service."

"You seem to be the only person chopping reeds. What are you doing, exactly?"

"Making a level. It's a tool we learned about from the Greeks. They say it was discovered by Archimedes, I think."

"Don't let me interrupt your work, Yusuf son of Yakob." Miriam knelt down, almost presumptuously, as she asked "You don't mind if I watch a while, though, do you?"

"That would be alright," agreed Yusuf, trying to conceal his pleasure for such attractive company. Miriam was a radiant presence. Her sandalwood complexion and softly cascading coal black hair seemed to glisten, even in the shade. Her facial features were attractive, and as much as one could determine by watching her move while fully clothed her body was well proportioned as well. She seemed slightly forward, a quality with which Yusuf was intrigued.

"How does the level work, and what will you do with it?"

"I'm creating the mosaic courtyard for your brother's addition. We need to make sure the ground is perfectly level, and packed down as hard as possible, before we create a slab. Then, we need to make sure the slab itself is level before we lay any tile."

"So, how does it actually work?"

"These sections of reed lay end to end inside a long strip of hide," answered Yusuf. He pointed to a small stack of materials nearby. "Then I'll sew the hide shut around the reeds, creating a flexible tube to contain water. Each end of the tube ties onto the nib on one of those specially thrown clay jars, and we have a level."

"I'm not sure I understand how to use it," said Miriam.

"We hang each jar on an identical wooden staff. One staff remains at the reference point, and the other can be moved anywhere inside the work area."

"I follow that."

Yusuf raised and lowered his hands to assist with the description. "When we want to test for level, we pour water into the jar on the reference staff. If the other jar is lower, it will overflow before the water level in the reference jar reaches the brim. If the other jar is higher, the reference jar will be the first to overflow. When both jars fill exactly to the top without overflowing, the staffs are at equal level."

"Seems pretty simple!" exclaimed Miriam.

"It is. Many time, the best tools are the simplest. I don't know how we'd level such a large area any other way."

Yusuf was not prepared for Miriam's next question.

"Can I help?"

Yusuf stammered in search of a reply. "Help with what, Miriam?"

"Help make the water level. It sounds fascinating. I am anxious to see it work."

Yusuf looked around, as if alarmed that somebody might have been close enough to overhear the unorthodox request.

"But… you're a woman!"

"Yes. For a moment there, I wasn't sure you noticed."

Yusuf blushed. "That's not what I meant. Building a water level isn't a woman's work."

"Cutting reeds? Stitching a hide? Women commonly do both. Come on, let me help. At least a little bit. What could it possibly hurt?"

"Sounds like something Eve might have said to Adam, under a fruit tree."

It was Miriam's turn to blush.

Yusuf continued, "It would outrage everybody. A lady of your position, laboring beside a hired workman? There would be trouble. If not for both of us, then at least for me."

Miriam spread open the hide and began to line up short sections of reed. "Nonsense, Yusuf. Besides, you're here in my father's service, correct? If anyone says anything, I will tell them I ordered you to let me help."

"Is that what you're doing? Ordering me?"

Miriam ceased arranging the reeds, shifted her kneeling balance toward her ankles, made deliberate eye contact with Yusuf, tilted her head, shrugged a shoulder and grinned. "No. Tell me to stop, and I'll go away and leave you alone."

Charmed by Miriam, and ignoring an internal feeling that trouble might be brewing, Yusuf replied, "No, don't go. I'm grateful for the assistance. The company too. I just don't want to embarrass either of us."

"If there's scandal, it won't be the first time," assured Miriam. "But I promise that I'll stand for the blame if anything is said. Looks like you have cut enough reeds, doesn't it? What about if I begin stitching hide from this end, and you from the other?"

Yusuf laughed softly. "In charge already, are you? Alright then, I'll meet you in the middle."

I, X
Separate Shadows

Yusuf and Miriam stitched up the hide from opposite ends. Yusuf became concerned as they approached the middle. He would soon be closer to Miriam, deeper into her personal space, than was customary or traditionally approved. She was the daughter of the richest man in Yudea, and he a lowly Tekton in her father's employ. To error on the side of caution might be wise. Splashing in Herod's pool cost him and his father their positions at Sephora. There were times when bearing the curse of Yeconiah made it difficult to find employment. Developing a further reputation for ignoring social protocol could prevent Yusuf and Yakob's future hire by other wealthy patrons.

Yusuf looked up from his work. His gaze carried across the cordoned space reserved for the courtyard. On the far side of his workspace, slaves and bonded servants hauled earth and stone in wicker baskets. Children scampered among the hectic thrall, bearing skins of warm water to quench thirst proclaimed in hisses and clucks from as far north as Illyria, syncopated throat rattles from as far east as Parthia, and in dusky rumblings from as far west as Tringitania, Tripolitania, Mauritania, and Numidia. An ochre dust rose wherever wood and stone collided to prepare the foundation, but no fortuitous breeze wafted the gritty cloud to conceal Yusuf's workspace from the pavilion of the master builder, Shimon of Accara.

A young man, recognizable as Miriam's twin brother, stood next to Shimon. The brother's agitated and concerned expression was evident, and only emphasized by his accusatory pointing. Shimon frowned, shook his head and threw up his hands to indicate confusion, motioned an assistant to join him, and walked toward the son of Yakob's work area. Aban followed on his heels.

The worried Tektons warned Miriam. "That didn't take long. Here comes your brother, along with the master builder. And they don't look happy. I guess I should have said 'no' when you offered to help.

Sorry about this."

Miriam didn't look up from her stitching. "Don't worry about them. I can handle my brother. And, I can handle the master builder. So far, we haven't done anything that I consider wrong. We hardly know each other, yet."

Yusuf stood to meet the arrival of the master builder and his companions. He bowed slightly. Miriam remained kneeling, stitching along the length of the hide.

"This is outrageous!" shouted the master builder. "What do they teach you, over in Nazareth?"

Before Yusuf could answer, Aban demanded of Miriam, "Has he hurt you in any way? I'll have him stoned if he assaulted you, or flogged if he so much as touched you at all."

Miriam stopped sewing to make a bewildered face at her brother. "Does it look like I'm here against my will? I'm interested in this device he's building, and I…"

Yusuf interrupted. "Please, Excellency, it's entirely my fault. Miriam is blameless. Nothing has happened. I'm sorry. I don't know what came over me." Yusuf felt sheepish at the partial lie. He knew precisely, and enjoyed, what came over him when Miriam approached. He suspected that Miriam knew as well.

Miriam wiped the dust from her cloak as she stood, assuming a position obviously and inappropriately close to Yusuf the Tekton. "Nonsense! I can speak for myself, and I will. I approached Yusuf to ask about his work. I found the answer interesting, and I offered to help. He turned me down, as you would expect. He said that making a tool of this type was not suitable work for a woman."

"He's right!" asserted the master builder.

"Not to mention the sight of my sister, a woman of your position laboring beside a man." Snarled Aban. "Any man would be unacceptable, but this one? This one and his entire family are cursed.

You could not have chosen a more unsuitable companion."

Yusuf looked beyond the master builder. Most of the workers were slowed or stopped, watching the confrontation unfolding across the designated courtyard. The Tektons saw his father press to the front of the crowd. The worried Yakob had his palms pressed together, and his face turned up toward the heavens.

"A curse, you say?" answered Miriam. "Even if that's so, it has nothing to do with this leveling tool. Did you know it was invented by Archimedes?"

Aban looked puzzled. "Archimedes? Who's that?"

"Never mind. The point is, Yusuf tried to send me away and I insisted on staying. He works for our family, does he not?"

"He works for our father, for me, and Shimon, sister."

"Are you telling me I have no right to ask him to let me help?"

Shimon spoke up. "Nothing can prevent a person in your position from asking, but he cannot and should not agree to allow it. There are laws, customs, and traditions to consider."

Miriam folded her arms across her chest and glared at Shimon of Accara. "You make no sense!"

Aban, Shimon, and the master builder's assistant gasped at Miriam's audacity. Her status as Eli's daughter did not confer the privilege of speaking disrespectfully to a person ranking as highly as the master builder.

Miriam continued. "If nothing can prevent a person in my position from asking, then what empowers a person in his position to refuse?" She lowered her voice to a whisper. "And Shimon, you talk about laws, customs, and traditions? What traditions are you and our servant, Rashiel, observing so secretly?"

Shimon was overwhelmed. "What? I mean, I have no idea what you're…"

"Spare me the lies, master builder. I've seen you together, in the gardens, in the middle of the night. You only thought nobody was watching. I could have brought the matter to my father. Trust me, it's only pity for her unhappy marriage and a regard for her future that has kept me silent. Otherwise I would denounce you and think nothing of it at all."

Shimon sputtered, at a loss for words and obviously guilty as charged. Aban shook his head and snickered softly. He had learned, long ago, never to underestimate his twin. Bringing the matter to Eli would result in some punishment for Miriam, and perhaps the discharge of not only the skillful tile setter but his master builder as well. This was not a good moment to replace Shimon. The situation would require some finesse.

Aban motioned to Miriam to join him away from the others. As they moved toward an out of earshot location in which to whisper, Shimon glared at Yusuf. "If you manage to survive this, you better keep silent about anything you think you heard about midnight visits to a garden. If it gets down to something between you and me, I'll warn you now to watch your back."

The Tekton folded his arms, defiantly, and said nothing.

The twins negotiated in their private huddle. "You have to stay away from him. He's beneath your station. You certainly can't lower yourself to do a tradesman's work! I can have him dismissed with a single word, and why shouldn't I?"

"I can do whatever I want. We haven't done, said, or planned anything to be ashamed of. I'm going to finish helping Yusuf with the tool. In fact, I'm going to ask him to let me help him use it. You'll say nothing to Father about this. Shimon isn't the only one here with secrets now, is he?"

Aban began to protest, then stopped. He realized there would be no point. Miriam missed very little that occurred around her. He dared not ask his sister what she had heard or observed. There were things that Eli had no need to know. Aban realized he was out maneuvered, and sighed. He jerked his head back toward the Tektons, the master builder, and Shimon's assistant. "Come on. I've got a plan." The twins rejoined the group.

"My sister and I have talked this over. She should not and cannot be in the company of our tile setter."

Miriam cleared her throat.

"Without permission," continued her brother. "I hereby give her permission to entertain herself and observe the work of the tile setter. I order the tile setter to allow her to assist, if she desires to do so, with light tasks that do not compromise dignity or modesty. I will have a chaperone stand by, close enough to hear any conversation that might pass between my sister and our workman."

Abani lowered his voice and spoke aside to Yusuf. "Thank her for your narrow escape. Keep at least an arm's length between you. If you lay even a finger on her, it will mean your life and your father's as well. Keep your place in mind. Don't even try to spark a friendship. Do you hear me?"

The Tekton nodded slightly. "I'm sorry for the trouble, Excellency. Of course I agree." Miriam's brother, the master builder, and the assistant walked back toward the pavilion. The instant they turned around, work resumed on the foundations for the new wing of Eli's estate in Caesarea. Yakob wiped his brow, glanced thankfully toward the heavens, and returned to work with the rest of the crowd.

"Sorry about all the outrage," said Miriam.

"Thanks for sticking up for me," replied Yusuf. "I know you said you would, but thanks just the same."

Miriam said something in reply, but Yusuf's mind was reviewing the conditions to which he had agreed. No touching. Keeping an arm's distance away from Miriam. Allowing a chaperone. All were reasonable precautions, given the differential in position and the social limitations applied to young women conversing with unmarried men. The last condition? "Don't even try to spark a friendship"? Yusuf realized it was already too late to comply. Far too late, indeed.

I, XI
Seedlings

South of the Roman port at Caesarea, low cliffs framed the eastern basin of the Mare Nostrum. The beach shriveled to a thin, sorrel strand- a wading ground for waxen storks- and vanished entirely at the highest tides. Nests of black backed gulls and sea sparrows hung precariously from every fissure in the tumble home crag.

Midway between the salt and the summit was a grotto. Fresh water trickled gently through the cavern, emerging to sustain incongruous mosses, meld with sunlight, and dribble into the sea. A stain from the smoke of a thousand cook fires smeared the upper lip of the cave, fading progressively into the rocks immediately above. This conjunction of earth, and fire, and water was home to Yetro, an apostate priest recently cast out by the Essenes.

Yetro squatted at the bright edge of his dark abode, celebrating the common grace of heat and light. He watched a red and black frigate bird swoop and dive, marveling that the creature's angular wingspan could sustain it aloft for a week at a time- yet The One God had not granted this master of the air an ability to either swim or walk. Each afternoon when the sun touched the cave, Yetro sipped an obscure tea and meditated. It was the hour every day when he found harmony with the universe; the triumph of spirit dreams over physical distractions. For Yetro, the confluence where twenty-three hours of illusion were reconciled by sixty-minutes of reality.

Yetro closed his eyes, and located the bright dot behind the bridge of his nose. As his artificial conscious constructs faded, the pure light expanded to surround his forehead, his, face and ultimately the space where he imagined his head must be. Shapes and sounds filled the vessel of virgin space. Shimmering visions of the Sefirot, the ten garments of The One God, swirled in a marbled, multi-colored spectrum of perfectly circular thoughts, connected by tangential lines.

Yetro celebrated the Sefriot from its peak. Keter, the crown, the father from which everything else was manifest. 'Hochma, the son of the father, seated at the right hand of Keter and the source of all wisdom. Binah, the divine will or holy spirit of the father, opposite and equal with the son and the point where wisdom is empowered to create change in the illusory physical universe. Yetro remembered this dream. There were seven more garments of The One God to consider, but a wind cleared the circle to make way for new vision.

A hand reached deep into a seed bag, rummaging along the bottom seam until finding a single remaining pit. With elaborate ceremony, the disembodied hand placed the seed on a flat, dry stone. Yetro noted a startling similarity between the visionary stone and the rock where he often courted young Nora, sharing with her and Miriam some secrets of the priesthood. There was no soil or water on the rock, but still the seed sprouted. The seed produced a green shoot, that became a stem, that became a trunk. A leafy canopy expanded across the sky, streaking in fire and thunder. Yetro rose on the wings of the frigate bird, higher and higher toward the sun. High enough to perceive, with enormous satisfaction that the tree sprouted from an infertile basis shaded all of Israel- Galilee, Samaria, and Yudea.

Laughter. Yetro heard laughter. He was almost certain he recognized the voice.

The vision of the tree evaporated. The hand, and a new seed bag reappeared. The seed bag was bright, white, and apparently freshly stitched. It tumbled in space, turning inside out in the process. There could be no doubt, the bag was devoid of seed. The sack collapsed into a new shape, and it resembled a sprouted seed. The sprout evolved into a green shoot, the shoot became a stem, and the stem became a trunk. Yetro again rose on the wings of the frigate bird, higher than ever toward the sun. He climbed until he could perceive that the tree sprouted from an empty sack dwarfed the tree that shaded Israel. The canopy extended across the Mare Nostrum, to Rome, Espangna, and Britannia. The shadow stretched in every aspect of a circle, disappearing into mists that enveloped those lands not yet imagined by Greeks, Romans, or Yehudim.

More laughter, and louder this time. An unfettered glee of celebration, victory, and fulfillment. Yetro recognized the voice. One of his former mentors, Zachariah, laughed exactly so. The face of Zachariah appeared among the still erupting tentacles of limbs, leaves, and wind rippled possibilities.

"Why?" cried Yetro. "Why would you bring a tree out of barren stone?"

The envisioned Zachariah looked puzzled. "Because there is no life in the stone, the life is from the seed alone."

Unsatisfied, Yetro demanded, "And why would you bring a tree from an empty sack, where never there was a single seed?"

Zachariah laughed until he lost his breath. His eyes were red as fire, and soft tears washed a light trace of dust from his aging cheeks. "Because even the seed is not life. It is a messenger of life. Our One God can send the message in other ways. Ways we cannot understand unless we dare imagine them. Words beyond even the holy alphabet of Yetzirah. Songs beyond the music of creation."

"Master, I'm not sure I understand."

"How does one see so much, but understand so little, Yetro? From what matter or substance did the One God Create the heavens and the earth?"

Before Yetro could formulate an answer, Zachariah continued. "From no matter, and from no substance. There was no absence, and no void, because there was no form or presence. The One God became the heavens and the earth, there was nothing else from which to work. If The One God can become the heavens and the earth, surely The One God can become a tree. Or a thousand trees. Or an eternal forest of trees."

Yetro jerked back into the illusory world of consciousness.

Zachariah and the universal tree were gone. But, what had Zachariah said? "Words beyond the holy alphabet of Yetzirah"? Such magic would transcend the very sounds with which The One God said "Let There Be Light."

Bathed in sunlight, Yetro experienced a freezing and foreboding chill. Many things stewing in his subconscious were suddenly clarified. He lusted after Nora, but now realized it was her friend Miriam whom he truly loved. Miriam, who had just declared her intention to visit Zachariah and his wife Elisheba. Zachariah, a master of Yetzirah, had a reputation as a spiritual radical. Was the old rabbi daring to wander so boldly into unexplored spiritual environs? The renegade priest was troubled by a sensation that Miriam was in danger. He sensed her life was about to take an irreversible turn. Perhaps, if Yetro could dissuade her from calling on the emergent fanatic, she might avoid entanglement in any fate from which she could not be rescued.

Yetro knew he would not be allowed entry to Eli's estate. There was an uncomfortable history. If anybody were to warn Miriam, if not too late and if she had not already departed, it would need to be Nora. It might be time to set Nora aside, but not before she carried a message to Miriam.

From the invisible black bowels of his cave, Yetro heard the laughter. It sounded like a celebration of victory and fulfillment. It sounded, for all the world, like Zachariah.

I, XII
Mazzeroth

Hamutal, wrinkled crone and bond servant of Eli, was assigned to chaperone Miriam and the tile setter. Her hooded cloak created a red and black frame around a perpetually dry scowl. She sat her post on a padded wooden bench like an owl surveying a pair of mice. Hamutal did not approve of the young tile setter. Clearly he did not know his place. Hamutal relied upon an established social order for security. The hierarchy began with Lord Eli, descended through his son, through the free laborers, and even through the ranks of servants and slaves. Miriam was amused that her brother, already adept in business, often overlooked important details in personal relationships.

Miriam smiled at Yusuf and raised a shoulder to suggest he look in Hamutal's direction. She laughed. "Speak Hebrew. Hamutal never learned Hebrew, but she won't admit it. You do speak the temple language, right?"

"Of course. Like everyone else, I studied the law until age twelve."

"Good. Then we can say anything we care to say. Not a word of it will travel back to my brother. That is, not unless you lapse into Aramaic, or Pashtu. Hamutal will give a favorable report, rather than admit her ignorance."

Yusuf was amused. His new friend was obviously a clever woman, and not above being devious when it suited her. While enjoying her acquaintance, it would be wise to avoid trusting her completely. At least not until he got to know her better; something that seemed rather unlikely.

"So," continued Miriam, "if the water level is done what's the next step?"

Yusuf motioned toward the roped off expanse of ground. "We'll use it to be sure the base is level where they are going to build the slab. But first, to keep track of which areas need to raised or lowered and by how much, we'll rough out the design. We also get an early look at how it is going to fit in the space."

"But won't it be covered when they create the slab?"

"Of course. Then it gets laid out again."

Miriam surveyed the tranquil rectangular vacancy surrounded by the chaos and clatter of construction. The grand courtyard would be the outdoor focal point of her twin brother's addition to their father's estate. Yusuf was only a few years older than herself. She wondered if such a significant project could be appropriately assigned to someone too young to be an experienced master.

Miriam looked around for any drawings, and found none. "Where are your plans, Yusuf? Shouldn't you be working from a drawing or something?"

Yusuf tapped his forehead. "The plans are here. Your father and brother approved a design I have done for two different synagogues."

Yusuf picked up a length of rope, two strands of cord and a pair of wooden stakes. "Everything we need to lay out a mazzeroth, you see here in my hand."

Miriam was shocked. Memories of secret meetings on the beach with Yetro and Nora erupted in her mind's eye. "A mazzeroth? My father and brother approved a mazzeroth? Father sits on the Sanhedrin. People have been stoned for telling fortunes from the stars. I doubt very much that my brother understands the cycle of constellations."

Yusuf was unflustered. He moved toward the center of the future courtyard. Miriam followed. "Try to walk lightly," he cautioned- instantly embarrassed that his remark insinuated Miriam could walk any other way.

"This mazzeroth will have nothing to do with fortune telling. As

I explained to your father, it's a calendar, with the twelve months of the year. And, each month corresponds to one of the twelve sons of The Patriarch, Israel."

"Did you explain to my father that each of those twelve months, and twelve tribes, is represented by a constellation in the mazzeroth? Did you even know?"

"Yes, I knew. No, I didn't explain about any relationship between the constellations and the tribes. Not exactly. He was satisfied that the design has been used in synagogues. Besides, the connection only applies if somebody is deliberately trying to make one. Otherwise, the constellations just indicate the seasons."

"How did you hear about it?"

"An old rabbi at the first synagogue told me all the stories while I laid the floor, but they're not usually part of Torah study. And you? Who told you about a link between the constellations and the twelve tribes?"

Miriam bit her lower lip. "Let's just say a not-so-old rabbi."

Yusuf stopped at a point marked with a previously placed black stone. The shape and color of the stone startled Miriam. It looked like a miniaturized version of the seaside rock where she kept many a midnight rendezvous with Nora and Yetro. Yusuf moved the stone just far enough to insert the pointed end of the stake into the ground. Yusuf wacked the top of the stake with the stone to drive it firmly into the soil.

Yusuf handed the ends of the rope to Miriam. "We need to find the exact middle. If you walk toward the edge of the plaza with both ends, I'll run out of rope when we get to the middle." Miriam moved ten steps. Yusuf found the middle point of the rope, and spliced a lightweight cord between the stands. Yusuf pointed to the splice and announced, "There it is, the mazzeroth."

"Hardly," objected Miriam.

"Well it isn't finished, but what we've got now is a tool to create a circle and divide it into twelve equal segments. So in a way the mazzeroth is already there, we just have to extract it. If you'd like to help, please come hold this middle piece on top of the stake."

Hamutal did not approve of Miriam's posture as she bent over the stake to secure the center of the rope. The servant was also curious about the process unfolding and after a moment decided to say nothing. Yusuf gripped the loose end of the rope and the second wooden stake. He walked an exactly defined circle around Miriam, scribing a line in the dirt as he progressed.

Yusuf joked, "So there you are, Miriam- how does it feel to be standing right in the middle of the heavens."

Miriam blushed, but did not respond. The middle of the heavens or not, she was much pleased to be sharing this time with Yusuf, the handsome tile setter.

Yusuf returned to the middle stake. "Now it's time to lay out the four directions. North, south, east, and west. If you take one end of the rope and walk to the edge of the circle, I'll do the same. As long as we keep the spliced cord over the central stake and the rope pulled tightly, wherever we both touch the edge the circle divides in half."

"Does it matter where?" asked Miriam.

"It will in the final cast of the Mazzeroth. Things will need to align. For now, we're only trying to get a sense of shape and scale."

The pair pulled the rope taut, each touching an edge with the spliced cord above the central stake. "Make a mark on the rim," suggested Yusuf. "I'll do the same. That will be north and south. The Greeks call these half circles 'diametros'- it means…"

"Two measures!" interrupted Miriam. "I'm a little familiar with Greek. So we could divide the circle again and have four parts. We could divide the four parts and get eight. Eight splits into sixteen. How do we divide the mazzeroth equally into twelve?"

"You're almost right about dividing the circle again to make four parts."

"I assumed. But I don't know how we figure out exactly where to make the next line of diametros. If it's too high or too low on the edge, we would have quarter circles that would not be equal in size." "

Yusuf grinned. "Yes, they probably would be uneven. That's why there's a secret step."

Miriam winked. "Excellent. I always enjoy a good secret."

"Why am I not surprised? Hold the spliced cord that marks the middle, and one end of the large rope. We need to find the middle point of the spoke, one half of the diametros."

Miriam laid one loose end of the rope next to the spliced cord. Yusuf stretched the resulting loop taut to locate the middle of the spoke. He spliced in a second cord to mark the location.

"It still looks like we're getting ready to divide evenly. Maybe even by quarters. I can't wait to see how you're going to turn this circle into twelfths."

"No need to wait," assured Yusuf. "Let's get started. Please take that original splice, the one that is the center of the whole rope, and lay it down where the diameter line meets the south point of the circle. I'll lay the rope in a curve, down along the outline, until we reach the length of the original spoke."

They began. Miriam kneeled to place the spliced cord where directed. Hamutal was alarmed. Miriam should not be kneeling lower than the tradesman. From her bench, she called out "Mistress, remember you place!"

Miriam ignored the chaperone. She watched Yusuf lay the rope. "You don't have enough length to work your way up to East."

"No, but where the rope ends we are exactly two-thirds of the way up the quarter circle from south to east. That second spliced cord? That's exactly half way of the two thirds, so it's one third of the way, and…"

"Wait, wait!" exuded Miriam. "I get it! We just divided one quarter of the circle into thirds."

"Exactly so. And if we measure from the…"

Miriam interrupted again. "If we measure from the point of the first third, that same two thirds length of rope will show us exactly where to locate one end of east and west, right?"

Yusuf was impressed. Miriam was bright as well as curious. "Yes. It works every time."

Miriam was pleased with her discovery. "Then we just divide the other quarters into threes, and we have an outline for the mazzeroth. Whoever thought of that must have had a miraculous mind."

"Euclid," said Yusuf. "Another Greek. But I doubt there's a miracle involved. A lot of times people want to see a miracle where there's just a well-kept secret. I'm sure there are a lot of actual miracles. But I think if we had a way to count, and always be sure of the differences, we'd discover there are many more secrets than miracles."

I, XIII
Butter and Smoke

A dust devil swerved through the sharp parch of the afternoon heat. Hiram of Dothan, as well as a servant and two guards, dismounted at the main entrance to Eli's compound in Caesarea. One of Eli's grooms accepted their bridles, and led the lathered horses to shaded rest and water in the stables. Eli's steward, Tadeis, approached the travelers and bowed slightly.

"Shalom, Lord Hiram. Lord Eli will be pleased to see you again. Will you be spending the night?"

Hiram considered the random reports of Zealots, lately attacking other Yehudim known to do business with the Romans. "We will, if it isn't inconvenient."

"It would be a pleasure. I'll have an apartment opened for your Excellency, and your guards will be welcomed in the barracks."

"Thank you. I'll need to shake off the road grime. If you would let Lord Eli know that I would like to see him this afternoon, at his pleasure?"

"Of course." Tadeis clapped his hands. A svelte, dusky, Egyptian girl responded, walking briskly to his side. She bowed to the arrivals. "Rehema, please escort Lord Hiram and his servant to our best guest chamber. See that he has everything he needs, and prepare a bath if he so desires."

Turning again to Hiram, Tadeis said "I'll let Lord Eli know that you are here. A messenger will come for you when it's time for your meeting."

Rehema bowed again before Hiram, executing a long, sweeping motion with her arm. "If you please, Your Excellency, I'll show you the way to your rooms" She walked gracefully through the hedges and ornamental gardens of the entry route, an oasis of songbird and shadow. Hiram, only a few steps behind, glanced appreciatively at the alternate thrusts of her hips. He knew it was understood by all that the steward's instruction for the servant girl to provide him "everything he needed" included quenching his lust upon request. Tempting as she might be, Hiram reluctantly resolved to avoid testing the limits of hospitality. His mission was too urgent for complications or distractions. The Feast of Tabernacles was only a few weeks away.

***

Miriam and Yusuf began surveying the twelve sections of the mazzeroth. Miriam held one staff of the water level at the center of the circle, while Yusuf measured four points in the center and three on the perimeter of every sign. As they worked, they tested and teased one another. It began with Nisan, the first month of the mazzeroth.

"Nisan," announced Yusuf. "Sign of the ram."

Before he could continue, Miriam added, "Tribe of Yehudah, known for royal leadership. Time of Passover."

Yusuf checked the water level inside his pot, and scratched a mark on a tablet covered with wax. "Isn't it a little strange that during the month of the Ram, and royal leadership, we sacrifice the son of the ram, a lamb, in the temple?"

"People have spent a lifetime puzzling over that," responded Miriam. "So if we are moving in order than the next is month is Iyar, sign of the bull."

Yusuf moved the water level to the adjoining sector. "Indeed. Tribe of Yissachar, legendary scholars of Torah."

They worked through Sivan, (sign of the twins, seafaring tribe of Zevulun, and representative of the unity of God with the chosen people). Partway through Tammuz, (sign of the crab, tribe of Reuven, focus on concentration to task), a hooded figure approached. He hissed in half whisper, "Miriam, I need to speak with you."

Miriam recognized the voice, and was startled. She drove her water level staff into the soil. "I'll be right back, Yusuf. I think this might be important." She stepped to the edge of the work area with the new arrival, arousing Hamutal's suspicions.

"What are you doing here?" Miriam demanded in a low voice. "You know what would happen if my father finds you. How did you get in?"

Yetro spoke without uncovering his head. "I sneaked in with some laborers. I tried to send Nora. She got upset and refused to carry the message for me. I've had a frightening vision, and I think you're in danger."

Hamutal called, "Is everything all right, Mistress Miriam?"

"Fine. I'll only be a minute."

Yusuf watched the pair as carefully as Hamutal. He experienced an unfamiliar feeling. Could it be jealousy?

One of Eli's overseers walked nearby. Yetro turned his head to ensure nobody in authority would get a glance of his face. "You said you were planning to visit Elisheba and Zachariah."

"Yes. I hope to leave tomorrow, if there's no more trouble from the Zealots."

"You shouldn't go," insisted Yetro.

"Why not? Maybe Nora isn't the only one who is supposed to carry a message."

The reference to carrying a message confused Yetro, but he decided to ignore it for now.

"It's Zachariah. He's always had an interest in Yetzirah, but I think he's taking it to a new level. He's going beyond any safe boundaries. Places we have all sworn never to go. I believe he's using the language to manifest things. Unlikely things. Impossible things. If The One God strikes him dead for his arrogance, everyone in the vicinity might be at risk."

Miriam remained silent for a moment, then answered tentatively, "I don't think I have a choice. I have to go to Elisheba. I'm supposed to carry a message."

"A message from whom?"

"He said his name was Ben-Gabar, or Gabriel, or Israel. But he also said that wasn't his true name."

"Miriam, you're using the names of an angel! How do you know him? Where could you have met him?"

"Do you remember the dead body you pulled from Mare Nost…"

A voice nearby cried, "There he is! Seize him!"

Yetro bolted for the gate, leaping over ditches and low piles of stone. His cloak flapped behind his back and his bare legs churned frantically for freedom. A stout Roman guard blocked his exit with shield and spear. Yetro sprang into the air, cleared the leveled spear, and planted both feet on the gleaming bronze shield. The astonished guard toppled backward, and Yetro was across the clearing before he collected his balance and regained a footing.

Yusuf the tile setter stepped to Miriam's side. "Who was that? Why did he run off like a thief?"

"Just a friend of a friend. There has been some trouble between him and my father. Lord Eli said if he ever set foot here again, he would be arrested and charged with blasphemy."

"What did he want?"

"He thought I might be in danger."

"From what, or from whom?"

"I'm not sure. It doesn't matter," said Miriam. She smiled. "But thanks for being worried. Where were we in the survey? Oh, yes; the tribe of Reuven, sign of the crab, Tammuz" ***

Bathed and refreshed, Hiram of Dothan entered the reception chambers to call on Eli of Caesarea. He carried a bindle, wrapped in fine red linen and tied with a golden cord. Hiram was presenting Eli with an elaborate gift, but hoping for much more in return

Eli greeted Hiram with a brotherly embrace. "It's always a pleasure when you come by for a visit."

"And a pleasure to be so graciously received. Thank you for that. I brought you something, from Damascus."

"That was kind."

Hiram extended the linen package toward Eli. "Here, open it please. I'd like to see what you think of it."

Eli accepted the package. He worked to loosen the knot in the golden cord. "So how goes the coal business, Hiram?"

"Very well. And no small thanks to you. The Romans have insatiable appetite to fuel their forges. I'll never forget how your influence opened so many doors."

The gold cord opened, allowing the linen to fall away. Concealed within was a box meticulously crafted from Acacia wood. The dramatic contrast between vivid black and yellow grains looked like butter blended with smoke. Eli opened the hinged lid to reveal a 12-inch dagger in a gilded scabbard.

Eli lifted the dagger from the box. It felt solidly satisfactory in hand. A gold pommel, shaped like the Star of David capped an onyx handle, inlaid with rubies. The guard was elaborately worked, and trimmed with gold. He slowly withdrew the etched blade from its protective holder, and held the knife so that rays reflecting from the afternoon sun pierced the dark shadows of isolated corners.

"It's fabulous, thank you," said Eli. He smiled, and winked. "Somehow, I suspect you may be here for something more than gifting me a beautiful dagger."

"There's no point trying to conceal anything from you, old friend. I'm here to speak for my son, Faramond. He's of age. You have a daughter. Our families have long been friends and allies."

"Faramond? For some reason, I hadn't thought… How well does he know Miriam? She can be very independent. It's going to take a strong man, or a loving man, to bring her to heel."

"They have met several times. Forgive me, Eli, but there are some who tell wild stories about your daughter. None of them could possibly be true. In our house, she would get a fresh start. There are only three brothers to inherit when I die. Faramond will be an excellent provider."

"I'll talk to Miriam. Soon. I will mention your son. Whatever I do, I won't force her to marry against her will."

"It isn't always useful for a woman to be willful, Eli."

"Perhaps not, but Miriam knows her mind. I said I will talk to her, and I will. So, tell me, Hiram, have you been able to buy enough labor to keep up your rate of production? And how about that new deposit at Bemeselis? The last time we spoke, you had some very high expectations there. I hope you were not disappointed."

I, XIV
Graining the Dove

Elisheba was weary. The annoying stone in her sandal could wait until she could set down her marketing. Her home, a dark silhouette crowned by the retiring moments of a late summer sun was less than a hundred steps away. Surely she could shift her gait to take some weight off the left foot, at least for a hundred steps. There was a silver haired figure profiled on the roof. He was turning in circles and flailing his arms, partially obscured by a swirling flock of doves. Elisheba scowled. Zachariah and his cursed birds; both more trouble than Elisheba needed or deserved. The priest would be graining his birds this late afternoon, but Elisheba was in no mood for patience.

"Husband!" she called. "Come down here and help me unpack the marketing."

"Just a minute. I'm almost finished here."

"Come down now. I've got a stone in my sandal. I need your help. Let the birds wait."

Zachariah mumbled something about approaching darkness. He placed his aging and rickety frame on the top step of a gopher wood ladder and teetered for a moment to collect his balance.

"Have you ever considered you might be getting too old to climb up there so often? One of these days you're going to miss your footing and fall. Let's hope, when you do, that it's from no higher than that top step. An old man can overreach, you know."

"Who's an old man?" muttered Zachariah. "I'm paying to ferry birds back to Crete and two ziggurats in Chaldea tomorrow. I need to be sure they are in good condition to make the journey."

Elisheba handed her basket to Zachariah. She placed a hand on his shoulder to achieve balance. She unlaced her sandal to liberate the offensive rock. "And probably paying too much again. How difficult can it be to haul a few birds in a cage? Field laborers work an entire year for less money."

"Perhaps. But the price is justified by the knowledge returned. Besides, it's too late to change my mind, the couriers are already here with birds that will fly to their homes with messages from me."

Elisheba removed her other sandal and placed it at the threshold. She kissed her finger, touched the mezuzah, and stepped beyond the shadows to her home. Zachariah followed behind.

Safe in the privacy of her home, Elisheba grew insistent. "I was happier in the first few weeks, when I didn't believe this was possible. I thought it was another of your crazy notions. That I was many years too old. That you were talking about "spiritual birth", not an actual pregnancy. I haven't bled in years, but there are other signs. A woman just knows."

"The One God works in mysterious ways, wife."

"It seems. And The One God is getting no small amount of mysterious help from you! I'm going to start to show pretty soon. How much longer must we keep this a secret? Not that any rational person would believe it, anyway."

"The messenger was very clear. We must tell nobody. The truth of this has been revealed to only one other. We wait until they came forward. That person is part of the larger plan, but without their faithful and voluntary acceptance nothing further can proceed. Once they seek us out and demonstrate belief, things will be very different."

"Different how? What's the larger plan?"

"Different that you can tell everyone you are with child. But you must never mention, to anyone, the means."

"There's no chance of that. I couldn't begin to explain the means. I'll never understand."

"It's more important, right now, to accept than to understand. And of course you can't mention that you know the child will be a boy. You could be stoned as a witch for less."

Elisheba thrust the back of her hands at Zachariah, emphasizing her frustration. "Why won't you at least tell me who this mysterious person is? Is it that you won't, or because you can't?"

"We must be patient, and faithful. The One God has an important task for us."

Elisheba rolled her eyes. "Well, I have an important task for you, as well. We're low on wood for the oven."

Zachariah raised a hand as he backed out the door. "As soon as I put the doves back on the roost, my love. Just as soon."

I, XV
Passage Through Samaria

The small group left at sunrise. The early morning hours would be cool and stress the donkey less. Miriam sat next to Moravius, who drove the cart. Eli's daughter was clothed in a humble gown and robe, appropriated from a servant. Moravius wore garments suitable for a tradesman, with a scarf wrapped over the lower half of his face to conceal his Roman features. Two chaperones and two more guards followed on foot behind, each dressed as a poor villager. Moravius hid deadly swords and spears under a pile of firewood in the cart, but as a final precaution ordered one of the guards to carry a beat up, rustic sword. "Just in case a lack of any weapons at all would seem as suspicious as traveling fully armed." There was no fresh news of any Zealots, last seen well to the south and east of their route and destination.

Yusuf the tile setter watched as the party left the compound. The last two days, shared with Miriam, had been happy times. He wanted to wish her farewell, or at least wave. But last night his father Yakob warned him, "Don't forget your place, son. She's played with you like a bauble, but that meant nothing. Whatever you might be dreaming of, it's impossible. She won't even remember your name in three days. There's still time to find you a wife. The One God will provide." Even so, Yusuf felt as though a portion of his heart was riding away from Caesarea, and probably out of his life forever.

Miriam looked briefly toward Yusuf's work area. She wished her father and brother were not hovering nervously about during the final preparations for departure. She ached to speak one last time to her new friend, perhaps even dare a farewell kiss on the cheek and make some vague commitment to resume their carefully monitored conversations upon return. She beat back the impulse, further attention or any sign of emotional interest might compromise Yusuf's future at Caesarea. She hoped Yusuf realized that she had feelings for him. But what did that matter? There could be no future for Eli's daughter and a tile setter burdened with the curse of Yeconiah.

As Eli instructed, they traveled directly through Samaria rather than east of the Yarden. The group rattled and walked through the fields and forests, on the Roman road through Narbata, Gita, and Yishub. Everywhere, the reception was the same. Villagers spat or turned their backs toward the travelers. Children were whisked off the street, with doors and shutters slamming. Marketers threw blankets across their wares, suspending sale until the group passed by. "Yehudim! How dare they trespass!" Skeletal, snarling dogs harassed the laboring ass. Disguised guards and chaperones kicked slobbering fangs away from weary ankles.

They were denied water, as Moravius anticipated. There were extra rations in the cart, but not enough to finish the journey. There was a traveler's well, just north of Capharsaba. It was unlikely they would be offered shelter in a Samaritan inn, but with a rotating watch it would be safe to spend the night at the edge of the forest.

That same morning, near the Tower of Aphek, eleven Yehudi patriots assembled a flock of sheep. The Romans took bloody revenge after the massacre at Yericho Ford, scouring every Yudean town and village for Zealots. Scores of Yehudim were arrested. Some known to be Zealots, some thought to be sympathizers, and others randomly selected to increase the reportable total of executions. Some victims were staked to the ground and eviscerated. Others were nailed to trees, and the outer walls of public buildings. The condemned screamed, then moaned, then silently embraced the mercy of death.

Duriel of Archeleus and his ten most trusted officers realized there was less risk of apprehension in Galilee. The sheep would be good cover. Wild beasts lurked in the forests, so the pseudo shepherds would carry basic weapons to protect the flock. The drive to Galilee, through Samaria, would be slow and dusty work. The sheep would require water every night. Duriel knew there was a traveler's well, just north of Capharsaba. That would be an ideal place to camp, the first night.

Mithraeum. He kicked aside the bones when she entered.

"The Samaritans haven't defaced the murals," said Moravius. "I can't do anything about the stench. Maybe the cat has protected them. So, you wanted to see this. The light is a little dim, but you can make it out. Take a look."

Low benches lined both sides of the cave, but the prominent feature was a painting that occupied the entire back wall. Protected from sunlight, the colors remained vivid two decades after the Romans abandoned the site.

The central figure in the painting was a man half astride a fallen bull. The left hand grasped the bull by the nostrils, pulling its head back to better expose the neck. A dagger in the right plunged to sever an artery, just above the animal's right foreleg. Other animals were depicted as well. A dog, a snake and a raven worried the dying bull, while a scorpion latched onto the testicles. Two smaller humanoids watched the ritual slaughter, each bearing a torch.

Miriam examined the mural. After a minute, Moravius said, "I'm pleased the temple hasn't been defiled. We should go now, if we hope to make the traveler's well by sundown."

Miriam was not satisfied. "Not so fast. I want to know what this means. We can wait a few more minutes while you explain the painting."

Moravius sighed. "As long as you have seen the god, you might as well know the story. Every temple in the empire has exactly the same painting. Some places, this scene is carved into the rock itself."

"Go ahead. I'll let you know if I get confused."

"Certainly, Mistress. You know that the year begins on the day when the daylight and darkness are exactly equal, right?"

"Of course. In the month of Nisan, under the sign of the ram."

"Right. It's under the sign of the ram now, but in the time of our fathers' fathers' fathers' fathers' it was under the sign of the bull. The great orb that surrounds the earth, upon which all the gods and goddesses have put their signs, was shifted. Mithras is so powerful; he exists beyond the orb surrounding the earth. He is mighty enough to grasp the orb and shift the heavens. And he did. That explains why Mithras is killing the bull, or the sign of the bull, in the painting."

"Interesting," agreed Miriam. "So the other figures in the mural? Are they heavenly signs as well?"

Moravius marveled that Miriam was so receptive. "If you look up to the heavens tonight, you will see the figures in the painting. They cross the sky in a line. The bull, we Romans call Taurus. The dog is Canis Minor, the raven is Corvus, the snake is Hydra, and the insect with the castrating pincers is Scorpio."

Miriam's mind raced ahead of Moravius' explanation. "And the two smaller figures, with torches? Do they represent the sun and the moon? Is that why the torches are the same size, because daylight and darkness are equal?"

Moravius regarded Miriam with admiration. "You just grasped, in a matter of minutes, what some who worship Mithras need years to understand. You are a quick study, Mistress."

Miriam smiled. "I have a good teacher."

They stepped back through the brush to return to the cart. Moravius scanned the vicinity for any sign of a returning cat. There was none.

"Forgive me, Mistress. Tell me if I assume too much or am out of line. Would it be alright if I asked a question about your god, The One God?"

"That would seem fair. You were kind enough to tell me about Mithras. I'm only a woman, of course, not a rabbi. I might or might not know the answer to your question, but if I do I'll be happy to tell you."

"We know the face of every deity in the Roman banquet of the gods. Jupiter, Neptune, Mars, Vulcan, Mercury, and as you just saw, Mithras. Why are there no images of The One God? How can you worship someone or something or some god that has no shape, form or face? Something that you can't see? Something that maybe nobody has ever seen? How would you ever be sure The One God is real?"

"Give me a minute to think about the best way to answer", replied Miriam.

Once reassembled on the road, the travelers proceeded toward the traveler's well at Capharsaba. Moravius assured everyone their destination was less than an hour away.

A late afternoon wind clattered through the skeleton of a broad leafed tree. "There's your answer Moravius. That's the face of The One God."

"The One God is the wind?"

"No, but The One God is like the wind. You believe in wind, right?"

"Of course, Mistress. Even a madman would have to believe in wind."

"Good. But you have never actually seen wind, have you? You can't weigh it, or measure it. How do you know it's real?"

"Of course the wind is real. We can't see the wind, but we can see the effects of wind. We can see things carried by the wind. We can see birds soaring in the wind. We can hear the wind, even when we can't actually see it. And we can measure wind. We can measure its force."

"Exactly. Consider The One God is like the wind. Unseen, but ever present. We don't need to see the wind to know it's real. Some things are seen, Moravius- like your god, Mithras. Other things are unseen, like The One God."

"But," objected Moravius, "we can feel the wind when it blows. When has anyone ever felt The One God?"

Miriam stopped walking, bringing the entire party to a halt. She placed her hand gently on the Roman captain's forearm. "Tell me, Moravius. At some point you must have been in love. What did love look like?"

"Love doesn't look like anything at all"

"But could you feel it? Was it real?"

Moravius shook his head to indicate disbelief. "I understand what you are saying. But forgive me, Mistress. I think I will hold fast to gods I can actually see. I hope you aren't offended."

"Not at all. We each need to listen to our own heart, "said Miriam. No sooner did she speak than she envisioned Yusuf, son of Yakob, creating a mosaic courtyard for her brother's wing of the family compound.

I, XVII
Goats and Lions

A scratch. Nothing more than an incidental abrasion, sustained at Yericho Ford. The lingering infection became aggressive on the walk from the Tower of Aphek. Duriel of Archeleus was weak with fever. He trailed behind the sheep, flanked by two compatriots supporting and, at times, dragging his sweating and trembling body.

The disguised Zealots drove their ersatz flock across the river Ajus and inquired for a rabbi. Tradition barred teachers of the Law and the Prophets from accepting payment for religious functions or spiritual guidance. Those without ancestral wealth followed a trade or profession, and many were healers, compounders of herbs, or physicians. But these were borderlands, where Samaria and Yudea converged. Rival theologies and philosophies swirled like olive oil and wine; stirred together yet refusing to combine.

The healer at Antipatris was disinterested and indifferent, but in exchange for a silver coin he bled the wound with a bronze dagger. He administered a bitter black potion to reduce fever. After an hour's rest, Duriel felt sufficiently revived to continue. No sooner was Antipatris out of sight behind them, the infection flared again and Duriel's fever soared. The leader of the Zealot band stumbled, badly.

Menachem, a man renown for enormous physical size, military acumen, and loyalty ordered the flock to halt. "We should go back. At least to Antipatris. I think that rabbi owes us a better result, especially at the price of a whole denarius."

"No, let's keep on," objected Duriel. "A night's rest at the well might be all I need. Besides, the Romans may still be inquiring about injured Yehudi men. Our learned friend back there could be trying to sell us to Caesar as we speak."

"I'm not so sure," countered Menachem, "but I'll do what you want. You have to agree to let me carry you, if it comes down to that."

"Yes, if it comes to that. But only for a little way. Maybe just until I recover my strength. Think of how that would look to…" Duriel lost consciousness and collapsed.

One of the Zealots asked, "What now?"

"Now we go on," replied Menachem. He bent down, grunted, and hoisted Duriel's limp form into his arms. "I asked him about going back to Antipatris, and his orders were to keep going to Capharsaba. Maybe we will find some help along the way."

***

The sun sank into the western hills. Shadows, destined to evolve into midnight, projected distorted shapes across the clearing. The small party traveling from Caesarea to Ain Karem stopped at the tree line.

"The woodcutters have been busy," grumbled Moravius. "It was never this far to the well. I'm not excited about making camp so far out in the open. There's more risk from other people than from wild animals, at least around here."

Lucanus nodded in agreement. "I'll unload some of the firewood. Then maybe Festus can drive the cart over to the well, refresh the donkey, and refill our water skins?"

Moravius was about to reply when he noticed a flock of sheep entering the opposite side of the clearing. "Hold up! Everybody wait. Something may not be right over there."

Miriam followed the gaze of Moravius. "All I see are some sheep and some herdsmen. What do you think is wrong?"

"Give it just a moment. We'll see."

Dusty white sheep filtered aimlessly from the woodland road. The grouping was uncharacteristically disorganized. The animals crowded around the stock trough, while the shepherds pressed up against the bulwark surrounding the well. Nobody was guarding the rear of the flock. A huge man brought up the rear, carrying a sick, dead, or dying body."

Moravius instinctively gripped his country sword. "There are far too many shepherds. Not enough sheep. The flock is out of control. The weapons are all wrong. Whoever or whatever those people are, they aren't what they're pretending to be. That makes them dangerous."

"We're not what we pretend to be, either," remarked Miriam. "Does that make us dangerous?"

"No, because we don't have a hostile intent. Until we know more about that group, we need to be very wary."

Festus thumbed under his chin and stared across the clearing. "If there's going to be trouble, we're badly outnumbered.".

"We must protect Lady Miriam at all costs," agreed Moravius. "Don't provoke anything, but be ready. Move most of the load. Make sure we can grab the swords and shields quickly."

"Perhaps we should just move on?" suggested Miriam.

Moravius shook his head to disagree. "As long as we remain on opposite sides of the clearing, we're safer here after dark than on the road. There could be bandits, or even Zealots, between here and Ain Karem. If we're camped tonight with bandits- and I suspect they are stealers of sheep- at least we know where they are at. We can keep an eye on them."

The Romans adjusted the load in the cart. Even outnumbered eleven to three, they remained confident their weapons, experience, and discipline would prevail in a skirmish. Still, they needed water and access to the well.

Moravius considered the options. "We will have Miriam's servants lead the donkey to the well and refill the water skins. This is a traveler's well, traditionally neutral ground, and a sanctuary. Nobody will bother two ordinary Yehudi women gathering water for a nearby camp."

"I can't let you send my chaperones unless I go too," objected Miriam. "I'm not going to hide at the edge of the forest while I put Yasminah and Hertzela at risk. Besides, the water skins and the donkey are more than any two women can manage on their own."

"I wish you would reconsider. If you go, I'll have to go as well," observed Moravius. "It's not that I'm afraid of that group. But who knows? Maybe if they realize there are Romans in your party something violent might erupt."

Miriam was already unhitching the donkey. "Then come if you must. I trust your judgment. You're responsible for me. I'm responsible for my servants. We'll all go to the well. You can hang back a little way. Close enough that they will know we have a guard, but not so close that they will know you're Roman. Whatever you do, don't speak where they can hear you."

Moravius stared constantly across the clearing as he adjusted the lacing of his sandals. He quietly exchanged his country sword for an Imperial blade, concealing it in the humble scabbard.

"As you wish, Mistress."

Moravius pointed at Festus and Lucanus. "If you see me draw my sword, come running. Be ready to fight. With luck, there will be no need."

***

The Zealots noticed a small party crossing toward the well. Three women, a man, and a donkey. Yehudim, by all appearance. They looked like simple country people, apparently tired and thirsty after a long day on the road. Two men behind them were busy setting up camp. There was nothing unusual about the group.

Menachem laid Duriel's body on the shadowed side of the bulwark. He took a linen cloth, dipped it into the water, and swabbed Duriel's brow. Duriel thrashed and moaned. The woman with the donkey looked up, hesitated for a moment, started to speak, thought better of it for a moment- and then asked, "What's wrong with him."

"He scratched his leg when we were shearing wool. It's swollen and red. He's hot with fever. We hope some rest and cool water will bring the fever down."

Moravius tensed. Every sheep in the flock was overdue for shearing. The account of the accident was probably a lie. He knew he should draw Miriam and the chaperones back, immediately, but weighed the risk of allowing the ruse to continue against the risk of revealing his party's identity. Eli's daughter must not fall into the wrong hands.

The woman with the donkey asked, "Do you mind if I take a look at him?"

Uriah, a Zealot from Yerushalayim, recoiled at the sound of her voice. Could it be? She was about the right age. If it were whom he thought it might be, during the portions of the year she resided in Yerushalayim her interest in the healing arts sparked rumors of witchcraft. Uriel had seen her and her retinue at market, only several months ago. She looked the part. But what would she be doing traveling in such humble circumstance?

Menachem was confused. "Why would you? You're obviously not a rabbi. What could you possibly do for him?"

"Perhaps nothing. Perhaps something. What have you got to lose?"

Uriah walked briskly around the well. He knelt to whisper in Menachem's ear, "I need to speak to you, right away. Where we won't be overheard."

"I don't want to leave Duriel."

"This is that important. We must speak, now."

Moravius grew increasingly alarmed as the two shepherds closest to Miriam walked a few steps away and huddled for private conversation.

"What could be so urgent?" asked Menachem.

"Do you know who I think that is?"

"Obviously not. Who do you think she is, and why would you even recognize some individual woman?"

"I swear that's Miriam. Daughter of Eli of Caesarea. I see her from time to time in Yerushalayim. I just can't figure out what she might be doing here."

"That's ridiculous. She's wearing a peasant's…"

Yigal, another Zealot tapped on Menachem's shoulder. "Hate to interrupt, but something's wrong. See that fellow standing over there, with his face partially concealed by a scarf?"

Menachem glanced briefly, hoping to be subtle. "Yes, what about him?"

"Look at his sandals. Have you ever seen anybody except a Roman soldier, preparing for battle, lace that way?"

Uriah confirmed the lacing, then whispered urgently. "We can take them. There are only three men. We can ransom the daughter. Maybe get a lot of prisoners released. Maybe even get the Romans withdrawn, at least from Yerushalayim. The One God has delivered this day to us!"

"Wait!" hissed Menachem. "She thinks she might be able to do something for Duriel. We should let her try."

Uriah looked around, as subtly as possible. He wanted to be certain there were no more Romans lurking among the trees. "I disagree. Duriel would be the first to give his life for a prize this rich. Even if he dies, and we don't know that he will, we could lose fifty or even a hundred times as many and accomplish less."

Menachem glared at Uriah, with a frightful countenance rigid as stone. He spoke slowly and singularly, emphasizing every word. "It is not your call. As long as I live, I am second commander here. If you have a problem with that, back it up with your dagger. One of us will be in charge when it is all over. We can let The One God decide which."

Uriah looked to the ground. "I'm no match for you, Menachem."

"Then don't challenge my authority."

Menachem stepped back to the well, where the young woman was already kneeling next to Duriel's body. "Go ahead. See what you can do. You won't do any worse than the rabbi in Antipatris. He's like a brother to me. I don't want to lose him."

Miriam placed her hands on Duriel's hot, sweaty body. She closed her eyes and identified the bright spot at the bridge of her nose. As she surrendered conscious thought, the small dot expanded to a larger circle. The empty light increased until it encompassed an area beyond where Miriam imagined her head must be. Forms and shapes were manifest in the sphere of light. She heard voices. Some were shouting.

Miriam experienced the man before her, mounting a horse. He scraped his leg on a thorn bush, before riding around a low hill. She saw Yehudim and Romans in deadly battle, and then she saw only Yehudim, standing in a silted river. It looked like the Yarden, at Yericho Ford.

Miriam knew the truth about her patient, and most likely all of his companions as well. Moravius was right all along to be suspicious, but it was now too late to react to the danger. If Miriam were to heal this man she must do so with light rather than darkness. It was darkness, itself, that was making him ill; a wicked spirit trying to claim victory over his body.

Aware that she could see more with her eyes closed than open, Miriam reached to feel the inflamed flesh on her patient's lower leg. In her light space, she beheld a festering wound. The flesh around the damaged area was even warmer than the rest of the body. Miriam prayed, "One God, show me what. One God, show me where."

Images in the light space shifted. Miriam viewed the area surrounding the well as if she were standing at the edge of the tree line, fifty yards away. At a location evenly split between the spot where Festus and Lucanus were setting up camp and her current position at the traveler's well, Miriam experienced a dark brown blossom with seven leaves.

Miriam didn't open her eyes, but merely pointed in the correct direction. She called to one of her chaperones. "Hertzela! The star flower, the anise. Find it where I point. Bring me a bundle."

Miriam's light space swirled with a vortex of galaxies, as if she were spinning through the heavens. A moment later she visualized a short green plant, low growing in the shade. Silky spikes covered the leaves and stems. She pointed, with eyes closed, to the opposite side of the clearing. She addressed her remaining chaperone. "Yasminah! The nettle. Find it where I point. Gather as much as you can. Use a hide or a wineskin. Don't get stung."

Miriam opened her eyes. Hertzela and Yasminah were already away on their gathering tasks. The party of strangers stood in a group, staring with mouths agape. Miriam knew that look. Too often it preceded rumors of sorcery or witchcraft; of speculations about dabbling in dark, forbidden arts. Miriam would deal with their reactions later. For now, acknowledging the guiding visions of The One God was all that mattered. Saving a life, even the life of a man who would consider her entire family mortal enemies, was her only concern.

Miriam's voice resonated with astonishing confidence and authority. She pointed at two of the men she now suspected as Zealots. "You, and you. Get water from the well and put it over the fire. Two containers. Make it hot enough to release the vapors, and hotter if you can."

Miriam pointed at Uriah. "You there. Take your dagger, and put the blade in the fire. Leave it until it turns red."

Uriah sneered. "Why would I do that? Give up my dagger?"

Miriam's voice shook with focused energy. "Because The One God requires it. Because we will need it to help heal your friend."

Menachem shouted, "Do it, Uriah!" Duriel's second in command then asked Miriam, "Why would we need heat? Heat is making him sick. That's why he has a fever."

"His body is trying to bake out the evil energy he took up with his wound," said Miriam. "That's why there's heat. There just isn't enough. There is only so much the body can do without help."

Miriam wiped her patient's forehead with a wet linen. Her chaperones found the plants described, exactly where Miriam directed them to look. The water above the fire was steaming and bubbling when the women returned to the well with bundles of vegetation.

Moravius was increasingly concerned. He turned to face Festus and Lucanus, held up his left hand to indicate a slow advance, and motioned gently with his right. His two cohorts walked slowly to his position, surmising that any rapid motion might escalate a dangerous situation.

"Soak the anise in one vessel," directed Miriam. "Put clean linen, and as much nettle as will fit in the second. Stir things around, to speed up the process."

Most of the Zealots stared at Moravius and his companions, sizing them up as adversaries. Menachem hovered over Miriam and Duriel.

Uriah kicked his dagger continuously, nudging it from one hot coal to the next. He smiled as he imagined sinking the blade into one of the three Romans standing remote guard over Eli's daughter and her servants.

Miriam wrapped her hand in linen and pulled the red hot blade from the fire. "You may need to hold your friend. He's sleeping now, but this is going to hurt, very badly, for a moment. The pain might wake him up. It wouldn't be useful if he thrashed around. Especially hold his leg still."

Uriah was skeptical. "The rabbi in Antipatris bled the wound. It didn't do much good. How is a hot blade going to make the difference?"

"Watch."

Miriam pressed the red hot blade to Duriel's wounded leg. He screamed and thrashed Only Menachem's firm hold on the injured extremity permitted Miriam to proceed. The air stank of searing flesh. The wound erupted, spurting blood and a greasy yellow puss that smelled like horse urine. The mess ran over his leg and into the soil. "You're going to kill him!" shouted Uriah.

"Not if I can help it," argued Miriam. "But he will carry the mark of this for the rest of his days." Miriam squeezed the extremities of the wound until only a clear liquid emerged.

"Give me the linen, soaked with nettle" said Miriam. She wrapped the cloth around the wound, binding it tightly to his leg. "That will drive out the evil energies - they don't like the prick of nettle. Next, we need to wake him up and give him some anise tea."

Menachem knelt next to Duriel and cradled his head against a bent knee. Duriel moaned and opened his eyes. "Sip this," said Menachem. "Careful. It's hot." Duriel took a few swallows and passed out again.

Uriah grew impatient. He whispered to Menachem, "He looks the same, or worse. She hasn't done a thing for him. Let's get rid of those Romans and take her hostage."

"Not yet. We may need her help again."

"Then when? We can't let this opportunity slip away."

Menachem whispered in reply. "Wait. The One God will tell us what to do."

Menachem returned to Miriam's side, where she continued to kneel alongside Duriel's motionless body.

"Perhaps I should stay here a while to watch over him," suggested Miriam.

"Excellent idea, Miriam," responded Menachem. "I was about to suggest the very same thing."

Miriam was alarmed. "How do you know my name?"

"You must have told us. Or perhaps one of your servants mentioned it."

"I am completely certain I did not!"

"Nevertheless, Miriam, and daughter of Eli, you will stay with us a while. At least until we see what fruit your witchcraft bears. Stand up, smile, and assure those lurking Romans that everything is fine. Tell them you will return to camp a little later, after your herbs and potions have a chance to run their course."

Miriam did as she was bid. Moravius was not deceived. He returned to the far side of the clearing with Festus and Lucanus, where he swore to plot a rescue. It would be too dangerous to attack these bandits with Miriam in their midst and at their mercy- a fact clearly evident to both sides.

I, XVIII
The Heresies of Lesser Nature

Miriam's twin brother answered a summons from their father. Eli's study was a grand compartment, situated on the topmost level of his palatial estate at Caesarea. There were windows on all four sides, to capture light at any hour of the day. Oil lamps, cast from an alloy of gold and bronze, enabled scholarship during times of darkness. The walls were paneled with aromatic planks of cedar, and eucalyptus. A carpet, knotted in Persia, interceded between the old patriarch's bare feet and an unforgiving slate floor below. Wooden frames held hundreds of scrolls, each carefully handled and returned to catalogued order after use. Incense smoldered on a bed of charcoal, contained in a tiny stone bowl.

On the central table was a balance scale, precisely calibrated and decorated by master goldsmiths. Here, in his study, Eli measured the laws and the prophets, as well as profits and loss. The richest man in Yudea recognized no conflict between his success in commerce and his membership in the supreme court of his people, the Sanhedrin. From Eli's perspective, the two roles were complementary. In fact, he was sure that his faithfulness to the One God and reverence for his laws were fundamental to his material wealth.

Aban entered the study to discover his father holding a scroll at an angle to intercept a shaft of light. The older man appeared to be experimenting with holding the text at a variety of distances from his eyes. "I think it's the One God's plan to keep us humble," grumbled Eli. "As we grow in experience and accomplishment, it becomes increasingly difficult to read."

Aban chuckled. "You have most of the important books memorized."

Eli nodded. "By the One God's mercy. That has been a gift. But, I didn't call you here to talk about my aging eyesight. It's time for me to make a decision about your sister's future. You know her better than anyone else..."

"I don't know, Father," interrupted Aban. "She may be my twin sister, but she's mysterious in a lot of ways. Sometimes, it's like I don't even recognize the woman she has become. And she was my constant playmate."

Eli shrugged. "She doesn't seem to know her place. All this interest in healing, and philosophy. The questions she asks! None of that will ever be of any use to her as a wife and mother. If she were your brother, and not your sister, she would have been a candidate for rabbinical studies. And still, she's too quick to sneak off and associate with religious radicals- heretics even."

"Ah yes. Would you include that fellow who was here two days ago, Yetro, as one of those heretics?"

"Absolutely. He repeats some heresy originated by Plato and Socrates. He tries to confuse simple people with a tale of how the earth, and all the planets, revolve around the sun." Eli raised his voice as he became uncharacteristically agitated. "The One God will destroy him for his lies! Besides, those long dead Greeks? They were all polytheists!"

Aban was not certain that he completely agreed with his father, but did not want to provoke an argument. He posed a rhetorical question. "Could the Greeks be wrong about the nature of God, but right about other things?"

"No, that would be impossible. If you err on the most fundamental truth, you err on all."

Aban pressed his thumb to his upper lip, glanced down, and nodded. "That seems reasonable. But you wanted to discuss Miriam, right?"

Eli folded his arms, and spoke with some reluctance. "Yes. I thought I had more time. But her attention to our tile setter is almost scandalous."

"She was much too forward," agreed Aban, "but their encounters were innocent. I had them watched. Constantly."

"As did I," confirmed Eli.

"Really? I didn't notice."

"You weren't supposed to notice. The tile setter honored her position, it's true. But an unmarried woman is likely to be ruined, eventually, by lustful impulses."

The conversation was intense. More intense than Eli anticipated. He fidgeted with the dagger gifted him by Hiram of Dothan, pulling the blade from the scabbard and setting it on one tray of his scale. The tray settled heavily on the table top.

"That's a beautiful knife, father. Where did you get that?"

Eli placed a stack of gold coins on the scale, attempting to balance the weight of the dagger. The scale did not move.

"Hiram of Dothan brought it to me. It's from Damascus. Expert workmanship, suitable for Augustus himself."

"Hiram of Dothan?" confirmed Aban. "No doubt he's looking for something in return."

Eli added another stack of gold coins to the high side of the scale. The dagger did not budge from the table.

"He is. He's got a son…"

"Faramond? Father, don't tell me you're considering a match between Faramond and Miriam. She would never consent. He's an unkempt glutton. Not at all bright. There are rumors of an unmarried servant girl who got pregnant, then mysteriously disappeared."

Eli added a smaller stack or coins to the scale. The dagger lifted, but only slightly. The treasure was still heavier than the coin.

"Surely they couldn't prove the father was Faramond," countered

Eli. "And if so, a least it demonstrates he's potent."

Four additional gold coins brought the dagger closer to level- but not yet in balance.

Eli continued, "Hiram controls much of the coal in Yudea. He trades spices with the Egyptians and Chaldeans. He pays his taxes to Caesar with sacks of polished gems. Miriam could do little better than a match with his son. Although now as I remember the boy, you might be right. He seems slow witted."

Aban was shocked. "Father, you have always said that you would never force either of us to marry against our will. Surely there must be somebody else. If Miriam were here, I know she would tell you Faramond is out of the question."

"We're running out of time. Your sister is impossible to control. It won't matter who I present as a match, Miriam will almost certainly refuse. It's time somebody made a decision. As her father, that decision falls to me."

"Father, she will never consent…"

"Oh, but she might," countered Eli. "You remember that renegade? Yetro? The one we were just speaking about?"

"What of him?"

"He and Miriam are acquainted," grumbled Eli. He looked accusingly at his son. "But, you already knew that, didn't you?"

"Father," began Aban.

The older man raised his hand to silence his son. "It doesn't matter. But what would Miriam think if we tracked Yetro to a cave just south of the harbor, arrested him, and were holding him for trial? Would she consent to marry a man of my choosing, in exchange for his release?"

"Father! You wouldn't do that."

Eli sat more coins on the scale, decidedly tipping the balance. The coin tray thunked on the table top, lifting the arm with the dagger to the highest possible point. "I already have. If no more promising prospect appears at the Feast of Tabernacles, she will weigh the death of Yetro against marriage to Faramond."

Aban sat down in utter dismay. He battled the urge to cry-something unthinkable in the presence of another man. "You're selling my sister to the highest bidder. You're scheming to manipulate her consent. How dare you, Father? How, dare, you?"

"I'm saving my wild child from the heresies of her lesser nature. How dare I not?"

PART II

II, I
Uranus and Neptunus

Three hundred years. Three hundred years earlier, the Tigris and Euphrates rivers converged at Ur. The wealth of Mesopotamia, Parthia, and Eastern Cappadocia spilled into the pungent bazaars and chaotic harbor. Oils, spices, grain, gems, fabrics, exotic animals, and slaves- all exchanged for golden coin amid battle cries of commerce. Contracts bought and sold. Promises kept, and broken. A Persian empire funded. A flowering of science and the arts, if only for a season.

As the Great Rivers swept wealth into Ur, they relentlessly silted up the future. Dredging worked, for a while, but now the river mouth was far to the south and east. Beneath a layer of acrid dust, the streets of Ur were deserted. Wild pigs sheltered in battered structures with doors long ago sacrificed for firewood. Emaciated jackals and dishevel-feathered ravens lurked in the shady edges of the market square, ready to pounce on an overly bold rat or random viper. Hot, withering, winds poured from the marshes, to be drowned in the muddy stream of persistent transformation.

Nothing remained of Ur, except the ziggurat once rebuilt by Nabonidus. A structure of colossal scope, featuring an ascending multitude of terraces. Each sweeping courtyard, and every step, carefully calculated in relative elevation and maintained perfectly level. To the uninitiated, the ziggurat would appear to be a temple, or a fortress, or even a palace. Indeed, there were occasions when it had been pressed into each of those uses. The essential purpose was an observatory. The parallel strata created a series of artificial horizons; ideal for accurately observing and recording the choreography of the heavens. Over two thousand years of observations were based on this location. Wherever the flood might shift the delta, the ziggurat must remain at Ur.

Grand Master Gaspar observed sunrise from an eastern wall.

Darkness dissolved, save the shadow of a reference staff, striking exactly on a predicted and previously marked location. One of the apprentices scratched a stylus against a block of wax, recording notes to be impressed onto clay tiles and dried in the afternoon sun. Few events were more routine than sunrise. Gaspar was free to turn his attention to the lens.

Suspended within a heavy timber frame, the bronze rimmed glass casting was shaped and polished over the course of a generation. Properly levered and braced on one of the upper levels, the instrument could survey any portion of the sky. The lens revealed mysteries of the universe invisible to the mortal eye. It expanded pin pricks of light to the size of small pennies and projected the images into a concave, silver mirror. The Greeks had a lens as well, at Rhodes.

Gaspar ordered the lens retired to a windowless chamber. The device that fostered knowledge during darkness could immolate the ziggurat during daylight hours. Once the lens was secured, Gaspar would be free to enjoy a well-deserved day's sleep. The scribes would mark the tiles as he slept, and he would check the accuracy when he awoke.

Gaspar was retiring to his quarters when he was interrupted by a subordinate.

"Master, there's a dove."

"There's always a dove. Take the scroll, band the leg, and grain it on the roost. Whatever the message, it can wait until this evening."

"Sir, this is a four-bird relay. It began near Yerushalayim. Zachariah. You told us to let you know whenever…"

"Whenever there's any news of, or from, the crazy old priest," concluded Gaspar. "Very well. Bring it into my rooms, let's see what matter is so urgent that Zachariah will spend the price of a four flight message." Gaspar sighed, and grumbled, "It will take a year to reset the birds."

Gaspar's apartment was simple and scholarly, with a sleeping couch and plain table. While there were few personal effects, there were scrolls and stacks of tiles neatly arranged around the perimeter. The Grand Master lit a utilitarian table lamp, adjusted the wick, and unrolled the tiny scroll delivered by the dove.

"His characters could hardly be smaller. How's your eyesight, Melchior?"

"Better than my Aramaic, Master. Be patient, if I mispronounce something."

"Go ahead."

"He writes from Zachariah, humble servant of The One God, Shalom. Inquiry: aspects and positions of Uranus and Neptunus on the following dates…and then there's a list of days. Uranus? Neptunus? What can he know? Is he an initiate?"

"Not exactly, but he isn't above trading secrets with the Greeks. He committed the Scrolls of Avram, the Yetzirah, to memory. There are wild tales of power and magic attending those documents. There's even evidence that some of the stories might be true. I'm cultivating Zachariah, in the slight chance he might have something to teach us in return."

Melchior re-rolled the tiny scroll. "For this information to be of any use, he must be a heliocentrist."

"Much to his peril. He'd be denounced as a heretic, and probably killed, if it came to the attention of the high priests or judges. I asked him about it once, in a message. His response was that his god, The One God, created the universe beginning with light and that puts the sun in the middle."

Melchior smiled. "It's funny how a simple deduction based on faith can accidentally agree with the best available science."

Gaspar extinguished the lamp wick. "Sometimes. But only sometimes. Have one of the novices transcribe the calculations. I assume we have enough birds to return the relay?"

"We can do the first leg, then it's up to the other posts of course."

"Of course."

Melchior began to leave, and then stopped. "Master, if Zachariah has been corresponding with the Greeks, he would know about Uranus. Hipparchus found Uranus about 100 years ago, but even though we can track its movements it's very hard to see."

"And, so?"

"So I am puzzled why he even mentions Neptunus. We can't actually see Neptunus, not on any night of the year and not with the best lens on Earth. We only know where it has to be because we see its effect on the orbit of Uranus. What possible significance can there be to something he cannot see?"

Gaspar threw back his head as he laughed. "Don't forget, Zachariah is Yehudi. The Yehudim have a long history of finding significance in things that nobody will ever see!"

II, II
Liquid mouse

Yetro sweltered in his tiny cell. There was not enough room to lie down, so he slept in a crouch. A tiny slit in the heavily reinforced wooden door admitted stale food, foraging vermin, and inadequate water. The jailer promised that every second day somebody would remove his waste bucket. It was well into the third day, the bucket was almost full, and no breeze from the Mare Nostrum successfully removed the stench. The prospect of potential death was rendered less dreadful by the miserable conditions to which he was reduced in life.

From the beginning, Yetro suspected there might be trouble associated with Eli's daughter. He was too quick to cave to Nora's entreaty and allow Miriam to join their clandestine studies, but he was also quick to recognize her unique aptitude for healing and spiritual matters. Had he been as quickly aware of his blossoming affection for the young woman, perhaps he would have made other choices. It made little difference now.

Eli could have ordered him arrested a dozen times. Why now? Was the old man's power so absolute that it could be arbitrary as well? He could be killed. He might even die in this cell. Eli could wait for months, or even years, before charging him in court.

Last sleep, there were terrifying images of Miriam wandering through pagan temples. He envisioned her despised in a foreign country. There were suggestions of corrupted shepherds, advancing a caravan of mournful ghosts.

Reviewing his dream, Yetro concluded that Miriam must have pursued her plan to visit Elisheba and Zachariah. He initially felt his premonition was of danger that would befall her after arriving at Ain Karem. Now it appeared, that something happened to her enroute.

Yetro kicked the waste bucket in frustration. A mouse scampered, and the odiferous contents of the bucket oozed through the small slit in the bottom of the door.

II, III
Headlong into Darkness

The fever broke. Duriel opened his eyes to a blurry image of a young woman, reaching toward his forehead with a damp cloth. He strained to croak "Where am I? What's going on? Who are you?"

Menachem was roasting chunks of lamb over a midnight fire. Each red morsel, speared with a stick suspended between two rocks, sacrificed molten fat to evoke sweet smoke from self-conflagration. Miriam motioned to attract Menachem's attention. "He's awake!"

"Praise The One God," said Menachem. He abandoned the cooking to confirm Miriam's report.

Rapidly rejuvenating, Duriel demanded, "Where am I and who are you?"

Miriam supported Duriel's head. She pressed the brim of the cup with anise tea between his lips. "You're at the traveler's well. At the southern edge of Samaria. I treated your wounded leg, and gave you something for your fever. You should drink a little more."

"And you are?" croaked Duriel.

Menachem interrupted. "Meet Miriam. Daughter of Eli. Eli of Caesarea. Since you live, so shall she. But she will bring an enormous ransom."

Zealots heard Duriel's voice and returned to the fire from the perimeter of the flock. An opportunistic wolf howled in the underbrush. The sheep panicked and broke, jogging in a ragged wooly knot across the clearing to where Miriam's companions were camped.

Festus, Lucanus, Hertzelah, Yasminah, and Moravius scrambled to encircle, calm, and collect the sheep. "I'm not sure how, just yet," said Moravius, "but their poor shepherding may break this stalemate."

"I won't second guess you, but I don't see why," said Festus.

"They've got Lord Eli's daughter. We've got a handful of dirty sheep. It's not likely they will trade straight across."

"Of course not. I was waiting for something to change. Any time there's a change, there's hope for better outcome."

Lucanus spat. "There are only eleven of them, and three of us. The odds would be in our favor, if Miriam were not in the mix."

Moravius nodded, glumly.

In the cavorting sparks of their respective fires, the Zealots and the Romans glared across the clearing at the traveler's well. One of the Zealots urged, "Give the word, Duriel. There are only three Romans and two women to deal with. It should be a short fight."

Duriel struggled into a sitting position. He swayed, until he braced himself with an arm. "No, not yet. I want to speak to Miriam."

"Be careful," warned Uriah. "There are many who swear she is a witch."

Miriam, still kneeling next to Duriel, silenced Uriah with a frightful expression. *Sometimes,* she thought, *it can be useful to be suspected of sorcery.*

Miriam offered Duriel more anise tea. "We can talk, a little. But really you should continue to rest."

"Do you know who I am?"

"Yes. You and these men you travel with are Zealots. They call you Duriel. I've heard of you. Everybody in Palestine has heard of you."

"So then why are you helping me? And why do you not seem afraid?"

"I'm helping you because you're hurt. Because The One God grants me the knowledge to heal and the gift to do so. We are of the same covenant. How could I turn my back on a fellow Yehudi?"

Uriah pointed wickedly at Miriam. "Your entire family is more Roman than Yehudi. The dog is defined more by its master than by its mother."

Duriel snapped, "Silence, Uriah!" He softened his to again address Miriam. "And why not afraid? Fear and I have a long acquaintance. There is little or none in you."

"Because I don't want anything from you. Because fear would only feed your thirst for blood. Because I am doing the work of The One God, and I believe I am blessed while I do it. Because of any of those reasons, or perhaps none of them. Because maybe I don't really know. But you are right, you don't frighten me."

Two of the wooden skewers holding lamb above the flames caught fire. The meat fell into the coals, to burn beyond the reach of fingers proven far too slow.

"So, Miriam, daughter of Eli of Caesarea, will I be able to travel without more nursing?"

"Very soon. Rest here one more day. Keep the bandage clean. There are more of them in the kettle, change your wrapping every day for the next week. Fill a wineskin with the tea, if your fever returns that will cure it. Nettle for the bandage, anise for the tea- in case you run out."

Duriel's thoughts became increasingly clear. His men were right, there were only three Romans. A fierce attack would likely dispatch them all, but at what cost? It was one matter to ambush Legionnaires wading across the Yarden at Yericho Ford, another to challenge three apparent veterans in a hand to hand brawl. Some Zealots would surely perish as well. Too many. Besides, the entire point of traveling to Galilee was to elude the Roman manhunt. Killing Romans in Samaria would shift the Imperial forces north.

And Miriam? Duriel imagined that had she been born a man she could have been one of his most trusted soldiers. She was truly without fear. Maybe, when the Romans are finally driven from Yudea, there would be some role for such a surprising and capable woman.

Duriel tried to rise, but lacked the strength to do so.

"It would be best if you don't put a lot of stress on the wound," cautioned Miriam.

Duriel nodded. "One of those Romans is probably in charge of the others?"

"That would be Moravius."

"Walk to the edge of the camp. Call him over here. Have him come alone, and unarmed. We'll see if he's as fearless as the woman he escorts."

"What will happen to him if he comes, unarmed?"

"He will be under my protection, just as you are now."

Uriah snorted his displeasure. It would be better to kill the Roman, especially once separated from the others.

"Your protection? I thought I was your prisoner."

"Have Moravius come over for a talk. Maybe we'll find out we're all prisoners of the same circumstance. Let's see if we can arrive at a mutual understanding. Menachem will walk out with you, to protect you, of course, from any sudden urge to run." Duriel smiled. "You could hurt yourself, you know, running headlong into darkness."

II, IV
Between Death and Dishonor

Moravius kept watch. Zealots appeared and disappeared in the palpitating ring of amber and amethyst firelight across the clearing. The total number did not appear to change. As long as all the Zealots were accounted for, there was no chance of a small party skirting the rim of dark forest. Little risk of a surprise attack on the rear of Miriam's party.

Festus slept, but only lightly.

Lucanus, as directed, quietly removed the swords and shields from concealment in the cart. It would be wise to have the weapons close to hand.

Moravius fretted about the archers. Before darkness reduced the entire universe to the dimensions of a clear cut around the traveler's well, Moravius noted that two of the bogus shepherds were armed with bows. If the Zealots decided to attack, one or two Romans might be felled before the sides could close in combat. It might be prudent to withdraw, but that option was unthinkable with Miriam in the clutches of the fanatics. Moravius would give his life, if required, to protect Miriam. He only hoped he wouldn't give that life to an unseen arrow fired from hostile shadows. He watched, worried, and listened for a whistle of fletched death.

New movements snared his attention. Two silhouettes walked to the very edge of the Zealot firelight. One was a woman. Miriam! The other was a very large man, guarding or escorting her. Could they be returning her?

The dark forms did not continue their advance.

Miriam called across the open ground, "Moravius!"

"I'm here! Are you alright?"

"I'm fine. The leader here, Duriel; he wants to talk to you."

The shouting awoke Festus. He sprang to his feet and moved to stand next to his commander. "Not so close," whispered Moravius. "Don't forget their archers. We're twice the target, side by side."

Moravius responded to Miriam. "Who's that with you? Is that Duriel? If so, send him over and we can talk."

"I'm not Duriel," yelled Menachem. "And nobody is going over to your camp. You come over here, Moravius. By yourself. Unarmed."

Moravius considered the situation. It was possible, perhaps almost likely, that once separated from the other guards that the Zealots would attack and kill him. Or try. Equally armed, a veteran legionnaire was the equal of several less disciplined and part-time warriors. Unarmed, the odds were dismal at best. Even so, if he remained alive long enough to reach Miriam's side he might offer some protection. Moravius had no desire to die, but if his death distracted the Zealots long enough for Miriam to escape their grasp then the sacrifice would be noble.

Still, there were the archers.

"Tell you what," shouted Moravius. "I'll come over there but only if you let me bring my shield."

"Just your shield? No sword? No spear? No dirk? Come ahead then. Just you. Nothing but your shield."

Festus hissed to his commander. "Are you crazy? They're just trying to split us up. They want to reduce our number. Try to even the odds. Don't go. Or at least hide your sword behind your shield."

"It's likely that you're right, Festus. I wouldn't go if they weren't holding Miriam. I was a fool to let her go with her maidservants."

"She is a strong willed woman. You would have had to tie her up to prevent it."

"Right again. One hopeful sign is that they don't have her tied up."

"It would be more hopeful if they simply let her go."

"Agreed. Maybe I can arrange that."

Festus frowned. "Maybe you'll die trying. Will you please take your sword?"

"Much as I want to, no. If they think I am trying to deceive them, Miriam will be in worse danger. If it gets to blows, I can probably kill the nearest one with the edge of my shield. You and Lucanus be ready to come running, and bring my blade. If I'm with Miriam, and I have my shield, I should be able to protect her for at least a few moments."

Moravius raised his shield to just beneath his chin. He started across the clearing, adopting a purposeful stride to appear confident. With every step toward the opposing fire, he discerned more dimly illuminated Zealots. There were the archers, with arrows nocked- but the bows were not drawn, merely ready. "I wish there were a better plan," thought Moravius. "But if I can reach Miriam before they cut me down, maybe we can manage her escape."

Moravius covered the distance and stood next to Miriam. They were immediately encircled by Zealots.

"Are you certain that you're alright? They haven't hurt you in any way?"

Miriam clutched Moravius, wrapping her hands around his bicep. "Other than not letting me go? I'm fine. Nothing has happened to me. But, I'm so glad that you're here."

"I had no choice. As a man, or a soldier, I had no choice."

Menachem motioned toward the fire. "Duriel is waiting for you over there. Let's go."

Miriam, Moravius, and the surrounding mob moved closer to the flames. Duriel was propped up against a stack of supplies, a blanket covering his bandaged leg. Duriel motioned to a spot on the ground a few feet away. "You must be Moravius? Sit here."

"I think I'll stand."

Duriel chortled. "You'll think you'll stand so you can use your shield as a weapon. Look around. If I wanted you dead, it would be done already. Sit! I insist. In fact, why don't you sit on your shield- and keep yourself out of the dust?"

Moravius laid his shield on the ground, and sat. "You must be Duriel?"

"So I am."

Moravius grimaced. "That was your work, at Yericho ford. There's a huge price on your head. Under any other circumstance, I would try to kill you."

"And I you. Roman wolves invade our lands and enslave our people. You defile our holy places."

"You're occupied, not conquered. You still have your own king."

"A king appointed by Augustus… but we're not here to talk politics."

"No, we're not," agreed Moravius. "Unless you intend to kill me now…."

"That would be a good idea!" interrupted Uriah.

Moravius continued, "As I say, unless you intend to kill me now there must be some other reason you are holding Miriam and asked for this talk."

"There is. Miriam saved my life. In fact, her potions and applications are working better than expected. Most of my men are in favor of killing you Romans, and then ransoming Miriam and the other women back to Eli."

"You might find Romans harder to kill than expected."

"Oh don't forget, Moravius, we know exactly how hard it is to kill a Roman."

"Yes, from cowardly ambush!" Moravius struggled to keep his temper in check.

Duriel did not take the provocative bait. He kept a calm demeanor. "We've got you, we've got Miriam, and so we've got the upper hand. That means I get to dictate the terms, and you get to accept them- or die."

"I'm warning you. Don't force me into a choice between death and dishonor."

"Let's see, shall we? We're en route to Galilee. We hope to make the journey without further loss of life. We can surely defeat three Romans…"

"You don't want to test that," interrupted Moravius.

Duriel continued. "But I'm realistic enough to know that destroying you would be costly. We're going to remain here one more day, while your group continues on. Miriam can rejoin your company. We're going to keep you as a hostage, instead."

"I'll never agree to that!" cried Miriam.

Moravius responded with his most authoritative tone and waggled a finger in her direction. "You'll agree to whatever is best for the larger party! And then what, Duriel?"

"Menachem will go with your group to Yerushalayim, to ensure nobody reports our presence here to the Romans. You travel north with us, and when Menachem returns safely and reports that we were not betrayed we will let you go."

Moravius mulled the options. There were few, if any. Miriam would be safer back among the other guards and her chaperones- away from the Zealots.

"I have a condition of my own," insisted Moravius.

"You're in no position to demand anything!" objected Uriah.

"Let him speak," said Duriel.

"While in Galilee, you avoid raiding Eli's estate or attacking anyone in his family."

A murmur erupted among the Zealots. Duriel asked, "Why would I do that? Eli's a collaborator, a lap dog for Augustus."

"Why?" countered Moravius. "Because I'm sworn to protect Eli and his household. Because you don't want to press me to choose between death and dishonor."

Uriah drew a dagger. "Let me kill him now! He demands too much!"

"No!" commanded Duriel. "We don't have the force, right now, to raid Caesarea anyway. Let's get all of our people out of here alive if possible."

Moravius was grudgingly impressed with Duriel's command of authority. He was in the hands of a master strategist.

Duriel motioned. An opening appeared in the crowd. "Menachem, you take Miriam over to her camp. Explain the arrangement. Tell them we're exchanging hostages, if that will make it sound more palatable. Oh, and tell them there's one last condition."

Moravius jerked to rigid attention. "Really, what would that be?"

"Tell them they need to send back the sheep."

II, V
Opus Caementicium

The Tektons, Yakob the carpenter and Yusuf the tile setter, reviewed their work. After Miriam's departure, Yusuf finished leveling the area reserved for the mosaic courtyard. He supervised compacting the soil, and then leveled the area a final time. The process was bittersweet. Miriam was burned into his consciousness. She helped him construct the leveling device, and now every moment of use reminded him of her presence. Her smile was in the sunlight, her song in the shadows, and her scent in the hide she stitched around the reeds. Her absence underscored his lament. The curse of Yeconiah made it difficult to marry- and even if that were not so he should never dare dream of a life with anyone of Miriam's social status.

Yakob pegged planks around the perimeter. Yusuf once again used the water level to ensure the top edges of the boards were perfectly aligned and uniformly above grade. A sloping berm of dirt was tamped along the outside, enabling forms to resist any bulging or breakage when filled with aggregate and mortar. Opus caementicium- the final slab would support the ceramic imagery.

Yakob smiled and nodded. "It looks ready, to me".

"Yes, I think you're right. If they pour tomorrow it can cure during Shabbat. Then I can trace the outlines on First day.

Yakob pointed through a cluster of Numidian masons chiseling an arched obsidian façade. Beyond them, a line of servants harnessed to baskets struggled to walk with 150-pound loads of rock and soil. Standing above it all was the pavilion of Shimon of Accara. Eli's master builder watched, suspiciously, and work continued.

"My old eyes aren't what they were," said Yakob. "The fellow standing next to Shimon looks familiar. Could it be…"

"Yes. It's Herod's master builder."

"I thought it was," said Yakob. "It's too far from Sephora for a casual visit. I wonder what he wants?"

The two master builders, each followed by an assistant, stepped down from the pavilion and walked toward the site prepared for the slab. "It looks like we will be finding out," said Yusuf.

Workers instinctively made way for the supervisors to pass through their projects. Although Shimon knew that Yakob and Yusuf were known to Herod's master builder, protocol required an introduction. An introduction would remind everyone of their official status.

"Yakob of Nazareth, Yusuf son of Yakob! Defer to the master builder of his Excellency, King Herod!"

The Tektons bowed, slightly, from the waist. They recited in unison, "Long life to King Herod and his master builder."

There was no verbal response. It was mandatory for the Tektons to acknowledge the master builders, but reciprocity was optional. Appearing bored and annoyed, Herod's master builder motioned toward the cement forms and carefully prepared grade. He ordered the two assistants, "Measure it."

Yakob and Yusuf stood aside while cords were stretched on two sides of the prepared site, and then diagonally across the middle. The assistants knelt in the dirt and called off each dimension in turn. Herod's master builder noted the sizes on a wax tablet, then announced a conclusion.

"You walk a dangerous line, Shimon. This is as everything else you showed me in Lord Eli's expansion. Only a tiny fraction smaller than similar features at Sephora."

Shimon bowed very slightly in reply. "I follow the exact instructions of Lord Eli."

"Then Eli walks that dangerous line. Herod will be displeased if this project outshines his in any way."

A scaffold collapsed nearby. Shimon scurried to assess the damage.

Herod's emmissary took Yusuf aside and asked, "You there, tile setter. What images or design will you lay here?"

"Only a mazzeroth. Like the floor of a synagogue. To glorify the work of The One God."

"Are you certain there is no profile of Eli, or of his son? Nothing similar to the work you did at Sephora?"

Yusuf looked at the ground and slowly shook his head. "Of course not. How could a mazzeroth compare to the portrait of King Herod? And I don't have the advantage of working under your master tile setter's instruction. I'll do my best for Lord Eli, but there's no reason to fear the results will be as impressive as we achieved for the King himself."

Herod's master builder glared at Yusuf. "I warn you, tile setter. See that they are not." He swiveled to return to Shimon's pavilion, with the rest of the inspection party in his wake.

II, VI
The Scent of Sacrifice

Festus and Lucanus walked ahead, where Menachem could keep them in view. The Zealot drove, with Miriam beside him. Miriam's maidservants and chaperones followed in the rear, and the cart rolled down the rutted Roman road from Samaria to Yerushalayim. Down from the low hills, where the timber gangs converted permanent evergreen forests to temporary Roman gold. Down through the low valleys, where surging, milling, seas of sheep were sustained on carpets of verdant grass. Up again through gnarled vineyards where pure waters, passed through roots of yesteryear, erupted into the wines of tomorrow. Through groves of fig and olive. Through waving, sun-crowned fields of sweet mustard, combed by the breath of The One God.

Miriam was concerned for the safety of Moravius, left behind in the hostage exchange. She pressed the Zealot, "Can we be certain they won't hurt Moravius?"

"No more certain than Duriel can be that your guards won't be killing me somewhere along this road. I don't know what came over Duriel. This is awkward. He went to a lot of trouble to justify letting you and your party go. I can't figure out why, but it's something he wanted to do. He couldn't lose face in front of our men."

Miriam frowned. "I wish I could be more confident."

"Duriel needs some time to recover. He's not ready for a fight. That's why we're getting out of Yudea for a while. As long as none of you send the Legion after him, I think Moravius will be alright. The sooner we get to Yerushalayim, and Duriel gets a day's head start, the sooner I can rejoin the patriots in Galilee, and the sooner they will let him go. Moravius seems like he'd be fierce, if it came to a fight."

"He can be. My father trusts him completely. By the way, we're not going to Yerushalayim."

"No?"

"We're heading to Ain Keram, not far beyond."

"I know the place. Why there, and not Yerushalayim?"

"I'm supposed to deliver a message to my cousin."

Menachem slapped the reins on the back of the donkey. "Seems like a lot of trouble, just to deliver a message. You could have sent a courier."

"No, not with this message."

A boy carrying a wicker basket emerged from a roadside cottage. Menachem reined in. The child looked to be seven or eight years of age, well fed and in clean condition. "Hot bread? Two loaves for a copper?"

"Fair enough," said Miriam. "Have you got four loaves?"

"I do."

Lucanus kept the purse. "Lucanus, give the boy two coppers. Come get two loaves for you and Festus. We'll have one on the cart. Hertzelah and Yazminah can share the other."

Miriam tore off a chunk of bread, releasing a cloud of fragrant steam from the soft and warm interior. She gave the bread to Menachem, who started the donkey again. "You know, don't you, that there are too many Romans? You can't possibly kill them all."

Menachem accepted the bread. "We don't need to kill all of them. Just enough of them. Enough that they will consider the cost too high. Enough so that they will leave. Enough so we will finally be free of them."

Miriam tore off bread for herself. "What if we could be free of the Romans without killing any of them at all?"

Menachem expressed his disbelief with a grunt. "Unless we kill the Romans they will continue to rule over us. Unless they leave, we will never be free."

Miriam offered Menachem another section of bread. "Maybe, unless we figure out how to be free despite the occupation. Maybe we could even figure out how to be free because of the occupation."

"You make no sense at all, woman. No wonder they accuse you of sorcery."

They spoke no more that afternoon. When they crested the ridge at Amasa to behold Yerushalayim beyond, the day star was weary in the west. A dusty red ray set sunset fire to the Holy of Holies. The scent of sacrifice was in the air.

II, VII
An Aureus for Mithras

The Zealots did not remain a day at the traveler's well. As soon as Miriam's party was out of sight, Duriel bargained with a woodcutter. He traded six sheep and a small purse of silver shekels for a cart and donkey. Not yet strong enough to walk a long distance, Duriel would ride in the cart. If Miriam, her guards, or her servants betrayed his Samarian presence to the Roman legions- an extra day's head start might be critical.

Moravius pretended to be asleep. He leaned against a stack of provisions, eyes closed but ears open. He was fully aware when Duriel assigned the militant, blood-thirsty Uriah as his guard. "If he makes any move to escape, don't hesitate. Kill him. Under our deal, we get Menachem back before we release him. We can be completely restored, even if the Roman is dead."

Uriah smiled as he wiped his dagger across his forearm. "We could kill him now, and save the work of guarding him. You don't really intend to let him go, once Menachem returns, do you?"

"I think I probably will. That woman saved my life. It would be shameful to break a pledge to her. Especially so soon after."

Uriah sneered with contempt. "It has to be almost as shameful to be healed by a woman. A probable witch, no less. She's not a rabbi, so what else could she be?"

"Would you rather I died, or was healed by a woman?"

"I'm glad to see you recovering, but that wound is healing more rapidly than normal. A lot more rapidly, in my opinion."

Duriel stretched his leg to full extension, and smiled. The pain and swelling were all but gone. "Well, rabbi or not she has succeeded where others failed. She is young, and gifted. She has skills that might serve us well again someday. And besides, if she is a witch it would be even more dangerous to offend her, wouldn't it? Go ahead and wake up the Roman. We're continuing to Galilee."

The Zealots assembled the bleating sheep into a milling cluster, immediately ahead of the cart. The warriors made poor shepherds, and the flock was restless for want of authoritative handlers.

Uriah kicked Moravius in the thigh, with much more force than needed to waken a sleeper. Moravius flinched in response, and feigned a groggy awakening.

"Get up!" ordered Uriah. "Duriel wants us to walk in the middle of the flock. That will slow you down some, if you try to make a run for it. Oh, and there's an archer on the cart- so be smart and maybe you will live to rejoin your friends."

The Zealots, the flock, the cart, and the hostage took the road to Galilee. They ambled and clattered, in a cloud of dust, through the lower reaches of Samaria. Moravius withdrew a gold coin from a pouch on his belt. He fingered it, as if he were nervous or anxious. Moravius hoped the coin would attract Uriah's attention, and it did.

"What's that you're playing with?"

"Nothing really. Just an Aureus. I count on it to bring me good luck."

"A lucky coin? You pagans will believe in anything. But as long as you have it out, let me take a look at it. I promise I'll give it back."

"Well, I don't know…"

"Let me see it, Roman. I won't ask nicely again."

Moravius suppressed a smile. His scheme was advancing. "Well, if you insist. But just for a moment. I think I'm going to need all the luck I can muster today."

Uriah grabbed the Aureus. "What's this? That's Octavian's likeness. I remember when I was a boy. Augustus recalled all of these. They were melted down, some copper added to cheapen the alloy, and then recast to honor Augustus."

"You're right. Augustus gathered up every Octavian Aureus in the Empire." Moravius paused for effect. "But there were others he could not find."

Uriah took the bait. "What do you mean by that? You still have an Octavian Aureus, but what makes you think there are others?"

Moravius tried to instill a tone of reluctance in his answer. "Well, I can't say for certain there are any others. Besides, it's a boring story." Moravius extended his hand. "Can I have my coin back, please?"

Uriah gripped tightly on the Aureus. He moved it to the side of his body farthest from Moravius. The Roman was pleased; Uriah's response could not be more perfect.

"Go ahead and tell your boring story," said Uriah. "Then I'll consider returning your gold."

"Looks like you have the upper hand. Alright, That Aureus was payment for my first two months in the legion."

"That had to be decades ago. You kept it all this time?"

"Not exactly. We had a tradition, in the Legion. We offered our first Aureus to Mithras. It was a major sacrifice, one-sixth of our first year's pay. But, in return, Mithras would intercede for us with Mars. If we died in battle, it would be a noble death."

Several sheep broke off from the flock. Waving frantically and shouting, four Zealots made poor work of frightening them, rather than herding them, back into place. Everyone stopped until order was restored.

"This isn't making sense," grumbled Uriah. "If you offered the Aureus to Mithras, how is it that you carry it around in your pouch?"

"My first posting was here in Samaria. In fact, our garrison was along this very road, and not all that far ahead of where we are now. There's still a temple to Mithras there, although once the well failed the legion abandoned the site. Nobody has used the temple for years. It's in a cave, concealed from the road by a thicket. I checked on the temple when we came by with Miriam. Sure enough, there was my coin. In the same crack in the rock where I left it, almost thirty years ago. My military career is over, so I picked it up. Can I have it back, now?"

Uriah was deaf to any petition from Moravius, but keenly invested in the tale of the temple. "Your coin was still there?"

"Yes. And I was surprised. The spot I placed my Aureus was a lot more visible than most. Maybe nobody has ever looted the temple. If they had, it's likely the more easily spotted coins would be taken first."

"When you picked up your coin, did you actually see others?"

"Yes, but only a few. Most of the Legionnaires did a better job of hiding their offerings. It was all the same. Mithras knew where every coin was placed, and each was equally honored. That's the thing about…."

Uriah interrupted. "And you say this hidden temple is along this very road, and not far ahead?"

"We should pass by within half an hour, but nobody would ever think to look for a cave beyond the thicket. Obviously, after all these years, nobody has."

Uriah glared menace at Moravius. "You will show me where to find this cave."

Moravius was excited by his success. He suppressed, as well as he could, an involuntary quiver. This was more than he dared hope for. A feint of supplicating defeat at this moment would additionally set his hook into Uriah.

"If I agree to do that, will you give me back my lucky coin?"

Uriah sneered as he passed the Aureus back to Moravius. "Of course. Here it is. Besides, if for some reason you don't survive the journey, I'll know what to look for in your pouch."

Progress stalled when the Zealots encountered three Samaritan goat herds, driving their animals south on the same road. The herd and the flock co-mingled. Moravius thought the bedlam amusing, as the always hostile Zealots and Samaritans cursed each other and struggled to separate the confused sheep from the indignant goats.

Not long after the trek resumed, the road dipped down into a low valley.

"Just at the base of the hill. It will look like a thicket up against the rocks, but step through the brush and behind it you will find the temple of Mithras."

"And the gold." Said Uriah. "I'm going to have a look for myself. If you value your life, don't tell anybody else about this cave. If I find enough gold, I'll share, of course. Not with you, though. With my fellow Yehudim."

"I don't want any trouble," said Moravius. "Count on me to keep my mouth shut."

Uriah called to one of the shepherds on the perimeter. "Zebina, come here and keep an eye on the Roman for a minute. I'm going to duck into those bushes and empty my bowels. Here, take my dagger. Use it on the Roman if he tries to escape."

Zebina assumed guard duty. Uriah turned to face Duriel on the cart. "Don't bother waiting for me. I'm probably going to be a minute. Too much of that grilled lamb, if you know what I mean. I'll catch up in a few minutes."

Duriel waved and nodded. Uriah stood aside as the flock, the cart, the Zealots, and the Roman advanced along the road. Only when all had gone ahead did he approach the thicket, press some limbs aside, and step through.

Moravius was unsure whether the roar of the attacking cat slightly preceded Uriah's death scream. It was over before any of the Zealots drew their swords and ran to rescue their companion. Uriah's throat was ripped out of his broken neck. The sheep panicked, and the cat fled over the rim of the valley. The archers each got off a shot, but missed.

None of the surviving Zealots discovered the temple of Mithras. Moravius, as promised, kept his mouth shut.

II, VIII
More for the Wine than the Candle

The taper was poured from corrupted wax, with the resulting light none the better. More smoke than flame swirled from the withering wick. Weak shadows danced erratically on carelessly limed walls. A pungent greasy tallow nimbus collected above the stone arched windows, randomly displaced by sea breeze from Mare Nostrum. The garrison bell chimed midnight. The appointed hour was at hand. The ancient jailer poured a cup of wine and honey. He mused, "The bees did more for the wine, than ever for the candle."

The outer door to an adjoining room groaned upon. There was the dissonant scrape and muffled clank of heavy chains sliding across a cobbled floor. Someone in the room called, "The prisoner is ready for interrogation, as ordered, sir. Do you want me to remain?"

"Not necessary. Just bolt the door on the far side when you go. I'll send for you when I've finished."

Minutes passed. The jailer poured more wine. Aban, son of Eli, was late. Understandable, perhaps. He would need to elude the sentinels at Eli's compound, and timing might be difficult to plan. However, if Aban were delayed too long the jailer's careful instructions for avoiding the garrison guards would be of little value. The prisoner in the after room shifted in his chains, smoke rebuilt above the arches, and Atticus savored his mead.

The entry door creaked open, but only far enough to allow a hooded figure to squeeze between the latch and the jamb.

"I was beginning to wonder," said Atticus. "Did you bring it? All of it?"

Aban pulled back his hood. He pulled a bulging sheepskin purse from under his cloak. "It's all here. Down to the last denarius. You ask an enormous price, jailer."

"You ask an enormous favor, Yehudi. Even now, I could take your purse, call for the guard, and have you arrested. How much more would your own father then pay, for your release?"

"In that case, it's my father who would set the price; and you paying- not him."

"No. I'm too practical. I expect, that over the years, you may need my services again. Just as your father has done in the past. I'll have the purse if you please."

"Not until I see the merchandise. How do I know he isn't already dead? Or too many bones broken to make an escape? If you have done business with my father, you know he is no fool. Nor is his son."

Atticus nodded. "I see the tree bears fruit after its kind. He's in the room beyond the inner door. There's no light in there. Let me get you a candle."

Atticus touched a fresh wick to the existing flame. It burned as foul as the former. Aban cupped his hand around the flicker, protecting it from the breath of Mare Nostrum. When the light stabilized, Aban nodded and approached the back door of the office. Atticus rose from his bench and drew the ponderous black iron bolt.

Two steps beyond the door, the feeble light stretched into center of the after room. There sat a filthy specimen of wretched humanity. Torn clothes were stained with bodily fluids. The face and hands were caked with black grime. Hair and beard were disrupted beyond any suggestion of deliberation. The chained figure looked up, with an expression of defeat and disinterest.

Aban scowled at Atticus. "This is disgusting. Much worse than I expected. Leave us- but keep that door open. It smells like hot sewage in here. Is there a bucket, if I get sick?"

"As you wish," said Atticus. "I'll put a bucket here at the door. It's only a few steps."

Atticus withdrew, and after a moment's clattering around placed the promised bucket in the doorway.

Aban turned his attention to the chained man. "Yetro? Is that you?"

"It might be. Or maybe it used to be. If it is, what of it? What do you want with me?"

"I'm going to take you out of here, tonight."

Yetro was animated by the answer. Chains clanked as he raised his head to take a careful look at this new arrival. Focusing his gaze beyond the flame, he was almost certain he recognized the face.

Yetro slurred, "Aren't you Eli's son, Aban? Why would you get me released? More important, where are we going? You have to know it's your father who put me here. Are you here on his business?"

"I'm here on my own. My father must never know about this. I'm going to get you out of Palestine. You can thank me some time in the future for saving your life."

"This makes no sense. Your father intends to have me tried for heresy. You could be put to death for helping me."

"I don't care anything about that. I'm not saving you for your own sake, but for my sister's."

Yetro jerked against his restraints. He was now intensely engaged. His speech clarified. "Miriam? What does releasing me have to do with Miriam's welfare? Has anything happened to her?"

"No, she's fine. Father plans to bargain your life for her agreement to marry against her will. I don't care what happens to a heretic, unless it affects Miriam. After your escape, he won't be able to pressure her into a disastrous marriage."

Slowly, awkwardly, and with obvious pain Yetro rose to stand. "Can I see Miriam? Is she here with you?"

"No. She knows nothing of Eli's plan. Nothing of mine. In fact, she's been sent to Ain Karem and Yerushalayim until after Tabernacles.

You may never see her again, but you will live."

"Never again? What if I choose to remain, and defend myself with the Sanhedrin? I could be exonerated, and freed."

"And I could be King of Numidia, Governor of Goshen, and Prince of Ethiopia. All at once, and equally likely. Stay and you will surely die, maybe even if Miriam agrees to marry Faramond."

"Where will I go? How will I live?"

"That's better," encouraged Aban. "A little self-interest right now will go a long way."

A span of silence bridged the gap between the two men in the jailer's after room. They arrived at a common intent and purpose.

Aban continued. "After your escape, which I have arranged, we will go down to the harbor. I have a small boat standing by, with a crew of three men who will carry you to Alexandria. You must never, under any circumstances, return to Yudea, Galilee, or even Samaria again. Never attempt to contact Miriam. At least not while my father lives."

Yetro stuck a grimy finger into the mess of his beard. "Alexandria? That would work. Our Yehudim brothers there are more open minded. They find nothing heretical about seeking truth through knowledge. I would be accepted. Maybe even earn access to the Great Library. I'll go."

"Of course you will. Your option would be to die here tonight, at my hand. I will not allow you to be used to force my sister into marriage."

Aban called into the jailer's office. "Bring the wrench, unbolt these chains."

"First the purse, young master."

"Yes, yes, of course. Here it is. Don't insult me by bothering to count. It's all there."

Atticus secured the purse in a wooden chest. He retrieved an iron wrench on a long handle, swinging from a peg next to one of the windows. "Bring him out here. There's a little more light, and I will be glad to close the door on the stench."

Like unhappy memories, Yetro's chains followed him into the outer office. The jailer removed two bolts on the manacles, and two on the fetters at his ankles. Yetro was free.

"We have no time to lose," said Aban.

Atticus agreed. "Especially as you were late. But the way out will be easier. Walk boldly. There are two guards you cannot avoid, but they have done business with your father as well. Tonight their eyes are blinded by a promise of silver. Tomorrow, their tongues will have no memory- once my promise is fulfilled."

"Fine. There's still time to get a boat out of sight before daybreak, and for me to sneak back into the estate."

II, IX
"The Stone Rejected by the Master Builder"

Yusuf was always amused when Malak arrived. The dusky Arab merchant dressed in billowing black robes and rode a chalk white stallion. Malak had a larger than average muscular frame, chiseled cheekbones, ear hoops of polished gold and eyes as piercing as any bird of prey. Men nodded as he passed by. Women blushed. He carried a scimitar secured in a scabbard covered with semi-precious stones; appropriate, considering his trade. Malak's entry to the construction area at Eli's compound spawned the easily predicted current of gossiping whispers.

The tile setter was not distracted. Malak was a necessary supplier, and not above using bluster and personal dynamism to close an extremely one-sided transaction. Most people who purchased his colored pottery, shells, bits of glass and chips of gemstone eventually learned to play the game by Malak's rules. None learned quickly enough. All would enrich the vendor beyond any reasonable level of recompense before their education was sufficiently, and expensively, advanced. Yusuf knew the dance, and was aware that it required careful footwork.

The merchant did not surrender his mount to the groom at the gate, but rode through the compound gardens and up to the construction zone. "Such arrogance," thought the tile setter. "For the fortune he expects to make, how hard can it be to act politely? He's as unchanging as any of his fancy rocks."

Shimon of Accara, the master builder, hurried from his pavilion to observe any conversation between the tile setter and the merchant. It was he, not Yusuf, ultimately responsible to Lord Eli for the cost as well as the final result.

Malak dismounted. He handed the reins to a random laborer, who accepted them but looked annoyed. "Shalom, Yusuf."

"Shalom"

"So you have advanced from the understudy at King Herod's palace to chief tile setter for Lord Eli? Congratulations on that."

Malak paced off the dimensions of the slab; his jeweled scabbard flashing in the sunlight with the swing of every step. "Only slightly smaller than the work you just finished at Sephora, isn't it? You will need almost the same amount of material. Maybe you should order the same, or a little extra. It pays to account for waste, or theft from the stockpile."

"It pays to be prudent with Lord Eli's resources," insisted Shimon. "We'll order no more than required. It will be Yusuf's job to use it wisely."

Malak executed the smallest detectable bow to Shimon, and made a sweeping gesture with an open hand. "Of course, master builder. I would expect no less."

Yusuf smiled. Malak was up to the charming tricks that earned his reputation. "What have you brought for samples?"

"Yes, down to business of course. I presume you will be working in traditional black and white, with a few accents? Let me show you some tiles of black sapphire, from the mines of Tunis. Lord Eli deserves nothing less."

"I'll be working with some black, but there will be no need for sapphire."

Malak pressed ahead. "The white then? You plan to save the more radiant pieces to accentuate the white? A wise choice. I can show you some dazzling examples of my white jasper, cut from select stones quarried in Cappadocia."

"Let me be more specific," said Yusuf. "For each hundred portions of tile and stone, I will require roughly thirty-five in blue. Twenty-five will be red. Ten each in yellow, black, and white. The final ten will be tin, to honor the family trade with Britannia and weather to green."

Shimon was shocked. "That's a very daring mix! I hope you know what you're doing, tile setter. This plaza will be a central point of the addition to Eli's compound, not a piss wall behind a bordello. The work you did for Herod…"

Yusuf interrupted. "The work I did for Herod is done. Lord Eli and his son have approved the general concept here, and left the details and choice of color to me." Yusuf pointed at his head. "I can see the finished work, right here. Fear not, Lord Eli will be pleased."

Malak turned to his horse, and began rummaging through his saddle pack. "So, for blue you will no doubt require lapis lazuli. Carefully sorted agate, of the finest grade, for yellow and white? Ordinarily, ruby is thought to be too expensive for red, but I acquired some surplus stones at a special price. As for the…"

The tile setter interrupted again. "Enough, please. I don't doubt that you can deliver enough gems to lay the entire mosaic in precious stones."

"And at favorable prices. Surely Eli will expect no less," agreed Malak.

"What Eli expects is the best. A spectacular result. Something that will enhance his son's addition to the compound. For that, I will require only a single material, in all the colors specified- except the copper, of course."

Malak appeared confused. "The only material available in that variety of colors is common clay, glazed and fired."

"So it is. Fire it to a gloss. We're going to use the most commonly available tiles to create a work worthy of the most exalted royalty. It's the line and the form that creates beauty, not the rarity or expense of the stone."

Shimon pulled Yusuf aside, to a point where he hoped Malak would not overhear his whispered admonishment. "Have you lost your mind? Clay tiles? Not even accented with gems? People will think Lord Eli was unable to afford better. You will bring us all to shame."

"I have had a vision, Shimon. The One God created mankind from mud and clay. Surely, The One God can instruct me to create a plaza that will honor Lord Eli and his son from the same material."

"You press to the edge, tile setter. You may press beyond. It's only my regard for Lady Miriam's high opinion of you that gives you a shaky grip on your situation here. The risk is all yours. If Eli disapproves once you lay the first portions- you will redo the work at no charge. And you, and your father as well, will bear the cost of the rejected tiles. It will be nearly a year's wages, even in clay."

Yusuf and Shimon returned to speak with the Arab merchant.

Malak appeared hopeful. "Now that you have had a moment to give it a bit more thought, can I show you some agates"

"No," said Yusuf. "Fired clay tiles. Make them uniform in hue, random in shape. We will want some red dye for the mortar. How quickly can they be here?"

"I have most of what you need in stock. I'll send some carts within the week."

"Fine," said Yusuf. "It looks like we are agreed."

Malak remounted his horse. The animal shook its neck. "It looks like I wasted a day on an errand for which I could send my most junior assistant. Clay tiles? I won't be making enough to cover my travel expense. You didn't need me for this."

"Maybe not," agreed Yusuf, "but I'm glad you came. It's always a pleasure to do business with you."

Malak's eyes gleamed as he grinned. His impatient horse turned in a tight circle as the merchant spoke. "So be it. Be sure we will be doing business again, tile setter. As will our sons, and their sons in their turn. Our accounts will square again and again, and long before we're finished. Shalom."

The merchant rode through the gardens, to the forecourt, and out the gate.

"You won't get far with those common materials," warned Shimon. "It will be your ruin. Lord Eli will order you to begin again, with stones of greater value."

"We'll see, won't we? Maybe the material normally rejected by a master builder will prove worthy. When it does, feel free to accept the credit."

"I warn you again. When it does not prove worthy, as I am sure it won't, I'm not going to accept any of the blame."

II, X
Challah, and a Good Red Wine

There was a busy market in Ain Karem. Vendors offering trays of spiced food, stacks of vibrant fabric, and fired clay jars of wine and olive oil left only a serpentine path through the center of the street. From every ramshackle lean-to and covered booth the shouts and adjurations of competing merchants swirled as marbled cacophony in a cloud of dust and incense. Here was a one-armed beggar. His face was painted white. Dressed in an absurdly lavish costume, he balanced on a tottering stack of wooden blocks. Passersby tossed coins close enough to be within his grasp- yet likely to pitch him off balance as he attempted to snag the coins in flight.

The donkey balked and would not be driven by rein. Menachem stepped down and grabbed the bridle. Festus and Lucanus parted the crowd to permit passage of Miriam's cart. Not far beyond the market was the home of the old priest Zachariah and his wife Elisheba. One of the holy man's apprentices sat in the shadow of the northern wall, praying over a scroll. Miriam's party stopped outside the gate.

"Are you the priest Zachariah?" asked Lucanus.

The apprentice rose. He eyed the Roman warily and began rolling up the scroll. "No, he's within, meditating. Do you have some business with him?"

Miriam answered, "I'm Miriam. My father is Eli, of the Sanhedrin. I've traveled from Caesarea to visit my cousin, Elisheba."

"Shalom, Miriam. Pardon me a moment. I shouldn't disturb Zachariah, but I will let Elisheba know you are here." The apprentice entered the house.

"Duriel and the patriots have a good head start," remarked Menachem. "Even if you raise the alarm now, the legion would be unable to find them. I'll work my way back to Galilee. Once I'm safely there, Duriel will release Moravius. "

"I'm going with you," said Festus.

Menachem was startled. "That wasn't part of the agreement."

"No. But making sure you survive the journey is important. If you don't live to return, they will eventually kill Moravius."

"I can travel alone."

"That's not going to be an option. Moravius ordered me to get Lady Miriam to Ain Karem. We're here. Lucanus will remain to guard Eli's daughter. I go north with you to be there when they release Moravius. I won't have him standing there alone when your friends realize they have no more use for him."

"Do you think we murder without honor?"

"What I think is not important."

Elisheba appeared in the doorway. Still slender of frame in her late 50's, she wore a yellow gown with a wide blue sash. Her silver hair was bound with black ribbons. Miriam immediately noticed the radiance; as if the rays on an internal sun projected from every pore.

"Could it be? The message I'm carrying for Gabriel- could it be true? Am I wrong, or does she have that look about her."

Elisheba expressed a satisfied smile. "Miriam! How wonderful to see you! Have somebody put the donkey and cart behind the house. Everyone, come in. There's enough room. Your timing is perfect, I have challah fresh from the oven, and a good red wine."

Zachariah and his apprentice emerged. "Shalom, Miriam. Is it only wonderful luck that brings you to our door, or did you come for another purpose?"

"Actually, I'm bringing a message, for Elisheba."

Zachariah clapped his hands together, closed his eyes, and nodded. "Excellent! I've been watching for a messenger- but until this moment I was not sure who it would be. The three of us must speak together, at an early hour in the morning. For now, though, rest and refresh. It's a long trek from Caesarea."

II, XI
Planets and Prophecies

A pink and orange glow carved in silhouette the eastern hills of Ur. At Gaspar's command Melchior moved the lens to a dark chamber within the ziggurat. Melchior was sure his calculations, and those of the scribe who assisted him were correct. With the night's work accomplished, this would be an ideal time to bring the phenomenon to the attention of the Grand Master. Perhaps Gaspar already realized- but perhaps not. Melchior would do no worse than appear to be a perceptive student, and there was a chance he had stumbled across a sign of substantial importance.

Melchior detoured to his dormitory. The freshly drawn chart was loosely rolled, and stored in a clay jar next to his sleeping mat. A shaft of early sunlight climbed the outside wall, crested the window sill, and tumbled to the floor exactly where Melchior was double checking his drawing. Yes, it was at is had appeared. The more one looked, the easier it was to see the relationship. Why else would the old priest send a dove to ask about this date? It could not merely be coincidental.

Melchior rolled up the chart and walked, with cautious optimism, to seek an audience with Grand Master Gaspar. He knocked, and was admitted.

"Grand Master, I would like to ask your opinion, if I may."

"Certainly. On what matter?"

"You remember the recent request from the Hebrew, Zachariah?"

"Yes, of course. Extravagant of him to waste a dove, wasn't it?"

"That's what I thought. So after the scribes prepared the response, I prepared charts for the dates he asked about. I didn't see anything of note in any of them, until I got to this one."

Melchior unrolled the chart. Gaspar repositioned a candle to provide a better view.

"And what day is this, exactly?"

"It's the fifth day of Nissan, at least on the Yehudi calendar. It's the same month the Romans name for their god of war and agriculture."

"So just over five months from now. What did you find?"

Melchior was pleased, but worried. Gaspar wasn't seeing the pattern. Had he actually discovered something new? Could it be that the pattern existed only in Melchior's imagination? At this point, there was nothing to do but proceed.

"Earth in Scorpio, Mercury in Capricorn, Jupiter in Taurus, Venus in Cancer. Remember my surprise that the old priest would ask about Uranus or even know about Neptunus? Neptunus will be in Scorpio, and Uranus in Pisces."

Gaspar studied the chart, and nodded approvingly. "That looks like a very regular distribution. What have you concluded?"

"Not only is the pattern regular, but the points are exactly 60 degrees apart. On the 5th day of Nissan these particular wandering planets will all be in identical, angular relationship."

"Your chart shows Mars in Libra, and Saturnus in Aries."

Melchior nodded eagerly. "Yes, and that disrupts the uniform angularity, unless we look at the chart and find two patterns."

"What have you found?"

Melchior laid a straight edge on the chart and picked up a marking coal. "If we connect Mars, Venus, Earth, and Saturnus, we create a square." Melchior sketched the connections.

Gaspar nodded. "And the remainder, do they form a circle?"

"Yes, if you create a ray from the sun. Connected directly, they form a perfect hexagon." Melchior traced the connecting lines.

Gaspar stroked his beard. "You're right, this might be auspicious.

A square, a circle and a hexagon on the same night. That has to be ridiculously rare. Good work."

Melchior was pleased with the praise. "But wait, Grand Master, there's yet another shape here. One that would only be possible on a night where the wanderers are in the exact positions." Melchior began tracing along the straight edge. "If we connect Earth to Mercury and Jupiter, and Venus to Uranus and Neptunus we get…"

Gaspar interrupted before Melchior finished his sentence or the second line. "We get the seal of Solomon!"

"Yes, we do. As a Yehudi, Zachariah would call it the Star of David."

Gaspar nodded. "That has to explain his interest in Uranus and Neptunus, and why he would spend the expense of a carrier bird. Zachariah must have made similar calculations. He's perceiving the same star shape in the heavens. No doubt he's expecting the fulfillment of some prophecy or another."

"The Yehudim must have a million prophecies," said Melchior. "That makes it easy to claim that no matter what happens a prophecy has come to pass."

"Entirely true. But how many of those prophecies would be fulfilled with the planets so uniquely aligned?"

II, XII
Complicated Equations

Miriam awoke to the sound of Zachariah graining his doves on the roof. She traced his muffled footfalls across the ceiling of her upper room. She smiled when she heard the birds began to coo and flap. No doubt, this moment was a highlight of the avian day.

Miriam closed her eyes again. She found that small white light behind the bridge of her nose. She allowed, willed, and experienced the light as it extended to inundate the surface of her unseen face. In rapid course, it inflated to engulf the area where she imagined her head must be.

Miriam fell into the glow, spinning weightless and warm. There was no reference point for ascent or descent. It was not clear, nor was it important, whether she moved through space or whether she remained still and space was effectively removed from around her. There was no presence of form, and no absence of void. Energies were extracted from white to meld sensations of freezing cerulean iron with the translucent celebration of flaming amber. She tasted green benedictions seasoned with sea salt. She smelled the sweet molded wood of umber husk. She touched an onyx horizon that exploded into an internal eternity of galaxies and fire.

Miriam's perceived universe vibrated with a reassuring voice.

"I am Elishua. I am Ben-gabar. Some call me Gabriel, or Israel, or Almodad. Only The One God knows my true name. Only The One God knows yours."

Miriam answered. "I am here. Just as you said I must, I am here to bear your message for Elisheba. I'm sorry to be so late. We ran into some delays; with Zealots and such!"

"Be assured that your timing is perfect. The One God holds you in the palm of his hand. All has been, and may yet be, as foretold."

Miriam sensed, but could not see, two hands gripping her wrists. "What has been foretold? Why is it what has been foretold may or may not come to pass?"

"Sometimes the will of The One God requires a conduit. Sometimes, the message requires a dove. When you speak to Zachariah, be open to possibilities. Remember, The One God holds you in the palm of his hand. Rejoice. Do not be afraid."

"I am seldom afraid."

Elishua laughed with a force that vibrated Miriam's new cosmos. "Then you are unique, indeed. The One God would have me leave you with a blessing. Bear it carefully in mind, when later you speak with Elisheba and Zachariah. At the time of all origins, there was The Word. The Word was with The One God. The Word was inseparable from The One God. The Word became flesh, is flesh and will become flesh, and The Word will dwell on the earth, among the Children of The One God."

Everything collapsed with a knock at the outer door. Miriam's eyes fluttered open. Had it been seconds, minutes, hours, days, or no time at all since she closed them? There was no sound of Zachariah on the roof. "Yes, come in!"

Yasminah entered Miriam's room. She sat a glowing brazier of hot coals against an outside wall, within a well-defined sooty crest. The smoke drifted through a window with adequate efficiency. "This will take off the morning, chill, Mistress." Yasminah replaced the partially filled privy pot with an empty duplicate. She was almost to the door when Miriam called out.

"Thank you. Did you sleep well?"

"Well enough, mistress. I got up early to bid Festus good bye. He and that Zealot left long before sunrise." Yasminah averted her gaze, and blushed. "I worry about Festus."

Miriam puckered her cheeks, tilted her head, and arched her

brows. "Festus? Really?"

Yasminah flustered. "Well, no, I mean yes, of course. I mean I suppose I mean just as I would worry about anyone else in Lord Eli's service."

Miriam smiled. "Well, that's perfectly fine. Just think of the complications, if there were anything more. I mean, he's not even Yehudi…"

Yasminah sighed, and interrupted with resignation. "No, he's not. And he's just short of twice my age. And they say he was married before. Some say he still has a wife in Pompeii, but he says that was never true…"

"You have talked with him about his marital status?" Miriam giggled as Yasminah hurried, embarrassed from the room. *The heart is a complicated equation.* Miriam closed her eyes again and briefly recalled a handsome tile setter, back in Caesarea.

Halfway down the outer stairs to the courtyard, Yasminah called, "Oh, and Rabbi Zachariah and Elisheba are waiting for you, at your convenience, mistress."

II, XIII
Price and Privilege

Nobody spoke. Father and son stood, toe to toe- each staring into eyeballs and defying the other to blink. A glacial age of silence, and then Eli drew a deep breath.

The elder man hissed, "You had no right!"

"I had every right. The priest was not formally charged."

Eli balled up his fists, and stood on tiptoes to gain a tiny height advantage. "He was my prisoner. Mine! And he's a dangerous heretic!"

Aban relaxed his stance and stepped away from the confrontation. *Sometimes, you demonstrate more courage by standing down.* "I'm happy to discuss this with you, when we're not both angry. I don't want to say something foolish I will regret. If this isn't the time…"

Eli lowered his shoulders, shook his head, and threw up his open hands. He took a seat at his counting table. He grudgingly motioned for Aban to take a seat as well. He admired the self-restraint and courage he had instilled in his son.

Another span of stressful quiet. Eli sighed before he spoke. "Now you know that the jailer can be bought. So learn that he cannot be trusted. Your gold freed the renegade Yetro, but my gold- and the tip of a sword at the base of his neck, bought the jailer's confession."

"I'll take that to heart. What will you do to the jailer?"

"Nothing for now. Besides, he's a Roman and that presents difficulties. He has been useful in the past. I may need him in the future. No doubt the next time or two I need a favor the price will be more than reasonable."

"Father, I am willing to beg your forgiveness, but I cannot apologize. I think I did the right thing, letting Yetro escape."

Eli pushed the balance scales aside, and leaned across the counting table toward his son. "He's a heliocentrist! A heretic! And he has too much influence over your sister!"

"There's some truth to that. But I could not let you maneuver Miriam into a marriage with Faramond, using Yetro as a lever."

"It's not your place to interfere. You will be a father yourself someday. Soon enough, The One God willing. You will find it isn't always easy, pairing up your children."

A silky breeze, scented with Jasmine, entered with a sun-warmed wink. It orbited the men like a busy blessing.

Eli continued, "Tell me where to find Yetro."

"He's gone. I sent him to Alexandria, and warned him never return. If he's smart, he'll continue on from there and be impossible to find. There should be no more trouble with Yetro."

"No more trouble, but no more use of him either. There's a price for your betrayal."

Aban shifted uncomfortably on the bench. He tugged on the sleeve of his robe, as if searching for salvation through distraction. "That would be?"

"You will support me, whatever decision I might make, about marriage for Miriam."

"You ask an enormous price, father."

"You presumed enormous privilege, son."

II, XIV
Master of a Dark House

Yakob fell.

The tile setter could not remember ever hearing his father scream, but from the leading edge of the first alarmed shriek, Yusuf knew it was his father in distress. He dropped his tools and ran to where the framers and joiners labored. The screech was beyond audible sensation. Like an invisible fist, it wrenched his heart and gut. Yusuf repeated, "No, no, no…" as he sprinted across the worksite.

Everything stopped. Shimon the master builder emerged from his pavilion. Basket men and water bearers flocked toward the gruesome agony. Yakob's fellow Tektons pressed the gawkers back. Yusuf forced his way through the circle, assisted by a fellow Nazarene who shoved people aside and cried, "Let him through! This is his son!"

Yakob's face was the color of wet mortar. The upper portion of his body shivered and convulsed, but there was no motion below the waist. Four of the workers joined arms under Yakob's torso in an attempt to move him. The anguished scream stunned everyone. It emerged from Yakob, but rang like the bell of a foreign tongue, chiming from someplace far, far, away.

"Leave him!" ordered Shimon. He pointed to a carpenter, "Run and find a rabbi." Shimon ordered his assistant, "Get the oil of poppy from my chest."

Yusuf knelt at his father's side. Yakob raised a palpitating hand, and Yusuf grasped it with both of his. "They have sent for a healer, father." Yusuf stopped himself from saying "You're going to be alright," in favor of a more realistic, "Help is on the way!"

A trickle of blood emerged from Yakob's mouth. "I heard the bones crush when I landed. My hip- it's shattered." Yakob's upper body shook violently. He groaned a thunderous wail. "My back- I think it's broken. The pain! It's all above the waist." Tears ran through the dirt on his cheeks, drawing lines that crossed his temples between his eyes and his ears. "I'm beyond any help."

Shimon's assistant returned, bearing a tiny jar covered with jewels. He knelt next to Yakob, opposite Yusuf. "Hold this for me. I'll put two drops on his tongue." Shimon's assistant inserted an ivory wand into the bottle and retrieved a drop of poppy oil. The bleeding from Yakob's mouth increased. The assistant administered first one drop of oil, and then a second.

The oil of poppy reduced the convulsions to a steady shiver. Yakob focused his eyes on Yusuf and coughed up blood attempting to clear his throat. He gurgled as he spoke, but his words were clear and his tone was determined.

"I'm going to a place. I can see it. I have been there before. So have you. Everywhere I look, I see brothers and sisters. Fathers and grandfathers. Mothers and grandmothers. Everyone there is a relative."

"Hush, father! Don't strain yourself!"

More blood, and darker, dribbled down Yakob's chin. "The One God calls my name. My true name. But I can see a promise! You will marry. You will have sons and daughters."

A ferocious trembling wracked Yakob's body. Blood pumped through Yakob's mouth with each beat of his failing heart.

"Give him some more oil of poppy!" insisted Yusuf.

"Any more will kill him," argued Shimon. "It would be murder."

Yusuf was still holding the jar. "No, it will be mercy." He tipped some of the contents into Yakob's bleeding mouth.

Yakob's stare intensified. He poured his remaining strength into his grip of Yusuf's hand. A momentary blush of color returned to his face and he summoned the strength to gargle. "Yeconiah! The curse! It's lifted. I can see it! Your first born son, he, he, h…."

Yakob answered the call of his true name, a moment before the rabbi arrived.

"Everybody, get back to work!" ordered Shimon. "And you, tile setter. Do you have any idea how much it costs for poppy oil? You couldn't of course. Take enough time to bury your father. When you return, we will expect a few days' work without wages to square accounts."

The crowd dispersed, each carrying away a tiny, unearned, piece of deadly darkness.

Yusuf remained. Kneeling in the dirt, the sawdust, and the shavings; he wept.

One of the framers brought Yakob's cart and donkey. The rabbi, a young stranger from Caesarea placed a hand on Yusuf's shoulder. "When you're ready, I'll help you take him home."

Yusuf stared vacantly, seeing through and beyond the rabbi. He spoke slowly, as if deliberately composing every syllable. "Thank you. I don't. Know how you. Got here so. Quickly. I think I could. Use some help."

The rabbi touched Yusuf on the forearm. "I assume you're going to bury him at Nazareth? I know of some women there who will dress the body. Then I will bless it."

Two Tektons lifted Yakob's corpse and set it gingerly in the cart. A joiner removed his cloak and laid it tenderly over Yakob's face. Yusuf grabbed the donkey by the bridle and turned to the rabbi.

"I'm going to walk him. To Nazareth. That's the last place we. Called home. Come along, if you like. I'd be grateful for the. Company. But, before we start off- know that it's a long walk."

The rabbi nodded. "Yes, but it's a shorter journey than Yakob made."

Yusuf retrieved Yakob's sword from their sleeping quarters. He secured it to his belt. Grieving son and sympathetic rabbi walked the cart through the gate. The axle squeaked softly. The ass plodded methodically, with head down, as if aware of his load. Every servant, worker, and Roman guard nodded respectfully as they past. A subtle sea breath nudged the travelers, over the crest of the hill on the road to Nazareth.

They walked for an hour before they spoke. Yusuf was too numbed for conversation. The rabbi appreciated the therapeutic value of silence.

Yusuf broke the silence. "So what becomes of my father?"

"We'll dress, bless, and bury him, according to our laws and customs."

Yusuf stopped the cart and addressed the rabbi over the neck of the donkey.

"That's not what I mean."

"Oh, I suppose you mean what happens to the spirit of Yakob, now that he's dead? What could I tell you that will bring you comfort?"

"The truth."

The rabbi nodded sideways, and cast his eyes along the road. "Let's keep walking. The truth is hard to pin down. Nobody seems to have all of it. A lot of us believe we might have some of it, even when we disagree."

Yusuf tugged the bridle. The donkey brayed, shivered, and trudged forward.

After a moment, the rabbi spoke. "You'll get a different answer to your question if you ask different people. Ask an Essene, and you will be told that everything is preordained. That we're each responsible to live in close harmony with The One God's plan for our lives."

"And when that life is over, what then? What now, for my father?"

"According to the Essenes, each life is a divine moment. Like a sunny day. The sun rises, shines, and sets. And then the purpose of the day is served. The sun is gone, but the work done that day endures."

Yusuf stopped the cart again. "Are you an Essene? Is that what you believe? That my father's sun has set?"

The rabbi shook his head. "No, most people call me a Pharisee. Like most Pharisees, I believe that physical death unshackles the spirit. Yakob was created in the image of The One God. Just like you. Just like me. It's Yakob's spirit that reflects and projects that image."

Yusuf sighed and resumed walking. "So nobody knows for sure, do they?"

"Truly? No. We think, we hope, we believe. We invest in different realities. Surely The One God must have some compassion for our attempt to understand."

"So if Yakob's spirit is released, where is it?"

"In a place, or a time, or a shadow where only spirits go."

"What's that place like?"

"Nobody knows. We think, we hope, we believe, and many of us fear."

"But, Rabbi, what do you believe? What do you hope, believe, or fear?"

"There was once a slave serving a master of a dark house. The slave searched the house for lamps. Finding some, he lit them all. The house glowed with light until the oil ran out. The slave went to the master and said, 'Master, the oil has run out. Give me some more, if you please.' The master scolded the servant for being foolish and wasteful, and told the slave he must do the rest of his work in darkness."

Yusuf considered the parable.

The rabbi continued. "As well, there was another slave under the master of a dark house. During the course of his work, the slave would often find lamps. To stave off want, the slave refused to light any of them. Eventually the master scolded him for fumbling around in the dark. His work would be better done with a little bit of light. Instead of wasting the gift of oil, he had wasted the discovery of lamps."

Yusuf asked, "How can anyone please such a master?"

"The master cannot be pleased by any decision. Not to light the lamps. Not to live in darkness. The master is perfect, and any decision will be imperfect. Perhaps the master will forgive the servant and release his bond. But if not, perhaps then the servant continues his work for another season, and in a garden of his own creation. Perhaps what we release in this world, we set loose in the next."

Yusuf fingered the hilt of his father's sword. "My father was a good man."

"Yes, he was. That's why I came when called. And why we're walking him to Nazareth."

II, XV
Yetzirah

Miriam pondered while she descended the steps to the courtyard. Elishua, Ben-gabar, Gabriel, Israel, Almodad charged her "Take a message to your cousin Elisheba. Tell her, she's with child." It was likely that mission would be shortly fulfilled. By why send her? Why all the way from Caesarea, and (as it developed) at no small personal risk? Zachariah said they were "waiting for a messenger, but we didn't know who it would be." If Zachariah knew a messenger was en route, could it be that he and Elisheba already knew what the message would be? How could Elisheba not know, or at least sense it, even at an age when she cannot possibly be fertile? In that case, why send a messenger at all?

Didn't Elishua mention that Zacariah and Elisheba might have a gift for me? I can't imagine what. Following visionary voices can be costly, exhausting, and dangerous. I don't understand any of this. Enough of this particular adventure for me. At least it's nearly over.

Elisheba embraced Miriam at the base of the steps. Just outside the lower door. "We're going to join Zachariah in his study. Consider that a privilege. Ordinarily, women would not be allowed in there. He makes an exception for me, sometimes. There would be trouble, if anyone knew, so we have to trust you will keep this a secret."

"Of course. By the way, speaking of secrets…"

Elisheba smiled. She touched the bottom of her nose with a finger across her lips. "Not yet. Not here. Not until we're alone with Zachariah."

The two women crossed the main room of the home, Elisheba knocked on the study door.

"Come in," called Zachariah.

The rabbi's retreat was a jumble of scrolls and amulets. Even though the sun was out, the window was covered and light pulsed from a fat and pungent yellow candle. Zachariah indicated a bench, next to his own, and invited the women to sit.

"Shalom, Miriam! Did you sleep well?"

"Yes, I was exhausted when we arrived."

Zachariah extended a plate of unleavened bread. "A piece of this to break your fast?"

Miriam took a piece of bread and extended the plate to Elisheba, who declined.

Zachariah filled two fresh cups from a jug, and then sipped from his own. "And try some of this. You might not like it. The Greeks often mix a little pine pitch into their wine. I enjoy it, but red wine and pine are an unusual combination for most."

Miriam took a tiny sip. She made a disgusted face, and set the cup down. "Sorry, but if death has a taste it must be a lot like that."

Zachariah was amused. "No problem. It can take some time to appreciate. So, Miriam, yesterday you said you came to us with a message. What is the message, and from whom?"

Miriam squirmed with slight discomfort. "This is probably going to sound hard to believe, But I agreed to carry the message, so here it is." Miriam swiveled to face her cousin. She reached out to hold both of her hands. "Elisheba, you are with child."

Zachariah and Elisheba cried in unison, "The One God be praised!"

Startled by this reaction, Miriam pressed on. "It seems like you're not surprised? Not to be rude or anything, but isn't this a little unlikely- given your ages? You will be the oldest parents anybody ever heard of."

Zachariah laughed heartily. "Not exactly. Avram and Sarai were much older."

"But Avram and Sarai? That was different. It was the handiwork of The One God."

Elisheba spoke, "So it was. But, so it is with every child."

"Wait!" insisted Zachariah. "Before we speak of anything else, you have to tell us who asked you to bring this message. We have to be sure."

"I don't know if I dare repeat his name. Or really names. He says he is called by several."

"Then give me one, child."

"Alright. He says his name is Elishua."

Zachariah nodded eagerly. "And did he mention Israel, Ben-gabbar, Almodad, and Gabriel? Do any of those names sound familiar?"

Miriam exhaled deeply, relaxing as she crossed her hands into the folds of her turquoise robe. "They do. I thought I was bringing you surprising news. Now it seems I might be here for something else. Like you're already playing some spiritual game I haven't been invited to join. You already knew, didn't you?"

Elisheba answered, "We have known since the very first day." She pressed her hands on her belly. "Four months now. We were told to keep this a secret, and we did. We were promised that a chosen one would be revealed, and by knowledge that only a chosen one would know."

Zachariah confirmed, "Bringing us the message proves that you can have a part in what you call the 'spiritual game'. But, it's only yours if you want it. Only yours if you accept it. If you aren't afraid to learn more, I will proceed. But if you are frightened or unwilling to explore a miraculous possibility, we won't go any further. In that case, The One god will choose another. In any event, you are welcome to stay with us until your family arrives in Yerushalayim for The Feast of Tabernacles."

In a moment of silence, Miriam gazed around the room. Although a humble abode, there was an aura of mystery and a sensation of scholarship. Why had Yetro warned her that Zachariah must never learn that she knew him? What extraordinary thing might potentially occur in this very ordinary space?

The young woman summoned her resolve. "I am not afraid. The One God holds me…

Zachariah finished the sentence in unison with Miriam, "…in the palm of his hand."

Elisheba chimed in, and all three exclaimed, "Rejoice! Do not be afraid!" The trio erupted in unrestrained laughter. Tears of mirth, and tears of peace. Zachariah's apprentice, as well as Miriam's servants and Elisheba's household staff stared toward the closed door, each speculating on the cause of such merriment.

Everyone caught breath. Merriam assumed a serious tone. "So, why am I here? Really? I bring you news that isn't news, and now you say that doing so means I can be chosen for something?"

Zachariah nodded. "Yes, it's time to tell you a profound secret. It's something only a very few rabbis know about. As a woman, you should never have knowledge of what I'm about to share with you. If you had been my apprentice, you would study with me until the end of your 29th year before you could take apprentices of your own. If I found you worthy enough to share what I am going to show you, you would first swear to keep this secret. Will you swear to keep the secret, Miriam?"

Miriam was annoyed. "And would you accept my promise? After all, I'm a woman, not a rabbi. I have not been your apprentice. I am well short of my 29th year."

"The One God has set you on this path. It may be fitting that you receive, by grace, what is withheld from even selected rabbis for 30 years."

"In that case, I promise."

Zachariah rose, turned, and picked up a long cedar box. Slowly, reverently, he sat the box on his study table. A rich perfume emerged as he removed the lid, and set it tenderly aside. The old priest lifted a scroll, wound on two mahogany spindles with gold finials. He raised the scroll to his lips- kissing it before laying it down.

"That looks important," said Miriam. "What is it?"

"The Sefer Yetzirah. Or at least my copy. It's the very language of The One God. It was a gift to Avram at the time of the Covenant. It was instrumental in Sarai's pregnancy, as well as Elisheba's. If you are willing, yours will be third and complete the circle."

Miriam suppressed the urge to scoff. "I'm still a virgin, but not a clueless child. How can anyone get pregnant by an old scroll?"

Zachariah frowned. "Not by the scroll, of course. By the language of The One God. The secret hides in plain sight. We use the language when we pray. When we read the laws and the prophets."

"Hebrew is the language of The One God?"

"It is. Not the only language of course. The One God speaks all tongues. But it's the language The One God used when saying 'Let there be light.' We have earth sounds, fire sounds, water sounds, and air sounds in our language. If one knows exactly how to combine them, it's possible to manifest anything in the universe. That was The One God's gift to Avram."

"Let me try to understand. You claim you can make somebody pregnant by speaking Hebrew?"

Not just any Hebrew. The mixture of earth, air, fire, and water sounds must be precise. Nothing can be created through Yetzirah that is not consistent with the will of The One God. It cannot be used for selfish gain, only to perpetuate a loving gift. The that end, the mother must be a Chosen One, and it cannot be accomplished against her will."

Stunned by possibility, Miriam reviewed her options in prayer.

Father is intent upon finding a husband for me, or rather pairing me up for breeding with some wealthy or politically connected family. I have feelings for Yusuf, the tile setter, who is so far below my social level there is no hope a marriage could ever develop.

I'm no longer perceived as a child, but rather a woman. That will begin excluding me from learning, and perhaps even healing. Especially if I marry. Nothing about the future seems inviting or promising. Must I surrender to a life where I will be servant to a husband unlikely to be my mental or spiritual equal?

I need to know more about Zachariah's methods, intentions, and purposes. I need to know what the Scrolls of Avram say, before I agree to be part of these mysterious birthings.

Elisheba and Zachariah waited patiently. Their kinswoman required an interval to absorb the gravity of their revelations.

Miriam took an initial step- overcoming doubt. "How do I know Elisheba is really pregnant? She looks radiant enough, but the belly might not mean anything. What if you're wrong? What if we're all wrong?"

Zachariah nodded eagerly. "It's only right that you should question." The priest sat a wrinkled wine skin on the table, a veteran container from which the hair had long since rubbed away. The leather, rendered black by age and grime, was creased with marks in every direction- as though it had fallen through a shaft of spider webs and the work of an insect left its mark. He withdrew a hollow wooden tube, as ebony as the bag itself.

"This is a tool from the Therapeuts down in Alexandria. Egyptians have been made good use of this for centuries. We can learn a lot from the Egyptians. Every healer should have one."

"What does it do?"

"It allows us to explore unseen portions of the body. Here, I'll show you." Zachariah stepped toward Elisheba and placed one end of the wooden tube at the edge of her left breast. He put is ear to the tube. Satisfied with what he heard, he held the tube in place and invited Miriam, "Come, listen".

Miriam placed her ear to the end of the tube. A steady drumming, roughly one beat per second, fronted fluid sounds of motion. Elisheba inhaled. A soft, low, hiss was added to the biological symphony.

"Can you hear her heart?" asked Zachariah.

"Yes! That and so much more!"

"In time, a healer learns the difference between healthy and unhealthy sounds."

Zachariah addressed Elisheba. "If you please, lay down on the bench."

Elisheba smiled, as though treasuring a secret. She reclined, as requested. Zachariah placed the wooden tube on her belly, and listened at the end. He shook his head and changed the location of the listening device. Two times, then three, he moved it, listening briefly after each relocation. On the fourth attempt, he placed his ear on the tube and smiled.

"There! Miriam, come listen. Don't move the tube. Tell me what you hear."

Miriam stooped to get an ear on the hollow tube. She heard Elisheba's heartbeat again, although less pronounced than before. She heard blood pumping through veins and arteries, as well as what must have been digestive sounds. Then, finally, she heard it.

Soft and persistent as the wings of a hovering butterfly, beating roughly twice as fast as Elisheba's heart, was the pulse of a second human being. There was a second heart in Elisheba's belly. Her cousin was certainly pregnant.

Miriam handed the listening tube to Zachariah. "I'm convinced."

Zachariah chuckled. "So you are, but only because you could

physically sense the truth. Trust me, child. If you adventure on with us, you will need to be convinced of things that you cannot see, hear, smell, or taste. The One God gave us the gifts of measurement and logic, but cannot be contained or defined by the gift he created for us. Likewise, the infant you will bear is part of The One God's plan, and cannot be contained by reason or measurement."

Miriam rubbed her palm across her brow. "If the scrolls are part of this, I would want to know what they say before I agree to go ahead."

Zachariah shook his head. "There are parts I cannot share. You are a Chosen One. You are a wise woman. But you're not an initiate. You're not a rabbi. You must be prepared to put faith in that which is unheard, as well as the portions I dare recite for you."

Miriam nodded. "I would need my faith to overcome my fear. Share what you can, and perhaps that will suffice."

Zachariah retrieved a cube of incense from the black wineskin. He set one edge alight in the flame of the candle, then blew out the flame to reveal a glowing and undulating crimson coal. He placed the incense in a stone dish. The air blossomed in olfactory celebration. The scent was simultaneously within and without the bodies of Elisheba, Miriam, and Zachariah- uniting them in a swirling, florid tapestry of smoke and spirit.

Miriam smiled. *And I thought incense was mostly for disguising smells. Obviously, I have a lot to learn from Zachariah, as well as the Egyptians.*

Zachariah did not unroll the Sefer Yetzirah. He closed his eyes, placed his hands gently on the scroll, and began to recite the text visualized behind his eyes.

"In thirty-two mysterious Paths of Wisdom did The One God engrave his name by three Sepharim; numbers, letters, and sounds. Ten paths are the ineffable Sephiroth. Twenty-two are the letters, the foundation of all things. Among the letters there are three Mothers, seven doubles, and twelve simple letters."

Three mothers, thought Miriam. *Could they be Sarai, Elisheba, and possibly me?*

Zachariah continued. "The Sephiroth are Ten, as are the Numbers. In man there a five fingers, pressed over against five, so over them is established The One God's covenant of strength, by opposing forces, by word of mouth, and by the circumcision of the flesh."

"The ten Sephiroth have ten vast regions bound unto them, boundless in origin and having no ending. They rule an abyss of good and evil, measureless in height and depth. The ten Sephiroth appear like a lightning flash, their origin is unseen and no end is perceived. The Word is in them as they rush forth and return, they speak as from the whirlwind."

"From the Spirit, The One God produced air, and in the air formed twenty-two sounds- the letters. Three are mothers, seven are double, and twelve are simple- but the Spirit is first and above these. From the sounds of the air The One God formed the waters, and from the formless and the void made mire and clay. He designed surfaces upon them, and hewed recesses in them. From the water, The One God formed fire, and made for himself a throne of glory. Auphanim, Seraphim, and Kerubim are his ministering angels. He makes his angels spirits, and his ministers a flaming fire."

"The three mothers are Aleph, Mem, and Shin- they are air, water and fire. Water is silent, fire is sibilant, and air derived from the Spirit is as the tongue of a balance scale, standing between contraries kept in equilibrium."

"The twenty-two letters are the foundation of all things, arranged as on a sphere with two-hundred-thirty-one gates. The sphere may be rotated forward or backward, whether for good or evil. From good comes true pleasure, from evil nothing but torment."

"The One God showed the combination of these letters, each with the other. Aleph with all, and all with Aleph. Beth with all, and all with Beth. Thus in combining all together in pairs are produced the two hundred and thirty-one gates of knowledge".

"And from the non-existent He made something, and all forms of speech and everything that has ever been produced. From the empty void The One God made the material world. By the power of His Name he made every creature and everything that is."

"The production of all things from the twenty-two letters is proof that they are but parts of one living body."

Zachariah stopped, and opened his eyes.

"Is there more?" Miriam asked.

"Yes, but not that I can share. There are more overviews, as well as specific passages of manifestation. One of which I shall silently intone, to rotate the sphere, if you are led in spirit to conjoin your will as well as your body with the breath of The One God."

Miriam cradled her forehead in hand. "But why? Why me? How can the infant I might bear be part of The One God's plan? Why now? Why would it be so critical that the child be born early next summer?"

Zachariah stroked his beard and smiled. "Not next summer, child. On or around the 5th day of Nisan, approaching the time of Passover"

"That's impossible! That's only five months away. The mother would need to be about four months along."

Zachariah picked up the incense, and blew on the coal to revive the fire. "Yes, or the pregnancy would need to begin at the 4th month."

"As I said, impossible."

Zachariah's tone was committed and confident. "Everything we're dealing with is impossible, yet is coming about nonetheless. The date must be the 5th of Nisan."

"I can't possibly be the right person for this," argued Miriam. "I'm too young. I'm not pregnant. Once again, I'm still a virgin. As Eli's daughter, my future is mostly predetermined. I may not like what that future looks like, but at least I can understand it."

Zachariah sighed, in resignation. "You're standing at a sort of crossroads. In the next few moments, you will need to make a choice. We cannot proceed against your will, or without your total and faithful trust."

Miriam wrestled with her thoughts and feelings. *This may be The One God's plan for me. Why else was I sent here, with the message? Zachariah seems empowered, but I can trust he means me no harm. I need another sign. Something more to confirm this remarkable possibility won't turn out to be a colossal mistake.*

Zachariah sensed her reluctance. "Do you know anything about the Mazzeroth?"

"Some," admitted Miriam, while remembering Yetro's warning that Zachariah must never learn that he and Miriam were acquainted. "I can always learn more."

"Normally, I would ask what you, a woman, could possibly know and how you were brought to the knowledge. But for now, let me show you something."

Zachariah pulled a leather tube from beneath the table. He removed a scroll. Even the incense could not totally obscure the faint aroma of recent ink. He unrolled the scroll, and set shining black stones on each corner to keep it flat.

"Take a look. This is a chart of the heavens, on the 5th of Nisan next spring. I went to no small trouble to have these calculations confirmed."

"And no small expense," grumbled Elisheba.

Miriam glanced at the drawing. Before she could restrain herself she blurted, "It's heliocentric!"

Zachariah scowled, "So, my suspicions are confirmed. I heard he fled to Galilee. Be careful. Any of us can be condemned for heresy, merely by professing belief that the earth circles the sun- rather than the reverse. Never discuss that, beyond the circle. Somebody, likely Yetro, has brought you to a place it is dangerous to go."

Miriam blushed, "I didn't really mean…"

"Never mind. Maybe The One God's purpose was to prepare you better for what I am going to share with you now. On the 5th day of Nisan, we find Mercury in the House of Zebulon. Jupiter in the House of Isaac. Earth in the House of Dinah. Venus in House of Ruben, with Uranus in the House of Naftali, and Neptunus in the House of Dan."

"Wait! What are Uranus and Neptunus?"

"Hipparchus discovered Uranus perhaps 100 years ago. The Greeks, the Babylonians, and the Egyptians- basically everybody with a lens, has been able to track it ever since."

"And what was the other name you used? I have never heard of whatever that was, either."

"Neptunus. An interesting case. Nobody has ever actually seen Neptunus, but we are able to know that it exists."

"How, exactly?"

"Even though we cannot see Neptunus, we can easily see how it influences the behavior of the other planets circling around the sun."

Miriam smiled. "That sounds a lot like The One God. Nobody can see The One God, but we can see the effects."

"You already see more than you should. Now see this. The positions on the Mazzeroth are exactly 1/6th of a circle apart. Look at the lines I drew to connect them, but don't look at one individual line. Look at all of them together. What do you see?"

Miriam startled. "The Star of David!"

"Exactly. The One God is redeeming Israel. The Covenant will be fulfilled. We will be free of the Roman oppressors, free to be closer to The One God. Why else would the One God arrange the heavens to so perfectly form our star?"

"That's when I'm due to deliver," said Elisheba. "The 5th day of Nisan. If you agree to join us, you will be due on the 5th day of Nisan as well."

"That's much less than 9 months!" insisted Miriam.

Elisheba looked at Zachariah for a moment, as if asking permission to speak. Before Zachariah reacted, Elisheba spoke anyway. "If The One God can create light in an instant, it will be no trouble to impregnate a Chosen One with a partially developed baby. Your son, and our son, will be born the same day. Our son, Yohan, will be the wind that sweeps a field before the storm. He will baptize with water. Your son, Yeshua? He will be the storm. He will be the sword riding on the storm. He will baptize with fire."

Miriam threw up her hands. "Redeeming Israel? Fulfilling the Covenant? Storm, and baptism by fire? It sounds like we're talking about The Messiah, or something."

Zachariah rose from the table. The room was so silent, that Miriam heard the tiny scrapings of his sandals as he crossed the stone floor to throw back the covering on the window. Sunlight filled the room. Miriam blinked, to help her eyes adjust. Zachariah said nothing for a moment, glancing furtively into the area beyond, as if to ensure that there were no potentially hostile ears.

Zachariah let the window cover fall back into place. He returned to the table. "Maybe the Messiah. Maybe not, exactly. Maybe it goes beyond re-establishing a sovereign state for The One God's Chosen People. Maybe it includes freedom from oppressions even more profound than Rome."

Miriam's mind raced back to a recent moment, when she was driving the cart with Menacham. Her own words now erupted in her mind. *What if we could be free of the Romans without killing any of them at all?*

Miriam hesitated momentarily, then concluded. "The One God holds me in the hollow of his hand. If everything is truly part of one living body, then I am a servant of that body. Let it be done to me according to the will of Our One God, even if it reduces me to a disgraced and lowly state."

Zachariah reached for Elisheba with one hand, and for Miriam with the other. All interlaced their fingers. Said Zachariah, "The circle is complete. We should each go, now, to a private spiritual plane. I will silently intone the passages to rotate the sphere."

"Rotating the sphere," whispered Miriam. "That's what Moravius said that Mithras did…"

"Hush, child. Find your spiritual plane. This will take, or already has taken an entire eternity. But for us, today it will seem like a matter of minutes."

Miriam closed her eyes. She found the white spot at the back or her nose, and surrendered her will while it expanded. She visualized the light expressing her features in shadow, perceived it shining on her face as warmly as a sun ray, and finally experienced it enveloping the space where she imagined her head must be. The space in the light began filling with images.

Miriam realized she had been here before. There were more stars, and brighter, than ever seen in a midnight sky. A wisping, flirting, spiraling light- devoid of smell, emanated from the stars and pulsed across a barren, cratered landscape. Something had changed from her previous visit. The shards of glossy pottery, fired with unnaturally vivid colors, were reassembled into glass orbs and crystals. The translucent shapes were layered, like multi-colored onions. They were swirled like wind dust in a stable corner. They were warm to the touch. They pulsed, in exact synchronization with her heartbeat.

Four figures were gathered around a fire. Miriam recognized the first. He was called Elishua, and Ben-gabar, and Almodad, and Gabriel, and Israel, but would always say that only The One God knew his true name. His was the only face Miriam was allowed to behold during her previous visit, but now the other faces were apparent as well.

The second and third were men, engulfed in a reality of peace and confidence- exuding an energy that transcended time or dimension. Miriam remembered the explanation given when she was unable to see their faces, "You have always known them, but have yet to meet them." On one level, Miriam was certain she had never seen either man before, yet on another they seemed closer than a shadow and more intimate than a breath.

The fourth face was a woman, no older than Miriam. After brief study, Miriam realized she was viewing Elisheba at a much younger age. Her cousin, still attractive after decades of life with Zachariah, had been a stunning beauty in her youth.

Elishua waved Miriam into the circle. "Shalom, Miriam. Blessed you are among women. You are a Chosen One, and in the favor of The One God. You shall conceive in your virgin womb, and bring forth a son, and his name shall be called Yeshua. He shall rule over the house of Jacob forever. To his kingdom, there will be no end. And he shall be recognized by men as the Son of the One God."

Miriam nodded. "Let it be done, according to the will of the One God. Your companions… I think I recognize Elisheba. I don't know the others."

Elishua smiled. "They form the circle. You will know them, soon enough, as Yohan and Yeshua. Yohan will be the wind that ruffles the grain before the storm. Yeshua will be the storm itself, and the sword that rides upon the storm. Yohan will baptize with water. Your son, Yeshua, will baptize with fire."

Miriam was amazed. "Can I speak to my son? Now?"

"You have been speaking to him since before you were born. You will speak to him long after he precedes you in the mortal destruction of these present temples. He has always been, and will always be, with you. Your perception of experience is sequential, but existence extends beyond the artificial boundaries of time and place. He will not need to speak, now, for you to hear his voice."

The circle of seated figures began to spin around the central fire. Faster, and faster, until the stars became streaking comets and the comets homogenized into an expanding cloud of uncorrupted frost. All thought and flesh sympathized with a deep, monotonous drone. Miriam suspected, and then was certain, she could smell Zachariah's incense. The circle stopped, then faded. Miriam was once again aware of her grip on the hands of Zachariah and Elisheba. She opened her eyes. All three laughed without restraint, like children released from a dream.

Miriam glowed. Literally, glowed.

"It's done," assured Zachariah.

Miriam took a deep breath. Her body was different. There were new pressures and presences. A scent of energy. "When Elishua told me to bring the message, he said you would have a gift for me as well. I had no idea."

Elisheba responded. "The prophecies are being fulfilled. Any gift to you, is a gift to us all."

II, XVI
Grief and Abundance

Yakob's funeral was a small affair. A tearful son, an itinerant rabbi, and a dozen women in white. There were as well a handful of men, paid by their fellow Tektons to guard the village while most others labored for Herod at Sephora or Eli at Caesarea. A wooden casket, simply styled but flawlessly constructed, descended into a dismal vault carved from the bosom of the earth. Yusuf the tile setter gathered a handful of moist pungent soil, hauled from the depths and warmed by a brief moment in the sun. He tossed the dirt back to its origins. It rattled down upon the coffin like a rolling dirge on a muffled drum.

The mourners disbanded. Two Tektons remained behind to refill the pit. Yusuf and the rabbi walked together between shaded houses, down the narrow, unpaved, gaps that passed for streets in Nazareth. Conversations stopped as they approached, held in check by respect. Murmurs blossomed in their wake.

Yusuf arrived at his small home to discover food and flowers; left, no doubt, by some group of older women. The house seemed abandoned without his father, as though the structure mourned the loss and ached with the knowledge that Yakob would never return.

Yakob's few domestic possessions lay neatly on some rustic tables and sturdy shelves. Yusuf would keep anything essential for housekeeping, and eventually distribute the rest to the poor. He would always treasure the sword, the cart and donkey, and the knowledge he had been deeply and unconditionally loved by his father.

"I'm going to return to my work," said Yusuf. "If you would like to use the house for a while, that would be alright. My neighbors could use a healer in Nazareth."

"Thanks for the offer. But the rabbi must appear where a rabbi is most needed, and now I am needed in Yerushalayim."

Yusuf shrugged. "There is no shortage of priests and rabbis in Yerushalayim."

"No, but I have special business there. During the Feast of Tabernacles. Some of it concerns you. In the end, your friends in Nazareth will benefit more from my absence than if I remain."

"Some of it concerns me? I won't be at Tabernacles this year. I plan to fulfill my obligation at Passover."

The rabbi adjusted the laces of his sandals. "Passover is the most popular time. But there are rumors of tax registration in the spring. I hear it may be mandatory. Herod wants a list of everyone descended from David, as you are and as am I. Perhaps we will meet again, before Passover. Maybe in Bet L' hem, the House of Bread."

"And the city of our common ancestor. Please, at least take some food and wine for your journey. There's far more here than I could ever eat."

The rabbi gathered some fruit, figs, and challah into a lambskin satchel. "Thank you for that. Abundance begets abundance. You, my friend, Yusuf bar Yakob, shall be abundantly blessed in return."

II, XVII
Plain of Gan Sarim, The Garden of the Prince

Duriel's band of Zealots, with Moravius held hostage, crested a stony outcrop northwest of Lake Tiberias. Warm winds wafted from the shores below, regaling both human and ruminant nostrils with an aerosol feast. Ripening grasses strutted the fragrance of fresh bread. The fish markets of Magdala teased the atmosphere with suspicious suggestions of cheap sacrifice, betraying a race among the salters to forestall the decay of succulent innocence. Patchwork orchards of olive, palm, walnut, and fig- variegated in texture and tinted like inconsistent emeralds- protruded irregularly from the plain of Gan Sarim. The men hastened step; lusting after the shade, the water, the fruit, and the fish to be found at the bottom of the slope. The sheep were undisciplined, and simply bolted for cool crystal creeks and lush pasture.

"How much farther are we going?" asked Moravius. "I can see Capernaum from here. It's only a few miles away. North of that, or at least much north of Beth Saida, we will be mostly among the Assyrians."

Duriel scoffed. "You don't need to know. You won't be going with us. We'll round up the sheep again, and make herdsmens' camp outside the gates of Tiberias. We can keep a watchful eye on the garrison, while we wait for Menachem to rejoin us. Once he does, we will decide your fate."

Moravius was disinclined to plead for mercy, but not above appealing to honor. "You seem to be walking very well. It looks like Miriam's attention to your corrupted wound was successful."

"No doubt. There should be a scar, but there isn't. It should take longer to heal, but it hasn't. Some say the young woman's a witch."

"She's not. Only a very skilled healer. Eli ignores reports of her abilities. He's desperate for her to assume a traditional role. It's not my business, but there may be some difficulty with that."

"Witch or not, she has some mysterious powers. It might be dangerous to break a pact with her. That's why you're still alive. Especially after the ugly death of Uriah. There is some talk among the men that you are to blame for that."

"He was killed by a lion. I was a distance away. Surrounded by guards, and a herd of sheep."

"True, but he appeared to be deliberately about some business, after his conversation with you. In a two days, or three at the most, we will know that nobody betrayed Menachem to the Romans. We will know that at least until he left Yudea to meet us at Tiberias, our former presence in Samaria was not revealed. When Menachem returns, we will decide. If he does not return, it is already decided."

Duriel's Zealots dispersed across the Plain of Gan Sarim, a place the Greeks in Assyrian Gaulinitis called Gennesaret and all considered The Garden of the Prince. They found their sheep wandering through open markets, or dining on fruit fallen from the orchards. Many bedded down in tall grasses, beside still waters. A handful were driven away by angry vintners, white wool smeared with a burgundy stain. Two were cornered by wolves, but rescued. One was ritually slaughtered, by mistake.

Before the day ended, the Zealots regrouped in a meadow just outside the walls of Tiberias. Collectively, they gathered far more sheep than originally lost. They established a camp at the very gates of their enemies in the Roman garrison, hiding effectively in plain sight.

II, XVIII
In the Image of the One God

Eli's morning contemplation was disrupted by a knock. "Master, some visitors have arrived. The lord Tadeo, with his wife Ruth and their daughter, Lydia."

The visit was not specifically expected, but neither was it a surprise. During feasts and festivals in Yerushalayim, Tadeo and his family frequently stayed in a separate wing of Eli's palatial apartments. Perhaps, with the sense of unrest in the land, and the recent betrothal, they thought it prudent to travel south to Yerushalayim as a group.

"See to their staff and animals," instructed Eli. "Offer them refreshment in the garden. I will join them in a few moments. Oh, and tell my son they are here. "

Eli stuffed his unruly white hair under a cap with gilded hems. The weather was cool enough to allow draping a dressed black and yellow leopard skin over his robe of sky blue silk. He exchanged his house slippers for his finest red sandals with braided silk laces.

The patriarch pretended he was not concerned with the crags and fissures etching the mirrored image of his face. Eli considered that a Greek, a Roman, or an Egyptian would have applied paints, powders, and ointments to appear more youthful. Yehudim believed that males, specifically, were made in the physical image of The One God. It would be nothing short of sacrilege to attempt any alteration.

Eli hurried to the garden. He found Tadeo, Ruth and Lydia sitting under an arbor, already served with fresh goat's milk and with challah dipped in honey. The guests rose as Eli approached. Tadeo embraced the host, while Ruth and Lydia bowed- slightly, but perceptibly.

"Shalom, Tadeo! Welcome, as always to my house. Blessings on you, Ruth. Lydia, you have blossomed from a pretty child to a gorgeous woman. Aban is a lucky man."

Tadeo responded, "And my Lydia is lucky as well. We thought it might be wise to travel together, from here to Yerushalayim. There will be thousands of pilgrims for Tabernacles, and the roads more tempting than ever to Zealots and bandits."

Eli ran his left thumb under his bearded chin. "Why not? My captain and two of the most trusted guards are gone. They escorted Miriam to visit our kinsmen in Ain Karem. Hiram of Dothan will join us as well. Combining our groups would offer more protection."

Aban approached. He overheard his father's remark and added, "Or perhaps by combining we present a more lucrative target?"

Only Lydia bowed, almost imperceptibly, as the son of Eli arrived. Aban noted that she had dressed with greater care and more ornaments than would be practical for the road. A bright orange and brown geometric pattern emblazoned her gown, tightly woven from premium linens. Aban focused less on the pattern than on the way in which her garment draped her figure. There were subtle hints of a rich banquet beneath, soon to be his to enjoy. His betrothed wore a hooded cape, framing a pure white veil secured by a ring of golden tassels. There were going to be certain delightful privileges bestowed upon Aban of H' ramathea.

Eli admonished his son. "It is our custom, and will be our privilege, to extend the hospitality and protection of our house. In fact, if it is agreeable with Tadeo, we shall leave for Yerushalayim a few days early, tomorrow morning. If we are going to entertain guests, it will be more comfortable for everybody to get away from the noise and dust of this construction."

Tadeo gestured broadly. "Speaking of, is all of this grand effort simply to create Aban's addition to your house?"

"Indeed," answered Eli. "We are making Lydia a magnificent home among us."

Though her face was partially concealed by the translucent veil, Aban was certain he noticed Lydia smile broadly- moist lips surrounding a treasure of pearlescent teeth.

II, XIX
Owl

Balthasar traveled by night. Decades formerly spent observing the heavens at the ziggurat transformed him. He was nocturnal. His breath a desert zephyr, his un-sandaled step a softened scratch across the sand. He leaned on a striped staff; acacia wood, crowned by a black scarab preserved in a tangerine amber orb. Balthasar memorized the heavens. When the dove arrived, he knew exactly which star would mark the course to Ur.

Forty miles from Ur to his secluded grotto, and many a year since his retreat to a contemplative retirement. The message from Gaspar, "Come at once," was cryptic with brevity, and unusual it was sent at all.

At once? Two nights will have to suffice. Fifteen miles to the oasis, then a day's sleep in the shade. Twenty-five mile the next night, if I start at sundown. There was a time I could walk this in a single leg. There was a time I wasn't quite so old.

The septuagenarian took shorter steps up a dune combed smooth by the wind. He left tracks; two rows of footprints beside the round heel of his walking stick. A visual rhythm, eroding in his wake. His shoulder chafed beneath his satchel strap, bearing the weight of two nights' food and a water skin.

What could they possibly need, and so urgently? The tables and patterns were established centuries ago. The duty now was only to observe, validate, and permit the next generation to believe they discovered everything anew.

A silhouette flashed across the moon. An owl, hunting from cliffs on the southern horizon, whooshed into the final moments of a viper's reality. The bird made musical whirring sounds; celebrating as it winged away with dinner. Balthasar paused to catch his breath. He could smell the sand, the stars, and the silence. It was good to be one with the desert. It was good to walk, to Ur.

II, XX
Short Tether

Yusuf of Nazareth lost track of time and space. After burying his father and bidding the rabbi farewell, the Tekton led his cart and donkey back to Caesarea. Waypoints along the road faded into a blur. He padded through a fog of unfocused thought, only occasionally conscious of the road before him.

With Yakob gone, Yusuf had no family left. His future was largely predetermined by the curse of Yeconiah. No clan would consider him a suitable candidate for marriage. Perhaps, eventually, he might do as his father and marry an older widow- a woman with few other options. Still, in Yakob's final delirious moments he claimed to see a vision of Yusuf with many sons and daughters. Through an older woman? An older woman might bear a single child, but not several children. Yakob's last attempt to speak was a mysteriously incomplete sentence. Through the pain, his father seemed excited about one of Yakob's future sons. Perhaps it was the pain, or the oil of poppy.

The short acquaintance with Miriam stoked a forlorn hunger within Yusuf. It was as if The One God were playing some sort of cosmic joke. Eli's daughter was as far removed from his social station as Damascus was from Yerushalayim. Now she was off to Yerushalayim, and if the gossip at Caesarea was credible Lord Eli was determined to find her a husband at Tabernacles. Phantoms of her face, her voice, her form and figure haunted Yusuf of Nazareth. Perhaps she was so desirable because she was entirely unobtainable.

If his father's dying vision was prophetic, Yusuf feared that he would spend his life comparing any accessible female to the woman with whom he had no chance. Asking a woman to compete with a fantasy would be unfair. If The One God had a plan for Yusuf of Nazareth, it was difficult to define.

Gulls aloft over Mare Nostrum goaded the orange sun as it sizzled into the sea. Yusuf descended the final slope to Caesarea, weaving through the grasp of shadows racing to the summit.

The Master Builder, Shimon of Accara, met Yusuf at the eastern gate.

"You took your time, tile setter. You should have been back earlier. Eli and his family left this morning, for the Feast in Yerushalayim."

"I went directly to Nazareth, buried my father, and returned. I took no more time than needed."

"Nevertheless, your materials are here. Malak's servants delivered them yesterday. Eli was bewildered when he saw the piles of fired clay. He expected far more expensive materials. Even accused me of buying on the cheap. Lucky for you, he was distracted by the visit of Lord Tadeo and his family."

Yusuf glanced across the construction site to confirm Shimon's report. Hides were draped across conical heaps next to the precisely calibrated slab. "Lord Eli would not be pleased if the world's finest materials created a mediocre result. He will not be *dis*pleased if these common elements combine with a stunning effect. This is not a guess, Shimon. It's not an experiment. I am recreating a vision."

"Then be about it. But you better know what you're doing. I'll stop you immediately if you lay something hideous. If you have to be replaced as tile setter, you will be liable for the price of these ordinary tiles."

"You already told me I need to work a few days to pay for the oil of poppy. You and I, we've had some issues. The tile is my responsibility, so give me some latitude."

Shimon turned to leave, shaking his head as he stepped away and making a dismissive gesture over his shoulder. "You're on short tether, tile setter."

II, XXI
The Coin is Spent

The Assyrian raiders remained concealed. The herdsmen's camp should be easy prey, even so close to the garrison at Tiberias. Once well dark, the Romans would not venture out unless directly under attack. Some chaos among the Yehudim would be dismissed as fractious discord of the semi-civilized. Shepherds carried only staffs, or the crudest of blades. Not only were the Assyrians all seasoned by close combat, the rumor spread among them "we outnumber these bumpkin sheep herders perhaps two to one." Lusting for murder, the raiders maintained a determined silence. Like angels of death, they dispersed among foliage and shadows surrounding The Garden of the Prince.

In the last hours, the sun rested against the wooded crest line of the Safed mountains before sliding away, unseen, somewhere in Mare Nostrum. The darkness began as a greyed half shadow at the highest peaks, gathering speed and becoming blacker as it tumbled toward Lake Tiberias. Birds concluded their business. The animal forms of daylight sought shelter, and nocturnal alternatives awakened. The shaded hand held Tiberias in its grasp. The shepherds added fuel to their fire, accentuating silhouettes for targeting.

The Assyrian bandits advanced. Not with cry and clatter. Not with ululating challenge. Not with any means to afford a warning, but rather with the stealth of stalking cats. The blackness of the night amplified their dark intention. Surely the herd, the provisions, and the purses of the shepherds would be theirs this hour. There was little risk, especially employing the element of surprise.

The raiders reached the perimeter of the herd. The shepherd encountered there stood courageously in place, and shouted a warning. With a deadly sounding "slish" he unsheathed an unexpected and wicked-looking sword. His companions rallied to his position, running eagerly toward the fray rather than fleeing.

The herdsman dispatched three Assyrians before taking a scimitar through the neck. The raiders realized they were in for more of a battle than anticipated.

Duriel and the rest of his Zealots responded to their companion's alarm. For the first time since the hostage exchange, Moravius was left unguarded. For a tortured second, he considered his options. As a veteran Legionnaire, he could appeal to the garrison for shelter. He could escape into the night and race toward Caesarea, or follow the road to Yerushalayim. He could warn Eli. He could protect Miriam. Or, he could respond to his warrior instinct.

Moravius jumped up. Unarmed, he ran toward the skirmish. He leaped over and dodged between knots of frightened sheep. When he reached the first body, he grabbed the available sword. The shouts, grunts, sharp clangs and dull thuds reverberated in the darkness, only a shadow's step ahead.

Duriel and two companions were back to back, surrounded by five Assyrians. There were originally six raiders, until a Zealot's blade ripped open an abdomen. The overpowered Zealots fought maniacally, but were tiring faster than the Assyrians. Duriel noticed another form emerge from the darkness. It was Moravius, the Roman. If the Legionnaire teamed up with the Assyrians it was unlikely that any of the three Zealots would live. If Duriel fell, the battle would be lost.

Moravius grabbed the hilt with both hands, pouring all available power into a single, deadly stroke. The decapitated head of an Assyrian flew into a wad of panicked sheep. The remainder of the corpse spasmed as it fell. A geyser of blood sprayed on the remaining combatants. The odds were now even, four to four. Moravius had chosen sides, and aligned with the Zealots.

One of the Assyrians turned to address the new threat attacking from the rear. That mistake was reward by Duriel's blade through his backbone, before the raider could raise a weapon against Moravius. The Roman flanked another Assyrian, and the Zealots shifted through the gap. The formerly encircled now surrounded their assailants. One by one, the Assyrians fell. Similar encounters elsewhere around the herd were resolved. Only two Zealots were killed, and two seriously wounded would likely survive. Nine Assyrians lay dead among the sheep, the rest faded into the shadows as soundlessly as they arrived.

Sword stabbed into the ground, Duriel leaned down against the guard. He stopped panting for breath long enough to puke. The Zealot leader spat the taste from his mouth, rose, and nodded to Moravius. "I didn't expect that. You could have escaped. But you didn't, and you made an important difference."

"I could have escaped the battle. Maybe I would never escape turning my back."

"Why would you care? The Romans and Yehudim are enemies."

"True, but I am Roman and yet I serve Eli, Yehudim."

Duriel sneered. "You serve for money. And because Eli serves Augustus."

"Yes, for money. But there's more. I respect Eli, and I have sworn an oath to protect him and his family. If I saw Eli killed by anyone, I would take revenge. Even knowing that with Eli dead I could not expect to be paid."

Duriel pulled his blade from the dirt. "We're on opposite sides, you and I. But somehow we share a sense of justice, and honor. How can we be so different that we must be enemies?"

Moravius shrugged. "Sometimes I think we fight more often over a difference of opinion than a difference of character."

"Well, there's good news for you in this, Moravius. It's possible you saved my life, but you most definitely saved your own."

"Was mine in jeopardy?"

"I was always determined to let you go, once Menachem returns to report your people kept their portion of our bargain. My men?

Maybe they would have taken their own hand in the matter. I don't know what might have happened, at the moment of decision. Your action here today gives me enough cover. You fought with us against the raiders. No Zealot will demand your death. When Menachem returns, you are free to go."

"If we're keeping bargains, "said Moravius, "let me remind you of another detail. You agreed that while in Galilee, you will not molest Eli, his family, or his house at Caesarea."

"Did I? That must have been something left of the fever. Very well. For you, and for his daughter the healer, I'll work around the hound of Augustus. You in turn must make no effort against us."

"Only in defense of Eli, his family, or his home."

"Then it's done. Ask no more of me, Moravius. Your coin is spent."

Zealots brought their wounded to the fireside and looted the slain Assyrians.

When Menachem and Festus arrived the following morning, Duriel provisioned the two Romans with bread and water for their journey. Eli's guards walked, double time, from the Garden of the Prince- choosing a route to Yerushalayim through Decapolis and Perea. They would cross the Yarden at Yericho Ford.

PART III

III, I
Prophecy and Sons of Light

The withered old man stooped more than stood. Zadok's back was almost as horizontal as a horse. He arched his neck to see a forward path. His tattered robe dragged in his wake, the hem shredded by friction and caked with dried mud. The bony knuckles of his left hand gripped the knob of an ebony walking staff, carved with a single snake; fashioned after the Rod of Asclepius.

Market crowds in Ain Karem grew silent as he approached, shuffling, tapping, and dragging himself toward the house of Zachariah. He was a figure unknown, yet easily recognized. Children fled, dogs hunkered and growled. Suddenly chilled merchants struggled to swallow through dry throats. The pilgrim was not concerned with public reaction. It was as it had always been, since a time before memory began. Patiently and inexorably, Zadok passed through the bazaar. People who dared not look at him as he approached stared at his trailing garment and counted every step until they felt he was safely and sufficiently distant.

Zadok crept up the final street to Zachariah's house. He used his staff to batter on the outer gate. "Zachariah! It's Zadok! I call on the hospitality of this house!"

Zachariah opened the window of his study. He leaned out and called, "Zadok? What a pleasant surprise! Quickly, somebody open the gate for our dear friend. Bring a basin of water for his feet, and some wine for refreshment."

Zachariah closed the window. Miriam was in the study, having begged her cousin's husband for permission to examine some unusual scrolls. "You'll have to go, child. I suspect I know why Zadok appears, just now. He's a strict traditionalist. Whatever he has to say, he will want to say in private. But, this likely concerns you, Elisheba, and the children. I'll leave the shutter open a crack. You will find a low bench along the wall. Sit there, quietly, and you may hear something of interest."

Miriam stepped out. Moments later, Zachariah's disciple propped open the door. Zadok hobbled in.

"Shalom, Zadok! I have sent for a basin, and some wine."

"Shalom, Zachariah. Save the basin. I haven't yet immersed for the day. I will enjoy the wine, and thank you."

Zadok took a bench, resting his elbows on his knees and tilting his neck to keep his host in view.

"I passed through Yerushalayim. It looks like Tabernacles will be busy this year. Those ceremonial tents and huts look out of place, especially in the upper city. For how many centuries must we pretend to be wandering pilgrims?"

Zachariah laughed. "Until The One God decrees otherwise, I suppose. You would know better than I do. You taught me so much."

"Apparently not enough. Here you are, not only a rabbi- but a priest in the High Temple. As much as you could have learned, you still sacrifice flesh for atonement. I always considered you one of my better students. I regret that so much of your potential was never realized."

"Flesh or fruits. That's the oldest argument in history. You're like Cain, Zadok. You live in harmony with the soil. You channel the energy of the earth. Perhaps that's why you are such an accomplished healer."

Zadok wagged a finger at Zachariah. "And you? You're like Abel. Asserting your will over a portion of the earth- herding and slaying lesser animals. Dining on death rather than absorbing life. Perhaps that's why so many are accomplished warriors."

Zachariah nodded. "Even so, I keep most of what you taught me close. Underneath these robes, there still beats an Essenic heart."

Miriam sat on the shady end of the bench, listening through the window to the discussion between Zadok and Zachariah. She was surprised to learn that Zachariah had studied among the Essenes. Yasminah approached. She appeared ready to call out before Miriam motioned for silence.

Zadok's hand shook as he sipped red wine from a bronze cup. "Then, it's to your heart I will appeal. There's a war, you know. A war between the Sons of Light and the Sons of Darkness. You and I, to the degree you remain Essenic, serve the Teacher of Righteousness."

Zachariah hastened to clarify. "Yes, I respect the Teacher of Righteousness, but I serve only The One God."

"It doesn't matter. We're all Sons of Light."

"Yes, that's true. Will this war ever end? Will we ever prevail over the Sons of Darkness?"

Zadok closed his eyes, and pointed two fingers into the air. "Victory is not the purpose. The purpose is struggle. Through the struggle, we are perfected. It's like purifying metal, by passing it through fire. I'm here today because I know you have engaged Yetzirah. I know how, and I know why. And, I have a request."

"I have utilized the Sefirot, and with the help of The One God exercised Yetzirah. How did you know?"

"When you speak the language of Creation, it's no small thing. It reverberates in a place where many ears can hear it. Some of those listeners speak to me. Some speak to you. Some speak to both of us, in common."

Miriam held her breath, afraid that even a light exhale might reveal her resting place. She was overhearing a profound conversation, and her heart beat quickly.

"So, Zadok, what is the nature of your request?"

"Before the children, Yohan and Yeshua, are two years of age there will be a storm. A Son of Darkness will search for them, without knowing exactly who or where they are. Your wife, and her cousin, will flee Yudea. You will remain behind. Elisheba's advanced age will make the birth of Yohan sufficiently remarkable. Your absence from the Temple might confirm something already suspected by those who would destroy the children."

"Who will try to kill the children? Where shall they go? Won't Eli protect his daughter?"

"All we need to know is that a Son of Darkness will seek their death. You must send them to Alexandria. I will arrange shelter for them among the Therapeuts. Miriam can learn much from them. That will protect the children, and serve the larger purpose as well."

"Surely two women cannot travel alone, all the way to Egypt. If I am to remain here, and Miriam is unmarried, who will protect them?"

"Even now, one has been chosen."

"Who has been chosen? And by whom? By Eli, I assume?"

"I cannot say."

"Cannot, or will not?"

Zadok turned slightly in his seat. He pushed open the window shutter with his copy of the Rod of Esclepius. "When you speak the language of betrothal, it reverberates where many ears can hear. Some of those ears are just beyond this wall, sitting on the shady end of a bench. She bears the Light. Let's not deprive her of every joy and discovery common to young women."

Zachariah was embarrassed that Zadok somehow knew he had stationed Miriam where she could overhear.

"Don't worry much about it," counseled Zadok. The old man placed his cane on the floor, shifted his weight across the support, and with a silent move that conveyed a mortal agony managed to stoop half upright again. "I must go, and bathe in Yerushalayim."

Zachariah watched his mentor struggle toward the door. "Forgive me for asking, Zadok. You spend your life surrounded by Therapeuts and Essenes. Why haven't you done something about your stoop?"

"You know there is no healing without prayer, Zachariah. For whom must we never pray?"

"We must never pray for ourselves. Prayer is only effective when it's a gift, to others."

"Exactly. You may seek redemption through the sacrifice of fleshbut obviously you remember the essentials. That's probably why you were chosen for your role. Sort of a bridge. A bond between Cain and Abel."

Zachariah rose to escort Zadok to the gate.

"When will we see you again, Zadok?"

"Whenever you have need of me, of course."

III, II
Blood Sacrifice and the Seal of Solomon

Balthazar slept. In his old chamber, swept clean in anticipation of his arrival, he slumbered. Deep were his dreams. The whimsical releases of tensions from a keen mind and comprehensive memory were as random sparks. Embers in the tail of a comet comprising critical portion of the cosmic clockwork. He saw the faces of a thousand souls. He heard echoes in a smoky fog, twined about the base of gaily painted ceramic cylinders. He heard laughter suspended among shadows, deep down in a mossy well of chimes. Every inhalation was another gift. Every exhalation, a prayer.

As Balthazar slept, so did most in the Ziggurat at Ur. The great lens, hidden from the sun, was guarded by a single watchman and polished by a solitary slave. Astral rays hammered on the bricks with no avail. Within the walls, the Ziggurat was dim, and the grey atmosphere was cool. A silent response to the insistent scream of Sol Invictus. The Ziggurat was more than a repository of knowledge, it was a sanctuary for night itself, where darkness defeated the dawn.

The low hills on the western desert gave birth afresh to the night. It crawled westward in its infancy, then sprinted in its youth. Before the flares disappeared entirely, the black edge raced across the desert floor like a herd of gazelle. As silent and powerful as thought itself a freshened ebony reality unveiled. The nocturnal dome was punctured by infinite songs of celestial celebration. One could read the signposts mapping the heavens. The windows of eternity were thrown wide open. Balthazar awoke.

"Come at once. Indeed. What could possibly be this significant?"

Old Amal, the steward, remembered. That wasn't a surprise. It was, this nightfall, as it had been for the decades when Balthazar was master at the Ziggurat. Just beyond his door were a handful of barley, a bit of roast lamb bathed in olive oil, and (in a familiar looking stone cup) a serving of fruit juice. Balthazar would eat no more before retiring again at sunrise.

With his repast finished, Balthazar joined Melchior and Gaspar.

Melchior greeted the master emeritus. "Welcome back!"

Balthazar smiled, but grunted. "It's like I never left. Everything is familiar of course. You two look a little older. Let's hope the wiser, as well. Why is it that you disturb my reflections and contemplations? Drag me across the desert for a walk of several nights?"

Grand Master Gaspar held up a parchment. "Zachariah sent a dove."

"Zachariah? That secretly heliocentric priest in Yerushalayim? The former disciple of Zadok?"

Gaspar nodded. "The same."

"The old Yehudi always wades in beyond his depth. But let me see that message."

Melchior handed the parchment to Balthazar. There would be no need to translate for the Grand Master Emeritus. Balthazar had a gift for language. He could find a common tongue in which to speak with almost anyone.

Balthazar moved the message closer to the candle. "He's inquiring about the positions of various planets, on the 5th day of the month they call Nissan. That would seem routine."

Balthazar frowned, then continued. "Except his references to Neptunus and Saturnus. He's schooled, but not an initiate. Have you been too free with some of our secrets?"

Gaspar shook his head. "The Greeks. They have some radical ideas about distribution of ideas."

Balthazar grunted again. "Well, if Hipparchus wasn't as much the braggard, we would never have known where to look for Saturnus."

"Or how to calculate the certain existence of Neptunus," added

Melchior.

"So you summon me from the farthest edge, because Zachariah asked about some planets. There's nothing unusual about his question. I can only guess there must be something unique about the answer. What have you found?"

Gaspar gave credit to his disciple. "Melchior noticed it first. Once he pointed it out, it cannot be denied. There's a constellation of planets on that day."

Melchior unrolled a star chart. "Grand Master, here are the positions of the planets on the next Nissan 5. When expressed in our two dimensional drawings, each is exactly an equal arc away from the sun."

Balthazar was intrigued. "Exactly? Not approximately?"

"Exactly," confirmed Gaspar. "We have checked everything at least twenty times. Exactly."

"So, your planetary constellation is hexagonal," concluded Balthazar. "Interesting phenomenon, but hardly worthy of a hike across the desert."

Melchior unrolled another chart, with lines connecting the planets. "But when we connect the planets, thusly..."

Balthazar nodded, "We get the Seal of Solomon, of course. Elementary geometry. Why don't we assume this is one of a million similar coincidences?"

"We're still doing some calculations," said Gaspar, "but we think this particular alignment occurs once every one-million, four-hundred-thousand years. There's likely some significance that a non-initiated Yehudi priest brought it to our attention. As you know, they call the Seal of Solomon the 'Star of David'. It might cause some trouble among the Yehudim. Maybe even change the course of history. You know the old Yehudi prophecies. We thought there might be something you could share."

Balthazar cradled his face within his hands, closed his eyes, and remained silent for about two minutes. Neither Gaspar nor Melchior dared interrupt his consideration.

Balthazar opened his eyes. They seemed to glisten, brightly. "Isaiah prophesied about a king. A king who would be of the house of David, yet born of a virgin."

Gaspar shrugged. "Everyone has their own fable about some virgin giving birth to a hero. Most of those virgins have to be young girls with gullible relatives."

Balthazar nodded. "The story is common enough, but Isaiah's king is not supposed to be a hero. He will be despised and spat upon. Widely rejected by those who should follow him. He will be put to death with criminals, and mocked as a blood sacrifice. If Isaiah is right, this king will be born expressly for the purpose of sacrifice."

Gaspar listened carefully, then asked, "Isn't blood sacrifice that way in which the Gauls, the Goths, and many other tribes dispose of their aging and infertile kings? Killing off the feeble old king makes room for the new young king, and restores the fertility of land."

Balthazar nodded. "You're right. It's very common. But this sacrifice won't be for the land. Isaiah claims that the sacrifice of this king will remove sin and sorrow from the nation of Israel. In fact, he claims that people from all over the world will worship his memory."

Melchior concluded. "So Zachariah is hoping to see some old prophecy fulfilled, and he thinks the Seal of Solomon forming in the heavens is a confirming sign."

Balthazar nodded. "Or, so it would appear. What if he's right? What if there's going to be some magical king that changes man's relationship to the universe? It's a very, very, remote possibility. But, one that we should investigate. Perhaps this king will be born under the sign, next Nissan 5."

Gaspar remarked. "If so, then we are likely to hear of it. Perhaps

Zachariah will keep us informed. How many children will be born to a virgin, on Nissan 5? How many of which Zachariah would be aware?"

Balthazar said nothing. He once again cradled his face in his hands and closed his eyes.

After some silence, the Grand Master Emeritus opened his eyes and continued.

"Over the years, I have had the same dream several times. Three figures, representing the past, the present, and the future, take a journey to find a child. Now, I realize that among Grand Masters of the Ziggurat, I am the past. Gaspar is the present. Melchior, if he succeeds in the rest of his studies, will be the future. I think we need to search for the child."

"We can't leave the Ziggurat," observed Gaspar. "How can we take a journey with you?"

"In my dream, there's a talisman. A small leather pouch. Each of you put a gift in the pouch. A very tiny amount will do. The largest quantity would make no difference. Melchior, you will put a pinch of frankincense into the pouch. That represents the prayers and hopes for the future. Gaspar, you are the grand master now, so your gift will be a gold coin. That represents the authority of the present. For my part, I will contribute some myrrh. It's the balm of Gilead, and a common dressing for a corpse. Appropriate, I think, to represent all of those whose lives are past."

"When will you go?"

"Soon enough. It's a long walk to Yerushalayim."

"Any idea where you will look when you get there?"

"Isaiah says the City of David. If I remember right, it's a little town not far from their temple. The Yehudim call it Bet L'hem; the house of bread."

III, III
Laughter of a Sparrow

Lucanus approached Miriam in the garden of Elisheba and Zachariah. His face was dry and wrinkled as sun baked papyrus. Nights of intermittent, fitful, sleep were taking a toll.

"Excuse me, mistress. If your visit with your cousin is finished, we might want to move to your family's compound in the Upper City. With Moravius and Festus gone, I'm your only remaining guard. I can keep you safer in Yerushalayim than here in Ain Karem."

Miriam nodded. Eli's household guards were genuinely committed to their assignments. Lucanus' concern was genuine, even when dangers were imaginary.

"I don't feel any danger here," said Miriam. "But my father will expect to find us there when the family arrives for Tabernacles. Yasminah and Hertzelah will get everything together. Zachariah's servant will hitch the cart."

"As you wish, mistress. If we depart by early afternoon, we can make the fifteen miles to Yerushalayim before sunset."

"Yes. We can be ready quickly."

A flock of five sparrows landed atop the garden wall. Miriam listened to their trills while she ran her hands down her blue gown and across her stomach. Loose clothing would conceal the definite bulge, for at least a while. Her breasts ached, and were tender to the touch. Whenever she contemplated the possibility of pregnancy, there had never been an image of fertility through an old priest and the Scrolls of Avram.

Miriam dreaded the unavoidable confrontation with Eli. His daughter, who was a virgin when she left Caesarea ten days ago was now four months pregnant- but virgin still. Perhaps Eli would accept the advanced stage of her condition as evidence. But, evidence of what? Miriam had a history of willful independence and disobedience. Her father would naturally conclude she must have been pregnant for the last four months, but kept a shameful secret. The risk she might be expelled from the family was very real, yet with that same risk came the possibility of an independent freedom.

She marveled that Zachariah could foretell the exact birthdate and sex of her child, but his predictions coincided with the stars. She quickly realized the feat was a minor accomplishment compared to the mystical impregnations of a post-menopausal woman and a virgin. Her son, Yeshua and his cousin, Yohan, were destined to be born the same day. Her instincts assure her that Zachariah was correct; the entire situation had to be consistent with the will of The One God. Even with the use of Yetzirah, none of this would otherwise be possible. None of this would be conceivable.

Miriam rose to make ready. The sparrow song changed to a familiar cadence. Where had she heard that rhythm before? After a moment, she recognized the pattern. It was exactly the distinctive laugh of the renegade priest and her banished mentor, Yetro.

Miriam shook her head and chuckled. *"How foolish can I be? I'm imagining things. But, only some things- to be sure."*

III, IV
Protocol and Horse

Eli of Caesarea, Hiram of Dothan, Tadeo the Greek, as well as their, as well as their families, guards, and adequate numbers of servants caravanned from the Roman port city to Yerushalayim. Their combined party represented more material wealth than could be found in the entire district of Samaria, through which they would pass.

In rare sections the tree line remained close to the road. Woodcutters ceased their labors at the approach of this train of privilege. They cleared their carts from the right of way, bowing slightly as Eli and Hiram's party passed. A Roman patrol approached in a dusty cacophony of clank. They held to road until the caravan was close enough the Roman Centurion recognized Eli. With a smart response to a single command, the troops split to opposite sides of the road to allow the caravan unrestricted passage.

The trek took a heavy toll on Faramond. Initially determined to ride with his father, with Eli, and with Eli's son; sitting astride the saddle aggravated and stressed his injuries. Within a few miles, Faramond asked Eli to order a stop.

Faramond leaned forward in the saddle, supporting his upper body weight with an elbow placed on a knee. Pain was evident in his voice as he directed his gaze at two of Eli's Roman mercenaries. "You two, there! Help me down off this wretched nag!"

Aban was offended. "That wretched nag is one of my own mounts. One of the best in the stable. And you should ask servants, preferably your own, to help you down. That's beneath the dignity of a guard."

Faramond spat. "One of the best? A proper horse would have a more civilized gait. And I will ask anybody I see for anything I want."

Eli turned his horse to intervene. Hiram promoted Faramond as a future son in law? Eli concealed his concern and disappointment. "I'm sorry the stallion is not satisfactory. Would you like to trade with Aban, or myself?"

Faramond blushed. The attempt to blame his distress on the horse, rather than his injury and physical limitations, would be wrecked if he accepted another ride and was still unable to continue. "The horse was ridiculous. We should never have left our own mounts to rest up in your stables. I'll ride in a wagon with the women for a while. Maybe after that we can change horses."

The guards summoned by Faramond approached, with a visible lack of enthusiasm. Hiram intervened. "Aban was right, son. We can call some servants up forward to help you down. It's not appropriate for hired guards."

One of the Romans responded, "That's alright, Excellency. What good do you think we would be in battle if we were put off by a small insult?"

Eli struggled to remain silent. He endured the sight of two tested, veteran guards dismounting an arrogant and entitled son of an aristocrat. One cupped his hands at knee level, providing support for Faramond's foot. The other supported the young man's weight and assisted with his balance as he slowly, and with obvious discomfort, brought his far leg across the rump of his mount.

One of Hiram's servants helped Faramond hobble to a wagon. Every few tortured steps, the young man berated the servant for throwing him off balance, assisting with too much force, or paying so little attention he might likely fall.

The caravan resumed, with Faramond's horse trailing a cart.

Eli was troubled. The more he saw of Hiram's son, the less suitable seemed the young man as a prospective groom for Miriam. *I'm glad my commitment to Hiram wasn't absolute. Perhaps The One God will reveal a better candidate during Tabernacles. It's time for Miriam to marry, but I must consider her happiness…if there's any way to do so…*

III, V
The Tree of Life

Yetro sought shelter from the midday sun. On the first terrace of the Great Library, between the outer gate below and the Roman Temple of the Muse above, were stone benches- marbled grey. Surrounded by flat white rocks, and in a line running parallel to a row of effusively green date palms, the temporarily shadowed seats were cool to the touch. The priests of the Museo remained dedicated to Ptolemy's vision of universal access to knowledge. "Worthy scholars" from every portion of the Empire, and beyond, gathered here to study.

Yetro enjoyed a view of the lighthouse, the Pharos of Alexandria. The structure soared 300-feet above the sea. Some claimed that with the pinnacle furnaces ablaze, the light was visible for 100 miles across the Mare Nostrum. Newer buildings adjoined the Pharos, but one prime building spot with a charred appearance was left unused along the quay. Yetro recalled the explanation by the Roman priest. "During the Egyptian civil war, Ptolemy's fleet blockaded Julius Caesar's troops. Caesar managed to set several Egyptian ships on fire. The flames spread to our warehouses. We lost 40,000 scrolls, but the damage could have been much worse. Nearly all were copies from the scriptorium, ready for export. Everything of enormous value was never in the warehouses. That was about 45 years ago. We have kept one site empty. It should be a lesson for us. Knowledge that is unshared, truth that is kept concealed, is at greater risk of loss."

Aristotle dominated the morning reading. Yetro struggled to reconcile Aristotle's theory of the soul with Torah, Talmud, and other sacred writings of the Yehudim. Aristotle correlated the human soul and body with an image impressed in sealing wax. Each impression was unique, but without wax the image could not exist. Without an impression, wax was nothing more than a bit of material, indistinct from every other. Among the Yehudim, the Pharisees, Sadducees, and the Essenes argued endlessly about the fate of the soul upon the death of the body. Aristotle infused yet another perspective on the subject.

Yetro's meditations were disrupted by a greeting. "Yetro of Yudea, as I recall?"

"Yes. And you are Philotheos, of Thracia, if I remember correctly."

A muscular man, with a shock of blazing red hair and thick beard took the bench immediately across from Yetro. He tossed his snowy toga casually over his shoulder, exposing calves and arms knotted with freckled muscles.

"I am. I noted you spending the morning with the works of Aristotle. He's a favorite of mine."

Yetro nodded. "That's easy to appreciate. He had so much to contribute. Amazing ideas, most of them. But something troubles me, just a little, about Aristotle."

"What would that be?"

"It has to do with his principles of logic, when applied to argument. Aristotle claims that the validity of any argument is determined by its presentation, not its content. That the conclusion of any perfectly logical argument is guaranteed to be true."

Philotheos stroked his beard. "Can you suggest an example where that wouldn't be the case?"

Yetro held his hands apart, approximately shoulder high. "What if a deliberately false proposition is argued with perfect logic? Can't there be some distance between perfectly logical and perfectly true?"

Philotheos smiled. "More things are perfectly logical than perfectly true. If a truth were perfect, it would automatically be accepted by everyone. Everything fanatically believed by anyone is rejected and condemned by somebody else. Maybe nothing is perfectly true, except maybe birth and death."

Yetro nodded. "And thus we come to the Temple of the Muses, and the library of Alexandria. Not to find answers, but to imagine additional questions."

A temple servant drew near. A dark Nubian woman in a long, colorful skirt., she carried a tan clay jar and a bronze ladle. "Some water?"

Yetro accepted the offer. When he finished the drink and returned the ladle, he watched the Nubian woman walk fluidly back toward the temple. He remembered nights on the beach with Nora, unconsciously lusting after her friend Miriam. Eli's daughter would never be far from mind. Neither would the risk to his life if ever he returned to the jurisdiction of Eli and his fellow judges on the Sanhedrin.

Philotheos put a finger on the bridge of his nose, then pointed at Yetro. "Aren't you among the Yehudim called the Essenes?"

"I was. I got expelled."

"Really? How is that possible?"

"The schools of philosophy aren't tribal. You aren't born as a Pharisee, a Sadducee, an Essene or a Therapeut. You are welcome as long as you stick to the dogma. Get too mentally or spiritually adventurous? You will be informed that you are no longer welcome."

"Even though you all serve the same god?"

Yetro sighed. "We all agree that The One God is the only god. But if our rival interpretations mean anything, The One God can appear very differently to even the most devout believers."

Philotheos contemplated Yetro's remark, then replied. "Perhaps we're not so different. In Thracia, we acknowledge many gods and goddesses. Still, I have dared to wonder if we are venerating individual entities or simply identifying various characteristics of an all-encompassing presence."

"Sefirot," said Yetro.

"Maybe," said Philotheos. "I've seen the diagram. Nobody has effectively explained it to me. What does it mean to you?"

"The Sefirot, the Tree of Life, displays the ten garments of the One God. None of these garments are The One God. Even the totality doesn't define or confine The One God. But The One God can appear, and does appear, as any of the concepts."

Philotheos opened his satchel. He pulled out a fresh wax tablet and a stylus. "Would you show me?"

Yetro slid to one side of his bench. "I'll try. Not everyone can explain it well. Come sit next to me and I'll sketch it out for you."

Yetro drew nine circles. Two parallel, vertical rows of three flanking three central circles. The upper most central circle was above the top circles of the outer rows, the lower central circle just below the outer rows, and the third central circle immediately above the lowest outer orbs. Yetro drew a tenth circle at the bottom of the central row.

"The top, middle row, circle is Keter. Some call it the divine crown. Others call it Heavenly Father. But even though we use different definitions, we have a consistent sense of the role and presence of Keter."

Philotheos nodded.

Yetro continued. "The three circles on the right represent the masculine side of The One God. It is the side of the provider. The One God provides goodness and generosity. The top circle is Hokhmah. Some call it the circle of wisdom. Those who call Keter the Heavenly Father often call Hokhman the Son. The next circle on the masculine side is Hesed. Most understand that as the garment of mercy. The bottom circle on the masculine side is Nezah, it represents endurance and eternal victory."

Philotheos winked. "In Thracia, we would make four different gods out of those same characteristics. Can I assume the left side is the feminine side?"

"You can. The right side is the side of provision, the left side is the execution of divine will, power, and uncompromising justice. The top circle on the left is Binah. It represents understanding. It connects in a triangle with Keter and Hokhmah. Some call this the Holy Spirit."

Philotheos pointed to the top of Yetro's diagram. "So wisdom and understanding are opposed?"

"Not so much opposed, as in balance," replied Yetro. "Below Binah, or understanding, we find Din. Din represents justice. Hod, below Din, is the circle of glory."

Philotheos contemplated the sketch. "So understanding leads to justice, and justice leads to glory?"

"Only when balanced with wisdom, mercy, and eternal vigilance. Any aspect of Sefirot, taken out of balance, will foster an evil result."

"There are three circles left, in the middle, below the one you call Keter. What are those?"

Yetro pointed to the circle two-thirds of the way down between the masculine and feminine rows. "This one is Tif'eret. It can be understood as beauty. It is balanced by the masculine and feminine sides, and connects to justice, glory, mercy, and eternal vigilance."

"And the two lower circles?" quizzed Philotheos?

"I described Sefirot from the top down. If we consider the Sefirot the Tree of Life, we begin at the bottom and work our way up. The very lowest circle is Shekhinah. It represents the presence of God in the world. You could say it is the basis from which the other nine aspects emerge, or you could say it is the natural product. Either way is equally correct."

"Leaving only the circle between the bottom of the male and female stacks...", led Philotheos.

"Yes. Yesod. If Shekhinah is the root of the tree, then Yesod and Tif'eret are the central trunk. Yesod is the foundation. Some call Yesod the Holy Mother, balancing Keter, the Heavenly Father. It is through Yesod that the aspects of The One God interact with Shekinah."

Philotheos rested his chin on his knuckles. "So, the Yehudim are not so different from the Thracians, if we compare the garments of your god to our family of gods and goddesses. But, I have one question. We have a goddess of love, Aphrodite. Where on this tree of life is love, Yetro?"

Yetro closed his eyes. He smiled broadly, expressing a total satisfaction. There was a tone of peace, and a victory in his voice when he answered, "Everywhere."

III, VI
Reunion

Festus and Moravius made haste. They arrived in Yerushalayim half a day before the families of Eli and Hiram. They abandoned formality and celebrated the reunion with Miriam, Lucanus, Hertzelah, and Yasminah with tears and hugs. Miriam noted the intensity and duration as Festus and Yasminah embraced. *An older Roman guard and Yehudi servant girl? That won't be easy for them. I hope he isn't trifling with her. Father will be concerned about tradition. But Father will soon have more to deal with than an unusual romance among his retainers. I still don't know how to tell him about my situation. What will he do? Disown me? Worse? I must wait until the time is right.*

The pilgrim caravan from Caesarea straggled through the Damascus Gate. A cavalcade of sweating animals, creaking carts, and ache boned hikers advanced slowly. Every street was filled with a churning congestion of clashing costumes, divided by language and conflicting intent. The travelers reached a crossroad. Hiram's group was bound for their rented quarters in the lower city, and Eli's larger body continuing to his compound in the upper.

Eli extended an invitation. "Of course you will join us for meals, Hiram."

"We wouldn't want to create extra work for your household."

"Nonsense. We have a spacious sukkoh, and Tedeo's family will be sharing our apartments. I wish we had room to house you as well. But we can easily eat together. The cooks will make a large meal just a little larger."

Hiram swept the air with an upturned palm. He bowed slightly. "You are most gracious, Eli. And maybe it would be good for Faramond to get better acquainted with Miriam."

"That's not entirely decided, friend. Your son will get fair consideration. As will any other suitable candidates. It would be wrong to promise you more. It is time for Miriam to marry. Perhaps there will be a decision this week. I will see Miriam this afternoon, but I will press the issue with her tomorrow."

"Thank you. And since you are the father, this will be mostly your decision, right?"

Eli shook his head. "Very little to do with Miriam has ever been my decision. She's headstrong. Don't wish a curse upon your son. A curse is what he would have if Miriam were an unwilling bride."

Hiram reined his horse toward the lower city. He turned his face back toward Eli, smiled and said, "Don't underestimate my son. The right man will bring her to heel." Hiram kicked his horse in the flank, and the caravan split into separate streams.

Eli brooded as his contingent buffeted the clogged streets. The guards made polite, but insistent attempts to press open a pathway with their shields. Results were mixed. The more crowded the road, the less obligation there appeared to yield priority passage to the privileged. The patriarch brooded. *Has it come to this? My son is to marry well, and most likely happily. His twin sister's most insistent prospect is an unfortunate exception in a good family. Perhaps if Rachel had lived…*

Hertzelah was in the market when she noticed Eli's caravan on the far side of the square. She ran back to the compound to notify everyone the Master approached. A quickly arranged reception line greeted the travelers as they arrived. Miriam ran forward to hug her father and her brother as they dismounted.

"Shalom, daughter! How was your visit with Elisheba?"

"Different than I expected. We will talk about that, soon enough. Moravius will want to speak with you right away. Everybody is here and nobody is hurt, but we did have some problems with the Zealots. That's probably the most urgent thing to report."

Eli stepped away from Miriam. He turned toward Moravius.

"Zealots?"

"Indeed, your Excellency. And likely more to come. They are sneaking around disguised as shepherds, and gathering more bogus herdsmen to their cause. There's much more to tell."

"Then we won't waste any time. Give me a quarter hour to refresh, and then come to my study."

III, VII
A Wink and a Blessing

Hiram of Dothan was not accustomed to begging an audience. Yet, here he was in the courtyard, like some itinerant peddler. Hiram sought distraction through the burbling marble fountain and the magical scents of fragile, polychromatic blossoms. He envied the industry of a fat, black striped bee. The insect was not delayed in his business of the day, not even by Simeon ben Boethus; High Priest of Israel and father of Herod's favorite wife, Mariamne. Hiram wondered whether Simeon was in fact "unable to break away from Temple affairs." His cousin would not be above making Hiram wait – if only to posture and assert control. An hour elapsed, and then another.

A servant assigned to his comfort was sufficiently attentive- but dared not appear apologetic for the lengthy delay. One of Simeon's musicians distracted the supplicant with glissando tapestries on a whispering harp. A sultry Phoenician courtesan paused for a moment. She relaxed her grip on her robe and covertly revealed a scandalous length of pleasantly sculpted thigh. Hiram wondered how such a woman secured a place among Simeon's staff, and then waved her off. He must concentrate on the important task at hand.

In the early afternoon, Simeon and two aspiring disciples entered the garden. The High Priest was dressed in gilded robes deliberately chosen to rival, but not surpass King Herod's attire. "Shalom, Hiram! I hope you have not been waiting long."

He knows exactly how long I have been waiting. Hiram played his role in the political game, "Not that long, really. Thanks for taking the time to see me."

"But it's a pleasure to greet a kinsman, Hiram. I assume you're in Yerushalayim for Tabernacles? Any luck finding lodging?"

"Less than usual. We're not even in the Upper City, but it's a fine house. There's a quiet second floor room, well furnished, with a large table and many windows. We could serve a memorable meal there, if it weren't for the less acceptable address. It would make sense to buy something here, if the best neighborhoods were not already staked out."

Simeon nodded. "That can be an issue, when the city fills up." The High Priest turned aside to one of his retainers, "Make a note to invite my cousin Hiram, and his family, to dinner."

"Thank you. That's very gracious."

"Not at all. Now, what brings you to my garden today? I suspect it might be more pressing than a dinner invitation."

The black and yellow bee flew against Hiram's cheek. He brushed it away, then replied. "I wanted to ask about your influence with Eli of Caesarea. He's on the Council of Sanhedrin, and I thought…"

"Eli is a judge, not a priest. I can get his ear when I need to. He considers my opinion when offered. But he considers others as well. How do you hope to influence Eli? If it's some commercial arrangement, I can't get involved."

"It's not about business, Simeon. It's about Faramond, my son. Eli's daughter Miriam is of age, and…"

"So it is about business," laughed Simeon. "She would bring a substantial dowry. And combining your households would multiply the wealth, and political influence, of both."

Before he could think better of it, Hiram said, "I am sure you are better prepared to evaluate that than I am."

Simeon looked annoyed, but decided that Hiram could not possibly be brash enough to reference the marriage of his own daughter to King Herod. "Ignoring that aspect, from the little I remember about your son and Eli's scandalous daughter, it would seem an unlikely match. Miriam tiptoes around the edges of heresy. There are constant rumors that she heals, without any authority. As a woman, not a rabbi, she is forbidden to heal. The One God surely disapproves. Her father's position protects her from arrest."

"Faramond can control Miriam. You should see him manage the servants. He doesn't accept any back talk. Some of the household respect him. Those that do not, fear him. He has the strength to establish his authority in a household. Miriam would learn her place, and be no further problem to the Temple."

Simeon stroked his beard. "Sometimes I wonder whether a husband's best strategy would be trying to manage his wife through strength and authority."

"It has always worked for me," answered Hiram.

"Aside from that," continued Simeon, "have you spoken to Eli?"

"I did. I even presented him with a spectacular Assyrian dagger."

"And he said?"

"He gave me no decision. There is some sentiment that Miriam will not be married against her will. But that's my point. Faramond has to be better than whatever other few young men would consider marriage to a suspected witch, even with dowry and all."

Simeon leveled a finger at Hiram, but it was apparent the High Priest was not shocked by the reference to witchcraft. "Careful, that's a serious and dangerous charge."

"As I said, suspected."

Simeon motioned down a pathway. "Walk with me."

The cousins, trailed by Simeon's disciples, meandered through a maze of hedges and scented vines. Rabbits scampered into the shadows. Tumbling clouds of songbirds roiled casually within the walls. The wind shifted, infusing the air with the smoke of temple sacrifice.

Simeon cleared his throat. "Tell me, does Faramond still suffer from that awkward walk? Not many people get injured in the Temple.

I have always felt badly about the accident."

"Well, everyone agrees it was his own fault. If he had not been so drunk, he would never have fallen down all those stairs. On his best days he walks with a serious limp. On a lot of days, he relies on a crutch. On his worst days, he cannot walk at all."

"That's unfortunate, at his age. What bout Eli's daughter? If Eli says he might not insist that she marry against her will, what does Miriam think of Faramond? Would she be willing?"

"I am not sure he has spoken to Miriam about it. From what I know about her, she's unlikely to agree to marry anybody. This is going to be one of those cases where a father must assert his authority. If he's going to pick somebody to match with Miriam, I want that to be Faramond."

Simeon shut his eyes and nodded. "I can't promise you much, Hiram. If I get an opportunity to talk with Eli about his daughter's marriage prospects, I will mention Faramond as favorably as I am able. But we both know that if Eli senses he is getting pressured or maneuvered into something he will dismiss any possibility."

"I would agree."

"In the meanwhile, consider very carefully whether this match would be best for your son. Miriam is notoriously strong willed. She might be harder to bring to heel than Faramond suspects."

"Thank you, Simeon. I could ask no more."

"But you may receive very little. I will look forward to our dinner this week. Somebody will send word when the exact day is arranged."

Hiram bowed politely and found his way back through the gardens. He approached the gate, where once again he encountered the courtesan. She winked, smiled, and pulled a hand slowly across her breasts. Hiram looked in all directions, to see whether he was being observed. Failing to notice Simeon watching from a shadowed corner, he motioned the courtesan to follow him and stepped fervently into the busy lanes of Yerushalayim.

A few paces into the crowd, Hiram turned to address his companion. She was gone. In her place, was a rabbi- who, with a wink and a word of blessing, disappeared as well.

III, VIII
Folds in the Curtain of Time

Opus Caementicium. Yusuf surveyed the perfectly poured, absolutely flat surface upon which he would lay the final version of the mazzeroth. He realized it only appeared to be exactly level, but sloped a nearly imperceptible amount toward a garden space on the southern border. Rain water would drain away, rather than pool up on the central courtyard of the new addition to Eli's estate. It was easy to despise the Romans. It was impossible not to admire their concrete. Some said it was the addition of volcanic ash, imported from the Apennine Peninsula. In any event, an exceptional result required such extensive attention to preparation.

Anyone else viewing the soft grey expanse would see only an unexploited, virgin opportunity. An empty space, suspended in time. Yusuf saw more. He saw a circular map of the heavens, originally scratched into the leveled subsoil. He knew every line, every angle, every arc and every quadrant by heart. He internalized the correlations between the twelve houses of the cosmos and the twelve tribes of Israel. He would draw the design again, before committing to mortar, stone and grout.

To the extent that Yusuf recalled the rough version scratched into the soil he remembered the past. Envisioning the next version of the drawing, he anticipated the future. Even so, everywhere he looked he saw Miriam. There were only a few short days to remember. She expressed interest in his work, and proved to be as bright as she was curious. She defended him against suspicions of impropriety- all the while unintentionally fueling his fantasies of an impossible and intimate relationship. Separated by wealth, by class, by social status, and with dissimilar prospects there was no practical expectation of any long term relationship between an itinerant tile setter and the daughter of the richest man in Palestine.

Only Yusuf heard her laughter and the music of her voice. He saw flashes of her form. Her scent was on the wind. It was as though she had moved into a portion of his soul. Now she was gone to Yerushalayim. Servants of the house gossiped that Eli was growing impatient to see his daughter wed. Speculation exploded when Hiram of Dotham and his household arrived. Everyone was well aware that Hiram's son, Faramond, might prove an auspicious match. Miriam could do worse, Hiram and his family were rich enough. Tongues rattled and eyelids winked when the families journeyed together to rendezvous with Miriam in Yerushalayim.

For perhaps the third, fourth, or even the fifth time since he last saw Miriam, Yusuf struggled to push her out of his consciousness. Dwelling on something, or someone, so inaccessible could only have a disappointing outcome. At the moment of his death, Yakob spoke to Yusuf about a happy future, with a wife and family. It would be best to put Miriam out of his universe, and remain open to the possibility of meeting the woman The One God truly intended for him. His mind insisted he put Miriam behind him, but his heart was unwilling to let her go.

Yusuf stretched two cords from diagonally opposite corners, noting the point of intersection as the mathematical center of his workspace. Next, he stretched a cord from the center point to the edge of the intended circle. Yusuf was ready to appeal to Shimon of Accara, the master builder, to assign a laborer to assist him. The moment he glanced around to find Shimon, he heard a familiar male voice. "It looks like you are in need of a little help."

Yusuf turned. He was to see the young rabbi who had walked with him to transport Yakob's body to Nazareth.

"Well, hello, I thought you had some business in Yerushalayim?"

"So I did. And in the courtyard of Simeon, himself. I amused myself there, with one of my favorite pastimes. I help people see whatever it is they most desire to see. Between you and me, it has more to do with their desire than my intent. As I said, my visit there had something to do with you. A man who would do you no favors will now find himself without an influential ally."

"Who could possibly mean me harm? I'm of no consequence, with no fortune and no hope for one. Who would bother?"

"In due time, Tekton. You're of the house of David, but cursed through Yeconiah. Justice is like water. It seeks its own level. My interest in your affairs involves a past you cannot remember and a future you cannot foresee. "

"It would seem you haven't had enough time to travel to Yerushalayim, accomplish anything, and return here."

"So it would. Remember, I help people see whatever it is they most desire to see. Know that I am a choir among a void that sounds like silence. I move between folds in the curtains of time. Not only have I been to Yerushalayim, but I am still there as we speak."

Yusuf shook his head. "How can you possibly expect me to understand that, or even believe it?"

"It's not important that you either understand or believe. What's important is that you create a masterpiece. That you pour so much energy into the mazzeroth that it will capture all who behold it. You are the artist. I'm here to assist you, and I'll be sure that Shimon of Accara, who opposes you, sees only what he most desires to see."

Yusuf was overwhelmed. "This whole situation grows crazier by the day. The only thing upon which we can absolutely agree, is that I can use some help. Do you know anything about tile?"

"Enough. And I know as much as anyone about the twelve houses, the twelve tribes, the twelve moons, and the mazzeroth. You won't regret our association."

"I have nothing to lose, even if I am reluctant to consider what I might gain. Other than "Rabbi", do you have another name?"

"Some call me Elishua. I have been called Ben-gabar. I am also Gabriel, Almodad, and Israel. Only The One God knows my true name, just as only The One God knows yours."

III, IX
Forgiven

Citrine ghosts and coral shades twisted smoking tentacles beneath the visor of the eastern night. Like an inexorable tide, the crimson, peach and cobalt vanguard flooded across the heavens. Soon the Day Star, too bright to be viewed would displace a vast penumbra, too dim to be seen.

From a seat in the ceremonial sukkoh, Miriam exalted with the rising sun. Like a blossom on a vine of expectation, she hungered for the heat. She longed for the light. *I'm living, and breathing for two now. It's a time to move slowly, and let the cosmic energy penetrate my swelling belly. Let me gather it in, like food to a nest.*

The scent of fresh cut palm fronds, woven to serve as roof on the sukkoh, spiced an underlying aroma of Yerushalayim jammed to capacity. The wind from beyond the walls carried news of ripe grains and fresh split cedar. There were notes of horses, cattle, sheep, and a spice caravan from Hindu Kush.

Miriam found the bright dot behind the bridge of her nose. She began ascending and expanding her reality. Her meditations were interrupted by footsteps. Miriam envisioned their approach, and noted the unusually syncopated rhythm.

She sighed softly. Her eyes remained shut. "Hello, Faramond. You're hours early for the morning meal."

"How did you know it was me? I've been watching your face. You never looked up at all. I thought maybe you were sleeping."

"Many times, I see more with my eyes closed than open. What brings you out so early, and all this way from the lower city?"

"I was hoping you might be here. I heard you often come here at sunrise. It might be a good idea for us to talk."

Miriam sensed the approach of an awkward situation. "About?"

"About what our fathers have been discussing off and on. Combining the house of Eli with the house of Hiram. Bringing coal and tin together, multiplying the value of each. Securing greater political influence for your brother, as well as me."

"And anything else? How do our fathers propose bringing the houses together?"

"Eli hasn't spoken with you?"

Miriam feigned clueless, seeking a few precious seconds before the conversation would become unpleasant. "He speaks with me every day when we're under the same roof. Spoken about what?"

"About me, naturally. Er, I mean about us. You're of an age to marry. I need a wife."

Miriam opened her eyes and glared at Faramond. He was startled, and jerked backwards.

Miriam spoke slowly, but not unkindly. "You say you *need* a wife? How does that work, exactly? Do you need a wife like you need a meal, or some fancy clothing? Like you need your house, your horse, your coin pouch, or your sword? In what way do you *need* a wife?"

Faramond stammered for a response. "I, I think, I think I might have been too direct. Maybe a little clumsy."

Miriam stared intently at Faramond. She could sense him wilting under her gaze. "There is some possibility."

"Let me start over. I am now a man. I have opportunities to do very well in business. I will inherit from Hiram. To be complete, in our tradition, I need to start a household and father children of my own. Our fathers will decide the matter of course. I was hoping that you might be willing."

Miriam shook her head. "No, Faramond. I wouldn't be willing. My father has always said he won't force me to marry against my will. Maybe he's getting impatient, but I don't have any reason to think he has changed his mind."

Faramond appeared discouraged. "It's my injury, isn't it? That has to be why you don't like me."

"Nonsense. Your injury isn't an issue. It isn't a matter of liking you, anyway. I like hundreds of people, but I can't think of a single one I'm likely to marry. That includes you."

Faramond considered Miriam's remark. "It looks like we're off to an awkward start. Most women enjoy my company. If our fathers reach an arrangement, maybe as time goes by you will come around."

Miriam closed her eyes and exhaled dramatically. "What do you really want, Faramond? Don't answer that you want to marry me. Maybe you don't really want to be married to anybody. But if there was one thing you really wanted, what would that be?"

"I want to be rich."

"That sounds like an honest answer. Is there anything else you really want?"

"I would give anything to walk normally again."

Miriam stared into Faramond's eyes. Again, the intensity of her gaze made him uneasy. "You would give anything? Would you give *up* anything, as well?"

Faramond was confused. "What are you saying?"

"If you were able to walk normally, would you give up this notion of trying to marry me?"

"It's not actually our decision. It's up to our fathers."

"Yes, but if Eli knows that I am unwilling to marry you, or anyone else, that will have to affect the decision. You can go to Hiram and tell him you realized that I am too stubborn and opinionated to make a good wife. I can't imagine them forcing the issue if neither of us are willing."

Faramond shrugged. "This is silly. Yes, I would give up the idea of marriage between us if it meant I could walk properly and without pain. But I don't see any connection."

Miriam spoke with calm authority. "Sit with me on this bench. Give me both of your hands."

"What for? There seems to be some mixed message here."

"You're going to have to trust me. I am going to be very quiet, for a short time. It's going to take more strength than ever before, but I believe I can take you with me."

"Where are we going? I'm not excited about a long hike."

Miriam shook her head. "We're not going to walk. There's something we need you to say. Over and over again. No matter what happens. No matter what you think you see or hear. Repeat Babaziah, Masmasiah, Kaskasiah, Sharlai."

Faramond pulled his hands away. "I will not! You know that some people suspect you as a witch, don't you? You want me to speak in some magic tongue! I cannot, I will not."

Miriam remained calm. "Babaziah, Masmasiah, Kaskasiah, and Sharlai are the angels of healing in the Talmud. There is no magic involved. None. Only faith. A whole lot of faith. I don't even know if what I am going to try will work, but if we can restore your health and call off this possible marriage then we will both get what we want. Now give me your hands again. Repeat after me."

Miriam noticed Faramond's hands were shaking as he extended them to her again. Both began repeating, "Babaziah, Masmasiah, Kaskiah, and Sharlai."

Miriam located the bright spot behind the bridge of her nose. At first, it remained small and localized. Miriam didn't give up. She kept repeating the angelic names. Faramond's hands grew steady, and while his grip was firm it was more relaxed. The white spot finally expanded to surround her eyes, her nose, her mouth. It engulfed the space where Miriam imagined her head must be.

Miriam was weightless. She tumbled in a vortex where light split as through a prism with every hue a note of music. Her fingers, enmeshed with Faramond's, were as sea vines- although they smelled of butter. Their chant, Babaziah, Masmasiah, Kaskiah, and Sharlai reverberated without decay. The layers of sound combined to create a drone. A black and yellow bee drifted motionless on the wind.

Translucent shadows shifted in and out of focus. Babaziah, Masmasiah, Kaskasiah, and Sharlai.

The shadows took shape. The shadow of central court of The Temple. Miriam's shadow. Faramond's shadow, a heaping wreckage at the base of the steps. A temple priest knelt next to Faramond's fallen form. The priest was dressed in a black robe. Everything else was rendered in contrasting shades of pink, accented with yellow and orange. Babaziah, Masmasiah, Kaskasiah, and Sharlai.

Faramond's subconscious thought screeched like the teeth of a hurricane, wrestling with the drone. "This is where it began. Where I fell. The day I was drunk in The Temple. That's me. This is the moment I hurt myself."

Babaziah, Masmasiah, Kaskasiah, and Sharlai. The priest arose. Miriam could see that he had no face beneath his shawl. He raised a bony finger and pointed to the west. "Go now, child. Take this son of Hiram with you. Return to the sukkoh. You have a message. All voices praise The One God."

Everything stopped at once. The light, the seaweed, the butter, the pink and orange shadows, the drone, and the black and yellow bee. Miriam and Faramond stopped chanting. The rising sun hatched shadows in the sukkoh- normal comforting shadows, of shapes well understood.

Faramond pulled his hands away. "What just happened?"

"Weren't you there? I saw you there, and heard you there. What do you think happened?"

"We were back at the day when I fell at the Temple. Only we

weren't there. But then again, we were. Why didn't the priest have a face? Why did he speak to you, a woman, but not to me? I don't understand."

Miriam spent a moment in thoughtful silence, then spoke. "Your injury. There are days when it is much worse than others, correct?"

"Yes, once in a while I can almost walk regularly. Other days, only with a lot pain. Some days, the pain is so great I cannot walk at all. Yes, some days are worse than others. Much worse."

"Faramond, when you fell you did not damage your body."

"But I did, I have not been able to walk like before."

"You damaged your pride. You were embarrassed, in front of many people you knew. People whose opinion you think might be critical to your future."

Faramond adopted a tone of indignation. "Are you saying I'm making this all up? Acting out for sympathy? How dare you? My pain is absolutely real. My father says it is The One God's punishment for behaving disgracefully in the Temple."

"Punishment? The One God does not punish us. But The One God will not interfere if we insist on punishing ourselves. That's what you have been doing, punishing yourself. But, I have a message for you. One that will change things for you, right away."

"That message is?"

"You are forgiven. Now get up and walk."

"What, right now?"

Miriam laughed. Tears streamed down her cheeks. "Yes. The gift is given. There's no reason to delay."

Faramond rose, uncertainly. He took a cautious step, then smiled. His pace quickened as he strolled back and forth across the sukkoh. "This is a miracle! I'm walking just like I did before the fall. There's no pain. None at all. Everyone will be amazed. What can I tell them happened here?"

"You must tell them nothing. As far as they are concerned, you are having an unusually good day. And tomorrow you will have another. And the next day, another still. Soon, they will begin to assume that The One God has chosen to restore your health. They will be right."

Faramond did a little dance. "How can I thank you, for this?"

"Remember your promise. If you could walk normally again you would speak to Hiram. You will tell him I am unsuitable as a wife."

"And I will. After all, if I am going to be healthy as well as rich, I can have any woman I want!"

Faramond hopped, and skipped, and ran down the hill toward the lower city.

Miriam smiled serenely. *One crisis avoided, assuming he goes to Hiram, and somehow I know he will. Now, I have to figure out how to tell Eli his first grandchild will be born in the spring- just five months from now.*

PART IV

IV, I
One Plus One Equal One Anew

Anchored. Like two ponderous marble galleons were Eli's original estate at Caesarea and the nearly completed addition for his son. The pillars, balustrades, corniches, finials, and cartouches of the original grand residence were emulated (but deliberately not exceeded) by the newer work. Not merely anchored, but permanently aground on a hillside overlooking the Roman port, and Mare Nostrum beyond. The older edifice had weathered for a generation. The scent of mason's lime and shards from stone cutters' shaping chisels swirled through the dust of the newer. Viewed from a distance, the older and newer buildings were each enhanced by the other. The combination more beautiful than the sum of the parts.

Not long after Tabernacles, there would be a wedding. The women gossiped, "Possibly two!" Aban, son of Eli would marry Lydia, daughter of Tadeo. Her dowry of real property would rename him "Aban of Ha'Ramathea. "Perhaps at Tabernacles Eli will make a match for the more rebellious of his twins. Miriam is more than of age."

Yusuf the tekton from Nazareth surveyed his workplace. The opus caementicium fully stabilized and the subtle grade confirmed for drainage, his canvas was ready days ago. Elaborate mosaic courtyards defined a splendid residence. It was unusual for one so young to be commissioned for an installation this significant. Despite the profound reservations of Shimon of Accara, Eli's master builder, masterful work on a similar project for King Herod at Sephora earned Eli's personal trust.

Shimon disapproved of Yusuf. He additionally distrusted the presence of an itinerant rabbi, ostensibly working as some sort of assistant. The stranger was not listed on the official payroll. It was unthinkable that Yusuf had any means to hire a subordinate. Shimon watched. Three days elapsed, while the tekton and the Rabbi picked up small handfuls of fired clay tiles and sat them temporarily in place around the slab. Material was piled, then removed. Sorted, then sorted again. Nothing was permanently in position, although the tekton and the Rabbi spent many hours in conversation. Eli expected the project completed when he and the family returned from Yerushalayim. The master would be displeased if the courtyard remained unstarted when the rest of the structure was complete.

Shimon's patience snapped. He marched from his booth to the empty slab. A bevy of quislings and assistants scrambled into hasty order and trailed in the master builder's wake.

The master builder interrupted a discussion between Yusuf and the Rabbi. "I've been right from the start. You aren't going to be able to fulfill your task. You stand around and talk all day, and nothing is accomplished. When Eli returns, your punishment will be severe."

Before Yusuf could respond, the Rabbi replied, "When Eli returns, the courtyard will be completed. The master will be pleased with Yusuf of Nazareth, and pleased with his master builder as well."

"Eli will return within the week! It isn't possible to lay this much tile that quickly."

Yusuf again deferred to the Rabbi. "Three days, Shimon. We need three days to finish here."

"Are you insane? Ten men couldn't lay this tile, properly, in two weeks. I'm to accept that the two of you will finish in three days? And what do you mean finish, you aren't even started."

Yusuf extended a hand. In his open palm were fired clay tiles of blue, yellow, and white as well as a bit of tin. "We have been sorting material."

Shimon sneered, "Oh yes, the common clay you insisted upon using. Do you know for how many years you will be indentured here, if Lord Eli takes offense at the use of this cheap material and insists you replace it at your own expense?"

Yusuf was unphased. "I have a vision."

The Rabbi agreed. "In fact, we have a mutual vision. Much of the courtyard is already finished, it simply needs to be moved to the common plane."

"Already finished? Do you take me for a fool? And who are you, exactly, anyway? I never hired an assistant for this man. He cannot afford your wages. Why are you even here?"

The Rabbi chuckled. "Certainly not for the money. It seems there isn't going to be any of that."

A freakish blast of wind swept across the slab. The gust tore at the hair and clothing of Shimon and his retainers. The breeze left unruffled the tekton and the Rabbi, only a matter of steps away. The squall fueled Shimon's frustration. Why were the tile setter and the Rabbi apparently immune of the laws of physics?

"Put up a partition," said The Rabbi. "Have some laborers hang something to conceal all sides of the courtyard from view. Leave the partition in place for three days. At the end of that time, take it down. I promise you will see what it is that you most want to see."

"I most want to see this project finished. And then I would most like to see you gone."

"Then get some laborers to string the partition. We can make all your dreams come true."

Shimon pointed toward an assistant. "Get these two fools their partition. All the better, anyway. We won't have to watch them condemn themselves with their incompetence."

Yusuf nodded deferentially toward Shimon, "Thank you, master builder. You won't be disappointed."

"Know that when the partition comes down, I will have guards on hand. Either the courtyard will be finished, as promised, or the two of you will be arrested for fraud. We will bar the gates against your escape."

The anomalous wind rose again, herding the flapping gaggle of Shimon and his entourage back toward the master builder's booth.

The Rabbi nodded confidently. "That will be the last we see of them until we're finished."

Yusuf scratched behind an ear. "This better work. We've spent more time sorting material than anybody would ever consider. I've been working with you pretty much on faith alone, but I think I'm ready to know why sorting down to groups as small as individual tiles is so important."

The Rabbi extended his hands, palms up, toward Yusuf. "Let me show you why. Put two tiles, of any color in my left hand."

Yusuf selected a blue tile and a white tile, and placed them where directed.

The Rabbi asked, "Now, what do you see?"

"A blue tile, and a white one."

"Now take away the white tile, and substitute it with another of the same color."

Yusuf complied. No sooner did the second white tile take the place of the first than the new combination emanated a subtle light. "Now, what do you see?"

"I don't see two stones anymore. Not really. I see something else. It's created by the relationship between two distinct pieces, but it forms a third presence. Each enhances the other. In the process, it's like the entirety is transformed. It was all a question of putting the right individual pieces together."

The Rabbi closed his hand. When he reopened his palm, there was only a single stone. It radiated a cheerful glow. "Lay your mazzeroth, Yusuf. Between your initial vision and what you have learned sorting these tiles, you are ready."

"We'll need to work very quickly, to be done in three days."

"Do what you can. I'll do the rest. Three days? That's actually much longer than we need. And the partition? That will save us from charges of sorcery. Shimon will more quickly believe what he cannot see than he will ever see what he refuses to believe."

IV, II
A House of Shame

The Sanhedrin maintained chambers for judges. Private compartments of moderate size flanked a terraced sandstone courtyard with black reflecting pools and potted palms. When in Yerushalayim, Eli frequently withdrew to these cloisters to contemplate aspects and arguments of cases before the highest court of the Yehudim. Popular courtesy afforded the judges some privacy, yet no guards barred entry to the quarters. It was here, away from her brother and beyond the hearing of ubiquitous household staff, that Miriam chose to inform her father. She stood in the doorway. She posed a raven silhouette, backlit by swirls of temple dust asail on rays of honey colored light.

Eli sat at a simple table, behind a section of unrolled scroll. He looked up from his bench and smiled at Miriam's arrival. His daughter was beautiful and fresh. Just now, in that doorway, Miriam in profile resembled Rachel. Miriam was almost exactly the age at which her mother and Eli were wed. Raising a daughter was not easy for a man with Eli's obligations. Too many months away each year, in Britannia, Tarshish, and Yerushalayim. Never entirely confident he was addressing all the needs of a maturing young woman. Had Rachel survived the birth of the twins…

'Father, can we talk?"

"Of course. These legal issues are tiresome. Your visit is a welcome break."

Miriam closed the door behind her. She crossed the room to kiss Eli on the forehead, then took a seat on a small bench at right angles to his own.

Miriam inhaled softly, then began. "There's been some discussion of marriage. You and Hiram of Dothan, hoping to make a match between Faramond and myself. I need to tell you that's out of the question."

Eli leaned forward, frowning slightly. "Out of the question? That's a rather bold statement from a young woman to her father. I decide how to define the question."

Miriam looked downward. Eli softened his tone. "It's time for you to marry. It would be better not to give you in marriage against your will. To avoid that, you need to let me know which prospects would be acceptable. I admit, Faramond would not be my first choice. It's why I have avoided giving a final answer to Hiram."

"I spoke with Faramond this morning."

Eli stretched a palm across his eyebrows and shook his head. "Without a chaperone?"

"It was entirely proper. I can tell you that Faramond doesn't want this marriage any more than I do. No doubt you will soon be hearing the same from Hiram. Any confederation of tin and coal, between you and Hiram, will need to be based on business, not marriage. Faramond told me given a choice, he would not choose me. He considers me too independent. Not sufficiently subservient to make a good wife."

Eli tossed up his hands. "I'll have to work quickly, then. There have been some inquiries. None as promising as Hiram's house, I warn you. I think you have met David, son of Amos of Emmaeus? The family has some modest estates. Nathan, son of Hezekiah of Nain? There's less money there, now, but the family has political connections and fresh opportunities. Then there's…"

Miriam interrupted. "None of them."

Eli tugged impatiently at his beard. "It is going to be one of them." He pointed his index finger at his daughter. "If, as you say, Faramond won't have you then I will make arrangements with another father. It can be your choice, if you will make it. But choice or not you will fulfill your obligation to The One God, to our people, and to your family."

"Father, I am afraid that none of these houses will have me."

"Nonsense! Our family is the envy of everyone in Palestine. You are beautiful. There isn't an eligible man alive who wouldn't...." Eli paused. His voice shifted to a darker and more cautious note. "Wait. None of the families will have you? What, exactly, are you trying to tell me?"

Miriam swallowed, but before she could answer Eli pressed again. "There can't be many possible reasons. Have you lost your virginity? Are you damaged goods?"

"I am pregnant, Father."

Eli jerked with shock. He gasped, and slumped on the bench. Neither father nor daughter spoke, enveloped by mutual despair yet separated by a chasm of hopeless dread. Eli used both hands to clear tears from his cheeks.

"None of the rest makes any difference. It's my shame as well as your own. I have failed you as a father. I should have taken another wife. Someone to give you better instruction."

Miriam blubbered and cried. She reached out to grab Eli's forearm. "You haven't failed me, Father."

"No? Don't forget, you could be condemned to stoning! There's no time to lose. How long have you known? If we get a groom drunk enough, maybe we can blame timing of this birth on an early arrival..."

"Five months, Father. The baby will be born in five months."

"You are four months along? That rules out the early delivery story. Who's the father? Your young Roman was gone long before then. Was it that priest, Yetro? If so, I will hunt him down. Tell me, who's the father?"

Miriam wept. *This seemed like a great spiritual adventure when*

Zachariah invoked Yetzirah. How could I have been so stupid? So selfish? How could I disregard the affect on my family? I dare not try to explain the details. Father is suffering a painful shame. He isn't prepared to accept or understand.

"I cannot say."

Eli erupted with anger. "What do you mean, you cannot say? Have there been so many? Are there multiple possibilities?"

"I dare not speak the father's name."

"What! So he must be married? If so, that makes you an adulteress! We will have to get you out of Palestine, quickly, before you're denounced. My position may not be enough to guarantee your safety."

Miriam wailed. "Are you trying to cast me out?"

"I'm trying to save your life."

Eli seized upon a strategy. "Tell no one. You think I will hear from Hiram to call off any further talk about you and Faramond. Let's count on that. I will deflect any inquiries by other fathers. Tabernacles is nearly over, and we will go back to Caesarea. I can call in a favor from Augustus and put you on a ship for Rome. Your brother and I will visit you there, on convoys to Tarshish and Brittania. If you return someday, let it be with a husband as well as a child. No one needs to know."

Miriam continued to weep. She stood up and groped for the door. Before she took a second step, Eli spoke in a comforting voice. "We'll get through this somehow. You're still my daughter. I have always loved you, and always will."

Miriam whirled toward Eli and held out her arms. Father and daughter joined in a trembling embrace. Tears flowed into tears, a passion of agony, regret, resignation, and commitment.

The embrace dissolved. "Thank you, Father. I have always loved you too."

Miriam turned to leave. She reached the exit when Eli called out, "Let me ask this one thing. Knowing that four months is a very long time… is there any possible chance you're mistaken?"

Miriam stood in the doorway. A raven silhouette, backlit by temple dust asail on rays of honey colored light. She stretched her hands across her belly, pulling tight the folds of her sky blue gown. She revealed the distinctive curve of the internal nest, the shape of a woman with child. "None."

IV, III
Disaster in the Upper Room

Dancing. There was no way Faramond, seldom able to walk properly, should be dancing. Hiram of Dothan beheld his son leaping, spinning, twisting and jerking across the upper room in the lower city. Although his balance seemed precarious, his limbs were supple and unrestrained. His grin, like the front door of an asylum for demons. The entire performance inspired, obviously, by an imprudent amount of wine. Hiram nearly slipped in a crimson puddle as he snatched away the slopping pitcher, disrupting Faramond's ecstatic revelries.

The young man drooled and slurred. "Fadder, gish me black my wine!"

"You have had more than enough. What's going on here?"

"I'm danshling. Anybrudy can shie I'm danshling."

"Yes, dancing. But why? And how?"

"Glish mebrack the wine!"

Hiram threw the pitcher against the wall. It exploded on the yellow brick, staining the proximity with a chronicle of his anger. The servants would deal with the wreckage. It was up to Hiram to deal with Faramond. He grasped his son by both shoulders and held him at arms' length.

"Come to your senses! Today is the day I press for Eli's decision. What if somebody from his house sees you behaving like this? And by what means are you able to dance at all? What about your injury?"

Faramond gasped and winced. His disorderly, dripping grin morphed into a grimace of distress. He put a hand to his belly, and jerked spasmodically. Hiram removed his right hand just in time to avoid a cascade of reeking, orange, acidic vomit. The servants were going to be busy, indeed.

"Blime shorry, Fadder."

Hiram renewed his demand. "How can you dance? And why are you dancing?"

"Ish Miriam. But I cansh shay morden it. I promised. I promised."

"You make no sense. Miriam got you drunk, and made you dance?"

Faramond shook his head. "No, … I gosh drunks by mystelth."

Hiram's mind leapt to rumors of witchcraft. Stories that surrounded Miriam like a malignant miasma. Tales that none dared repeat too loudly, given Eli's position. What could Eli's daughter have to do with Faramond's altered state? In Faramond's condition, subverting whatever promise he reports should not be difficult.

"What did you promise Miriam?"

"Nosh to tell."

"Tell what?"

"But I ams shaposhed to tell you. I donsh wanda marry her. Crawl it orf. She woshnot blee orbidarint denuf. She mache me promish to tells you thish."

Hiram shook Faramond. His son flopped like a rag doll, and puked again. Faramond groaned.

"And what did you promise not to tell me?"

Faramond slumped, apparently ready to faint. Hiram shook him again.

"Answer me!"

"She mache me promish notta tell arniebuddy. She healsh me. Ishcan walk now. Ishcan dansh. Ishcan gish any womunsh I wand. I am youngsh, hilthrey, and rish. I donsh needum womunsh who wonch ovrey meech. I donsh wand Miriam. Crawl it orf."

Faramond passed out. Hiram dragged his son to a corner of the room, leaving heel tracks through a stinking morass of ruby wine, bubbling grey bile, and spreading yellow vomit. Hiram propped the unconscious form against some cushions, to be cleaned up with the rest of the disaster in the upper room.

Hiram gathered first his thoughts, and then his cloak. If Faramond was healed, as it appeared, rumors would thrive. Too many people already knew that Hiram was promoting his son as a husband for Eli's daughter. There were important commercial considerations. Eli and Hiram were tin and coal- lacking only copper to control the age of bronze. A rejection of Faramond would be an insult to the house of Hiram. Eli might force Miriam to wed against her will, but as a man Faramond was less obligated to wed as instructed. A rejected Faramond, healed or not, would be disgraced. That disgrace would tarnish Hiram as well.

My family will not be shamed alone!

Like a devious rat with a purloined cheese Hiram crept through streets and alleys of the lower city. He ascended the shadowed steps to the Roman district, nearest the temple. Blasphemy must be denounced. Simeon must be informed. Perhaps the marriage might still be salvaged, in order to avoid a prosecution.

Faramond can be brought back in line, once he sobers up.

A heavy door barred entry to the high priest's compound. Hiram hammered his fist against the planks. There was no response. "Hello? Hello? It's Hiram of Dothan. I have urgent business with the high priest!" Hiram pounded until his knuckles began to bleed. Still there was no response. He cried out again, and thumped the door some more. Passersby kept their distance, but pointed and stared.

"I must speak to High Priest Simeon! It's an emergency!"

The door opened, slowly, cracking far enough to reveal a steward's face beyond. "The High Priest sent me to ask about the nature of your business. You are disrupting his meditation."

"The nature of my business? A report of scandal and blasphemy. An affront to The One God right here in the streets of Yerushalayim.

Tell Simeon he will definitely want to hear what I have to say."

The door shut. Hiram waited. Onlookers dispersed.

Several minutes passed. Hiram dared not knock again.

Perhaps I have been dismissed?

The door eventually opened, wider this time. The steward motioned for Hiram to enter. "High Priest Simeon says he has very little time to discuss anything with you, so please try to state your business briefly."

Hiram followed the steward to Simeon's chamber. The steward opened the door, and motioned Hiram to enter.

Simeon's tone was cordial, but not convincingly polite. "Shalom, Hiram. I thought you might be here about my agreement to talk with Eli on your son's behalf. I admit, I have not yet found an opportunity. Now, what's this report of something you think might be scandal and blasphemy?"

"It's Miriam, Your Eminence. She has bewitched my son."

"I have warned you before, about that same accusation. We charge blasphemy based on evidence, not rumors or disgraceful gossip."

"I have evidence. As clear as summer sunrise, I have evidence. Faramond is healed. He walks again. Normally. He told me Miriam is responsible. She's a woman. She is not a rabbi. She cannot heal by the authority of The One God. Witchcraft is the only remaining explanation."

Simeon tilted his head. He ran his thumb and index finger across closed eyelids.

"That's a disastrous charge, Hiram. Eli's daughter? Think very carefully before you advance this any further. And even if what you allege could be remotely true, why aren't you celebrating Faramond's good fortune, instead of trying to condemn the woman you maintain was an instrument in this supposed miracle."

"It's not a miracle. It's a spell! I don't want to see Miriam condemned, or put to death. I am hoping that you will counsel Eli to insist on her marriage with Faramond. Once they are wed, we can hope she will assume her appointed role as a proper wife among the Yehudim. There would be no need to prosecute, were that the case."

Simeon shook both hands at Hiram. "You're impossible. First you insist she's a witch, and then you say you want her to marry your son nonetheless? What right have you to claim a high regard for The Law? Do you remember your last visit here?"

"Of course, Your Eminence. You received me very graciously."

"I tried to do so. But you dishonored my hospitality. You shamed our association. I have no idea where she came from. Nobody recalls ever seeing her before, but when you left my courtyard on your last visit it was in the company of some tawdry harlot. I saw that. I had somebody follow you, to see what sins you might indulge. They lost track of the whore in the crowd."

"I did nothing."

"And I choose to do nothing now. Go home to your wife and family, Hiram. Make whatever arrangement with Eli you can, but it will be without any help from me. If Faramond is healed, it is by the grace of The One God, not a spell cast by Eli's daughter."

"Must I make a public outcry?"

"At your peril, Hiram. Marriage or not, you're well advised to cultivate a good relationship with Eli. He helped you get your franchise from Augustus. Don't let damaged pride destroy everything. If Faramond is truly healthy again, you should have no trouble finding another woman for him. He's going to be rich enough, if you don't make an enemy of Eli."

IV, IV
Straw Heart in a Stone House

Claudius, garrison commander of the Roman fortress on Lake Tiberius, was startled by Eli's message. Zealots in the Garden of the Prince. Rebels disguised as herdsmen, and drawing others to their cause. Claudius doubled the guard and hired additional spies. Now he walked the ramparts in a frosty dawn, inspecting the sentries. To the east, beyond the lake, the sun emerged from slumber. A shaft of silver light sliced the inky surface, releasing a spreading puddle of crimson and pink. Grain and citrus, sheep and fish, left scented tracks weaving wattles in the waft.

Nobody could remember so many shepherds in Galilee. Even in The Garden, the grass would not sustain the herds for long. But if Eli's information were accurate, and some not herdsmen at all, an urgency fostered by a shortage of forage would only aggravate the political situation. There would be dissension among the Yehudim. Confrontation was inevitable. Claudius dispatched a rider to Mount Carmel, requesting reinforcements. The criminals responsible for the massacre at Yericho Ford were likely hiding in plain sight. It wouldn't be possible to arrest and interrogate every shepherd. The backlash would be catastrophic. The spies might prove effective. In any case, before the grass runs out, someone might find the courage to betray the imposters.

Thus it was throughout the Empire. The heart beat strong in the capital. Imperial power surged through the central arteries of commerce and culture. It was only places like Galilee, on the farthest extremities, where a lack of circulation bred contempt. The Picts, the Goths, the Gauls, the Yehudim, and scores of other remote nations were unlikely to march on Rome. Distance was the equalizer. Costs were constrictive. Defending a front that extended hundreds of miles inland from the Mare Nostrum strained even a Caesar's capacity. The tribes always would nibble at the excess flesh of the perimeter.

Claudius resumed his inspection. He always gazed beyond the faces of his men. It was wise to avoid familiarity. War is a ravenous concubine, scything her price without warning. Command required a straw heart in a stone house.

IV, V
A Future Unforeseen

The Rabbi proved correct. It would not take three days to lay the mazzeroth. Yusuf the Nazarene was astonished, even somewhat alarmed, at the speed with which they worked. The Rabbi troweled the mortar. Yusuf set the clay tiles, pieces falling perfectly into place as if on their own volition. House by house and tribe by tribe they worked around the circle.

Shimon's partition, draped over a hasty frame, concealed the mosaic from view.

The tekton stopped for a sip of water. "They are taking bets, you know."

The Rabbi chuckled. "Of course they are. Making odds on how much of this work will be done when the partition comes down. Wagering whether you will be whipped before you are fired. Even betting whether Eli will discharge Shimon for failure to supervise this signature installation. What they assume would be the worst bet? That will prove the best of all."

"How is it possible to work this quickly?"

"You have been laying the mazzeroth your entire life, Yusuf. The days we spent sorting tiles and stones? Handling the materials repeatedly? That was part of it. That created discipline. It established structure. It's that same structure that has now set you free."

"But we're not even taking steps to be meticulous."

The Rabbi stretched his hand over the completed sections. "Here's the house of Gad, sign of the ram. How do you think it looks?"

"It looks flawless. It radiates energy, much like those two stones in your hand when we finished sorting."

"I agree. As will Eli. As will anyone who sees your finished work. Next, the house of Isaac, sign of the burdened beast."

"It is as the sign of the ram. It looks like a week's work, only better than anyone might dare expect. There were the few tiles that you placed, in the house of Isaac, forming the sign for Jupiter."

"Yes, Jupiter in the house of Isaac. Earth in the house of the virgin, Dinah. Neptune in the house of Dan, the scorpion. Venus in the house of Rueben, the home of all waters. Mercury in the house of Zebulon, the fish."

Yusuf nodded. "Yes, but why these specific houses? Why so extremely important?"

The Rabbi turned to his trowel and concentrated on the spread of mortar. "You may, or you may not, see the plan as it falls into place. But, if not, when Miriam returns from Tabernacles, she will know. Ask her then. If you do not see it for yourself, she should be the one to say."

Yusuf scoffed. "I will be lucky to get her attention for anything more than a courteous nod. Rumors are that Eli won't leave Yerushalayim without securing a husband. Her mind will be occupied elsewhere."

The Rabbi scooped fresh mortar from the board. He addressed Yusuf without looking in his direction. "Yes, rumors are. Know this, Eli failed to arrange a marriage for his daughter."

The Nazarene's heart leapt in his chest. For a moment, before he returned to the sobriety of his intellect, he harbored wild, impossible thoughts of a chance for a future with Miriam. But what was he thinking? What possibility could ever exist for the daughter of the richest man in Palestine and an itinerant tekton serving her father?

"But, Rabbi; how can you know this?"

"It's enough that I know it. How I know it is not significant. And, by the way, Eli's family returns early from Tabernacles. There was some unpleasantness with a business associate, threatening to make a public scene over some issue or another. The High Priest gave Eli leave to go, and in fact suggested he do so."

Yusuf thumbed his chin. "It's enough that I trust you. No matter how unlikely the sound of anything you say; over and over again you prove yourself correct. When will they return to Caesarea?"

"Within a few hours after you complete the mazzeroth. There's no reason for additional delay, and the plans do not include an early arrival."

Yusuf returned to placing tiles, rapidly and instinctively. "You make me think I'm involved in some grand plan or something. Surely that cannot be the case."

Above the scraping of his trowel, The Rabbi replied, "As I have said, my interest in your affairs involves a past you cannot remember…"

Yusuf finished the statement, "And a future I cannot foresee."

The partition parted. Shimon the Master Builder inserted his head through the gap.

"We were not supposed to be disturbed," grumbled Yusuf.

"And you won't be. Not by anyone except me. There can be no secrets from the Master Builder."

Shimon stepped into the enclosed workspace. "Well, I have to say I'm pleasantly surprised. Obviously, you changed your mind. I was expecting a mazzeroth, and you're creating a dual portrait of Eli and his son. Eli will be very much pleased. The quail around the edges? They remind me of the work you did for Herod, at Sephora. This is a better concept for a nobleman's court. Even the cheap tiles work better than anyone would hope."

Yusuf was confused as well as annoyed. "Now that you have had your look, please go away and leave us to finish."

Shimon bowed elaborately, and backed out through the partition. "Indeed. And at the amazing rate you're going, you just might make good your boast of three days."

The Rabbi suppressed his laughter until Shimon departed entirely.

Yusuf was concerned. "What did we just do? What's Shimon talking about? There's no portrait of Eli or his son. There are no quail. He doesn't see our actual work. Have we deceived the Master Builder?"

The Rabbi pointed skyward. "Yusuf, what have I said my greatest service to you was going to be?"

Yusuf nodded. "Ah yes. Helping people see whatever it is they most want to see."

"And so it is. Let's return to work. Your blessing, within the structure created by your preparation enables us to work quickly, but even so we must continue. The mazzeroth will not complete itself."

IV, VI
The Forge and Mustard Seed

Light folded in upon light. Silvers and whites spun yellow and orange. Sunset approached. The ziggurat at Ur awakened.

Elderchild, apprenticed to the clerks and stargazers, hurried toward the Master's chambers. His task was completed, the talisman in hand. Given the sparse contents, the leather pouch seemed unnaturally heavy. The stone passageways, worn smooth by seer and scholar, were always warm when the evening work began. By morning, the energy would dissipate. Everyone would sleep again, as the edifice recharged under the fires of the Day Star.

The apprentice knocked at Gaspar's door for admission.

"Come in."

A feeble candle in a bronze bowl cast an unsteady glow on Grand Master Gaspar, his personal apprentice Melchior, and withered old Balthazar. The three were huddled in consultation above an unfurled map with green silk ribbon alongside. Balthazar gestured. "I will follow Euphrates, north toward Babylon. At the right point, I will go west to Damascus, then pick up the incense road to Petra."

Gaspar placed a hand on the map. "Directly to Damascus? That takes you across the desert. Why not follow the caravan route from Babylon northwest to Palmyra, and then southwest to Damascus? It's longer, but safer."

Melchior nodded, indicating agreement with Gaspar.

"Safer, how? The road is lined with thieves and toll collectors everywhere from Babylon to Damascus. Certainly both sides of Palmyra. An old man, traveling alone? I know what dangers lurk in the desert. I dare not imagine the evil that dwells in the heart of man."

Melchior asked, "What about water? What if you get lost?"

"I am no stranger to the sands. I can smell an oasis many miles away. And lost? How could I possibly get lost? I travel at night. The heavens point the way."

Elderchild discreetly cleared his throat. Gaspar looked up from the map. "I assume you finished?"

The apprentice bowed, slightly. "Yes, Grand Master. It is as you ordered."

Gaspar took the talisman from the apprentice. He held the diminutive leather pouch and attached strap close to the candle for examination. The fresh skin still smelled of tanning urine, as well as exotic spice. The scratchy strap was hard and etched with dry cracks. "The stitching is well done. Very precise. The edges are firm and tight. Nothing should spill out. Confirm for us, did you enclose everything, as instructed?"

"Yes, Grand Master. Everything I was furnished. One small gold coin, a pinch of frankincense, a thimbleful of myrrh. Would I be permitted to ask about the purpose of my labor?"

Gaspar said nothing. After a moment, Balthazar spoke. "There's no harm. The boy is here to learn, isn't he?"

Gaspar consented. "If you think it's a good idea, then by all means explain it to him."

"Very well. A Yehudi priest inquired about a star chart. Specifically about an arrangement of planets on a day the Yehudim call Nisan 5. The configuration forms the Seal of Solomon, something the priest and his people call The Star of David. This event coincides with an old prophecy about the birth of a king. In a city the Yehudim call The House of Bread. There's at least some chance this event may be exceptionally significant. I am taking a gift to a magical child, who will grow up to be a king among the Yehudim."

Elderchild dared inquire, "It sounds like you are planning to walk? And will this king be impressed with so little myrrh and frankincense?

Will the king not be insulted with only a single gold coin?"

Gaspar frowned at the youngster's impertinence.

Balthazar tipped the candle to drain off melted wax and expose fresh wick. A momentary effusion of yellow light generated black silhouettes on the stones in Gaspar's chamber.

"Yes, I will walk. Part of the gift is delivery and presentation. As far as the quantities, let me ask you a question, boy."

Elderchild bowed again. "I will answer if I can, sir."

"How much gold is there in the world? How much myrrh? How much frankincense?"

Elderchild considered the question, then replied. "I have heard there are kingdoms with storehouses filled with gold."

"You have heard correctly."

The apprentice continued. "Caravans of myrrh and frankincense are traded nearly every day. Enough to create enormous fortunes."

Balthazar nodded. "Correct again. Would you say it is true that no matter how large our gift to the king, it would still represent only a tiny portion of each element?"

"Of course, but still it seems like larger amounts would be appropriate."

Gaspar stood and pointed toward the door. "Thank you for stitching the talisman. Darkness is at hand. Your regular duties await."

Elderchild turned to leave. Balthazar called out, "Wait! A good question should not go unanswered."

Gaspar looked confused, shrugged, and sat down. "As you wish, Master."

The boy faced the table again. Balthazar continued, "If the amounts are not significant, what aspect might be important?"

"The combination?"

"Exactly. Hear this, there is a limit to what anyone can buy; but no limit to what anyone can become. Gold is the present, myrrh the past, and frankincense the future. Combine these elements, in the proper forge, and transcend all of your self-imposed limitations."

"The proper forge?"

Gaspar cried, "Enough! He's an apprentice, and only a boy. You will confuse his studies. He is not ready. Some are never ready."

"I will be gone from here in an hour, Gaspar. At my age, and from this quest, I may never return. Indulge an old man. Let me share a simple folk tale with this apprentice, and then I will go."

Gaspar did not reply. He rolled up the map, secured the green ribbon, and passed the bundle to Melchior.

Hearing no further objection, Balthazar resumed. "You asked about the forge. There is a sect among the Yehudim, called the Essenes. Ever hear of them?"

Elderchild replied, "No, Master, I have not."

"There's really no reason you would have. Are you familiar with the mustard plant?"

"Yes, Master. It is harvested in the north, near my hometown."

"How would you describe a mustard plant?"

"Master, the mustard plant is a grass or a stalk. Much like wheat, but with bright yellow blossoms."

"The Essenes claim from the proper forge, the tiniest of seeds can become not the slender, fragile stalk we expect, but a giant tree, dwarfing all other trees. An enormous network of branches where birds can build nests. Workers can rest in the shade."

The boy nodded, eagerly. "So like the elements in the talisman, the difference is not the seed or the size of the seed, but rather the forge. Where can I find this magnificent forge?"

"Nearer than you might imagine. Continue to apply yourself. Listen to and respect Grand Master Gaspar. Study the stars. Measure and record everything. Eventually you might realize you have known the answer all along."

Elderchild sensed his instruction was over. He bowed deeply, and disappeared to his nightly responsibilities.

Balthazar picked up the talisman. He combined the ends of the strap with a simple knot and draped the loop over his neck. "This will keep me safe enough, even across the desert. Our three gifts will be mine, for a while, before they are his."

"Send me a dove from Babylon, Master. And another from Damascus. We have birds in both locations. We will know that you crossed the frontier, safely."

Balthazar stood and embraced first Gaspar, then Melchior in silent farewell. He followed the warm stone passage to his customary chamber. The servants provided the two skins of water requested the previous sunrise. He draped them over his left shoulder, one sloshing sack hanging cool on his chest and the other down his back. The old stargazer collected his walking staff, extra sandals, and a leather bag almost too heavy with smoked fish and dried fruit.

The great lens was rolled from storage as Balthazar descended the blackest stairway of the ziggurat. *I have a haunting feeling I am standing here for the last time.* The wizened seer knelt to kiss the lowest step. Weighted with supplies and the immensity of the journey ahead, he stood slowly and deliberately, assisted by his walking stick. Balthazar disappeared into darkness. He began tracking the soft gurgle of the Euphrates, north toward Babylon.

IV, VII
Rubies on the Road to Yafo

Lucanus scouted ahead, and wondered. Eli's departure from Yerushalayim was earlier, and hastier, than anticipated. In some sense, it seemed like a retreat. Eli's family and key servants gathered horses and wagons hours before the first meal. Several of the staff remained behind, as Tadeo's family would remain in Eli's apartments until the conclusion of Tabernacles. Eli's explanation involved "urgent business in Caesarea". If that were truly the case, Lord Eli, and perhaps his son, could return horseback to Caesarea in a single day's hard ride. The wagons would require two full, slow, days, tracing the shoreline of Mare Nostrum.

Recent experience with the Zealots inspired Eli to choose a more prudent return route. The coastal road from Yafo to Caesarea was the safest choice; more Roman patrols and fewer bandits.

There was sudden secrecy surrounding Miriam. They hustled her into a fully enclosed cart. Hertzelah and Yasminah shielded her with a yards of yellow silk as she walked quickly and silently from her apartment to their conveyance. What prompted Eli to conceal his daughter? If her handmaidens knew anything, Festus should be able to coax the information from Yasminah. Festus would at least enjoy the attempt.

Moravius ordered Lucanus to ride the road from Yerushalayim to Yafo. "If you see anything that looks like an ambush, don't engage. Turn around and warn us. By the time you reach Yafo, we will be a few hours behind. Get a fresh mount from the Procurator's barracks at Yafo, then ride back to join us. We will spend the night as guests of the Procurator. Festus will ride scout tomorrow."

Lucanus heeled his mount through Yafo Gate, narrow and set at a protruding right angle to the city wall. The 90-degree bend in the gate provided security against invaders. It also spooked livestock.

There was no exit visible when entering the inner gate. Stubborn pack animals, like donkeys and camels, often balked. Traffic often backed up as cursing merchants pushed, pulled, and whipped their beasts of burden through the awkward opening. Caravans from Mare Nostrum were known to take alternate routes to enter the city. Traders nicknamed the unwieldy entrance, "The Eye of a Needle".

The road was uncrowded at this early hour. After Caesarea, Yafo was the Empire's most significant port in Palestine. Trade goods bound for Yerushalayim swapped piers with lumber needed in Rome. Trading caravans tracing the spice and silk roads from Parthia, Bactria and beyond wholesaled their treasures to Roman agents on the shore of Mare Nostrum. The stew of languages, cultures, faiths, and traditions that brewed in the Yehudi inns and Roman brothels of Yafo was eclipsed only by the diversity of Yerushalayim. The colorful cultural contrasts and perpetual chaos often surged along the terrestrial artery between Yerushalayim and her port.

Lucanus noticed swirling dust in the Valley of Gihon. There should be horses, or camels, or sheep nearby to create such a cloud. There were not. In the two years since Lucanus last rode between Yerushalayim and Yafo, woodcutters spread the tree lines on either side of the road. Eli's scout heard the chunking axes. Trees groaned in protest as they capitulated to gravity. Whips cracked and carters shouted commands to obstinate donkeys. The sounds originated much farther up the hillsides than Lucanus remembered. That was good. The road was still within an arrow's flight, especially from altitude, but the clear cuts reduced the risk of close quarter ambush.

The dust continued. Lucanus wiped his lips, but still the spectral shade of human mud flavored every swallow. The stallion blinked repeatedly, shaking his head, snorting, and flicking his ears to protest the gritty atmosphere. Stoic faces on an opposing route momentarily emerged. They were similarly annoyed with the dust, disinclined to exchange greetings, and quickly enveloped by the brown and yellow miasma.

Two hours west of Yerushalayim, a solitary tree remained along the roadside. Lucanus dismounted. A few minutes of rest would be beneficial. Lucanus closed his eyes, promising himself it was only for a moment. He awoke as his stallion whinnied and reared. Lucanus rushed to grab a handful of saddle and mane. The horse broke free and ran back toward Yerushalayim. The dismounted Legionnaire instinctively reached for his sword.

Was he still dreaming? Coiled in the center of the roadway was a gargantuan serpent. Never had Lucanus seen its like. Not in Rome, nor in Thracia, and certainly nowhere in Palestine. Nothing ever this large. Nothing this colorful. The scales were larger than the hand of a child. Every surface surrounding the snake was the same ashen beige aswirl throughout the atmosphere, but the ophidian was unaffected. His skin was vividly green, brilliant blue, and daringly yellow and orange.

The nostriled head was as large as a goat. Bolts of crackling flame coruscated in the eye slits. A crimson ruby, larger than a pomegranate and translucent as a summer sky, lodged between the curved fangs and the distended lower jaw. Lucanus swore he heard laughter in the wind as the snake swerved it head, and the gem, slowly back and forth above its coils. With a single, well considered stroke Lucanus could slay the monster and claim the prize. But perhaps this was no ordinary snake. Perhaps the ruby an illusion. There was a possibility his blade might have no effect. Lucanus hesitated. The serpent did not.

Slowly, intentionally, and without any suggestion of fear the behemoth stretched its horrifying head toward Lucanus. The veteran was distracted by the odors, or lack thereof. The serpent's breath smelled of incense, or perhaps spiced honey wine in an autumn orchard. Transfixed, Lucanus could not find the will, or the courage to raise his sword.

The ruby was only inches from the eyes of Lucanus. He stared into the red and purple depths. The surface of the stone fogged over for an instant. When it cleared again, Lucanus beheld his own reflection, permanently etched onto the gem. Laughter on the wind again, but louder this time. Much, much, louder.

In the shroud of amber dust, Lucanus was uncertain whether the snake slithered away, or simply vanished. Within moments, the dust settled. The atmospheric clarity seemed pristine, perhaps virginal. Lucanus was covered with a layer of soil, without his horse, and amazed by what he had seen. Or, did he see it?

Lucanus had no memory of sitting again at the base of the tree, yet there he was.

The old veteran considered his options. Without a horse, he would be unable to continue effective scouting. If Eli and his party encountered the empty horse along the road to Yafo, they could become unnecessarily alarmed. Decades of discipline dictated that he should continue his assigned mission, but how?

A voice called from behind Lucanus, from the direction of Yerushalayim. "Hello, there!"

Lucanus turned to behold a young rabbi, leading his fugitive stallion. The animal walked docilely on the bridle, clearly calm and relaxed.

"I caught him before he got very far. Something must have spooked him badly, but I think you'll find he's alright now. What happened?"

Lucanus walked to meet the rabbi's approach. "There was an enormous snake in the road. We didn't see it until we were right up on it. There was too much dust in the air."

"Really? I wasn't that far behind you. I didn't notice any dust. None at all. But now that you mention it, you're as grimy as a Bedouin. Funny, isn't it, how things can be so localized? Almost personalized, sometimes."

Lucanus mounted his horse. "I suppose you could call it funny. Here's a coin. A token of appreciation for recovering my horse."

The Rabbi waved off the reward. "Keep it. You will see a beggar outside the gates of Yafo. Give him the coin. He needs it, more than I. I don't deal much with gold and silver, in any event. I trade in gemstones. Rubies, mostly."

Lucanus heeled his horse forward. He found the Rabbi's remark about rubies rather unsettling. Lucanus scouted ahead, and wondered.

IV, VIII
Yellow Silk and the Family Name

Miriam wept. It was too hot in her cart, rigged with a temporary canopy and draped. Eli ordered her to remain concealed until they reached Yafo. Deprived of a breeze, the air was hot. This tumbril, purchased hastily in Yerushalayim, must once have belonged to a tanner. Sweeping and scrubbing have little effect when the stench has penetrated the wood. Eli ordered her confined behind the drapes. She was not to emerge until arrival at the Procreators estate at Yafo. Miriam, accompanied by her hand maidens, was hauled like embarrassing cargo. No one would suspect that any member of Eli's family rumbled along in the baggage train. "It's for security," said Eli. "Miriam may be in some danger."

In the stale, odiferous, roasting shade, Yasminah sat cross legged in front of Miriam. Yasminah gently held her mistress' hands. Miriam leaned to put her head on Hertzelah's shoulder. Hertzelah softly stroked her hair. Still, more from distress than discomfort, Miriam wept. Despite the sisterly attention and affection, Miriam wept.

Only a few miles beyond the gates, at Amasa, emotional exhaustion dried the tears. Miriam slept. Hertzelah and Yasminah laid her gently on some soft bundles. Gently, tenderly, and carefully to cushion her against the effects of an unsprung axle telegraphing the texture of the old Yehudi trail.

Yasminah took a tiny sip of spiced wine, and handed the skin to Hertzelah. "Once we reach Yafo, we will be on the Via Maris all the way home. The Romans worship lesser gods, but they build better roads."

Hertzelah put some wine on a cloth and pressed it to Miriam's dry lips. Her mistress did not awake. "You don't think Lord Eli will make us ride in this stinking cart a second day, do you? Wasn't this supposed to be about keeping Miriam's location a secret?"

"More secret her condition, than her presence, in my opinion. How do you think she managed?"

Hertzelah giggled. "Managed to get pregnant? That's been done in the same way since the beginning…"

Yasminah interrupted. "No, silly. Managed to keep it from us. We spend more time with her than anyone else. Did she seem pregnant, to you, before we went to Ain Karim? Not to me. Not at all. And who? Nobody seems that likely, especially when she's supposed to be in the fourth month."

Hertzelah shrugged. "I couldn't guess the father. The young Roman has been gone too long. She does a poor job hiding her feelings for that tile setter, but he's much too recently arrived. Faramond? He would have to take her by force- even if they were married. Praise The One God, at least that's out of the question now."

Yasminah nodded. "But we don't really know where she went all those nights when she sneaked out from Caesarea. Perhaps she had a secret lover. Some gorgeous man, down at the port. Maybe from some exotic nation."

Hertzelah moistened Miriam's lips, again. "Yasminah, the romantic. I'm hurt that she kept this secret. And I think the father might be somebody important. Remember what she said when we first asked her about it?"

"Yes, that she dares not name the father."

Hertzelah tapped the air with her index finger. "Exactly. Not that she could not name the father. That she dares not. Maybe she's at risk from the father. Maybe that's why Eli left Yerushalayim so quickly. But who does Lord Eli have to fear?"

One wheel dropped into hole. The cart rocked, brutally. Miriam awoke with a moan. Hertzelah and Yasminah assisted her return to a sitting position.

Miriam stretched her arms. "I need to relieve myself."

Yasminah pulled a pot from the corner. "Here. I'll ask the person leading the donkey to stop, so the cart doesn't rock around."

Miriam waved off the pot. "No. I'm going to do it outside if I can. Let's crack back the curtain and see where we're at. Let's hope we're not in the middle of some village."

"Nothing on this side," reported Hertzelah. "There are some woodcutters, up toward the top of the hill. They are too far away to see anything, especially if we hold up some of that yellow silk."

Yasminah grumbled. "Yellow silk. Well, that won't give anybody any idea what might be going on now, will it?"

Miriam stretched the seam in the draping. The fresher, cooler air spilled in like a blessing. Yes, it was time to get out of the cart, and for a totally defensible reason. Miriam noted a group of mounds, no more than a dozen steps from the road. They resembled giant fistfuls of soil, similar in size but random in shape. They were tall enough to conceal a squatting woman from prying eyes. There were woodcutters on her side as well, but none directly opposite the road.

Yasminah ordered the cart stopped. Festus, riding guard in the rear of the caravan, spurred his horse forward to investigate. "What's wrong, why have you stopped?"

Yasminah responded. "Lady Miriam needs a private moment. Go around us. We can catch up."

"Lord Eli would have me flogged if I left you behind. We will wait. Be quick about it, please."

"Well, the quicker you give us some privacy, the faster we'll be back on the road."

Festus remembered his duty. "Where do you plan to take her?"

"Over there, on the far side of those dirt piles."

"Wait. We can't see the other side. I will ride over first, then I'll ride off so you bring Lady Miriam after I tell you it's safe."

Miriam scolded. "You can be such an old woman, Festus. Look how close they are to the road! You also need to be quick about it. I can't hold much longer."

Festus reined his mount away from the road. Miriam, Hertzelah, and Yasminah did not wait as instructed. They were only a few steps behind when Festus raised the alarm.

"Get back! Get back! Get back in the cart! Get back now!"

Festus dismounted. He drew his sword, and backed up. He stood between the women and the mounds of dirt- as if to defend a retreat. Miriam and her hand maidens scrambled up the wheel and back through the curtain.

Miriam lost her bladder as Festus held his ground. He shouted. "Everybody, keep going up the road. Catch up with the rest. Don't stop. Don't slow down. Go, now!"

The rear section of the caravan advanced. When the final cart was a spear's throw away, Festus mounted his nervous horse and rode forward to check on Miriam. He came up on the tumbril, and called through the draping.

"Is everyone alright?"

Miriam poked her head through the curtains. "Yes, but what was that about?"

"Snake den. There must have been a thousand baby snakes. And there were bones. A donkey, a sheep, and what might have been part of a camel, or a person."

"Snakes? Perhaps a thousand? It's usually very easy to smell out a snake den. The stench from the musk glands of just a few snakes will gag a buzzard. But from a thousand? I didn't smell anything, except this miserable cart, of course. And how do baby snakes drag sheep and donkeys into a den?"

"I don't think the babies dragged anything. There was a wide, flat track. At first I thought it was from the woodcutters, dragging a log.

Then, I noticed it swerved, like a serpent. If a snake laid that, it would be the largest viper anybody ever saw."

Yasminah's head emerged, just below Miriam's. She smiled. "Thank you Festus. That was brave of you to stand guard until we got away."

The forward portion of the caravan slowed to allow the stragglers to close the gap. Festus bowed slightly to Lady Miriam, then turned his horse to resume his position guarding the rear. "I for one will be glad to see Yafo this afternoon. There's some sort of curse on a country that breeds odorless snakes."

Aban broke off riding with his father and Moravius at the head of the column. He walked his horse against the flow, until he came upon Miriam's humble cart in the baggage section. "Yasminah, Hertzelah. Are you both in there?"

Hertzelah leaned out through the curtain. "Yes, we are."

"Get out and walk for a while, please. I need to speak to my sister, privately."

The donkey leader stopped the cart.

Yasminah stepped down first. "Shall I walk your horse, Lord Aban?"

"I can tie the horse to the cart."

"Of course, sir. But Lord Eli says we are protecting Lady Miriam from enemies. Would your horse look conspicuous, hooked to a baggage cart? Perhaps if I walked your horse next to Festus, riding rear guard…"

Miriam's brother winked. "Fine, then. Walk with Festus."

Hertzelah emerged with energetic delicacy. Her sandals gracefully tapping the hub of the axle as she seemingly floated to the ground. She smiled and bowed, very slightly, and went forward to help lead the donkey.

Aban clambered up the wheel and over the side of the cart. Upon his order to continue, the after portion of the caravan rolled along the road to Yafo.

Miriam sat in a corner, leaning against a roll of linen. She waved a frond of silk, gathered into a handle of pearls and gold wire, to fan away insects and heat. She greeted her brother with bright eyes and a weary smile. "Have you come to ride with the outcast?"

Aban experimented with squatting, rather than committing to an actual seat in the old tanner's wagon. The cart lurched across a hole in the road, throwing Miriam's brother off balance. He perched decisively, and directly, beside his sister.

Aban laid a hand gently on Miriam's forearm. "Everything happened so fast. We haven't had a chance to talk at all. Simeon warned Father that Hiram of Dothan was likely to denounce you as a witch. Some say that Faramond is healed. That you did it. Simeon suggested we get you out of Yerushalayim. Not a bad idea, anyway-considering what Father just told me about your condition."

"Condition?"

Aban reestablished his gentle grasp. "Pregnant. Four months pregnant. That condition."

Miriam removed her brother's hand. "It's not a condition. It's a gift. In fact, it's an honor."

Aban choked down his astonishment. "An honor? You're unmarried. Not even betrothed. It's as opposite honor as you can get."

Miriam crossed her arms, pulling away from her brother's grasp. "You don't understand."

"Understand? Miriam? What I don't understand is who, exactly. You have been watched so carefully. Four months ago? Unless it was a complete stranger, it had to be Yetro. I followed you enough times. I thought he was involved with your friend Nora."

"He is with Nora. Or at least he was before he was arrested. It wasn't Yetro."

Miriam's twin exhaled loudly and shook his head. "Father was right. He said you refuse to name the father."

Miriam shoved Aban to almost an arm's length. She clenched her fists, and pounded them into his chest. "You're too predictable! You haven't bothered to ask anything about me! Nothing at all! No, 'how are you feeling, Miriam?'. No 'what can I do to support you right now?' All you want to know is who dared disgrace the family name."

Aban gripped Miriam's fists. "I know very well who disgraced the family name. Father wants to send you to Rome. I would miss you. It would be better if you stayed. If you will name the father, perhaps we can claim you were secretly wed by a rabbi, a sufficient number of months ago. Nobody will have any problem believing you would defy your father. We can make use of Yetro's name, should anybody ask about a rabbi bold enough to wed outside of tradition."

The caravan stopped. Voices shouted in the vanguard. Aban leapt up. "Sounds like trouble. One of the leading carts broken down. I've got to get back up front with Father and Moravius."

Aban backed out through the curtain. "We will talk more. I can't approve of what you did. But you're my twin sister. I still love you. None of your outrageous antics will ever change that. I see now, I should have said that first."

Her brother was gone. Miriam pondered his last statement, and smiled.

PART V

V, I
Ambush of the King

Woodcutters. Along the road from Sephora to Mt. Carmel, Duriel and fifty Zealots were disguised as woodcutters. For two days, they hauled timber to the roadside. The aromatic stands of pitch-fresh cedar and sycamore lay parallel to the road. There were a thousand similar stacks in Galilee awaiting transport. King Herod and his Roman escort would have no reason to suspect the ambush.

Across the road, a dozen Zealot shepherds tended a ragged flock between the King's road and the tree line. Fifty archers milled among the animals, ready to crouch out of sight.

Herod's scouts would be overconfident. It was as if the King's authority bestowed invincibility, rather than hostility. As Herod's scouts crested the hill and followed the curve to the left, the main column would be out of sight. The Zealots planned to remain concealed, among the sheep and behind the timber, until the scouts were beyond their trap and Herod's column hard abreast.

Three blasts from a shepherd's horn. It was a common and meaningless sound to Herod and the Romans. Duriel heard the lookout's signal. In another 100 yards, the scouts would be able to see the sheep. The archers crouched, belly down, in the primal dirt and the fresh manure- moving slowly to avoid spooking the flock.

Duriel and two lieutenants continued stacking wood. Forty-eight Zealots laid in ambush, concealed behind the timber. Swords and spears, but no shields, were at ready hand. Duriel ordered, "No shields. They would only slow us down. Stay behind the wood piles until the archers loose two flights. The sheep will panic, and confound the Roman horses. The Roman column will address the archers, and then we will attack from behind. But we must be quick. Archers are no match for mounted Legionnaires."

Two scouts approached in syncopated trot. One an old veteran with scarred limbs and the eyes of a suspicious hawk. The other was much younger, but of higher rank. The visible woodcutters and shepherds faced the road, and bowed very slightly.

The scouts reined in. The veteran called out, "Keep those sheep off the road, King Herod approaches. Show him his due respect!"

The shepherd nearest the road grasped his staff for support and rested on one knee. "As you command sir. His due respect."

Both scouts heeled their horses along the road. Duriel was pleased. The situation was unfolding as planned. After only a few yards, the younger Romans pulled up short. He rode toward the shepherds. "In fact, we'll take a lamb for supper. Let me select one. You can kill it before the King's column arrives."

Duriel caught his breath. One of his shepherds answered, "No need to trouble yourself, sir. I know which will be the tastiest young lamb. I will slit its throat this minute. It will be well bled before Herod's supply train passes by."

The scout turned his horse to resume his ride along the road. "See that you do, and be quick about it!"

The younger scout caught up to the old veteran. "I got some fresh lamb for dinner."

The elder Legionnaire stopped his horse. "Don't turn around. Something's wrong."

"What could be wrong?"

"We're in Galilee, aren't we?"

The young scout pressed impatiently. "I don't see what that has to do with…oh, wait! By Zeus! We're in Galilee, but that shepherd! He speaks with the tongue of one from Yerushalayim."

The older scout nodded. "He does. We're on notice to watch for Zealots from the south posing as shepherds in Galilee."

"Then, on my command let's wheel and run the shepherds down.

There are only a handful." The young officer put a hand on his sword. The older veteran leaned and reached to grab his hand before the blade cleared the scabbard.

"No, sir. We should not. We could handle twelve shepherds, if shepherds they are. Twelve armed Zealots would be less certain. There may be more hiding nearby. There may be many more. Don't forget, our mission is to protect the King. We have reason to suspect an ambush. Our duty is to warn the Centurion."

"Take your hand off my wrist! On my command.... now, charge!!"

The scouts galloped toward the shepherds, steel drawn. The sheep panicked. Fifty archers covered in primordial mud and fresh manure rose in response. Fifty arrows sailed, and many found a mark. The scouts were swept from their saddles. One horse died instantly, while the other ran through the ambush and back to Herod's column. Arrows protruded from the neck, ribs, and rump.

Upon Duriel's signal, the Zealots all fled into the woods. Marshalling surprise, there was a high probability of victory. Duriel's Zealots were no match for an equal number of Legionnaires under disciplined command.

Herod's Centurion ordered the King's column to a halt. One badly wounded horse, and no sign of a rider. There must be an ambush ahead. Without a scout, there was no way to know whether there were four in ambush, forty, or four hundred. On this road, on this day, his mission was to protect the King.

Herod bawled from his gilded pettoritum, "Why have we stopped?"

The Centurion rode to Herod's carriage window and bowed. "Your majesty, it looks like there's an ambush ahead and they took down both of our scouts. Judging by the number of arrows in the horse that managed to escape? I think there might be a large force ahead of us. We may be riding into a trap. I can't recommend we continue."

"Why can't you march up there and clear them. Surely the local rabble are no match for the Legion. Not in a fair fight, where you aren't taken by surprise."

"Your Highness, the Emperor himself commands me to keep you safe. If there were no risk to your person, we would go up this hill and engage."

"Fair enough. Your record speaks for itself. You're no coward. What do you recommend? Shall we return to Sephora?"

The Centurion passed his thumb below his lower lip. "I suspect they may have another ambush in place behind us, somewhere between here and Sephora, just in case we did turn back. No, we need to do something unpredictable. Only a quarter mile behind us a road branches off. I think we can make that quarter mile, and once we do we should take the other route."

"Does it take us to Mount Carmel?"

"Eventually, Your Highness. But by way of Caesarea. There's a small garrison there. We can resupply."

"Fine, then. By way of Caesarea. I can impose on Eli's hospitality if you think it wise to wait for reinforcements from Mount Carmel."

V, II
Enriched by What is Given Away

Bedlam subsided as Eli's edifice arose. Arcades of arched and crested columns, topped with proud parapets and supported on polished marble bases, defined three sides of a square. Obligatory relief carvings depicting the Emperor's military triumphs hovered high above, chiseled into the tympanum. Shimon the Master Builder paid off the Tektons working in stone. The workers departed for Damascus, Alexandria, Yerushalayim, and Nubia. A coarse, cyclonic dust laced with quicklime lurked commeasurably among sunlight and shadow.

Perimeter beryl pools and sapphire fountains rippled and gurgled softly. Relentlessly repeating ancient secrets in a virgin hall. Shimon paid off the plumbarii. Workers of lead returned to Nicomedia, Galatia, and Tarsus.

The gardens were a gift from Augustus. Hedges of assertive briar, effusive hibiscus, purple broad leaf castor, and eruptive oleander instilled blush and bouquet. Winds raked perfumed pollen from polychrome blossoms. Tentative birds explored the sylvan snags and twiggy tangles. Shimon dismissed the Emperor's workmen. The gardeners walked down to the wharf to exercise an Imperial warrant and claim passage on the next ship to Rome.

Smooth cedar panels lined each apartment. Every breath became a celebration. Cedar and sycamore jambs and lintels framed the hatch work lattice from which criss cross shadows swept the floor. Pith and pulp black beams encased, in a resin dissolved in the oil of terebinth. Tekton shapers and joiners who worked with wood, accepted payment from the Master Builder, gathered their tools and departed.

Like a chain of ants hauling dew drops and honey, the carters ferried furnishings and provisions from the maritime warehouses to the grand home newly built for Eli's son and his betrothed.

In the exact center of it all, Yusufs mazzeroth remained concealed behind the partition. It was the morning of the third day. Shimon, trailed by two scrambling scribes, swept down from the disassembly of his booth. For the second time, he presumed to part the curtains concealing the heavens. For the second time, Shimon beheld the universe and saw only what he most wanted to see.

The Master Builder cleared his throat. "I'm shocked. You said the two of you would create this in three days. It looks like you have done so. Am I right? Aren't you polishing off the final grouting."

Yusuf of Nazareth and the Rabbi rose from hands and knees to acknowledge Shimon. Yusuf made a sweeping gesture across the virtually completed work. "You are right, Master Builder. Everything will be finished in three days, as promised."

Shimon pointed. The Rabbi and the Nazarene laid a central sun, surrounded by the twelve houses of the heavens. Each house represented a tribe of Yehudim, descended from the sons of Yakob. As before, Shimon instead saw a dual portrait of Eli and his son, surrounded by geometric patterns and quail. "I will admit that I was wrong. I was sure your choice of such common materials would spoil the overall result. If anything, it improves it. The tiles work together, don't they? Each piece is the sum of itself and everything immediately next. Somehow, there's a gleam to the overall effect. Very clever, tile setter. Your results exceed the quality of materials used. Eli should be pleased."

The Nazarene and the Rabbi bowed. "Thank you, Master Builder."

"How soon can we get this partition down? There were two riders this morning. Eli and his family return from Yerushalayim. They were in Yafo last night. They will be here before sundown. King Herod approaches from the Northeast. We weren't expecting the king, but it will be well to have everything completed before his arrival."

The Rabbi replied, "Three days, Master Builder. While it looks as though we are almost finished, and we are, we will require the entire third day upon which we agreed. Why not leave the partition up until Eli and Herod have each arrived? You could preside over a grand unveiling. It will be a moment that should bring a Master Builder great honor. If you are to be honored, how better than in the presence of Herod himself?"

A smile bloomed across Shimon's customarily sour countenance. "Honored? Why, yes of course." He turned to his scribes. "Lay some better fabric over this crude partition. Prepare for a grand reveal!"

Shimon stepped away to leave, then retraced his steps in afterthought. "Tile setter, will you be returning to Herod's service, now that your task is completed here?"

"I labor at Lord Eli's pleasure. Who can say what that will be? The One God has a plan for all of us."

Shimon stepped back through the partition, leaving the heavens to the Nazarene and the Rabbi.

"How do you do that, Rabbi? You explained your gift is helping others see what they most want to see, but Shimon sees the same illusion every time. Is it because his desires have not changed? And what if they did? Would he notice a difference in the illusion?"

The Rabbi knelt somewhere in the house of Zebulon. He balled up a coarse cloth and polished a film of grit from the faces of fired clay tiles. "Lust knows no history. It lives only in the present moment. It rewrites the map of memory as required. Had Shimon now perceived an image of Leviathan swallowing Jonah, he would be certain it was exactly what he remembered it to be."

Yusuf chased specks of grit from the house of Ruben. "I get the sense that if the Master Builder is ever undone, he will be victim to his own greed and ambition."

"Yes. Take note. We are destroyed by whatever we choose to keep. Strengthened only by that which we give away."

They worked without speaking, polishing the heavens. The Rabbi lingered over his inserts defining the planets on the upcoming Nisan 5, when their positions relative to the sun formed the Seal of Solomon and the Star of David. Although Eli condemned heliocentric cosmologies, he, like Shimon, would behold the mazzeroth and see only what he most wanted to see.

The Rabbi touched the shoulder of Yusuf of Nazareth. "Let's say this is finished."

"But, there is still more polishing to do."

The Rabbi nodded. "There will always be more polishing required. We will finish with a blessing instead. The results will be the same, if not better. Come join me in the middle."

The Nazarene tekton and the Rabbi knelt in the center of the heavens. The rabbi extended his arms, palms up. "Grab my wrists. I'll grab yours as well. We will align our energies for the blessing."

The two men reached across the sun.

The Rabbi spoke. "Before I call down a blessing you should know I will be gone before either Herod or Eli arrive. The One God has a plan for us all. You have a role to play. For the rest of the day, for the rest of your life, be bold and live without fear. A great treasure may be yours."

"Great treasure, rabbi? Is that desirable? If we are destroyed by what we keep, and strengthened by what we give away?"

"Sometimes the opportunity and the will to give, without condition, can be the greatest treasure of all. Now, close your eyes for the blessing. Abba Disnya, yithqadash sh'mk. Tethe malkuthak, tehwey ra-uthak. Pitthan d-coark, hav lana yomden. Wa shubuq lan hobenen, hek anan shbaqin l-haibenan. W-la ul lan l-nisyon. H'amen."

Suddenly, the tekton's hand were empty. They grasped no rabbinical wrists. Yusuf opened his eyes. He was alone.

The mazzeroth. Somehow the mazzeroth was not only completed, but slightly changed. The mysterious glow observed from the original placement of the tiles was richer, brighter, and more pronounced. It was as if pure water, or music, were transmuted into light. Stunned by the disappearance of his companion and the transformation of his work, Yusuf sat down and closed his eyes. He noted a bright spot behind the bridge of his nose. As he watched, it expanded. Soon the radiance encompassed the entire area where he imagined his head must be.

Yusuf reflected on something The Rabbi said. "Only The One God knows my true name. Just as only The One God knows yours."

V, III
Into and Out of Egypt

Zadok walked quickly and confidently down the gangplank. His back was erect. He gathered the hem of his freshly laundered robe with one hand, using his ebony Rod of Asclepius for neither balance nor support. The ancient Yehudi priest was well known in Alexandria, but in any living memory he was so crippled to be only marginally mobile. Never so agile. Never so energized. Never had his countenance glowed so brightly. Was he reborn, or merely reinvigorated?

The charred vacancy of the warehouse lay on the far side of the quay. Zadok paused. He remembered the rebellion. He could still smell the smoke. He could hear the screams of scribes daring one too many dashes into the conflagration in a vain attempt to rescue more texts. Most were copies. Zadok shook his head, regretting the waste.

Vendors of trinkets, keepers of harlots, and destitute supplicants clustered on the wharf. Zadok ignored the pleas for coins. A ragged woman squatting against a cask of olive oil cried out, "Mercy, good priest! Spare me a blessing!"

"What troubles you, child of The One God?"

"It's my left ankle. It twisted. I can't stand, so cannot deliver the oil. My master will beat me if he finds me here and my task undone."

Zadok planted the black staff in front of the injured woman. "If you believe you can be healed by prayer, and only if you are willing to pray for me in return, wrap your hand around the Rod of Asclepius."

The woman winced. Shifting her weight enough to grasp the rod put pressure on her injured joint. "I believe. I don't know what I can accomplish, but yes, I will pray for you in return."

"Then close your eyes. Be silent for a moment. The process is short."

Energy jolted through the injured woman's body. Within seconds, the pain in her ankle vanished. She opened her eyes. Zadok was favoring his left leg.

Zadok balanced against the staff. "Now, child. Pray for me. The affliction will be removed from both of us."

"What exactly do I say?"

"It doesn't matter what you say or even how you say it. You don't even need to say it out loud. The One God reads your heart, not your mind. Close your eyes, and ask a blessing in return for me."

Energy bolted through both bodies. The woman arose. Zadok stood confidently, and without pain. "Thank you, priest. How can I ever really thank you?"

"Don't thank me. No more than you thank the wind for carrying birdsong. No more than you thank the riverbed for a drink of cool water. Use your restored ankle and complete your task."

The woman shouldered her cask. Zadok watched her walk away, smiling at the beautiful music of her hips. There had been a time…

Zadok scurried up the low slope to the Great Library. Familiar faces among the crowd were astonished by his nimble gait. "What's come over Zadok?"

Through the outer gate. Into the terraces, fountains, and gardens surrounding the Temple of the Muse. Parting swarms of silent butterflies, inhaling the lavish cologne of floral abundance, appreciating falling water sparkle-speaking every known language at once. Zadok visualized Yetro, and followed the paths where the energies seemed best expressed. The grand master found his renegade priest in a room of modest size and furnishing, meditating among scrolls of prophecy.

"Shalom, Yetro."

The voice, familiar as well as unexpected, startled Yetro. "Master Zadok. I did not expect you. I have honored my expulsion. Why do you seek me now? And what has happened? You're standing, not stooped!"

"The proper voice prayed for me. A voice without expectation. A voice without price. A voice of unconditional gift. In fact, you had much to do with her enlightenment."

"Miriam? It could only be Miriam! What is happening with her? I miss her. How is that you asked her to pray for you?"

"Praying for myself never relieved the burden. Asking others to pray for me brought no relief. The load was too entrenched, too historic, too profound. My burden was lifted by an unconditional gift. I did not ask for her prayer, but I knew she overheard me when I reminded Zachariah that I could not heal myself. I did not know exactly what to expect. Within three days, the pain was gone."

"Praise the One God, Zadok. But why are you here? You have already cast me out from community. There's no more punishment within your power."

"Don't be so certain. But it's promise, not punishment, that brings us together again."

Zadok leaned his ebony staff against a sand colored wall and squatted on a mat, opposite Yetro, with the scrolls of prophecy between. "With all you have been through, and what more you have learned, would you say you are still Essenic?"

"At the root, grand master? Yes. I will always be Essenic. We both know what happened. I could not conform to the small restrictions. I dared allow The One God to whisper secrets in my sleep. We disagreed only on detail, not the fundamentals."

Zadok squeezed his upper lip between thumb and forefinger, then pointed at Yetro. "That's what I needed to hear to proceed. You mentioned Miriam. You will see her again. It's part of the plan."

Yetro brightened. "When will I see Miriam? What plan?"

"There's going to be new age, Yetro. A new covenant. The old truths will change."

"What do you mean, change? Truth cannot be refuted."

Now fully relaxed, Zadok gestured with both hands. "Of course truth cannot be refuted. But it can be expanded. Just as we can expand the number of people who recognize it. We enter the time promised by the Teacher of Righteousness. The war between the Sons of Light and the Sons of Darkness is upon us. But there's a new battlefield. That battlefield is the individual human spirit. We will all be purified as we struggle for righteousness, even if victory is elusive."

"But what has any of this do with me, or with Miriam? Will I return to Galilee? Is she coming to Alexandria? How soon will I see her again?"

Zadok shook a finger to scold. "Your desire is apparent. Put it aside. It's a distraction. Miriam is not destined to be yours. In fact, she's with child, as is Elisheba, the wife of Zachariah."

Yetro was astonished. "Miriam? Isn't she still unmarried? Who's the father? And Zachariah's wife? She's always been barren and now she's far too old!"

Zadok shrugged. "Didn't I tell you the old truths would change?"

"So you did. And there was never a realistic chance for Eli's daughter and a disgraced priest. Not if Eli had anything to say about it. And of course, he does."

"Miriam remains unmarried, for now. The father's name is a secret, for now. Secret as well, I will eventually send Miriam, Elisheba, and their two sons to Alexandria. The Sons of Darkness will try to destroy the infants if they remain in Palestine. You will be charged with their care. That will require a special community."

"A special community?"

"Yes. While I am in Alexandria, I will reach out to Melchizedek of the Therapeuts. We will form an alliance. Protect the infants. Instruct Miriam in the way of the spirit. Melchizedek will pick up where you left off and bring her forward as a healer. She will emerge as one of the most effective healers. She will eventually help instruct her son, who will in turn surpass her."

"Miriam's son will be a healer?"

Zadok nodded. "On many levels."

"Forgive me, Grand Master. Caring for all these people will cost money. I'm a poor man. Is Melchizedek prepared for the expense? I would doubt it. And what about the second child? Is he to be a healer as well?"

"The One God will provide. So will Eli. In the end, he won't turn his back on his daughter or his grandson. He can fund the new community for a year with only a single day's income. Meanwhile, it will be up to you and Melchizedek to prepare a way. Pave a path for the new age. It's why you were cast out, Yetro. It's why you escaped to Alexandria."

"And what of Elisheba, and the other child?"

"Teach the other child the laws and the prophets. Prepare him to be a warrior among the Sons of Light. Elisheba will not long survive. The two cousins will be raised as brothers, by Miriam and her husband. Their initial destinies will be as one."

Yetro initially did not reply. He concentrated on rolling a papyrus scroll, gently tapping flat the ends, and wrapping it with a red silk ribbon. Failing to suppress a tone of bitter disappointment, he asked, "You said she remained unmarried. Who is that husband to be? Who is the father of Miriam's child?"

Zadok rose, gracefully, and picked up his Rod of Asclepius. "You will know the answer to your first question quickly enough. As for the second question? You cannot know the answer until you are prepared to accept it. You cannot accept it before you are prepared to know it."

"I'll do as you say, Zadok. Protect and school the infants, help

Miriam continue her studies. I'll even welcome her husband, whomever that proves to be. As far as that last riddle? You never offered a riddle that didn't lead to enlightenment."

Zadok made a sweeping gesture, palm up, and turned to leave.

Yetro called, "When will I see you next?"

"Whenever I'm in Alexandria. Or, whenever you need me."

V, IV
Unwelcome Guests

Herod. Eli stewed about news that Herod waited at Eli's estate in Caesarea. Interactions with the king were frequent enough. They were also obligatory, cordial, and guarded. Amicable relations with Herod were a political necessity, not a personal joy.

Herod was not invited to Eli's estate. Herod didn't technically need an invitation, but custom and courtesy dictated precedent. The King should not presume to encamp, with a retinue, at the home of any judge of the Sanhedrin. The King should respect Eli's wealth, on par with The King's own. Obviously, Herod did not.

Not only was Herod presumptuously accepting Eli's in-absentia hospitality, his timing was dreadful. The Imperial Diplomatic transport to Rome, the ship guarded by heavily armed galleys, would not sail from Caesarea for nearly a week. Eli loathed the thought of shipping disgraced Miriam to Rome with less security than a full military escort, yet it would be very difficult to keep her condition secret from Herod or the petty spies among his entourage. Herod would find a way to use the information to his advantage. If not right away, then at some time when Eli least expected.

Miriam. Always enough trouble for both twins. If only she would reveal the father's name, and if the man were eligible, Eli could demand a marriage to save her reputation. It was a father's right. Especially a wealthy father's right. Eli teared and sniffed. For all her independence and obstinate delinquencies, he often felt better connected to his willful daughter than his more orthodox son. He would miss her terribly, between his infrequent visits to Rome.

Eli reached a conclusion. He would make a final appeal to Miriam soon after arriving in Caesarea. While he would be required to formally welcome King Herod to his estate very shortly after returning home, it would be possible to keep Miriam temporarily out of sight. "Yes, Excellency. It's a joyous event and we're making final arrangements for a wedding" was far more acceptable than, "Yes Excellency, and sadly enough she refuses to name the father."

Herod, Miriam, and saddle sores. His place was still at the head of the column, flanked by Moravius and Aban. Were it not for custom, expectation, and appearance Eli would rather most days ride in a cart than sit horseback. Were it not for custom, expectation and appearance, perhaps there would be a great deal that Eli might choose to do differently.

V, V
Hawk at the Fountain

Servants wheeled away the final loads of construction debris.

A man arrived with eight live fish in a basket. A wedding gift from the proconsul at Crete. Slow bulbous specimens, splattered with red and white and black and yellow splotches. The aquarist released them in a creamy marble pool beneath a fountain of fiery bronze.

The King took advantage of Eli's absence. He walked through the arcades, the gardens, and the apartments of Eli's addition. In every location, two clerks scampered frantically to opposite corners, measuring for area. A third servant recorded the results. With each calculation, Herod mentally compared Eli's accomplishment to his own new palace at Sephora. Herod was pleased. Eli respected decorum. His structures were slightly smaller in scale than Herod's. The King grudgingly observed they were no less grand.

Like a starving hound, Shimon the master builder followed in Herod's footsteps. The King did not bother to conceal his annoyance, but took advantage of the shadowing Shimon to verify assumptions regarding the materials and techniques employed.

"This curtain around the courtyard, when will it be coming down?"

"If it please Your Highness, we are planning a grand reveal after Lord Eli returns."

Herod grunted. "We could insist on seeing it, of course, but as we've arrived unexpectedly perhaps it will be my pleasure to wait and view it's official unveiling. Let me consider. Do I recall sending Eli a tile setter? Some young man who dared wash his bloody hands in a royal pool?"

Shimon bowed slightly. "Indeed. A young Nazarene and his father."

Herod snickered. "Ah, yes. Lord Eli promised to teach them some respect and discipline. How has that worked out?"

"The father is dead."

"Well then, it would seem Lord Eli was sufficiently instructive. And the son?"

"The young man may have come around. He did a decent job creating a double portrait of Eli and his son."

Herod rolled his eyes. "That's dangerously similar to his work at Sephora. Any of that superstitious nonsense about a graven image?"

"Your excellency?"

"When the Tektons did the courtyard with my portrait there was some grumbling about creating a graven image. Something about contrary to the laws of Moses. We paid, or more likely overpaid, a couple of sympathetic rabbis to persuade them it would be alright, as long as nobody actually *worshipped* the image."

Shimon bowed slightly. "Perhaps the lesson was well learned, Highness. I have seen the courtyard at Sephora. It is stunning. Be assured that what the Nazarene created here barely rivals and certainly does not surpass any similar feature of your palace. Even so, I believe my Lord Eli will be pleased."

"Fair enough, master builder. You are almost as clever with words as you are with labor and materials. We will indulge your whim, and wait for the grand unveiling. It's nearly midday. What does your master keep for wine?"

Shimon bowed and gestured toward the main house. "Allow me to introduce you to the primary steward. I am sure he will show Your Excellency to Lord Eli's reserves."

Herod's group turned to follow Shimon. A circling hawk dove on the fountain pool. The black raptor struggled to rise, with a fat, colorful perch in his talons. Relentless flapping amidst frantic splashing. The bird rose slowly from the chaos, and lifted its oversize prey to a luncheon site on a warm rock not far from the compound walls. Seven fish remained.

V, VI
Healing the Flesh and Blessing with Water

Three nights into the desert. No track or trail interrupted the wind-blown swells of grit brown sand, save one. A cloak supported on a walking stick created Balthazar's customary canopy.

The aged mystic slept naked through the heat of the day, burrowed under a shallow layer of sand. The earth was a partial shield against the merciless solar inferno. Balthazar unconsciously fingered the leather amulet. A pouch containing a single gold coin, a pinch of frankincense, and a sprinkling of myrrh.

Balthazar was not too old or cynical to wonder. Why did he feel so compelled to seek out this magical child, supposedly destined for birth in the spring? Of all the old prophecies circulating among the Yehudim, why had this one resonated so? There was no doubt, the planets aligned to form the Seal of Solomon. It had to be more than a coincidence.

Balthazar realized this was likely his final quest. Some of his learned friends discovered stars and planets. Balthazar hoped to find a child, confirm a prophecy, and additionally validate the order of the heavens. It required courage to test belief and the assumptions considered foundations of knowledge. If he failed to find the child, the prophecy might be false. If the prophecy were false, then perhaps everything Balthazar believed and taught others to be true was in error.

The mage dreamed grand visions of a long-delayed return to Yerushalayim. Sweet Yudea, with fragrant forests, lush meadows, and abundant streams of water. Water so pure that it was invisible. Water that could not itself be seen, only the flaming refractions of ray and rainbow across the ripples of its surface. The One God of the Yehudim. A rabbi among the Essenes once suggested to Balthazar that The One God was like the water of Yudea. Even when it was not possible to see the water, the fertile and cleansing effects were visible in all directions.

If The One God of the Yehudim were actually water, instead of like water, then The One God was absent in the desert. Except for that in the skins, from which Balthazar sipped like a miser.

On this third day in the desert, buried naked in the sand in the shade of his cloak stick canopy, Balthazar was not alone. He was deep in slumber when a lone scorpion skittered across the sand. Each footfall as soft and trackless as a spider scaling slate. Like Balthazar, the scorpion was a creature of the night. Unlike Balthazar, the insect last ate almost a year ago. Something smelled of flesh. Moist flesh. A being still alive, or recently so. It was enough to draw the scorpion up from his burrow. Enough to risk the broil of the sun for a rare opportunity to dine.

The prey was found lying in the surface, and in its own private shadow. Out of the sun, there would be time for the scorpion to inject the paralyzing venom, and then extract liquid nutrients from the flesh. Balthazar slept. The scorpion crept to within inches. The poisonous tail whipped forward, and struck the water bag. The scorpion gnawed patiently on the skin. Vibrations of his feasting awoke fellow arachnids. They blossomed from the sand, attacking the water skins as well. Within an hour, they gnawed pinholes in each bag. Balthazar slept. The water drained. The satiated insect culprits fled.

Deadly hot in the daylight, the desert was uncomfortably cool after dark. Balthazar normally awoke in response to a change in temperature. He rolled to shed the sand from his body and habitually reached for a water skin. Empty! And the other? Empty as well! The sand was still damp below the bags, but Balthazar was now without water.

The mage recalled the star map observed just before bedding down in the morning. It would be three sleeps back to the Euphrates, and three sleeps forward to a known oasis. Three dry sleeps. One sleep was not a problem. The second would be difficult. The third impossible for a man of his age, traveling afoot. Yes, this was definitely his last quest. After a full life, his destiny would be a slow, miserable death in the desert. He should have followed Gaspar's advice, taking the longer route through Damascus.

Balthazar would not wait on death. Perhaps if he increased the tempo of his steps, slightly, he might make the oasis or Euphrates in time. He considered the options, and choose to press forward. Better to die deep in the desert and never be discovered than somewhere near the busy banks of the Euphrates. Better to endure as a mysterious legend than a pathetic old victim.

Roses faded from the western sky. Uncountable silver sparks emerged from the black canvas of the cosmos. Balthazar followed the heavens across the desert, while a soft wind groomed the rolling tops from dunes and whispered secrets to the sand.

Several hours without water, and then, a mirage? A mirage is a feint. A curious gambit promulgated by sunlight. Once, he awoke to view a vast ocean complete with a galley under sail. This mirage was different, beyond the rarity of occurring at night. Another man, walking toward him in the desert, wearing only lightweight garments and carrying no visible provisions.

Balthazar sensed the stranger was probably not a mirage when a voice cried out, "There you are! It's a good thing I found you. It's a long walk to the next oasis. How's your water holding out?"

Balthazar changed course to meet the unexpected fellow traveler. His feet slipped in the sand, He regained his balance by using his staff. "I'm in trouble. The water is gone. Something pierced both skins while I slept. If you have any to spare, I would be indebted to you. Where did you come from?"

"I was recently in Caesarea."

"I meant directly. There are a thousand places between here and Caesarea. You cannot have traveled far. Your robe looks freshly washed. If you carry anything at all, it's beneath your cloak. Is there a town or village nearby? If so, I'm lost. It's very unusual for me to be lost, but I would be thankful for a well."

"You're not lost, Balthazar."

"What? How do you know my name? I don't recognize you at all. Who are you?"

"Me? I am called Elishua, and I am called Ben-gabar. Some call me Gabriel, or Almodad, or Israel. Only The One God knows my true name, it's even secret from myself."

Balthazar fell to his knees. "I recognize some of those names. The Yehudi Talmud claims they are messengers from The One God of the Yehudi. Are you an angel? That would explain a lot."

"Get up off your knees. There's no reason to kneel to me. To keep things simple, call me Rabbi. Most people do. As for whether I am an angel, that isn't important. What's important is healing your water skins, and refilling them. You carry a talisman to Bet L'hem. Gold and frankincense and myrrh."

Balthazar was aghast. He rose so quickly he lost his balance and staggered to the left. "Is there anything you do not know about me or my quest?"

"Your journey is a minor, but very important piece in a plan with universal significance."

"Will I find the child of the prophecies? The despised king?"

"If you persevere. The talisman will prove essential to his future. And it's your long walk to Bet L'hem that empowers the gift. It is in our common interest that you succeed. Now hold out your water skins."

Balthazar unlaced the top of his leather bag containing smoked fish, dried fruit, and the ruined water skins. The Rabbi put the skins between his hands, and rolled them into a ragged ball. "Something chewed through, didn't it? It's a good thing this is sheepskin, it's a simple case of healing the flesh."

"But the sheep is dead! Long dead! How can the flesh be made to heal?"

The Rabbi unwadded the bag. "The sheep lived within and by means of a greater presence that was never born, and cannot die. Look, I believe your water skins are as good as new."

Balthazar turned the skins over, several times. It was as The Rabbi said, the holes were gone.

"I don't know what you just did, but the water skins look fine. Now, if only I had some water."

"Who would be cruel enough to give a brother a water skin, but deny him water in the desert? Are you hanging on tightly to the bags?"

Balthazar nodded.

The Rabbi placed his left hand on Balthazar's forehead. "Brother, your sins are forgiven."

Immediately, the bags were heavy, wet, and cold. There was now a supply more than adequate to sustain Balthazar's journey to the oasis."

Balthazar rejoiced. "I can't believe this! You just created water, out of nothing!"

The Rabbi shook his head in denial. "No, not really. Water is a basic element. Only The One God can create water. The best some of the rest of us can do is move it around a little. Especially someplace where it's needed."

"What can I do to thank you?"

"I'm glad you asked. On your way to Bet L'hem, call on Herod. He will be in Yerushalayim. Tell him you have seen a sign in the heavens. Ask for his help locating a newly born baby, destined to be King of the Yehudim."

Balthazar laced up his bag. "There's something going on here that I don't comprehend. Why would I ask Herod where to find the child, when we already know he will be born in Bet L'hem?"

The Rabbi laughed softly. "Perhaps because we gave you water? And because more than a long walk is required to empower the talisman."

Before Balthazar could respond, The Rabbi shimmered with waves of distorted light. He was momentarily transparent, then evaporated progressively from head to foot. It had, after all, been a mirage! Balthazar panicked, but only for a moment. There, next to his leather bag, were the waterskins, cool, and moist, and full.

PART VI

VI, I
Consigned to Augustus

Eli's caravan stopped, just beyond sight from Caesarea. The patriarch rode back to survey the line. The day's march cast a smudge. The livestock were tired, wheels dirty, and canopies dusty. Gaps were raggedly uneven. Most of the time, none of this would matter. Today, King Herod waited at Caesarea. It would be a matter of honor. Eli's retinue must arrive with discipline, and with flourish.

Eli dismounted outside the cart in which rode Miriam and her attendants. "Hertzelah, Yasminah, carry some of this silk up forward. Moravius will drape it from a pike and create a banner. Everyone else will be cleaning and repositioning. Help where you can. I need a few minutes to speak with Miriam."

Miriam's handmaidens clambered down the wheel, their dainty sandals landing silently in the mustard colored dist. They bowed slightly, then backed away with a bundle of yellow silk. Eli began climbing into the cart.

Miriam said, "I need to get out of this cart and stretch my legs. Why don't we talk outside?"

Eli surveyed the vicinity. The woodcutters were halfway up the nearest hill, with a wide clearing left behind. There was enough space to the right side of the road to create privacy for quiet conversation. He nodded, and extended a hand with which to assist Miriam's descent down the cartwheel.

Eli was puzzled by Miriam's smile. Despite her scandalous predicament, she seemed almost radiant. At peace with herself and her situation. Miriam was always the first to test every boundary and the most reluctant to be satisfied with common reality. Now she was more relaxed, and if possible even more self-confident.

A short walk off the road, Miriam asked, "So, father, are you still planning to banish me to Rome?"

Eli cleared his throat. "You leave me no choice. You aren't the first unmarried Yehudi girl to be pregnant before marriage. It's embarrassing, of course, but we normally arrange a quick marriage with the father. That's socially accepted, even if outside a strict reading of the Law. If you refuse to name the father, you can't remain in Yudea or in Galilee. You need to disappear, among the gentiles."

Miriam looked tenderly upon Eli. "You are so certain that if I named the father, everything could be worked out. I would name the father if that were so. It's more complicated than that."

"Only if the father is married. Even if you won't reveal his name, please tell me that he isn't married. Nearly every time I sit my term with the Sanhedrin we order some woman stoned to death for adultery. Lying with a man before marriage is a sin. Lying with a married man is a crime."

Miriam frowned and shook her head. "Only for the woman. A woman caught in adultery is condemned to death. The married man is subject only to humiliation, and a fine payable to the temple."

Eli thumbed his beard and stared at the ground. "You act as if that is unfair. The man usually has a family. The woman tempts him to shirk his duties to them. He shames his family with his sin. Why punish them twice by removing their provider? I ask again, is he married?"

"He has no wife."

Eli chuckled with resignation. "With you, it's always the puzzle. Never a simple yes or no. I will accept 'he has no wife' to mean he is not married. In that case, name him. Does he even know you're pregnant? He might be eager to fulfill his responsibilities."

"Father, the responsibility is mine."

Eli choked up, suppressing and then abandoning anger... He failed to suppress his tears. "Please, daughter, it will break my heart to send you away. I would miss you. I yearn to know my grandchild. Give me a name. I swear on the memory of your mother that I will excuse you from any consequences. Shelter you from any gossip. Defend you against any wild charges Faramond's father or anyone else tries to bring. I will provide a generous dowry, enough to sustain you for a lifetime. Please. All I ask is a name. That will set everything right."

Miriam cried as well. "Nothing will be set right. This is more complicated."

Eli waved his hands in frustration. "Complicated how? In the normal order of things, a man has a wedding and then receives a virgin bride. As it is, the father has received the virgin bride, and is therefore obligated to the wedding. We make reluctant exceptions for this reverse order. We always have. It's been the way of our people for countless generations."

Miriam hesitated to respond, carefully considering the amount she was prepared to risk. She crossed her arms, and wiped her cheeks with a thumb and forefinger. "Father, what if I could still be someone's virgin bride?"

Eli was shocked, and aghast. "What!?"

"What if despite being with child, I am still a virgin? Have me examined, if you like. I can't actually explain…"

Eli interrupted, alarmed. "And don't even try. I turn a deaf ear to rumors. There are some people, jealous of my wealth, who would bring me down by accusing my daughter of witchcraft. Such a wild tale plays right into their hands. No child is ever born to a virgin. Never say that again, to anyone. My enemies would bring you to judgment. You might even destroy us all."

Miriam balled up her fists and wept with frustration. "Are you forgetting about Isaiah? About the prophecy?"

Eli recoiled with panic. He glanced jerkily in every direction to ensure that nobody was close enough to hear Miriam's remark about Isaiah. "Blasphemy! My own daughter condemns herself. If we were in court, I would have no choice. I would have you put to death. We're not in court. My other choice is to send you to Augustus. You refuse to name the father. Let's get you out of Palestine while I still have both choices."

Eli grasped his daughter's hand and dragged her, more than led her, back to the cart. The line of march was reshaped. Moravius rigged a banner. An orderly, if not entirely magnificent entry was assured. Yasminah said something to Festus, riding rear guard, before scampering to rejoin Hertzelah and Miriam in the cart.

Eli remounted his horse. "Miriam, we will be in Caesarea very shortly. Get out of sight and stay out of sight. If Herod asks about you, I will tell him the truth, that you are indisposed. It probably won't be long before his gossiping spies bring him the details. He will be pretentiously gracious enough not to press the issue."

Eli's entourage rumbled up the road. As the procession drew near the gates of Eli's estate at Caesarea, two trumpeters on the wall sounded a fanfare. Servants scampered into position, endeavoring to appear busily engaged with the task nearest at hand.

Behind the enclosure, a Nazarene tile setter paced nervously across the mazzeroth universe. Eli had returned. Miriam would be with him, of course. When they finished the courtyard, the Rabbi assured Yusuf that Miriam remained un-betrothed. How could the Rabbi know, for sure? But if she was not promised to another, there might be some chances to speak with her again. Among recent memories, none were more dear than the time spent showing Miriam the water level, conspiring with her to speak Hebrew and evade the prying ears of the chaperone, and subsequent days spent discussing the twelve houses of the mazzeroth and the corresponding tribes of Israel.

There could be no future at all for the daughter of the richest man in Palestine and a poor tekton from Nazareth. Even if Yusuf were not born into the curse of Yeconiah. Miriam was too special. Too unique for an ordinary working man. She ignited feelings, almost magical and previously unknown feelings. Even if there were no future, perhaps The One God would grant him a short extension of the recent past. If she was not betrothed to another, he should be able to speak with her again.

VI, II
The Handmaiden's Ruse

Trapped. Miriam, Hertzelah, and Yasminah brooded in Miriam's private quarters. Eli hustled his obviously pregnant daughter and her attendants out of sight, immediately upon returning to Caesarea. Festus guarded the door.

Miriam paced up and down her soft, wool, crimson rug and grumbled. "This is ridiculous. My father is hiding me as if he's ashamed or something. Right now, he's giving Herod the grand tour of my brother's new addition. I too would like to see how everything finished up."

Hertzelah laughed. "Especially the mosaic, right? Is it the tile, or the tile-setter you hope to see?"

Miriam blushed.

Yasminah frowned at Hertzelah. "Be nice. The Nazarene is probably hoping to see Miriam as well. I have an idea. Festus is guarding the door. Let's just say I know how to distract him, long enough for Miriam to sneak out. Miriam, take my servant's cloak and throw it over your gown. Be sure to keep your head covered. Blend in with the staff. You should be able to get a glimpse of that, ahem, *tiled courtyard* you find so fascinating."

Hertzelah nodded with approval.

Yasminah took off her cloak, revealing her lightweight, form flattering shift. She was now too casual for a proper appearance in public, but better prepared to distract Festus. She handed the outer garment to Miriam. "I'll take Festus around the corner to the right. When you hear me giggle, loudly, that will mean the coast is clear. Get out the door, and go left."

"Easily done. I have sneaked out of these quarters a hundred times. And I need to see what's happening."

VI, III
Thirsty for The Rabbi's Gift

Hot. The delay was more unbearable in the heat. Shimon instructed Yusuf to wait next to the partition surrounding the courtyard. The master builder escorted Herod, Eli and Aban through the marbled arcades and fragrant gardens. Eli nodded approvingly as Shimon scampered around to point out a variety of highlights. Exotic woods were sanded smooth as a maiden's cheek, and illuminated with layers of oil and resin. The sun fired rays through jeweled embellishments. Although Herod had previously inspected all of the work except the mosaic, he participated graciously in the tour. Shimon was saving the grand reveal of the finished mosaic for the final moments. Simultaneous efforts by several servants would bring down the partition in a single motion.

Yusuf waited. He scanned the crowd, hoping to get a glimpse of Miriam. She wasn't with her father and brother. Wouldn't that be unusual, during a visit by the King? And not a word. Not even a brief "hello". Yusuf would trade almost anything, at this moment, just for the sound of her voice.

Something about a servant, on the outskirts of the throng, came to Yusuf's attention. At first glance, there was nothing remarkable about her appearance, but something was familiar about her movements. Was the servant the same size as Miriam, or was Yusuf so wishful of her appearance he was imagining similarities? The figure pinched the hood of her cloak as tightly as possible around her face. She looked about. With head facing downward, she began moving furtively toward Yusuf. Could this indeed be Miriam? Why would she be dressed as a servant? Why sneaking around her own home?

Shimon cried out, "Now for the grand reveal of the central courtyard!" Eli, Herod, and their retinues advanced toward the partition. Servants scampered through the joints and folds, waiting for the final signal to drop and remove the coverings. Halfway to Yusuf's position, the mysterious figure turned abruptly and disappeared into the assembling shadows.

Yusuf bowed, deeply and respectfully, as Eli and Herod approached.

Herod remarked, "There's a familiar face. We trust you aren't washing your hands in the pools. It will be interesting to see what you created, on your own, without help from an old master."

"I hope you find the results pleasing, your Excellency. Just as I hope the lords Eli and Aban are pleased."

Shimon sought the spotlight. "Be assured, your Majesty, that this young tekton has been carefully supervised. The work represents his labor, but every part of the design and all the materials involved were approved by myself, or one of my top assistants."

Herod slowly stretched his hand, palm up, toward Shimon. "Of course, Master Builder. As carefully as you had to oversee the rest of this work, you no doubt supervised the mosaic as well. But if you want to claim the credit, be prepared to take the blame. We are about to see how the center of this compound turned out."

Shimon agreed. "Indeed we are." The master builder yelled, "Drop the curtains!"

Flumpf! Low breakers of creamy dust crested away from the tile work. Within seconds, the servants dragged away the collapsed partition. When the view was clear, it was as though everyone inhaled at once. Some people stood with mouths agape. Others pointed and shook their heads in joyful disbelief. A cacophony of excited chatter swelled and pulsed. Two of Herod's retainers scrambled to take measurements.

Afternoon rays caressed the courtyard like a blessing. The ordinary clay tiles seemed to create, as well as reflect a radiance. Shapes and shadows, darks and lights, forms and voids. Everything vibrated like a living being. Color became light. Light became fluid and connected until it twisted and swirled about on itself like a marvelous music.

Shimon remained focused on Eli and Herod. The more astonished the reaction of the crowd, the more he basked in the glow of his own ego. This was his moment. Time to steal the credit from Yusuf. "Look at the quail! And the…"

King Herod motioned to silence Shimon. "We would take a walk on this courtyard, to inspect it more carefully. But what are you saying about quail? We see none."

For the first time in broad daylight, Shimon turned to survey the finished work. There was no dual portrait of Eli and his son, surrounded by quail. There was, instead, a mazzeroth. Shimon recalled seeing something similar, years ago, on the floor of a synagogue. But no mosaic he had ever seen rivaled this work at Caesarea. This was once-in-a-lifetime special. All the more glory to steal from Yusuf.

Shimon faced Herod, and bowed. "Forgive me, Excellency. Was I so excited I said 'quail'? Truly, I meant to say 'quality detail'. I apologize for misspeaking."

Herod appeared skeptical, but was so enthralled by the work he overlooked the master builder's weak excuse. The king spoke to Eli. "Our assistants report that the courtyard is properly smaller than at Sephora, but there's some chance it may be even more impressive. I am sure you meant no insult. However, we will be pleased only if you assign this master builder and tile setter to create something equally stunning for our new palace in Yerushalayim."

Yusuf remembered something The Rabbi told him. Some reference to seeing him again in Bet L'hem. The House of Bread was his ancestral home. If he were indeed going to work for King Herod in Yerushalayim, he might find lodging in nearby Bet L'hem.

Eli, Herod, their closest relatives, and senior advisors walked, reverently, around the mazzeroth.

Yusuf answered questions. "Yes, these are the twelve houses of the heavens. Yes, there is one house for every tribe of Israel, or maybe that's one tribe of Israel for every house. No, the tiles were not expensive. It has more to do with how they are used than it does with their price."

Herod smiled, slyly, and posed a question as well. "Eli, old friend. What is here in the center of this design, surrounded by these houses of the heavens? There isn't any chance that might be the sun, is there?"

Eli responded quickly. "Of course not, Excellency! That would be heliocentric, a blasphemous belief popular only among some pagans and gentiles. Our teachings are very clear. The sun and all the heavens revolve around Earth. The One God made it so. No theory or speculation will change that. We can be sure the Earth is the center of the universe. And Earth is at the center of the mazzeroth."

Yusuf remembered something else The Rabbi said as they labored together on the mazzeroth. "My gift is helping people see whatever it is they most want to see."

I could use some portion of The Rabbi's gift. Right now, I most want to see Miriam.

VI, IV
Aching Heart, and Feet of Clay

Miriam watched from behind a pillar. Why did her friend Yusuf seem so vulnerable in this moment of triumph? Perhaps because he was surrounded by men who made their way in life by taking from others. She longed to be at his side. Maybe even scandalize everyone by holding his hand. Ready to whisper advice should his overly trusting nature begin leading him into a trap. Her heart ached, but her feet were still. As far as Eli knew, she was still "resting" in her quarters, behind a guarded door.

Miriam intuitively sensed a significant event about to unfold. Although harboring doubts about the immediate future, Miriam realized there was no longer any doubt about her feelings for Yusuf. Maybe if he felt the same way, they could run off together. Out of Palestine. Maybe even out of the Empire. Somewhere where Eli, or Herod, or even Augustus would not find them. But that's almost silly. Yusuf never said he wanted Miriam. After all, a man of his humble status would never dare. And if he had ever wanted her before, what about now? What about now, with a child to be born in just five months?

Miriam wrapped her hands around the pillar. Clinging, desperately, for a sensation of solidity at a moment that seemed confusing and unstable.

VI, V
Greater and Lesser Rewards

The crowd circled around the mazzeroth. None dared step onto the surface while the parties of Herod and Eli continued an inspection. But they pointed inward from the edges; discovering, comparing, smiling and exclaiming. Shimon strutted, as much as he dared in the presence of the king. Yusuf remained quiet, humble, and wondering about Miriam. He spoke when spoken to, and politely answered questions.

Ten gold rings flashed in the sun as Herod extended his arms from his shoulders. "Quiet, everyone! We would have it quiet, please!" The babble died rapidly to a murmur, then a total and contrasting silence. One heard the trickling of a fountain, and the low splash of a bright-colored carp seizing an unfortunate insect.

Herod continued, "Shimon. You have rendered our friend Lord Eli magnificent service. A fine example for others. We are impressed. A gift is appropriate. We shall relieve Eli of his obligation to reward your efforts by granting you a boon from our own reserves. "

Eli recognized Herod's cleverly disguised insult. He struggled to remain silent. Aban noticed the change in his father's stance and demeanor. He placed a hand on Eli's forearm and almost imperceptibly shook his head. *No. Not now, Father. Do not speak from anger.*

Shimon bowed responded to Herod, but failed to conceal his glee. "Your Majesty is too kind!"

"Come then, Master Builder. Name a gift. If it's within my power to grant, it shall be yours."

Shimon glanced around. At the edge of the mazzeroth was a servant carrying a cypress water bucket with a bronze ladle. "Your majesty, my wish would be enough gold coins to fill the water ladle, three times."

"And you shall have it! Call on us at Sephora, with your ladle, and we will open our treasury and fill it for you, brimming over, thrice."

Shimon bowed so deeply he almost lost balance. "Thank you, Your Majesty."

Everyone around the mazzeroth bowed as well.

Herod smiled. "We would retire now, to some more of that delicious wine."

The crowd began dispersing. Eli brooded over Herod's insult. Yes, Shimon was entitled to a reward. Eli had no need for Herod to fund a boon for his master builder. It was clearly a maneuver to make Eli appear less wealthy than the king. Herod could be such a miserable jackass. This could not be allowed to stand, but Eli dare not reward Shimon after Herod had done so. If the gift were greater, Herod would be insulted. If the gift were less, Herod's point would be reinforced. Eli realized that Herod was fully aware of his predicament, and without doubt enjoying it very much.

Before the opportunity was lost, Eli cried out, "Wait, please!"

Herod was already two steps toward the edge of the courtyard. He turned around. The king looked annoyed.

Eli bowed, almost imperceptibly. "Your Highness, perhaps there's another reward due here today. While I can obviously not compete with your magnificent generosity, I would like to make a similar offer to the young tekton. He laid the tiles that created the courtyard. The courtyard is the crowning glory of the entire addition."

Shimon squinted and frowned. The tekton from Nazareth would get some glory as well. Shimon grabbed Yusuf by the shoulder and hissed into his ear. "Be careful here. Do not ask for as much as I received from Herod. You will embarrass the king. Perhaps one handful of silver coins. Two, at the most. Anything else, and you may be in peril."

Eli raised his voice. "So, then, tile setter from Nazareth. Name a gift. If it's within my power to grant it, it will be yours!"

Yusuf the Nazarene knelt before Eli. He remembered the advice of the Rabbi. (Be brave, show no fear). His heart pounded like a mason's hammer, his breath heaved like the bellows in a forge. Tears welled up. He struggled to keep his voice steady as he replied, "My Lord Eli, the gift I ask is to take your daughter Miriam as my wife."

Herod shouted, "That's an outrage!"

Shimon kicked the Nazarene on the side of the head, sprawling him out on his own masterpiece.

The master builder hastened to apologize. "Lord Eli, I am so sorry. I have no idea what came over this man. This lowly tile setter dares insult you, and your house, and your daughter. I will have him dragged off and flogged right away and…"

Herod interrupted, "And if he lives, give my guards a turn as well. It seems washing his hands in my pool was the most innocent of his low desires."

VI, VI
Fear of Flogging

Miriam could endure no more. She released her grip on the pillar and took the first step toward the confrontation on the mazzeroth. She had to intervene, if she could. She could not stand by while her beloved was flogged, or possibly even killed, especially not now. Not if he cared enough to ask for a marriage. She could heal his wounds, if he survived. Could she heal his heart if they beat him senseless, or beyond?

Before she could take a second step, she felt a hand on her shoulder.

A familiar voice said, "Wait, child. It's not yet time."

Miriam kept her attention on the mazzeroth. She didn't turn her head when she replied, "You are Gabriel, Almodad, Elishua, and Israel? I know your voice. This is the first time you have spoken to me, outside of a vision."

"Who knows, for sure, what is a vision and what is not? Too many draw lines across reality, presuming authority to divide and define. Surely, you have learned that. Hot, cold, wet, dry, life, death; all are part of a broader cloth."

"I should go to Yusuf! They're planning to kill him."

"Stay, daughter. Stay. These are steps of a complex dance. Your young man is in good hands. Stronger than yours, better than mine. Your love for him empowers and validates it all. Go, wait outside your father's window. Let no one see you. Remain silent there. You will know when, and if, to speak."

VI, VII
All Options Considered

Eli and his son looked at one another. Each knew they shared a common, if improbable thought.

Eli commanded, "Wait! There will be no flogging. At least not yet. Pick him up. Take him to my private quarters. I will speak to this over bold tekton. I would understand why he presumes to make such an outrageous and improper request. When I have judged his answers, you may get your chance to flog him."

Yusuf was too dizzy to stand on his own. Blood poured from his nose and upper lip. Shimon signaled for two servants to support Yusuf. "And wipe some of that mess off his face. We can't have him bleeding all over Lord Eli's furnishings."

Herod turned away in disgust. "You will never have any discipline if you coddle people. We will be in the garden. Send us some wine. Don't forget, when you get tired of beating him we are willing to take it up for you."

Yusuf tried, and failed to walk. He was dragged by the shoulders into Eli's study. One servant placed a cloth on a bench so that he might not soil it. Another gave Yusuf a cloth. "Keep this pressed into the blood. Do not let any of it stain Eli's room or belongings."

Miriam hunkered down outside Eli's window, concealed by a hedge. Her heart yearned to cry out to her beloved Yusuf, but she found the discipline to remain silent. Silent, as instructed. Silent, trusting that her beloved was sheltered in the profound grip of some invisible hand.

Eli entered. Miriam heard him shuffling manuscripts on his study table. Someone else entered the room. Miriam assumed it was her brother. Her suspicions were confirmed when he spoke.

"So, tell my father what possesses you to ask for my sister as a wife?"

Yusuf's speech was affected by his injured lip. "If it please, your lordships, I knew it was a risk. I knew it might result exactly this way. But if I did not ask, I knew would I spend the rest of my life regretting my silence."

Outside the window, Miriam suppressed a gasp, but not a blush.

Eli crossed his legs and rested his chin in his left palm. "The rest of your life might not be all that long. Especially if Herod gets his way. You are barely acquainted with my daughter. You would be a ridiculous match. She comes from the richest family in Palestine. You come from no family at all."

Aban added, "And you're born into the curse of Yeconiah! No son of yours will ever sit on the throne of Israel."

Eli countered, "That old curse was lifted, officially. But look at him. No son of his will ever sit on the throne of Israel in any event. Not unless we anoint carpenters and tile setters King."

Yusuf summoned the courage to gasp, "They once anointed a shepherd."

Eli was emotionally exhausted. He would never tolerate such a reply in court. Under the circumstances, he chose to be amused rather than offended.

The patriarch launched his index finger toward the blooded Nazarene. "This is about money, isn't it? It's always all about money. What if I offered to pay you to change your request? By the way, this is where you ask me how much I have in mind and perhaps we can get down to business. Take some money, and I'll make sure there's no flogging."

Outside the window, behind the hedge, Miriam drew a breath.

"Your excellency, it's not about money. As far as no family? I don't expect to join your family. Miriam and I will start our own. And I know Miriam as well as most of the sons of wealthy men who might seem better suited as a match."

Miriam grinned, and exhaled.

Eli put his chin back in his hand. "It would be about money to this degree. If ever I should lose my mind and consent to wed Miriam to a man of your status, there would be no dowry. That shouldn't matter to you, if you claim you would be marrying for love. And that's a ridiculous idea. Nobody can live on love."

Miriam frowned.

Yusuf grew bolder. "Maybe it's more foolish to try to live without love than to live without money."

Miriam smiled with serenity.

Eli laughed, reluctantly. "Well, a philosopher tekton. You may be wise beyond your station, young man. Pity that random accident of birth. You might have had some chance to be remembered someday."

Aban spoke. "Father, go ahead and tell him. Tell him about Miriam. Even if he were of a proper class, and he's not. Everyone will know soon enough, anyway."

"Tell me what about Miriam? She's alright isn't she? Why haven't I seen her since your return from Yerushalayim?"

Eli cleared his throat. "I'll put this bluntly. She's with child. In fact, she's in her fourth month. She won't name the father. She can't remain in Yudea or Galilee as an unmarried woman with a baby, so I am arranging to send her to Rome. In a couple of days, she will no longer be in Galilee. For most purposes, she will have disappeared. No honorable man will have her. You may be impulsive and foolish, but you stand by your misguided principles. I will consider you among that list of honorable men."

Yusuf was stunned. Miriam? Pregnant? What other secrets was she keeping? He squirmed on the bench. What should he do? What should he do? He recalled the voice of The Rabbi, ("do not be afraid").

From her hiding spot behind the hedge, Miriam counted every second as an eternity.

Eli and Aban let Yusuf stew on the news. Each found some small amusement in his discomfort.

Finally, Yusuf the tile setter of Nazareth, son of Yakob the carpenter, and excluded from the throne of Israel by the curse of Yeconiah reached a decision.

"Considering that there will be no dowry, that I will not be welcomed into your family, that Miriam carries another man's child, and knowing full and well that perhaps my life depends on my decision…. I ask you again, Eli of Caesarea. I ask for your daughter, to be my wife."

Behind the hedge, Miriam folded her hands in prayer.

Eli took a full minute to respond. The three men stared uncomfortably at each other, aware that he who spoke first would likely be the loser.

Eli spoke first. "Despite it all, you would press ahead? It's not too late to have you flogged. But Miriam has always been unusual. More than a little rebellious. She has enough wit and character she could have been a second son, instead of a beautiful daughter. Maybe such an unorthodox match is just the thing for such a unique woman. My guess is you would treat her well. I care for her, very much. That's important to me."

Miriam's brother interjected, "Father, are you seriously considering this?"

"I am. In fact, I'm inclined to agree. She has few options, given her circumstances."

The bloodied Nazarene bowed as well as he could from his seat on the bench. "Thank you, sir, thank you!"

Eli put up a palm. "Not quite so fast. Since she has been old enough to understand, I have assured my daughter I would not force her to marry without her consent. If she agrees, you can be married right away. It will depend entirely upon what Miriam has to say."

Just outside Eli's window, somebody gasped and began weeping with joy. The men turned toward the window in time to see Miriam's upper body thrust into the room, arms spread wide as if embracing the universe. Tears flowed liberally across her cheeks. "Yes! Yes! Yes! Miriam says yes!"

Epilogue

Nissan 1.

King Herod's avarice and jealousy ultimately outweighed his animosity toward Yusuf the tekton. Every time he closed his eyes, he envisioned Eli's spectacular mosaic courtyard. Surely, the king's own palace required something equally grand. And larger.

Herod dispatched a detachment of royal guardsmen to call upon Yusuf in Nazareth. "His excellency, Herod the Great, requires that you relocate to Bet L' Hem within the week. You will then report to his palace in Yerushalayim to begin the redesign and expansion of the central courtyard."

Yusuf protested. "This is not the time. Miriam is too pregnant to travel. I won't leave her by herself. Not with the baby due any day now."

"King Herod ordered us to accept no excuse. Your wife can stay if you choose. There will be women here to help her when it's her time. We will take you by force, if we must."

Miriam pulled Yusuf aside. She whispered into his ear. Yusuf looked skeptically at his wife. "Are you that certain?"

"Yes. Our child will be born on Nissan 5. Absolutely. No sooner and no later. We can take the cart at a slow pace. As long as we're in Bet L' Hem by sundown on Nissan 4. If we leave in the morning, we can make the inn at Bet L' Hem in plenty of time."

Yusuf stroked his beard. Few women would be that confident of an exact delivery date. Perhaps the ride in the cart would induce an earlier labor. But Miriam was an extraordinary woman. Yusuf concluded that she was most likely right about the date of the impending birth. Miriam had a knack for knowing the unknowable.

Yusuf consented. "Return to King Herod. Tell him I will be in Bet

L' Hem by Nissan 5, and will begin service to His Excellency on the seventh."

"See that you do, tekton. See that you do. Should we ever have to come looking for you, there will be lives at stake."

****

Nissan 4.

The sun crawled relentlessly toward the western horizon. Yusuf flinched every time the cart joggled across a rock or dipped into a hole. Miriam smiled stoically, balancing on the seat and supporting her great belly with both hands. Her eyes were closed. Yusuf knew there were times when Miriam was physically present- but mentally or spiritually some other place entirely. This was such a time. All the better, perhaps. Yusuf suffered her share of the anxiety in addition to his own.

Perhaps a mile from Bet L' hem, the road was obstructed with sheep. Yusuf stopped the cart. A bleating, surging, swirl of soiled wool ruminated across the path. Something about the shepherds seemed unusual. They walked more confidently than most sheep herders. Some on the outskirts of the flock were more than typically concerned with keeping a watch on the surroundings. Perhaps there were rumors of wolves, about.

One group of shepherds approached the cart. Among them, a man noticed Miriam and was taken aback with surprise. "Forgive me, but is that Eli's daughter?"

Yusuf was no less startled than the shepherd. "Yes, how is it that you know my wife?"

"We encountered her in Samaria. She healed my leg wound. Probably saved my life."

Miriam recognized the voice. She opened her eyes. "Duriel? How have you been? This is my husband, Yusuf."

"Shalom, Yusuf"

"Shalom, Duriel"

Yusuf noticed how awkwardly Duriel handled his shepherd's crook. Carried it more like a club than a staff. There might indeed be more to this group than met the eye. The prior acquaintance between Duriel and Miriam was unusual, but reassuring

Duriel waved toward the flock. "We'll be clear of the road in a moment. We plan to camp very near here tonight."

Yusuf nodded. "Miriam is due to give birth."

Duriel appeared perplexed. "Due? But there have only been… never mind. It's not really my business. We need to make camp. It's getting dark, and there are Romans nearby."

Yusuf continued. "We're pressing on to the inn at Bet L' Hem, just ahead."

Duriel thumbed toward Bet L' Hem. "I wish you luck. There's an Imperial revenue squadron there. Several tax collectors, a centuria of legionnaires, and of course there's the swarm of vendors and harlots. Most of the lower ranks are camped outside, but the officers and tax collectors might have filled up the rooms."

Miriam frowned. "I wonder why they stopped at Bet L'hem?"

"It's not easy to know. They say Augustus is on a mission to tax everyone in the world. Bet L' Hem is the home city for the House of David. I have heard they're checking the records. They also say Herod is making lists of everybody descended from David. One thing is certain; they have collected enough gold and precious cargo in those wagons to fund a large army on a long campaign."

Miriam rolled her eyes. "No doubt, you will be keeping close watch on those transports."

The last of the sheep crossed the road. Yusuf and Miriam wished Duriel well, and rolled their cart into a cavorting miasma of dust. Out of earshot from the shepherds, Miriam confided, "They aren't really shepherds. Not in the true sense. Duriel and his friends are

Zealots."

"I'm not that surprised. Something didn't seem right. Do you think they will try to attack the tax collectors?" Joseph brooded. "Maybe it's not safe for you at the inn."

"There's no serious danger. Duriel won't attack such a large force. But in some remote circumstance where one wagon is isolated and the guard is divided, who knows? Duriel still believes the only way to be free of the Romans is to kill them all."

The leading edge of the sun touched the western horizon. Miriam's water broke. "It's time. Our baby will be here very soon now."

Yusuf leapt down from the cart. He grabbed the startled donkey by the bridle. Yusuf ran toward the inn, literally dragging the donkey, the cart, and Miriam down the final stretch of the road. He found space to stop the cart, immediately outside the door.

****

Micah, innkeeper at Bet L' Hem was excited to host a full house. The tax collectors and the Roman officers spent lavishly. Why not? Provincial tax collectors kept notoriously sloppy records of receipts. Even Augustus pretended to ignore that most of his revenue agents lived well beyond any means afforded by their meager stipends.

Platters of food passed in constant circulation. And wine. So much wine that Micah sent two different requests to Yerushalayim for resupply. Musicians on lyres, bells, drums, and whistles blended an aural tapestry against which two slaves from Nubia jumped and stretched in scandalous poses.

In thirty years of inn keeping, never had there been such an evening. Money was everywhere. Accumulating in boxes, on shelves, in cups, in Micah's empty cap, and glimmering in random stacks in dusty corners. A few more hours like this, and Micah would be set for life.

Above the noise and confusion, distracted by his cash receipts,

Micah almost failed to hear the desperate pounding on the front door. *Perhaps the harlot master needs more wine. He should use the back door.*

Micah jerked open the upper half of the door. There stood a man looking very concerned, immediately in front of a cart. A woman, apparently in some distress, was moaning and squirming on the seat.

"Please sir, we must have a room. My wife is going into labor. The baby will be born tonight."

Micah pondered the situation. Everything was full. Well, almost everything. There was that small room under the steps. The place reserved for the servants of rich travelers. It was too small and crude for a tax collector, too ignoble for an officer. Perhaps the family could be accommodated there.

But no. Not here. Not tonight, of all nights. A woman in labor, possibly screaming, would disrupt the mood. The golden stream of prosperity would dry up to a trickle, if it flowed at all. Servants, musicians, and cooks would be distracted. The platters would stop circulating. There would be less demand for wine. No. Not here. Not tonight of all nights. Accepting this family would be too costly. Too inconvenient.

"I'm sorry, but we're completely filled up. It's the tax collection. They will be gone by tomorrow night, if that's any help."

"You don't understand. We need a room tonight. Not tomorrow night. My wife is in labor as we speak. Surely you must have something? Even a store room. Maybe even a big closet?"

"A big closet? Tell you what I can do. There's a stable around the side. The whore master is entertaining some of the legionnaires out there, but I am pretty sure I can get them to move somewhere else. You can use the stable. The price of a room tonight is 15 denarii. Do you have the price?"

"You're going to charge us 15 denarii to sleep in the stable?"

"Take it or leave it."

Yusuf grumbled, "I'll take it. It looks like we have no choice. It's been a while since it felt like I really had a choice about much of anything."

"Fine then, let's go around the side and I'll tell the whore master he has to relocate. It's not like I'm heartless, you know. I'll send a servant to fetch the village midwife. I'll send out some warm food, and some blankets. Normally, I could have taken you in. But not tonight, of all nights. I just can't. The timing didn't work out."

****

Just over a mile from Bet L' hem, Duriel rose from beside the shepherd campfire. He yawned and stretched. Some strange voice in a dream spoke about good tidings and great joy. What could that mean, exactly? He had an inexplicable urge to walk into town and see whether Miriam and Yusuf managed to find lodging.

It would be best not to go alone. Duriel kicked Menachem gently in the thigh. "Wake up. Gather a few of the others. Let's go the Bet L' Hem and spy out the revenue carts. We can check on Miriam and what was his name? Yusuf? Maybe they didn't find a room. If not, we can offer them shelter in our camp.

The End

CPSIA information can be obtained
at www.ICGtesting.com
Printed in the USA
FSOW02n1357140617
35204FS